MW00620533

METAL WOLF

WARRIORS OF GALATEA #1

LAUREN ESKER

Metal Wolf
Published by Icefall Press, June 2018

Copyright © 2018 Lauren Esker/Layla Lawlor
All Rights Reserved

ONE

SPACE BATTLES WERE beautiful from a distance, Rei had always thought. Artistic, almost: a dance of light in the darkness. He could imagine painting it. And this one was no exception, even though he knew each kaleidoscopic whorl of light was a pilot fighting and dying in hard vacuum.

The Galatean battle fleet hung in star-speckled darkness, framed by the great arch of a gas giant's rings and, beyond it, the double suns of this system, winking past the planet's curve. Against that glorious backdrop, dying ships and battlepods blossomed like flowers as the smaller, faster Kk'rek craft swarmed them. So far, none of the Kk'rek armada had turned towards Rei's formation, but they would get here soon enough. His craft was in front of the attack, along with all the other slave-piloted battlepods—humanoid cannon fodder to keep the Kk'rek from reaching the fleet's battleships.

The waiting was the worst. He tried to rely on his inner wolf at times like this, keeping himself focused on the present without allowing his mind to drift, like the hunter that he was at heart. His arms were pushed to the elbows into the control cradle of his battlepod, sweat-slick hands wrapped around the control handles and shoulder muscles taut with anticipatory tension.

Rei! The call came not over the comms, but through his telepathic link with his bond-brother, the dragon Lyr. They were supposed to be maintaining comm silence, but nobody else could tell when Lyr was using his telepathy, so it wasn't like anyone could stop them. *Hostiles coming in on your nine!*

There were so many distractions to follow in the chaos of the battle, even with his augmented senses, that he hadn't noticed the two incoming Kk'rek craft on his ship's 360-degree heads-up display until they were almost on top of him. Rei wrenched the controls of his battlepod, swinging it around, and took out both with a one-two punch that started in his brain and was directed through his control cuffs to the ship's cannons. The Kk'rek vessels bloomed against the void in a bouquet of silent fire.

That's two for me so far, dragonbreath.

Lyr's laugh came across the link, strained but genuine. *Seven for me, four for Rook. You napping over there? Keep lazing around and the after-battle drinks are on you.*

Just had the bad luck to get stuck in a sleepy backwater of the fleet this time, asshole. Not like you lucky saps over there in Onyx Formation.

Wordless sarcasm came over the link. It felt like Lyr was having to concentrate, so the direct link winked out, leaving only the warm awareness of Lyr's presence—attenuated by distance to little more than a thread, but still soothing, like the reassuring pressure of a hand on his mental shoulder.

At least Lyr was okay, so far. Rei had no idea which of those little dots in the swarming flecks and numbers on his HUD represented his friend; all he could see was whether a craft was a friendly (blue) or an enemy (red). Nobody thought slave soldiers like Rei needed to know irrelevant information like "where are my friends?"

But, as usual, Lyr was keeping track of *him* through the link. As for the dragon's current physical location, Rei guessed he was somewhere in the vicinity of Rook, the sole remaining member of their childhood sept. Gentle Rook had never been more than an adequate battle pilot. Rei and Lyr (and the others, when they were still alive) had always taken turns watching their friend's back.

Back in the days before Haiva's death, before they lost Skara, before Selinn fell, and Kite—back when it still felt like a game and the deaths on their screens were nothing more than numbers—Rei used to tease Rook about his lack of flying skill. Ironically, Rook could fly just fine without any technological help at all; his species had wings sprouting from their otherwise humanlike shoulders. Meanwhile Rei, the best pilot in the group, was a werewolf from the primitive ice world Polara, who had never even seen a spaceship until the Galateans drafted him at the age of nine.

Rook insisted that being able to fly on his own was exactly why he wasn't good at piloting a ship. "It'd be like you putting on a furry costume and crawling on all fours and calling it hunting."

"It's nothing like that and you know it, birdbrain."

But it had long since stopped being a subject to joke about. Rook wasn't a skilled pilot. He'd originally been trained for ground combat, utilizing his wings as a natural resource, the same way Rei had specialized as a pilot and Skara had been trained as an assassin. But the focus of the war had shifted, their entire sept was moved to battlepod duty, and ...

And I'm the only one who's really good at it.

His heart was racing now, his hands shaking in the control cradle, and he realized to his horror that he'd lost some time, slipping back into the past. In a battle situation like this, a moment's inattention could be lethal.

Would that really be so bad? asked a small, cold corner of his mind.

He didn't know if he still believed in his people's concept of an afterlife, and anyway, the Polaran afterlife, with its forests and snow-covered hunting lodges, probably wouldn't be pleasant for someone like Skara or Kite anyway. He had no real hope of seeing his dead friends again. The best he could hope for was oblivion, because then he wouldn't miss them anymore.

Steady, came Lyr's thought down the link. *Steady, little brother. Keep on.*

Lyr couldn't have known what Rei was thinking, not unless he'd been lying all these years about reading emotions but not true thoughts. But he would have sensed Rei's stress and agitation, and he was dividing his attention to help Rei, taking vital resources away from his own battle.

Self-loathing twisted Rei's stomach. His inattention problem had been getting worse and worse, which meant Lyr had to spend more of his concentration in a fight helping Rei focus, and that meant less to spare for protecting himself, or for helping—

ROOK!

It was a searing cry of pure horror, tearing through Rei's brain. Rei screamed, wrenching his hands out of the control cradle to clap them over his ears, as if that could shut out a scream coming from inside his head.

No—not only from inside. It was coming over the

comms too. Lyr, normally a model of discipline, had lost control so badly that he had broken radio silence.

"Rook! *Rook!*"

The anguish in Lyr's voice was unbearable before it snapped off abruptly. One of their superiors must have cut off Lyr's comms.

"No," Rei said aloud. Lowering his shaking hands from his ears, he stared out at the battle. Was one of those dustings of glitter, so beautiful among the stars, the remains of Rook's battle pod?

Lyr certainly seemed to think so.

And Lyr was the one person who would always know for sure. Only two things could sever his link with any of them—a very great distance (such as the distance between stars, not merely within a solar system) ... or death.

Rei became aware, through a haze of emotional shock, that he had a splitting headache. Cautiously he touched his face and then his ears, finding them sticky. His nose and ears were bleeding from the force of Lyr's psychic scream.

As he felt cautiously at his face, trying to concentrate past a headache so severe it throbbed in time with his heartbeat, he bumped his slave collar by accident.

It moved.

Startled, he fumbled at his neck. The collar, like the bracelet-style cuffs around his wrists, was connected to his nervous system at all times by tiny wires beneath the skin. The difference was that he could take the cuffs off. The collar might as well have been welded on.

The only times it was ever loose was when an overseer deactivated it.

Rei's heart rate accelerated out of control. He felt at his control cuffs. Those rotated freely as well, without having to mentally detach them.

The whole system was connected to his nervous system, which had just taken a hammer blow from Lyr's psychic blast of grief and despair. It was impossible, *had* to be impossible ... but it felt like the collar and bracelets had both burned out.

Rei pushed his hands back into the control cradle and sent a mental command to connect to the pod.

Nothing happened.

He was hanging here dead between the stars—perhaps soon to be *actually* dead, if a Kk'rek got the drop on him while his battlepod drifted on autopilot. But if his collar was as dead as the control bracelets seemed to be, then the containment system that normally prevented him from traveling a certain distance from the fleet would also have been deactivated.

He could flee.

He could escape.

Lyr? he sent out into the void.

All that came back was incoherent grief and rage.

Looking at the HUD, Rei realized that a swath of the battlefield was lit up with an unusual flare of activity. Was *Lyr* doing that?

He'd known the dragon was powerful, but he had never seen him go all out like this before. Kk'rek ships winked out like dying campfire sparks, vanishing in clusters, along with sporadic Galatean ships all over a particular sector of the grid.

And then Rei realized why. If the backlash of Lyr's pain had burned out *his* slave collar, then Lyr would have burned out his own collar too. And Rei knew, because Lyr had once told him, that the collar served as a limiter on his power.

Even with his bare eyes, he could see something among

the glitter of the ships that blazed like a tiny star. He was witnessing the true power of a dragon unleashed.

We're free. But did Lyr even realize it, or was he too far gone in rage and grief?

Lyr! he sent desperately. *Lyr!*

But Lyr was beyond hearing, and with dawning horror, Rei realized that the dying Galatean battlepods were also victims of Lyr's destructive frenzy. Lyr would never do something like that on purpose. Swept away in a tempest of fury and grief, Lyr was immolating himself to destroy the Kk'rek fleet, along with any Galatean battlepods unlucky enough to be in the area.

Lyr didn't expect to survive.

And now, after distracting Lyr at a crucial moment, after all but causing Rook's death, Rei could do nothing but watch.

Or escape.

Leaving Lyr to die.

Leaving Rook's remains to float between the stars ...

But what else could he *do*? Stay here and die with them? This was his one chance to get away, with his collar dead and everyone distracted by the dragon flaming out in his death-throes on the other side of the battle fleet.

Rei swallowed through a desert-dry throat. His trembling hands steadied as he began going through the emergency procedure for taking manual control of the pod. The manual system still worked; the controls folded out of the wall, and he clenched his fingers around them.

Now or never. The collar hung loose around his neck. Rei started to initiate the jump process, then stopped. Without the fine tuning of his mental controls, let alone the ability to connect back to the ship's computers, he had no ability to calculate a jump destination. He'd simply have to set it to random coordinates.

The pod's range was limited and only had enough power for one short jump before it needed to recharge; it was normally used for dropping the pods into an enemy system a few minutes ahead of the main fleet for a distraction. It certainly didn't have the range to get him out of the Galatean Empire. The automatic failsafes would try to drop him near a system, not into the heart of a star or the cold void of interplanetary space, but an inhabited world would return him as a deserter, while an uninhabited system most likely meant being stranded for a slow, lingering death.

If he killed himself doing this, he'd probably deserve it, for killing one friend and abandoning another.

But even if the human part of him was ready to lay down and die, his wolf wanted to live. It was the wolf that clawed its way toward survival, refusing to let him stop.

His hand hovered over the button to initiate the jump.

If he was wrong about the collar, it would blow his head off as soon as he jumped.

And if he was right, he would be the worst kind of traitor. Not to the Galateans, to whom he owed nothing, but to the only person left in the universe that he loved.

Lyr, he tried, one last time.

Suddenly his HUD flashed with a light so bright that he had to close his eyes briefly in shock. When he opened them, squinting, the error lights on his console had come on, and a message was flashing at the bottom of the HUD:

Security override engaged.

Pure horror shriveled his soul. Someone back on the fleet ship had noticed his collar had gone off the grid. They were going to pull him in—recollar him—

No!

He flicked switches, shutting down the HUD along with the rest of his non-manual systems. Sudden darkness swallowed the interior of the pod, leaving only the dull red glow of the emergency lights.

Without the HUD, he didn't have even minimal control over his jump.

But he was willing to try. The wolf inside him would rather die free than submit to being dragged back to the ship and collared again.

I am so sorry, he thought into the void where Lyr had been—where Lyr still was, at least for now, lost in pain and fury, and soon to be utterly alone. *I am so sorry, my friend, my brother. I will come back, I promise. I'll find you, no matter where you are, if you still live.*

He pushed the button.

The pod's jump drive powered up, and the stars smeared to greasy, colorful trails. Rei's whole body wrenched agonizingly, like every cell was being turned inside out all at once.

Then he dropped out of jumpspace and hit atmosphere.

Rei yelled aloud in shock. Still in the dazed post-jump state, he fumbled at the controls, trying to stop the pod from tearing itself apart in the gravitational forces tumbling it like a child's toy. He'd come out in the upper atmosphere of a planet. The only thing saving him from instant death were the shields, already at full strength from the battle.

It looked like he was coming in for a hard landing ... wherever the hell he was.

TWO

SARAH METZGER HUMMED QUIETLY to herself as she went through her familiar farm chore routine. Wisconsin autumn was always glorious, and this had turned out to be a particularly nice one. The colors were starting to pass their peak, but the October air was crisp and clean and sharp as the edge of a knife, carrying a faint, acrid hint of woodsmoke.

The sun was setting behind the outbuildings as she dumped the last bucket of feed into the milk cow's trough. Not a cloud marred the deep blue sky, where the first stars were beginning to emerge. It would be a chilly night, so she shut the horse in the barn and made sure the chickens were all in their house. But with that clear sky and the moon not yet risen, tonight would be perfect for stargazing.

"Hey, Dad?" Sarah called, pulling off her muddy boots in the farmhouse kitchen. "I'm going out to the lake tonight, all right?"

She came into the living room to find that it had been annexed by another of her dad's projects. Wide, flat pieces of metal and a variety of electrical and engine parts were spread out on newspapers that had been put down to protect the old hardwood floor, and Gary Metzger was sitting in the middle of it with a wrench in one hand and what looked like a heap of printed-out instructions from the Internet, stained with black fingerprints.

"If I was any other little girl's daddy," her father remarked gruffly without looking up from his project, "I'd think you were gonna head out there to Lover's Leap and hook up with some town kid."

Sarah couldn't help laughing. "I'm twenty-six, Dad. Hardly a kid. If I wanted to hook up with someone, not that I do, I wouldn't have to go out to Lover's Leap; we could get a motel—"

Her father made a protesting sound and a show of blocking his ears. Sarah laughed again.

"Wouldn't mind, you know," he added gruffly, wiping his hands on his grease-stained sweatpants. "You ought to do something for yourself for a change."

"I'm not hooking up with anyone, Dad."

"I know. It's *you*, so I reckon you're goin' out there to look at the stars."

"That's right. It's the Orionids tonight. I'm hoping to see some meteors." She stepped carefully over what appeared to be a crankshaft. "Are you still working on turning the old gristmill into a hydroelectric plant for the farm?"

"That's right. Finally got the alternator pulled from that ol' truck out back of the barn, and the water wheel is just about put back together." He scratched his ear, then looked ruefully at the parts on the floor. "Okay, not quite. But I got the bearings I needed, so she'll get there. Eventually."

"Well, have fun. I'm looking forward to hearing all about it. And looking forward even more to putting an end to those stupid power outages whenever we get a snowstorm." She kissed him on top of his balding head. "Don't wait up."

Her father shifted his weight, wincing as it tweaked his damaged hips, and set the printouts aside. "You shouldn't be havin' to look at the stars through a telescope from the lake. I know you were always wild to be one of those astro-whatevers—"

"Astrophysicist," Sarah said with a smile, turning back at the bottom of the stairs. The old pain was dull enough now that she could talk about it, even laugh about it, without hurting. That was the thing about childhood dreams. You imagined all kinds of wild things about your future, and then you grew up and learned to have smaller dreams, simpler dreams, the kind that were easy to achieve.

"You deserve the stars, Sarah," her father said quietly. "You shouldn't put it all on hold to take care of me and the farm."

"I'm taking classes, aren't I?" Sarah said with a lightness she didn't quite feel. Part-time, true—at the rate she was going, it would take her twenty years to get a degree—but a couple of days a week were all she could manage while still living at home, with the long drive to the university in Eau Claire. "Now I'd better get going or I'll miss the show."

She hurried up the stairs, as much to get away from the conversation as to avoid missing a few minutes of meteor-watching.

It doesn't matter. I probably wouldn't have been much of an astrophysicist anyway. I'll eventually marry some local boy just like my mom did, and settle down to raise sheep and take care of the family farm. I'll still have the stars in the evening. That'll be all right.

Small dreams, she reminded herself as she packed the telescope into its carrying case. Small, easy dreams, the kind of dreams that couldn't be upset by your mom getting a terminal cancer diagnosis when you were fifteen or your dad having a bad farm accident a couple of years later.

Just because she had once dreamed of the stars didn't mean she couldn't learn to enjoy a life on the farm. She had once imagined the universe, but now its boundaries had narrowed to the borders of a rural Wisconsin county, and that was okay too. Or so she told herself. The stars were still up there, old familiar friends keeping her company in the autumn dusk.

She trotted down the stairs with her arms piled high with her skywatching gear. She had her telescope and tripod, DSLR camera for taking night shots, night sky field guide, camp chair ... what else was she going to want? A good jacket, she thought, shrugging into the heavy sheep-skin-lined one that always hung on a hook by the kitchen door. And a sandwich and thermos of coffee would probably be a good idea, too.

Her father, busy with his project, didn't seem to notice her leave. She loaded her kit into the passenger seat of the farm truck and pulled out of the driveway onto their little rural road.

The road to the lake skirted the edge of Sidonie, Wisconsin, pop. 1092. A truck laden with laughing teens roared around her, spraying gravel from its rear tires. Going to one of those bonfire parties along the lake that her dad was worried about, she thought with a smile. She'd been to a few of them as a teen, but she liked the peace and solitude of stargazing better.

She turned off the lake road onto a rutted dirt access road that took her down to the beach. This late in the fall, the lake was nearly deserted. The summer houses had been boarded up for the season, the boats pulled out of the water.

Far down the beach she saw a small flicker of light and heard tinny strains of music from what was probably the end-of-season bonfire that the kids had been going to. It looked like it was the only one.

Good. Better star watching for her.

She set up her camp chair and her telescope. She had a bigger and better telescope at home, but the portable one with the carrying case was good for traveling because she didn't mind if she bumped it when she was throwing it into the truck or hauling it through the woods. She'd had it since she was a kid. Through the old plastic eyepiece, she had gotten her first glimpse of Saturn's rings. She'd watched comets and meteors, and experienced a rare view of an aurora borealis straying far enough south to light up the northern sky in shades of red and green.

"We've come a long way together, haven't we, old gal?" she murmured, patting the telescope as she looked up at the sky. Just as she looked up, a meteor flickered briefly, and Sarah smiled. That was a good sign of a nice display tonight.

The Orionids weren't the most spectacular meteor shower on the calendar, but they were the last one before the weather got cold. So far, the October night wasn't too bad. She'd been able to see her breath as she packed the truck, but the sheepskin jacket was keeping her warm. She tucked her hands into her pockets, curling one of them around the thermos of coffee she'd poked in there. It was, as she'd hoped, a good night for stargazing, clear and dark. There was some light pollution from the town off to the west, but it wasn't too bad with no cloud cover to trap and reflect it.

Another shooting star appeared and vanished in the dark sky over the lake, arcing between the stars, there and gone. Two so far, and she'd hardly been here ten minutes—

Wait—what was *that*?

This was a bright reddish light in a part of the sky where she knew there shouldn't be a star, not one like that. It was in the wrong place for Mars or Venus too. A satellite, maybe? Sarah reached for her telescope.

Several times in her night-sky watching excursions, she'd had the rare treat of seeing a meteor explode. Twice it was a bright flash, too high to see any details. Other times she'd gotten to see them pop like fireworks as they plunged into the Earth's atmosphere.

And there was always some small part of her that hoped to see a UFO. Not that she believed in UFOs, not in the alien spaceship sense. But if you spent a lot of time staring up at the night sky, sooner or later you might see something a little out of the ordinary, something you couldn't quite identify. That was the actual meaning of UFO, anyway: unidentified flying object. There was a lot of interesting stuff up there—space junk, military aircraft, satellites, experimental rockets, weather balloons.

Maybe this was her first UFO.

The telescope didn't make it any easier to identify; it just made it brighter. It was a vivid red flaring to yellow-white at its center, the color of an object heating up on contact with atmosphere. Through the telescope, she could make out a little of the comet-trail of hot air and debris that it would be leaving behind, but only a truncated hint of it. An object like this should be leaving an incredibly long trail, like in footage she'd seen of space shuttle reentry.

If the tail looked so short she couldn't even see it with the telescope's aid, that meant it was headed almost directly for Wisconsin.

Sarah straightened up from the telescope. The object was so bright now that no one looking up at the night sky, even in a cursory glance, could possibly miss it. As she stared up at it, the air shivered around her with a sudden, low rumble.

Sonic boom, she thought. *It was going faster than the speed of sound when it hit the atmosphere. Probably still is. Just like the space shuttle.*

It seemed shocking that an object this large could have slipped into Earth's atmosphere undetected. NASA tracked everything of significant size that might risk a collision with Earth, and Sarah followed several sites and message boards devoted to near-Earth objects. She would definitely have heard of anything large expected in Earth's neighborhood tonight. However, she also knew from following those message boards that new objects were discovered all the time. There was always a chance—not a large chance anymore, but still a chance—that an object large enough to cause the extinction of all life on Earth could slip through the network of official space observatories and amateur astronomers guarding the night skies to plow into the planet undetected. Space was unspeakably huge, after all.

Maybe this *was* that extinction-causing object.

Yet she wasn't scared. Wonder filled her instead. This was why she'd wanted to be an astrophysicist in the first place. If this was going to be the giant asteroid that wiped out humankind, she was getting to *see* it. She was getting to watch it land.

Possibly right on top of her. It was shockingly bright now, lighting up the trees around her, bright enough to cast shadows. Far down the beach, the music cut out, and she heard distant, startled voices.

All Sarah could do was stare. She could hardly even blink, even though it was so bright it made her eyes water.

She didn't want to miss a second of this. Especially if these were her last moments on Earth.

If this is how I die, what a way to go.

She could hear it now, or rather, feel it, the way she'd been able to feel the sonic boom a few moments earlier. The air around her seemed to tremble.

And then it was upon her. Heat washed over her, and Sarah belatedly realized she'd have a better chance of surviving this if she got down on the ground. All she had time to do was throw her arms over her head before the object hit the water with a tremendous *CRACK!*

The shockwave hit her an instant later, knocking her down. As she sat up dazedly, covered with sand, she was just in time to see a wave racing inland, topped with foam, high enough to blot out the dark line of trees on the opposite shore.

Her telescope! She made a desperate lunge for it, just as the wave caught her and she was suddenly underwater. The wave rolled her like a pinball into the woods. She tumbled into the brush with a painful crash, disoriented and terrified. Somehow she maintained the presence of mind to throw her arms around a tree trunk, stopping her from being battered to death among the trees. Water was all around her; she couldn't tell up from down. And then the wave receded, leaving her shivering and coughing at the edge of the woods.

She clung to the tree until it was clear no more waves were coming and then sat up, stretching out each of her limbs at a time. She was dripping wet and slightly bruised, but nothing seemed to be broken. It took her a couple of attempts to stand up on her shaking legs, and then she tottered out of the trees onto the beach.

High waves still lapped up the sand, but no worse than

she'd seen in winter storms. Her truck was still where she'd parked it, too big and heavy to be moved. Her little skywatching nest was completely gone, telescope, camp chair and all.

Maybe the telescope had been pushed into the trees, Sarah thought dazedly, rather than being sucked out into the depths of the lake. She would have to come back in daylight and look for it. At least she hadn't gotten around to taking the DSLR camera out of the truck yet, so she hadn't lost that.

And ... there was something out among the waves, bobbing on the lake.

She walked on rubbery legs down the beach until the purling waves lapped at her boots. The lake was starting to settle down now, rocking gently like the surface of a giant tub of water. The floating thing on the lake was about thirty yards offshore. She could see it mainly because it still glowed a faint, dull red from the heat of its reentry. It seemed to have broken apart when it hit the water; she could see bits and pieces floating on the surface, sinking rapidly out of sight.

The biggest intact piece of the object was vaguely roundish and maybe the size of one of the small outbuildings on the farm, not barn-sized, more like chicken-house-sized. It bristled with oddly angled parts, although she couldn't tell if that was because it had a bunch of antennas and things poking out, or because it had been crumpled and damaged in its crash landing, so she was looking at pieces of its exterior that had been broken and partly torn away.

It was getting harder to pick out the object from the dark water. The red glow was fading as it cooled, and more than that, she realized it was sinking into the lake. In moments it would be gone from sight.

Something moved abruptly, a large section of the main body of the thing flipping up and outward. For just an instant, Sarah glimpsed what was unmistakably a figure starting to clamber out—

—and then the whole object heeled over and sank very abruptly beneath the waves. Water rushed into the space where it had been.

Sarah stood and stared, even as a higher wave of displaced water swamped her up to the thighs and made her stagger.

There had been a *person* in that thing.

A test pilot?

An astronaut?

Whatever she'd just witnessed, whether it was a torn-off piece of the International Space Station falling to earth, or the crash of an experimental military test plane, or something else entirely, there had been a person in it. And they weren't coming up.

Sarah threw her sodden sheepskin jacket onto the beach and kicked off her boots. She ran into the water and met the next wave head-on, diving into it.

The October lake felt like ice, even to her already chilled skin. She was courting hypothermia; she couldn't stay out here long.

But she was a strong swimmer, a legacy of hot summer days at the lake, when she and the other kids from neighboring farms used to paddle around in the water to cool off. Back in her teens she'd been a strong enough swimmer to make it all the way across the lake. Those days were behind her now, but working on the farm kept her in good shape, and she was naturally buoyant even with her soaked sweater starting to weigh her down.

She stroked hard, swimming toward where she had

watched the object go down. Something jostled her under the water, a piece of floating debris that slid away from her when she reached for it; she felt a sharp edge of metal brush her fingers. In the cold water, it was slightly warm to the touch.

Abruptly, something alive and struggling broke the surface just in front of her, thrashing in a spray of water droplets and then going under.

Sarah dived after that struggling figure. She caught a fistful of what felt like hair and kicked toward the surface.

They splashed into the air together. She released her grip on the other person's hair, but he clutched at her, starting to drag them both down again.

"No!" Sarah gasped, shaking him. Her head went under the surface and she kicked up again, gripping him by a— bare?!—arm. "Relax! Try to float! I've—augh! blerk!—got you!"

She had no formal lifeguarding experience, but her gym teacher, Mr. Mancuso, had made sure that if the kids were going to spend the summer down by the lake, they'd all know the fundamentals, not just for rescuing each other but also because summer people often came out to the lake without knowing how to properly swim. He'd also warned them that drowning people could easily drag you down with them. And that seemed to be what this guy was doing. Her hands slid off his torso, catching on bits of metal or plastic; he was wearing some kind of slippery body suit that left his arms bare, which didn't give her any good purchase to grip, not like a jacket or sweater would have.

But then he went limp, as if he'd suddenly figured out what she was trying to do, or perhaps remembered his own water rescue training. It immediately became obvious that he was too heavy and dense to float on his own—guys often were, according to Mr. Mancuso, because they typically had less body fat and more muscle than girls—but Sarah got her arm under his shoulders. She felt him start to struggle again as his body tipped back in the water, then relax (kind of; he was still tense as hell), and a moment later they were drifting in a rescue position, with his head against her shoulder.

"That's it," she panted. She was starting to shiver. They had to get out of the water as fast as possible or they'd both be in trouble. "I'm just going to swim toward the shore. Float with me. Okay?"

She couldn't tell how out of it he was, but he understood enough of what was going on to let his body trail in the water as she towed him toward the beach. His wet hair rested against her cheek, his head on her shoulder. She could feel him breathing in short, shallow gasps.

"Slow breaths will make you panic less," she told him between strokes, dredging up another fragment of Mr. Mancuso's lifeguarding wisdom. She was going to have to look up her old gym teacher and thank him someday. "If you hyperventilate, it makes it worse. Try to slow your breathing if you can."

There was no answer, and his breathing didn't slow down, but he seemed to relax a little more, as if her voice itself was calming to him.

She was shivering hard by the time her feet finally touched the lake bottom. From here it was a desperate scramble onto the beach, with Test Pilot Guy clumsily helping. Together they stumbled out of the waves and fell onto the sand in a tangle of limbs.

"Oh my God, oh my God." It was half profanity and half prayer; she was laughing in relief as she unwound herself from her rescuee. Now that they were out of the water and he didn't seem too badly hurt, the impact of the adventure was starting to hit her, leaving her dazed and giggly. It really *was* an adventure, the most amazing one she'd ever had, a million percent better than getting chased by the Wazlowskis' bull at age eleven or that time she got lost with Jeremy McManus in the woods behind the lake. "Oh, my God, can you believe this is happening? Can you believe you survived that? Can you believe we're actually—*erk!*"

In the middle of her giddy babbling, Test Pilot Guy erupted from the ground, a sudden explosive movement so fast she had no time to react with anything but a startled, strangled cry as she was slammed into the sand. The next thing she knew, she was flat on her back with his knee jammed into her chest and something sharp and hard pressed to her throat.

THREE

SARAH STARED up at her captor in mixed panic and disbelief. In the darkness, all she could see was a black silhouette framed against the dim glow of the lights from town.

"Are you *kidding* me? I rescued you! Jerk!"

... was what she *would* have said, had she been able to breathe. Instead, she could only squeak for air, trying to flap her hands in distress as he held her pinned.

The only self-defense she'd ever learned was how to chase off a stray dog threatening the sheep. Having a big, heavy guy kneeling on her chest, pressing a knife against her throat (and where had it even *come from?*) was so far beyond all her experience that her mind was a humming, panicked blank.

Test Pilot Guy, now downgraded to Potential Rapist Asshole, stared down at her in total silence. Or at least she assumed he was staring. She couldn't see anything except a faint glitter of his eyes somewhere in the shadows blotting out his face.

Black spots were starting to blot out *everything*. She

really couldn't breathe. Just as she teetered on the edge of either total panic or passing out, the guy suddenly jerked away from her, scrambling backward in the sand and falling onto his ass.

Sarah gasped and coughed and sat up.

The stranger said something. Sarah couldn't understand him at all. She spoke a little Spanish from school, and a little German from Grandma Metzger, but it definitely wasn't either of those. His voice was soft and a little baffled and, as far as she could read his intonation, sounded apologetic.

Then he went suddenly limp, like a puppet with its strings cut, and keeled over on the sand.

Sarah stared at him for a long moment. She tried to stand up and fell right back down, her legs were shaking so hard. So she crabwalked backward until she'd made it twenty feet or so up the beach, leaving a trail through the sand. *Foreign* Test Pilot was nothing but a dark heap at the edge of the water. Farther out, pieces of his shuttle or plane or whatever it was glimmered on the waves as, one by one, they sank out of sight.

Sarah sat for a moment with her arms wrapped around her sodden legs before she forced herself shakily to her feet.

It was time to let someone else handle this.

She was halfway to her truck before she realized that she was missing a couple of vital things, such as her truck keys, and her phone.

Her discarded jacket was lying on the beach some ten or fifteen feet from Asshole Foreign Test Pilot. She retrieved it, keeping her eyes on him the whole time, and felt in the pockets for either of those missing items. All she found was a squashed granola bar and a couple of soggy feed-store receipts.

The phone was big and heavy enough that it had probably washed out of whichever pocket she'd stuck it into. She patted herself down thoroughly while she wobbled toward the truck, finding nothing except some random pocket change and sand.

She clambered into the truck anyway, locked all the doors, and sat shivering behind the wheel.

Okay, something that bright would absolutely have attracted attention from town. The sheriff would be out here soon. All she had to do was wait in the truck.

Her hands were sticky. She opened and closed them. Whatever it was felt warm. Was she bleeding? She reached up and switched on the truck's dome light.

There was something on her hands, all right. It looked like dark blue paint, streaked with water.

How had she got something like *that* on her? Did it come from his plane?

She turned her hands over, staring at them. Cautiously she raised one hand to her nose and sniffed it. There was no paint smell, just a kind of faint metallic scent that seemed slightly familiar.

Hoping she didn't regret this, she touched her tongue to the back of her hand.

As soon as she tasted it, the familiarity of the smell clicked into place. It was blood.

Blood … that was blue. Vivid blue. Not veins-under-the-skin blue, but deep indigo paint blue.

Or, at least, it was something blue that tasted and smelled like blood. Butchering season on the farm had left her very familiar with what blood was like. If she closed her eyes, it was indistinguishable.

Sarah wiped her palm on her jeans and got a flashlight out of the truck's glove box. Leaving the truck door open and the dome light on, in case she had need of a hasty escape, she hopped down and walked towards Foreign (Alien?) Test Pilot through the sand.

The feeling of the sand through her wet socks reminded her that she hadn't bothered to stop for her boots in her flight to the truck. She hadn't gone far before she stepped on something hard and pokey.

"Ow!"

She hopped on one foot for a minute, then bent down and felt around until she located her truck keys. They must've fallen out of her pocket during her inglorious escape from being kinda-sorta attacked.

I'm really not thinking very clearly tonight, am I?

But her head was starting to clear as her adrenaline rush and panic faded. And now she was desperately curious.

Foreign Or Alien Test Pilot still lay in a huddled dark shape on the sand. Sarah squatted next to him and shone the light over him.

He was blue, all right.

Not a *little* blue from being dunked in the cold water. He was actual, full-on, what-the-effing-hell-have-I-gotten-myself-into *indigo*.

His hair was black, or at least dark enough to look black in the flashlight's beam, very thick and long enough to plaster all over his forehead and neck. He was lying with his cheek pressed into the sand and his body twisted to the side. On the visible sliver of his face, the flashlight's beam reflected off a pattern of gold dots, starting just under his eye and curving down his cheek in a graceful arc.

His muscular shoulders and arms were bare, and glimmered in her flashlight beam with silver threads zigging and zagging all over his skin. Tattoos? She'd heard it was possible to make tattoos with unusual pigments, though having grown up in Sidonie, her experience with tattoos of any kind was limited. More oddly, she could see no sign of the knife he'd held on her. Had it even been a knife? Maybe she had mistaken the edge of his hand for a weapon.

But it had really *felt* sharp. She'd felt the point of it, pressed against her skin.

He wore a sleeveless jumpsuit of some clingy, gray material. There was a necklace or something around his neck, made of dull silver metal, like pewter or lead. Sarah poked at it hesitantly with a finger. It didn't seem to have any seams; it just ringed his neck like one of those solid bracelets that slides over the hand.

And he had those too, one solid silver-colored bracelet on each wrist. They gleamed under the flashlight with a luster like brushed steel.

His feet were bare. For some reason that was what finally broke through her curiosity and fear, leaving only a deep pity. He just looked so vulnerable like that.

He'd attacked her, she reminded herself.

But he hadn't meant to. She was sure of that. Whoever he was, *whatever* he was, he'd come to his senses in a strange place, with a stranger touching him and babbling at him in a language he didn't appear to speak. She would probably have tried to attack too. He'd stopped as soon as he'd realized what he was doing.

And he didn't seem to be armed, in spite of whatever she thought she'd felt earlier. It must have been his bare hands.

She looked up at the distant wail of sirens. Sounded like someone had managed to rouse the sheriff from his favorite bar. All down the lake, lights had begun come on at scattered cabins along the shore. Most of the summer people were gone, but there were always a few year-round residents. She could hear voices along the shore from the direction of the now-extinguished bonfire.

Pretty soon, half the town would be out here to check out what was going on.

"Hey there," Sarah whispered, shaking the guy's shoulder. His skin was terribly cold. "Mister? Are you awake?"

By all rights he should be in a hospital, and possibly locked up. But dozens of books and movies about alien contact flooded her mind. Alien autopsies. Area 51. Evil government agents.

You know that's fiction, right? she scolded herself.

But ...

If she let the sheriff's department have him, what were they going to do with him?

He could have alien germs. He could hurt me, or Dad, or the animals. He could ...

He could do any of those things, but he's lost and scared and hurt. If I were stranded on another planet, or escaped from a government lab, or whatever happened to this guy, I'd hope that a friendly alien would find me, instead of some government goons that'd lock me up and poke me to figure out how I work.

"Mister?" she said again, shaking his shoulder. The sirens were getting louder.

Sarah stood up, hooked her hands under his shoulders, and started dragging him toward the truck.

Years of working on the farm, throwing around sacks of feed and hay bales, had left her with flat, strong muscles in her shoulders and stomach. She was able to manage Alien Test Pilot's muscle-heavy bulk okay, though the trail he left where she'd dragged him through the sand made her wince; the sheriff would have to be a total idiot not to notice something had happened here.

Heaving him into the truck through the passenger-side door was considerably harder, but she had helped string up beef cattle at butchering time, and after her dad's accident, she'd done most of the necessary in-home health care, including helping her dad into bed or the shower. This guy was heavier than her dad; he seemed to be made of solid muscle. Still, with effort she got him into the truck, slumped over on the wide bench seat. She climbed in on the driver's side and pushed his head over to make room for her leg.

She really wanted to take a better look at him under the dome light, partly to find out where the blood was coming from, and partly because *he was blue*. But the sirens were loud now, and the urgent desire not to get caught by the sheriff with an alien in her truck made her stamp on the gas, fishtailing off the beach in a shower of gravel.

She had to slow down on the bumpy dirt road, and then killed her headlights—mouth dry, heart pounding—as red and blue flashing lights tore past on the main road. They didn't even slow down. Must be heading for the main access road to the lake, she guessed. They would find her little access road and the tracks on the beach soon enough, but for now she pulled out onto the main road with no one the wiser, turning away from the distant flashing emergency lights.

Now that she had committed herself, doubts beat at the back of her brain. Had she left anything at her stargazing sight that could identify her? Heck ... what *hadn't* she left there? Somewhere in the woods was her telescope, her camp chair, and worst of all, her *phone*. And she'd left tracks all over the beach. Didn't they have forensics nowadays that could match tire treads to specific cars? And what about DNA?

It's a rural county sheriff's department. They're not exactly CSI.

But even if she didn't get caught ...

She glanced down at Alien Test Pilot, slumped sideways on the seat with his head resting against her leg. She couldn't see much of him in the dark, but she'd seen enough earlier to be quite sure he wasn't human.

His species might kill and eat humans, for all she knew.

Or maybe she'd accidentally started an intergalactic war. Maybe his people were going to think she'd kidnapped him.

And yet, she couldn't leave him out there, any more than she could've left an injured accident victim alongside the road.

AS SHE GOT CLOSER to town, headlights on the road became more frequent. All of the traffic was headed the other way, going out to the lake to get a closer look. Little did any of them realize that the main attraction had just passed them in a nondescript, beat-up farm truck.

Her heart rate accelerated every time headlights flashed by. She felt like the words I HAVE AN ALIEN IN MY TRUCK were painted two feet high on the side of the truck bed. But none of the other vehicles slowed; no brake lights flashed in her rear-view mirror. When she turned into her driveway, no one turned in behind her.

The lights in the house were off. Her dad didn't like to admit it, but he got tired early these days. Tonight it was a relief. At least she could save one awkward explanation for tomorrow.

She drove slowly through the yard and around behind

the barn. Here at last, out of sight of either the road or the house, she turned on the dome light for a proper examination of her alien passenger.

The first thing that struck her, oddly, was how very human he looked. If not for the blue skin and blood, and the gold dots on his face—which looked organic rather than metallic, like the iridescent whorls on a peacock's tail—he could actually *be* human. The silver threads that glimmered all over his skin appeared to be some kind of adornment, if not tattoos then bits of metal imbedded in his skin. With some face paint and a set of decent clothes, he wouldn't raise eyebrows just walking down the street in downtown Sidonie.

Well. Except for those shoulders, and those arms, and all that ... everything. These were probably inappropriate thoughts to have about a guy who was bleeding all over her truck seat, but especially after bodily hauling him into the truck, it was impossible for her to avoid noticing that he was *built*. His sleeveless silvery-gray coverall was tight enough to give her a good look at his defined chest and flat stomach.

Outer space must have some good gyms.

Remembering how deftly and easily he'd overwhelmed her, she wondered uneasily if this guy could be an alien bounty hunter or space pirate. He could be a soldier from an invading army, or some kind of cyborg killing machine ...

But whatever he was, he bled. And he'd tried not to hurt her once he'd realized what he was doing.

Now that she was getting used to the deep blue tint of his skin, she could see he'd gotten more banged up in the crash than she had realized on the beach. His entire right shoulder was one huge purple-blue bruise, and his arm was scraped, with clotted dark blue blood welling along the gash, and—

... glimmering?

Sparkling?

Baffled, she leaned closer. His injured arm appeared to glitter under the dome light. Very gently and carefully, she picked up his forearm so she could study it up close. With her nose almost touching his skin, she thought she could see something effervescent fizzing along the gash, as if his blood itself was gently bubbling—

The arm in her hands jerked, and before she had time to react, a strong hand closed over her wrist, twisting it. She gave a gasp of mingled surprise and pain, jerking away, and just as quickly, in apparent reaction to the noise she'd made, he released her and sat up.

His eyes, she discovered, were a startling gold, reflective as a cat's. They would have shocked her more if one of them hadn't been almost swollen shut, a very human touch of vulnerability. He was squinting against the truck's dome light. Maybe such catlike eyes could also see in the dark.

The entire side of his head that had been pressed to her truck seat was clotted with blood, and while she couldn't get a better look without getting closer, she didn't think it was her imagination that the bloody area seemed to fizz gently, just like his cut arm.

It's healing, I think?

He'd bled all over her seat, and all over her, but he wasn't bleeding now, except for a bit of sluggish oozing. There was blood on his jumpsuit, quite a lot of it, but it didn't seem to be getting worse. Which was weird; with that much blood, she wouldn't have expected that it could have clotted already. Maybe the fizzing was some kind of ... leak-stopping measure?

He said something, causing her gaze to jerk back up to

his face. His voice was soft, the words lilting, but no more familiar than at the lake.

"I'm sorry," she said. "I can't understand."

He frowned. Touched his ear. Said something else, to the air more than to her. Talking on a radio, maybe? But from his worried look, he wasn't getting an answer.

Sarah cleared her throat, getting his attention again. "Sarah," she said, planting her hand on her chest, and then pointed to him.

She wasn't prepared for his reaction. He jerked away until his back slammed into the truck door, brought up his left hand in a fist in front of his chest, and pointed his right hand at her with the fingers together in a straight line with the palm, like the "paper" in "rock, paper, scissors" but rotated sideways.

Sarah jerked away too, more startled by the sudden motion than scared.

The alien lowered his hands slowly, easing out of what was, she thought, almost certainly some kind of martial arts position. Did he think that's what she had been doing, too?

"Sarah," she said again, tapping her chest.

He jerked at the sound of her voice. Sarah gasped aloud when she realized the patterned spots on his face had turned blue, almost matching the indigo tone of his skin. As she watched, their former gold color began to return.

And then ... he smiled. It was just a slight tug of his lips, but it made her smile back, because it was so recognizably human.

"Reian," he said, touching his chest in a near-perfect emulation of how she'd done it.

"Rain?"

Her clumsy attempt to pronounce the lilting syllables with their sleek, gliding vowels made his smile widen, just wide enough that she glimpsed a wholly unexpected dimple in his left cheek before he turned solemn again—though the faintest hint of that smile continued to lurk in his golden eyes. "Reian. Rei."

"Ray," she said. "No. Rei?" She tried to swallow the initial consonant and lift her tone at the end, just as he'd done.

"*Na*," he said, with another brief smile. "Sairah."

He made her ordinary name sound exotic.

"Yes, Sairah," she said, and they grinned at each other in a moment of shared triumph. He seemed to be just as delighted to achieve communication, however rudimentary, as she was.

FOUR

IT MIGHT BE EXHAUSTION, it might be fatalism, but Rei didn't think the native was going to hurt him.

He could tell by the way she looked—human features, curly blonde hair, freckle-splattered skin—that this world was a Birthworld planet. That made things easier. Most intelligent beings in the galaxy, including his people and the Galateans, were derived from DNA taken from Birthworld, the unknown planet where humankind evolved. This woman was relatively unmodified, from the look of her. That meant he could probably eat her people's food, breathe their air, and live in their dwellings without needing any special accommodations.

It would be easier to think if a blinding migraine wasn't splitting his head open. The pain in the rest of his body was relatively easy to ignore, or at least more familiar. He was used to hurting. The faint tingle of nanites combined with the hollow, hungry ache of his body's own healing ability let him know that it was being taken care of.

But the headache was different. It seemed to have a

presence of his own, pressing on the insides of his skull like an expanding balloon.

Lyr? he thought experimentally.

There was no answer, no thread of comforting warmth, not even the thready but still reassuring sense of Lyr's presence that he could sense when his friend was asleep or unconscious. Wherever Rei had ended up, he must be well outside Lyr's range. Either that, or—

He pushed the thought down. He couldn't think of Lyr, couldn't think of Rook. Each moment had to be taken one at a time.

Right now he had a friendly native with him who seemed to want to help. If only he could understand her properly. Either his translator had been fried by the same power surge that had fried the cuffs and collar, or this world's language wasn't one of the languages stored in it. Possibly both. He had thought a minute ago that she'd been lining up an energy blast from her cuffs, but no, she didn't actually seem to *have* cuffs. He couldn't see anything under her sleeves, and when he'd moved into a defensive stance of his own—by habit, having forgotten that his cuffs weren't working—she didn't act afraid. Which meant they were on a planet that the Galateans hadn't "pacified" yet.

She turned away from him and opened the door of her primitive land vehicle. Cool night air washed in. Rei automatically flinched away from it, trying uselessly to activate his personal shield to protect his face and lungs. Nothing happened, of course. And anyway, if this world's atmosphere was poisonous to Polarans, he was already doomed.

What was she doing anyway? Getting a weapon? Going for help?

Instead she circled around and opened his door. She

said something calmly and softly in a "talking to children and invalids" voice. Apparently some things were a human universal, even on a possibly-uncontacted planet.

When she laid her hand on his arm, Rei jerked away, his nerve endings lighting up with an instinctive fight-or-flee response. He had to squash his attempt to deploy his body's defenses—what few he had left.

The cuffs didn't work. That meant no shields, no guns, no cutting blade.

He had his natural claws—which he'd held to her throat earlier, fingertips half-shifted through pure instinct—and his scant handful of completely physical mods independent of the cuffs, like his healing nanites. And that was it.

He'd never felt so unarmed.

But she had pulled away as soon as she realized he didn't want to be touched. Taking a step backward, she gestured to the dark structure behind her and went on speaking in her singsong language, as if she thought he could understand her.

She wanted him to go in. That was plain enough. He stepped down carefully from the vehicle, holding onto the door for support and working hard to make sure she couldn't see how weak and disoriented he really was.

He was someplace rural; that much he could tell. He didn't know what kind of manure he smelled, but he'd bet it was from a domestic animal, and there was minimal light pollution to hide the unfamiliar constellations in the sky. A bright white light behind the outbuilding lit up the yard, but they were hidden in the building's inky black shadow; even his sharp Polaran night vision had trouble penetrating the gloom.

This planet didn't seem to be as undeveloped as his native world. From the smell of her vehicle, they possessed some sort of combustion engines. His people were still at the "boats and foot travel" stage. Still, this world's technology, what he'd seen of it so far, was a long way from hover-trains and jump-capable ships.

I bet they don't have spaceflight, he thought as he walked carefully toward the dark building, with Sarah hovering anxiously at his side, not quite touching him. *They're not used to strangers here. Primitive farming planet, I guess ... at least this part of it.*

Polara technically had a spaceport, after all, and when he'd left his homeworld, galactically advanced technology had been drifting outward from the cities, spread by trade and warfare among the many native villages and tribes. This world might be similar. And it had to be relatively close to the system he'd jumped out of, which meant he was probably still inside Galatean space.

But there were a lot of primitive worlds in the galaxy, officially within the domain of one star-spanning empire or another, yet unexplored and sometimes even undiscovered. He thought he might be on one of those.

It's possible no offworlders have been here since the Founders seeded this planet.

Rook would have loved that. He would have already started asking a thousand questions, by gesture language if necessary. The culture and history of other planets had always been endlessly fascinating to him.

Rei swallowed hard against a surge of nausea, smothering his emotions under a glacial calm. It helped that his headache was still trying to expand to fill his whole awareness. He let himself focus on the pain. It was better than thinking about anything else.

(Rook's *bright intelligence and gentle spirit, snuffed out in a war he'd been drafted into as a child, never given a choice—)*

Sudden light made Rei stop in his tracks. Sarah was just removing her hand from the wall, where she had flipped a switch. *Electric light,* he thought, squinting as the light stabbed his night-adapted pupils and worsened his headache. This technology must be common, if it was being used in a storage shed which, his nose told him, was used for keeping beasts. But it was also a very basic use of electricity. The lights were nothing but glowing filaments enclosed in glass, lighting up a large space containing equipment, piles of hay and grain, and enclosures for animals.

Homesickness for the world of his childhood punched him in the gut. This wasn't exactly the same, but it was closer than the sterile spaceships and stations where he'd spent most of his life.

Sarah moved forward to pat one of the piles of hay. She pointed to it, then to him; he tensed, starting to raise his hand in a defensive gesture, but this time he arrested the automatic response in mid-motion. As before, Sarah seemed unbothered, clearly unaware he had started to point a weapon at her. She touched her chest, pointed to the door, then pointed at him again, and to the pile of hay.

"I should stay here, right?" he asked, though he knew she couldn't understand him. He pointed at himself, and at the pile of hay.

Sarah vigorously bobbed her head. At least half the humanoid species of the galaxy had a gesture of affirmation like that, including Rei's own people. Some used it for negation, but she was smiling that infectious smile, so probably it meant "yes."

"Leyt," Sarah said, pointing to the electric switch and then to the light bulb overhead. "Leyt." She mimed flicking something up and down before touching the switch, plunging them into darkness, and turned it back on. "Leyt."

"Leyt," Rei dutifully repeated. It could be the local word for off/on, for electricity, or for the light itself. Either way, he got that she was telling him how to turn it off.

Sarah smiled again. She said something incomprehensible while pointing to herself and to the door, then held up her hand with all five fingers spread. With another smile, she turned quickly and went out the door.

Rei followed her and tested the door. She had not locked him in, and the door had a simple latch mechanism operated with a lever-like handle, easy enough to figure out. Rei cracked it open and peered out. He caught a glimpse of bobbing dark blonde hair and the pale collar of her coat as she jogged toward another structure nearby, a house of some kind.

She might intend to call the Galateans, having recognized him as a deserter. Or perhaps she was going to summon this world's authorities, which would amount to the same thing if they were in touch with Galatea.

Sarah glanced over her shoulder, and waved her arms wildly with an expression of alarm. She pointed to the house, then to him, and emphatically mimed closing the door.

Rei did so.

She wasn't going to sell him out. He would bet money on it in any of the gambling games common among the warslaves. She wanted him to hide. She did not want him to be seen from the house.

She was helping him.

He still didn't know why.

Rather than sitting down, he walked slowly around the interior of the structure, exploring. Movement helped activate the repair nanites, which weren't going to expend as much energy on an inert soldier as a mobile, functional one. Everything hurt, but he was used to pushing through pain.

The outbuilding was a large one with a dirt floor, smelling of animals and dust, cluttered with tools and junk that offered many opportunities for improvised weapons. He automatically located the exits, which consisted of another small door like the one Sarah had used and a wide set of double doors for animals or equipment. Everything in sight was mechanical with large, clunky parts and not the slightest hint of nanite tech or computers. The most advanced technology in view, other than the lights, was a big piece of farm equipment with large wheels and an engine, or what he guessed was an engine, made up of large, heavy components gleaming with oil and grease. There were other engines, partly disassembled, and some cut lumber, and more tools. Clearly this building served many of the farm's construction and repair needs.

A ladder led up to the shadowed loft. Rei climbed it, wincing; this was a lot harder with his injuries than just walking around. Above the main floor of the structure, he found a large space containing hay and assorted items such as boxes and broken pieces of furniture. One end was open to the night.

This place wasn't defensible in the slightest. At least it had a lot of options for escape.

A high-pitched crying sound from the shadows made him jump and extend his hand in the useless defensive stance again. The creature that emerged from the shadows of the loft was surprisingly familiar, a small gray and white cat.

"Huh," Rei said, lowering his hand.

Felines were one of the Birthworld species that had

been sampled by the Founders and used to populate the galaxy, so a lot of the worlds that had humans also had cats. Since he wasn't sure if it was unmodified or had been given offensive capabilities such as venom, he left it alone. It followed him down the ladder with surprising ease, navigating handily from rung to rung, and trailed him at a discreet distance as he explored the rest of the barn's main floor, poking into the corners he hadn't gotten around to yet.

He had thought the slatted stalls along one side of the barn were empty, but one of them turned out to contain a hoofed animal, lying down, that resembled one of the centaurish Hnee people from the shoulders down. He'd never seen the whole animal that the Hnee had been made from. It turned its head toward him, pricking its ears forward, and made an inquiring noise, blowing its breath out.

"Just exploring," Rei told it quietly.

An enclosure at one end of the barn turned out to contain several dozen fluffy domestic birds, with their own exit to the farmyard. They crooned at him sleepily when he opened their door. The cat seemed very intrigued by this. Rei pushed it back with his foot and closed the birds' door.

There was nothing else downstairs except animal feed and junk. Rei climbed back up to the loft and walked carefully across the treacherous floor—it was made of boards with gaps between; in places he could see down into the barn below—to look out the open end.

From here he could see that the clear, stark white light was coming from a light at the top of a pole in the yard. It lit up a pasture lined with trees, where some other animals of different sizes were bedded down for the night. Through the trees, he glimpsed the lights of neighboring houses or farms. None were close, but he made a note that they might still be able to see him if he wasn't careful.

An approaching rumble made him tense up, recognizing a similar sound to the engine of Sarah's vehicle. But it passed without slowing down, somewhere out of sight on the same road they'd driven to get here.

He hadn't seen any flying vehicles so far. Was it possible they only had land travel?

Somehow he was going to have to get himself back to space. If this planet didn't have native space travel, repairing the battlepod was his only option, unless he wanted to build a spaceship from scratch, using the primitive tools in the barn.

Or I could live on this world for the rest of my life ...

It didn't look like a bad world to live on. The cool temperate climate was compatible with Polaran life. There were forests, and there were animals similar enough to the ones he was familiar with that he could probably eat them without poisoning himself. If all the natives looked like Sarah, he couldn't pass as one of them so he'd have to avoid them, but that didn't sound so bad. He could live in the woods by himself.

Leaving Lyr all alone, out there where the war was still going on ...

But there was no war here. No Galateans. No slave collars—which reminded him of his own collar, a presence so familiar he hardly even felt it anymore. He fingered it, worried. He needed to find a way to cut it off as soon as possible, in case it wasn't permanently disabled and still contained some kind of tracker. The idea of the Galateans being able to reassert control over the collar sent an icy chill through him.

He was free for the first time since he was nine. He wasn't going back.

Also, with the collar off, he could shift again without explicit permission—not just the claws and teeth, but his entire self. He could have his *wolf* back.

His whole body shuddered, for an instant, with desperate want.

A light blinked on suddenly outside the house. Jolted out of his thoughts, Rei looked down at Sarah's head of dark blonde hair as she trotted back toward the barn, carrying a bundle in her arms.

He didn't want to be caught lurking in the loft, so he scrambled down the ladder, landing with a painful jolt that made one of his legs nearly buckle under him. His knee must have been twisted in the crash. He wished he could run a proper diagnostic on himself, but everything seemed to be down except his most basic nanite self-repair functions.

There was a sharp tapping before the door opened and Sarah pushed her way inside, using her elbow and shoulder since her arms were full. She'd changed out of her wet clothes into a thick, fuzzy shirt and a different pair of the blue, ridged trousers that must be customary garb of her people.

She greeted him with a smile and cheerful babbling in her own language. She was so—open. So happy. He wasn't used to being around people like that. It made him want to avoid her clear, open gaze, as if she could see into his soul and see how twisted and damaged it was.

Were all of her people like that, or had she led an unusually sheltered life?

At the very least, these people didn't live in fear. He'd seen no sign of walls or defenses around the farm, not even any signs of the frequent small-scale warfare prevalent on his native planet.

Sarah was still smiling at him, looking at him with her bright blue-gray eyes, fringed with sandy lashes, and holding out her soft bundle at him. She gave it a little shake.

Hesitantly he took it. When he started to unroll it, more items dropped out. Sarah giggled and then covered her mouth with her hand, making apologetic noises.

She had brought him a large, fuzzy blanket. Wrapped up in it were some clothes of the same general manufacture as the ones she was wearing, a large open-fronted shirt with a red and blue striped pattern and some trousers like hers, but larger.

The smart-fabric of his jumpsuit was dry enough, so he put the shirt on over it. He wasn't particularly bothered by cold—being Polaran, he was inured to it, and anyway, ignoring discomfort was second nature by now. But he was shivering, and warming up his body would allow his healing to concentrate on his injuries rather than on keeping him warm. He'd spent too long on space stations and ships; he no longer knew how to deal with the changeable weather of a planet's surface.

She'd brought him boots as well, but he left his feet bare. He was used to walking barefoot around the ship, and the dirt-and-gravel floor of the barn felt good on his soles, another echo of his childhood.

Sarah had vanished off to a different part of the barn while he put the shirt on, but now she returned, holding out her hands with some packaged objects in them. She squatted down and started spreading things in front of her. Looking up, she spoke again, beckoning him with her hand.

Rei crouched down awkwardly as she tore open one of

the paper packets. It contained soft fabric squares. She held these out toward him. He just stared at her, baffled.

Sarah sighed; exasperation, it seemed, was the same the galaxy over. As she unscrewed the top of a bottle, Rei found himself entranced with the slant of her lashes, the soft curve of her freckle-dusted cheek. It must be exhaustion. Just as he'd lost himself in exploring the barn, now he was lost in the springy curls brushing her cheek, the pinkness of her lower lip as she pursed her lips in concentration ...

Sarah cleared her throat, getting his attention. The open bottle released a sharp, pungent smell, and when she pressed one of the cloth squares to its mouth and turned it briefly upside down, dark orange-red fluid saturated the cloth. She dabbed the fluid on the back of her hand, then held it out to him again and pointed at the side of his face.

Oh.

This looked nothing like the medicine he'd grown used to—injectors, spray sealant, nanites. But it was not unlike the primitive first aid methods of his childhood planet.

He didn't know how to explain to her that his injuries would heal more quickly and readily if he just let the nanites do their work. After the third time he batted her hand away, Sarah gave up in visible frustration. She recapped the bottle and left her primitive medical supplies spread out on the floor. A few gestures to the supplies and to him got the point across: he was welcome to use them if he wanted.

Saying something, she led the way to the nearest pile of hay, carrying the blanket. She spread it on the hay and patted it.

"Yeah, I get it," he said. "Bed here. Yes."

She seemed to understand that, or at least he got

another smile out of her. She smiled so easily. What would it be like, to be so free with emotional gestures?

And now she was talking again. She liked to talk, it seemed. He didn't mind; she had a pleasant voice, even if he couldn't understand a word.

It took him a moment to realize that she'd repeated the last set of sounds a couple of times, looking at him with her big blue-gray eyes as if she expected it to mean something to him. He'd been distracted by—Actually, he wasn't sure what was distracting him. He'd just drifted, listening to the pleasant cadence of her voice.

She said it again.

"Goodnight?" he echoed.

"Goodnight," she said again, smiling at him, and backed up to the door, making him realize the words were a ritual goodbye of some kind. With another smile, she said something else, and then "Goodnight!" again, and left quickly.

Rei waited until he could no longer hear her footsteps before testing the door handle again. It opened just as before. He was not locked in. No point, really, with so many exits to the building she'd put him in. If she wanted to make him a prisoner, surely she would have chosen somewhere more defensible.

He was desperately, achingly tired, but he still wandered around a bit more before settling down. Sarah hadn't brought him any food or water, but he found a tub of clean-looking water in the hoofed animal's pen and drank it from his cupped hands. Water that had already been sampled by the animal-body half of a Hnee didn't bother him; he'd had worse. When his thirst was slaked, he dipped palmfuls of water and washed some of the blood off his face and arms.

The animal watched him from large, liquid eyes. Its ears

swiveled forward when Rei thanked it quietly for the water. He doubted whether it was intelligent enough to under-stand conversation, and it wouldn't know his language anyway, but he felt that it never hurt to be polite.

He was too tired to be hungry yet, though he knew he'd be ravenous in the morning, after his body's healing factor had worked all night. Maybe he could eat some of the animals' feed. If he really got desperate, he could eat one of the fluffy domestic fowl, but that seemed like a rude way to repay Sarah for helping him.

But right now, sleep was the biggest priority. He could have suppressed his body's need for a couple of days, but he'd also learned that it was a good idea to take advantage of any opportunity for sleep when possible. And it would help him heal.

He took the blanket up to the loft, feeling safer on high ground, and curled up in a pile of hay in front of the loft's open end.

It had been a long time since he'd slept anywhere but a bunk on a spaceship or station. The only times he'd spent any amount of time on planets in the last fifteen years was during infantry combat operations, and as a pilot, he hadn't done very many of those.

He'd forgotten how quiet planets could be, how steady they were underfoot. There were always sounds on a ship, always the hum and vibration of the engines, always distant voices and the clanging and banging of mechanics else-where on the ship.

He kept feeling as if the pile of hay under him was swaying. Knowing it was only his own inner ear trying to cope with the lack of motion didn't help much.

Sleep, he ordered himself, closing his eyes, but that didn't help any more than the other hundred thousand times he'd done it throughout his life. Some of his sept-mates, the other boys and girls he'd gone through training with, had the enviable ability to fall asleep instantly, anytime, anywhere. Rei couldn't. Even as exhausted as he was, his mind kept spinning, his gritty eyes coming open whenever he closed them.

He gazed out at the stars, but that didn't help. It only made him wonder about the battle going on around one or another of those tiny pinpricks of light, where Rook's ashes were scattered in a glowing orbital trail, and perhaps Lyr's as well.

He didn't recognize the prickling in his eyes and the tightness in his throat, at first, for what it was. It had been a long time since he'd cried: his septmate Haiva's death, to be exact.

Lyr and Rook had held him, that time. They'd all wept together in the privacy of their quarters, the last three survivors of their sept.

Who would hold him now?

The stars blurred and swam in front of him. He swallowed the sobs, forcing himself to be silent with the habits of a lifetime. In silence, he cried for his dead brothers and sisters.

Once there had been seven besides him. They had been his lifeline, his courage, his heart. Three sisters, four brothers. Lyr, Haiva, Skara, Rook, Kite, Selinn, and Thorn.

Now he was the only one left.

Something jostled his ankle. Rei flinched away from it, though it had been too soft and tentative to set off his combat reflexes. He sniffed and wiped his eyes with the back of his hand, wincing as his hand brushed across the healing scrapes and bruises.

The light touch came again, and then small paws

pressed into his leg as the gray and white cat stepped on him, climbing into his lap.

"Well, hi there," he murmured. He didn't know how to pet a cat, but he remembered that Haiva used to like having her ears rubbed, and Galateans were made from cat and human DNA. When he rubbed the cat's ears, she arched into his hand, vibrating softly.

He was glad she didn't have Haiva's pattern of leopard spots. That would have been too much to bear.

Yet somehow it felt a little like having his dead sister back. As if she was trying to comfort him from beyond the grave.

With the cat purring gently in his lap, he closed his eyes, and was finally able to sink beneath the tidal wave of sleep.

FIVE

SARAH GAVE up on sleeping around 5 a.m. after waking every half hour from dreams of meteors mixed with half-remembered scenes from science fiction movies. It was still dark, and the thermometer outside the window read just above freezing. She dressed quickly and went down the stairs on stealthy sock feet to avoid waking her dad. When she grabbed one of last night's biscuits from the lidded tin on the countertop, she realized guiltily that she'd forgotten to offer any food to Rei last night.

What did aliens eat? She didn't want to poison him. For all she knew, his people were like pandas or koala bears, and only ate a single type of plant that grew on his home planet. Or maybe, as space travelers, they could no longer survive on regular food at all; perhaps he needed an intravenous nutrient formula or something like that.

But he seemed so much like a human. He had teeth like human teeth, not a beak or a specialized apparatus for consuming pollen. It was possible that everything on Earth would be poisonous to him or that he had extreme food taboos, but if he stayed on Earth for awhile, he'd have to eat the local food or he was going to starve to death.

She loaded a plate with samples of every different kind of food she could find in the kitchen: a biscuit, sliced ham, leftover bacon, an orange and an apple from the fruit bowl, saltine crackers, a carrot, a cup of yogurt, a few half-stale shortbread cookies from Grandma Metzger's last Christmas care package, some slices of cheddar cheese, and a handful of pepperoni. There should be *something* here he could eat.

Sarah examined her handiwork, and then another thought occurred to her. She hurried to the living room and pulled books off the shelves until she found the one she wanted. Then she stamped into her boots in the kitchen. The sheepskin coat was still damp, so she put on an over-sized denim jacket of her dad's instead, and opened the door with her elbow.

She loved this time of night, the crisp final hours before dawn crawled up the sky. Clouds had rolled in to blot out the stars, and the predawn darkness was nearly absolute. The air felt sharp as a knife blade when she sucked it in through her nose, breathing out through her mouth in curls of steam.

She knocked lightly before opening the barn door, wondering if Rei even knew what knocking meant. The interior of the barn was dark and perfectly silent except for the sleepy murmuring of the chickens. Sarah took a careful step inside. If he was asleep, she'd leave the plate and go start her morning chores—

"Sairah," said a soft voice at her elbow. She stifled a gasp and nearly dropped the plate.

"Jeez! You're so quiet!" She could just see the glimmer of his eyes and the silver tracery on his skin. "I'm gonna turn the light on, okay? Light?"

"Light," he said quietly. "Goodnight, Sairah."

She shut the door and flicked the light on. He was still wearing her dad's shirt over the gray coverall, and his hair was tousled, with straw in it. His eyes sparkled at her; he looked amused. The swelling and bruising around his black eye was noticeably less than it had been yesterday.

"Oh, yes, very funny, scaring me out of a year's growth, and as my dad would say, I don't have a lot of growth to lose. Are you hungry?" She set the plate on top of a barrel. "Food? Eat?"

She picked up a piece of ham and took a bite to demonstrate. His eyes tracked her movements, with a certain desperation in them; the spots on his skin blanched almost white.

"Eat," she said, pushing the plate toward him.

"Eat," he repeated softly. He picked up the ham and ate it rapidly in small, quick bites, flashing very white teeth. She was about to demonstrate the same process on another piece of food, to show him he could eat anything on the plate, but he'd already grabbed the biscuit, so apparently he was figuring it out. And from the look of things, he was ravenous. Didn't they feed him on his spaceship?

Maybe he's a refugee. He might have traveled for a long time to get here.

Frustration at the language barrier nearly strangled her. How could they communicate? She wanted so desperately to ask him questions.

I wish universal translators weren't just science fiction ...

She felt like she should give him privacy to eat, but instead, she couldn't help watching him. With his head bent over the plate, he ate like a ... *like a hunted animal,* she thought. His eyes darted around, and he looked at her often, as if he feared she might tell him to stop.

Her gaze drifted to the silver collar around his neck. Did he escape from captivity? Perhaps someone had been abusing him.

They probably hadn't made a habit of starving him, though. She didn't think you got that kind of muscle and those smooth, athletic movements from being malnourished.

He also didn't wolf his food. He wasn't taking big enough bites to choke on. He was just eating very, very fast. Like he'd had manners drilled into him so thoroughly that he couldn't eat rudely even when he was desperately hungry.

He looked up again, met her eyes with a quick flash of his amber ones, and stopped in midbite. After swallowing, he pushed the plate toward her. "Sarah?"

"Oh, no, that food is for you."

But he showed no signs of resuming, even though he flicked a still-hungry gaze at the plate. There were crumbs on his bottom lip; she had an odd, quick urge to reach out with her thumb and brush them away.

"Okay," she said with a smile, wrenching her gaze away from his mouth, and picked up the apple. She pushed the plate back in his direction.

He didn't need any encouragement to finish the rest of it. The yogurt cup made him pause. At least he didn't try to bite through it; he knew it was packaging, just not how to open it.

"Here," Sarah said, opening it for him before realizing she hadn't brought a spoon. This didn't seem to faze him. He just dipped his fingers into it. Maybe they didn't have spoons on his homeworld.

And, okay, watching him lick yogurt off his fingers was unexpectedly distracting.

Sarah ate one of the shortbread cookies and grimaced.

Dry as sawdust and just as tasty. Grandma Metzger always gave Sarah and her dad a big tin of them every Christmas. Maybe they tasted better if you'd grown up in the Depression.

Rei didn't seem to mind. He ate everything on the plate, including the orange, which he ate like an apple, biting through the peel. Sarah started to tell him to stop, but decided it didn't make enough difference to be worth trying to explain. After all, it was normal to eat an apple skin and all; why not an orange?

She wandered over to feed her apple core to Princess. The old dapple-gray mare was lying down in her stall, but put her head over the half-door to take the treat from Sarah's palm with her soft lips.

"So what do you think about having an alien in your barn, old girl?" Sarah asked, scratching the mare's forehead.

Princess blew out her lips and snuffled around Sarah's hand for more apples. She had a tremendous taste for them. If Sarah and her dad would let her, she'd scavenge windfalls at this time of year until she gave herself colic.

"Sorry, no more. Gotta get back to my guest, old gal."

In her absence, Rei had finished everything down to the crumbs. "Good?" Sarah asked.

"Good?" he repeated.

"Yep." She looked critically at the side of his head. He didn't appear to have used the first aid supplies she'd left him—they were still sitting on the floor—but he seemed to have cleaned himself up a bit. At least he wasn't leaving blood everywhere anymore. And his bruises looked like they'd faded noticeably overnight, though it was hard to tell with dark blue-purple bruising against blue skin.

"Hey, Rei," she said to get his attention, and moved the plate out of the way so she could open the book she'd brought, a world almanac from her high school days. She flipped through it until she found the world map. Rei looked on with interest as she pointed to Wisconsin.

"Sarah," she said. "Rei. Here. Sarah and Rei."

Rei said something in his own language, frowning in concentration as he examined the map. He touched the blue part of the map that represented the Atlantic Ocean, and then the blue splash of Lake Michigan, and looked up at her. "Rei-*ket* Sarah?"

"Yes, this is where we are."

Rei tapped Lake Michigan emphatically, and the thought dawned on her that, if he'd already grasped blue was for water, he might think the enormous lake was the lake he'd crashed in. "No," she said, shaking her head. "No, that's a different lake. Uh, the world is ... big?" She touched the map and spread her arms out wide. "Big!"

Rei looked baffled, then pensive. He looked around and pointed to the light bulb. "Light," he said, his musical, lilting accent making the word sound foreign. He held his fist above the map. "Light." His fist moved down in an arc to thunk against Lake Michigan. "Rei."

"No," Sarah said firmly. She turned the page to the U.S. map, and taking his hand, she tapped his fist to the map a hair westward from the lake, in the blank space that made up most of Wisconsin. The map was much too large-scale to pinpoint Sidonie's location in anything other than the broadest terms, somewhere vaguely in the central-western part of the state. "Rei." She turned back to the world map and then back to the U.S. map, pointing to the same place, trying to demonstrated the equivalence between them.

Rei frowned thoughtfully and then crouched on the barn floor, stretching one of his legs out to the side as if bending the knee hurt him. Sarah sat down, curious, and watched him draw with his finger in the dirt. She could still feel the texture of his skin under her fingers when she'd gripped his fist, not thinking about it until after; it almost felt as if his hand, soft yet ridged with calluses along the edge, had left a warm imprint on her skin.

Rei drew an irregular blob in the dirt. What was *that* supposed to be—a sun, a world, a continent? Not like she could ask. Anyway, he was drawing something else above it, something round, with stubby fins ... and she sucked in her breath when she recognized the intact version of the craft she had glimpsed floating on the waves before it was sucked under. It was round and fat-bodied, with short wings-like things sticking off. For something sketched in the dirt with his fingertip, it was actually a really good drawing, easily recognizable even though she had only had a brief look at the craft, badly damaged, in the dark

"You're a good artist," she told him. Rei flicked a glance at her—*Damn it,* she told herself, *you know he can't understand you!* Turning back to his drawing, he sketched a gently curved line arcing down from the craft to the odd-shaped blob, which she now realized must be the lake. Not only that, but she realized from her astronomy studies that he'd connected them with a parabola. Rei was not only an artist but understood basic orbital mechanics too.

"Hey," she said, and Rei looked up again. "I have a better idea than drawing in the dirt. Hold on, let me get something."

There were some carpenter's pencils with the rest of the hand tools in the workshop part of the barn. She couldn't find any paper, so she flipped the almanac to the title page, which had some blank space on it. "Here," she said, holding out the pencil. When Rei merely looked at it, Sarah made a mark on the paper and then pointed at the drawing in the dirt.

Rei's face went ... *bright*. That was the only word for it. He lit up, and Sarah's breath caught in her throat. She hadn't even realized he could look like that, animated and genuinely happy.

He pulled the almanac toward himself and made a quick copy of his earlier drawing: lake-blob, ship, parabolic arc. With the pencil and paper, his movements were quick and sure. On a blank space near the lake, he drew a recognizable though weirdly distorted version of her truck, and a couple of squarish buildings complete with perspective.

"Is that our farm?"

The tip of the pencil traced a pale line from the farm to the lake. Rei pointed to himself, to her, and to the wall of the barn. He touched the truck drawing with the pencil and pointed to her again.

"You want me to take you back to the lake," she guessed. "Oh, no. That is not a good idea. No. *Bad* idea." She shook her head vigorously, hoping he understood that gesture.

Rei's face went blank. He tapped the drawing of his ship with the pencil tip. Pointed to the sketch-truck. To her. To the drawing of the lake. To the ship. And the lake again.

"You ... want to get your ship?" Okay, that made sense. If she were stuck on an alien planet, she'd want to fix her spaceship and get home as soon as possible. Except ... "Rei, it sank in the lake. What are you going to do, dive down to it?"

Uncomprehending stare. He pointed to the lake, truck, her—

"I get it! I know what you want! That's not the problem." She crossed her arms. "Rei, maybe you don't remember, but it's at the bottom of the lake. We'd need divers and a really big winch to get it out. Anyway, there's probably cops and scientists and God only knows what else out there now."

Rei tapped the pencil on the paper to get her attention. He pointed to the sketch-farm and to the lake. Then he pointed to the wall of the barn.

Sarah stared blankly as he turned in place, finger pointing to each wall of the barn, one by one. He gave her an impatient look, tapped the pencil on the lake, and continued pointing to different walls until she figured out what he wanted.

"Oh. The lake is that way." She pointed in the approximate direction. "But—how are you going to get there? No, no. How can I make you understand 'no'? This is a bad idea."

Rei laid the pencil down on the book. He smiled at her, touched the empty plate, and smiled again with a brief flicker of his dimple. Then he turned and walked—limped, rather—toward the door.

Sarah hesitated for the barest instant before she sprang to her feet and dashed after him. She got in front of him and blocked his forward progress, planting her hands against his chest. He was very heavy and solid. She knew he could have pushed her aside if he wanted to, but he didn't try; instead he gave her a quizzical look from his odd, gold eyes.

Gorgeous eyes. Cat's eyes, amber threaded with green and gold and subtle hints of violet ...

She had to tear her gaze away. "No!" she said to his lips —which wasn't any better; this close, she could see how the blue continued all the way inside his mouth, not like grease-paint alien makeup, but a million subtle shades of blue and purple, just like human skin. "No, it'll be light soon, and people will see you. And it's *miles* to the lake, with houses and farms and roads. I know all you can see from our farm is trees, but it's not all like that."

Rei quirked a brow quizzically. He took her by the shoulders and carefully, but effortlessly, moved her out of the way. She'd been right about how strong he was.

"No!" she protested. "You'll get caught!"

He was fumbling with the door latch. Sarah closed her hand over his, and was arrested once again by the contrast of her small, square pink fingers against his blue ones. She blinked and looked up into those serious, intelligent cat's eyes.

"I'll take you," she sighed.

REI SEEMED to understand readily enough what she wanted, even when she threw a pile of empty feed sacks into the passenger side of the truck and gestured him down to the floor before putting a couple of the old sacks on top of him. Heck, she hadn't gotten this much comprehension out of her high-school boyfriends even though they both spoke the same language.

He pushed himself up far enough to look out the window as she turned out of the driveway. It was still very early, brightening from night into a cool gray dawn. Sarah didn't blame him for wanting to look around, not that there was much to see out here. But maybe for an alien, a road lined with trees and farms was as exotic as his spaceship seemed to her.

Whenever headlights approached on the farm road, she murmured "Down" and gave him a push below the level of the windows. After the first time, he understood what

"Down" meant, ducking and covering up whenever she said it.

Well, he's brighter than most of the dogs in town, she thought, and tried not to laugh.

She avoided the town and cut over to the lake by the back roads. So far she'd encountered few other cars, just the usual handful of farm vehicles or people driving to early jobs in town, but flashing lights on the lake road caught her attention. There was a sheriff's car parked sideways across the road up ahead.

"Oh no, I knew it," she whispered. "There's a police barricade."

She slammed on her brakes. It was light enough now that she could see a deputy in a wide-brimmed hat next to the cop car, smoking a cigarette and looking in her direction. If she turned the truck around and hightailed it out of there, all she'd do was make them suspicious and maybe get in her very first police chase.

"Down, down!" she hissed at Rei, covering him with more feed sacks. "Be quiet. Quiet!"

Although she knew he couldn't understand, the heap of feed sacks was utterly still and silent as Sarah pulled up to the police car and rolled down her window. "What's going on?" she asked with her best and most innocent smile.

"You live around here, ma'am?" the deputy asked. He glanced into the truck, his eyes passing over the cluttered interior without much curiosity.

"Sure. My dad and I have a farm over on the other side of town." *Don't look at Rei. Eyes forward, Sarah. You can do this.*

A drop of sweat trickled down her back. As a teenager, she'd hated being in trouble with the school authorities. She'd never been arrested. She'd never even smoked pot!

"License and registration, please?"

She dug it out of the glove box, reaching across the heap of feed sacks. Her arm brushed against Rei's shoulder, warm and solid under the camouflage.

"See anything weird last night, Miss Metzger?" the deputy asked as he examined her license.

"Weird like what?" Sarah asked brightly, and then tried not to wince at the realization that the whole town had probably seen Rei's spaceship crash. Indeed, the deputy was giving her a puzzled look now. "We go to bed and get up early out at the farm," she explained. "If anything happened after dark, I wouldn't know about it. Were those stupid town kids causing trouble again?"

After another long look at her, and a second glance into the truck, the deputy asked, "What's your business out at the lake this morning?"

At least she had a decent excuse for this. "I lost my phone out here yesterday. I wanted to look for it."

"How'd you do that?"

"We were boating, and either it fell in the water or got lost on the beach. I wanted to walk around and look for it." Inwardly, she patted herself on the back. For a person who rarely lied, that was a pretty good one if she did say so herself.

"Late in the year for boating, with the weather gettin' so cold."

"We were out on the lake looking at the fall colors," Sarah explained. "Me and my dad." *Don't call and check. Please don't call and check.* "Listen, if the lake's closed right now, I can just go home and try to find my phone some other time. But it's my *phone*, you know? I don't want to have to buy a new one and change my number everywhere if it's just laying on the beach somewhere."

At this point she almost hoped he told her to leave—her nerves were a wreck—but he looked thoughtful and then handed her license back. "Go ahead. If you find anything else, something funny-looking, bring it to the sheriff's department, okay?"

"What sort of funny-looking?" Sarah asked—innocently, she hoped.

"Weather balloon fell in the lake last night, it looks like. Weather service wants it back, that's all. So if you pick up any pieces of metal or anything else that's not supposed to be there, bring them down to the sheriff's office."

"Okay, will do," she promised, and he waved her through.

As the truck got up to speed on the lake road again, the pile of feed sacks lurched. Sarah reached over, groped for the top of Rei's head through the camouflage, and pushed him down. "Stay," she ordered. "There might be cops on the beach. If we're not alone down there, I'm turning right back around, okay?"

She knew he couldn't understand a word, but he stayed where she'd put him as she bumped down the dirt road to her favorite beachside lookout. It was full daylight now, but the light was flat and gray, a heavy cloud cover shrouding the sky. If it had been like this yesterday, she'd never have come out here, never have met Rei, and missed out on the biggest adventure of her life.

There was no one on the beach, so she parked in her usual place, where the woods gave way to sand but before the sand got soft enough to trap her tires. When she opened her truck door and hopped down, she could see that people had been tramping around. There were boot tracks all over the beach, scuffing the sand where waves hadn't smoothed them away. A boat anchor had left a deep divot on the beach. Importantly, though, they weren't here now.

"It's okay. You can come out." She leaned back into the truck through her door and pulled the topmost feed sack off Rei. He sat up, his hair standing up in tousled tufts. "But we can't stay for long, all right? They might come back. And ... why am I still talking, you don't understand any of this."

Rei was already groping at the inside of the passenger door, trying to figure out how the handle worked. "It's—" she began, but he gave up and came out her door instead, sliding gracefully past her. His body brushed hers, and she was reminded all over again that he was a very sexy man.

For someone who was blue. And an alien.

He looked around, and Sarah tucked her hands into her pockets, watching him. The wind off the lake was bitterly cold, late October with a promise of November, and he was still barefoot. Maybe his people didn't wear shoes?

Just as she was wondering how he could possibly be warm enough in nothing but his rumpled silver coverall and her dad's plaid shirt, he shucked off the shirt, dropping it in the sand. Her surprise turned to shock when he began popping open a seam of sticky tabs down the side of his coverall.

"Wait," she squeaked, but he peeled out of it with a quick, smooth motion, leaving it in the sand like a snake's shed skin.

He wasn't wearing anything under it.

He was blue all the way down, she thought dazedly. And he had a pattern of gold dots down his back, a double row on either side of his spine, patterned in gentle whorls like the ones on his face.

Rei looked over his shoulder at her and said something incomprehensible. He gave her one of his quick, sweet smiles ... which had a whole new impact on her entire body, coming from a guy who was stark naked.

"Rei! People are going to see you!" *Like me, for example!*

Ignoring her, he strode forward, muscles rippling smoothly under his blue skin. He seemed to have no self-consciousness at all about being naked. Sarah didn't mean to stare, but she was entranced by his flexing calf muscles, the tight buttocks, the firm curve of his spine—

He strode into the water and now she was getting alarmed.

"The lake bottom drops off really quickly!" she called. "Be careful!" Like he understood a word of that.

When he was thigh-deep, he dove forward, arcing into the water with a splash. Sarah held her breath until his dark head popped up farther out in the lake, bobbing on the gray surface of the water. He dove again and emerged a little way farther along for a breath before going under once more.

Last night, she had assumed he couldn't swim. Apparently the problem had only been that no one was an especially good swimmer after an emergency crash landing on an alien planet. He swam with the same grace and physical confidence that was evident in every move he made.

Sarah watched for another couple of minutes to make sure he was going to be okay. He was treading water now, far out on the lake, and she remembered all too well how cold the water was. But he seemed to be fine, so she started searching the beach and the edge of the woods for any sign of the things she'd lost.

She couldn't find her telescope, or the camp chair either. The wave had probably dragged them both out into the lake. They'd resurface in front of some vacation cabin's boathouse with the November storms hit. She did find a few twisted pieces of metal and plastic washed into the edge of the trees. She wasn't entirely sure if they came from Rei's ship or if they were just flotsam, but she put them in the truck bed just in case.

And amazingly, wonder of wonders, she found her phone, buried in damp leaves and sand near the base of the tree she'd managed to hang onto. *Thank you, patron saint of cell phones!* She tried powering it on, and was unsurprised when nothing happened. If you dropped your phone in the toilet, you were supposed to put it in a jar of rice to draw out the moisture, right? She decided to try that when she got home. But cell phone, yay! Good news for once.

Rei splashed suddenly out of the waves in the shallow water near the shore. Sarah looked over, only to be smacked in the eyeballs, not to mention the reptilian hindbrain, by a naked and strapping specimen of blue humanity striding out of the water.

... well, limping, actually. With his clothes off, she could see that his left knee was bruised and swollen. There was also a dark slash across his abdomen, probably where all the blood on his coverall had come from. He looked way better than yesterday, but that was a *lot* of damage his body was trying to repair.

He dropped a gray plastic case, about the size of a brief-case, in the sand at the water's edge, and turned immediately to dive back in. Sarah slogged through wet, heavy sand down the shoreline and picked up the case. "Do you want me to put this in the truck?" she called after him, but he was already back out in the lake again, visible only as a dark, bobbing spot against the gray waves.

The case was heavier than it looked. Toolbox? Luggage? She might have tried to open it if she could figure out how, but since she couldn't, she put it in the truck bed. By that time Rei had returned to deposit what looked like part of an instrument panel above the reach of the waves. He came back several more times, dropping off pieces of junk made of metal or rugged plastic, trailing wires from their ragged edges. Sarah ferried them all to the truck.

On the last trip he collapsed to his knees in the sand. Sarah hurried down the beach, shrugging out of her denim jacket, and threw it around his shoulders. She wished she had brought the warmer sheepskin.

Rei nodded in acknowledgement and, perhaps, thanks. His teeth were chattering, and he sat in the sand for a minute, head bowed, while Sarah carried the latest piece of junk to the truck.

As she was stowing it under a feed sack in the truck bed, she heard the drone of an engine. There was a motorboat out on the lake, angling toward them across the gray water.

"Whoa, gotta go!" She ran down the beach and tugged on Rei's arm. Seeming to understand her urgency, he stumbled to his feet. Sarah grabbed his clothes and opened the truck door for him when he fumbled with the handle.

The motorboat was close enough now that she could see people in it, including one standing up. And they were looking this way. Cops? Curious residents? She didn't want to be caught by either one, especially with a naked alien in her truck.

"Down!" she told Rei, tossing a feed sack at him, and revved the truck. As she jolted into the trees, she glanced into the rear-view mirror and saw the motorboat closing on the shore.

Well, now she'd *really* find out if it was possible to identify a truck from its tire tracks. She hoped no one had been able to get her license plate. It was bad enough they'd seen the truck. Luckily, beat-up old Ford farm trucks weren't exactly rare around here.

Rather than going through the police barricade again, she took a back way she doubted if the sheriff's department had bothered to block off, since it went through the Mullers' cow pasture, utilized a couple of old logging roads, and came out behind the Dairy Queen downtown. There were advantages to living in the same small town for her whole life. Just to be on the safe side, she took a roundabout way back to the farm.

"I hope you got what you needed," she told Rei. He'd poked his head up enough to look out, peering with curiosity at bits of outlying Sidonie as it sped past them. "And try not to be seen, okay? We don't have very many blue people around here."

She knew he couldn't understand, but at the sound of her voice, he glanced at her and flashed her a brief grin.

SIX

THE FIRST SIGHT that greeted Sarah when she turned into the farm driveway was her dad, leaning on a cane and loading items off the front porch into a wheelbarrow. He waved to her. Sarah waved back and pulled around behind the barn. At least Rei had the sense to stay low.

"That was my dad," she said as Rei looked up at her from his seat on the floor. "I'm going to distract him while you unload the—oh, what the hell, you can't understand me anyway." She tapped her fingers on her knee for a moment, and then pointed into the back of the truck, at the recovered debris from his ship, then at the top of the barn. "Dad goes in the barn sometimes, but he can't climb the ladder. Do you understand? Up." She mimed climbing a ladder, pointed into the back of the truck and at the loft again.

Rei nodded. Sarah hoped that meant *yes*. Maybe it just meant *I don't understand*. He slipped her jacket off his shoulders, where it had been inadequately teetering on the edge of falling off anyway, and held it out to her.

The jacket was damp with lake water, but the rain that had threatened all morning had finally begun to fall, so she was bound to get wet anyway. She left Rei with a final whispered, useless caution to stay out of sight, and went to see what her dad was up to.

"Hey, glad you're here, punkin. Give me a hand with this." He was dragging a dirty plastic tarp by one wadded-up end, tottering on the cane.

Sarah decided it wasn't worth scolding him for using just the one cane—he was supposed to use two, one in each hand, to avoid twisting or tweaking his back—and instead helped him cover the wheelbarrow. Large pieces of metal and plastic jutted out of its bed, making her think of the spaceship junk they'd retrieved from the lake. "Is this for the hydroelectric project?"

"Yeah, spent the morning at the mill, figuring out how to run the lines. Where were you at today, kiddo?"

"I lost my phone at the lake last night. I went back to look for it."

"Find it?"

"Yep. It got wet, though. I'll need to see if it's okay when it dries out."

Gary grunted as he tucked in the edge of the tarp. "Heard on the radio this mornin' there was some kind of plane crash or something out there last night. Prob'ly some townie with a pilot's license, flying around after dark like an idiot. You see anything like that?"

"No, it must have happened after I left," she said quickly. "I did see some cops out there this morning and I wondered why."

Her belly squirmed with guilt. She hated lying to her dad. But what could she tell him: *I found an alien and I'm hiding him in the barn?*

"Damn fools," her father scoffed. "Give any young hothead a license these days. Damn lucky they didn't get anybody else killed along with their own fool self. Now where's the—ah—"

He reached for his second cane, leaning on the porch, and started toward the barn with a fast, stiff stride that Sarah had trouble keeping up with. After the tractor had rolled on him and crushed his back and hips, the doctors had said he'd never walk again, but they hadn't counted on hardheaded Metzger determination.

Right now Sarah wished he wasn't moving quite so fast. "Dad? Are you going to the barn? Can I get something for you? I—uh, I was going that way anyhow."

"Just need the toolbox out of the truck. You wanna start rolling the wheelbarrow out to the mill, I'd sure appreciate it."

The truck. Oh *no*. Some people might believe her if she said the stuff in the truck bed was trash she'd picked up at the lake, but her dad, with his mechanical aptitude, would be instantly fascinated—and he'd know in a moment that it wasn't anything at all like Earth technology.

"Dad—wait—"

Too late: he'd already rounded the corner of the barn. Sarah let out her breath in a relieved sigh when she saw the truck bed was already empty except for some straw and feed sacks. Rei had been fast.

"Now how many times did I tell you, sugar," her dad began in an exasperated tone, just as Sarah noticed the side door to the barn standing open.

"I'm sorry," she said, quickly hurrying to close it. "I was in a rush." She peeked quickly into the barn as she shut it, seeing no sign of Rei. He was good at vanishing into the shadows when he wanted to.

"If Princess gets into the Haverfords' hayfield again,

you're the one gets to catch her. You know she can open the latch on that stall."

"I know. I'm sorry, Dad." She reached out a hand for the beat-up metal toolbox as he got it out from behind the truck seat. "How 'bout I go put this in the wheelbarrow and meet you over at the mill?"

Her dad shook his head, and the creases in his weather-beaten face deepened in a smile. "You got homework for your college classes? I don't want to keep you away from that."

"My homework will keep. I'd love to see how the mill project is coming along. You can tell me all about it."

And if it keeps you away from the barn, that'd be fantastic ...

ALTHOUGH SARAH and the other native soon left for other parts of the farm, Rei spent the afternoon in the loft anyway, feeling safer up there than down in the main part of the barn. Rain pattered gently on the roof of the barn while he spread out the items he'd retrieved from the battlepod and went through them carefully, cataloguing his assets.

He'd managed to retrieve most of the instrument panel, along with assorted pieces of the battlepod that had broken off in the crash. His heart sank as he looked at the motley collection of metal and plastic junk. He didn't even know what half this stuff *was*. He wasn't a mechanic; he was a pilot. Maybe Skara or Thorn could have looked at his salvaged finds and all the stuff down in the main part of the barn, put it together, and built a functional spaceship out of it. Maybe he could have even done if he could've used his bracelets to hook up to the galactic 'net and found instructions somewhere.

Well, Skara and Thorn are dead, and my bracelets don't work, so I guess I'm just gonna have to deal with what I've got.

The best find by far, and probably the only thing of actual value, was the emergency repair kit. It was designed to float, and he'd found it just below the surface of the water. Most of the pod had sunk in the deeper part of the lake. Hopefully that would keep it out of the hands of the natives, at least for now, until he could figure out a way to retrieve it and, through some miracle, make it flightworthy again.

It really would take a miracle, with his limited repair skills.

But he couldn't think that way. It was like surviving a battle. You had to just keep moving, focus on the immediate task at hand, and not think about the sheer impossibility of the whole thing. Otherwise you'd lie down and never get up again.

The kit contained equipment for repairing simple malfunctions in the pod and in Rei himself. Along with a basic array of tools, a portable power cell, and that kind of thing, there was an injector with a case of medications. Rei flipped the case open. Stimulants, painkillers ... and, *yes.* A backup translator chip.

It was possible their communication issues were because his chip had been fried in the same surge that had knocked out his collar and cuffs, but he thought it was just as likely that Sarah had never been fitted with a chip of her own. He hadn't had one himself until he was taken by the Galateans at age nine. If his chip was working and her language was in its database, he ought to be able to understand her even if she couldn't understand him, but it was no surprise if her planet was too primitive to have been properly catalogued yet.

All he had to do was think of a way to convince her to let him inject something into her head while sharing no common language. *That* sounded like fun.

He reached for the book Sarah had brought him, the one with maps. She hadn't taken it back to the house, so he had brought it up to the loft with him. The Galatean Empire was mostly paperless, but Rei had enough experience with different planets' versions of books to know what it was. Most of it was useless to him, since it was all text and charts in a script he couldn't read, but it contained an insert with a bunch of maps and pictures in the middle.

When she'd first showed it to him, it had taken him a moment to figure out that all those irregular shapes of many colors represented maps. The large blue areas had tipped him off; he vaguely remembered seeing a lot of ocean as he was struggling to guide the damaged pod through the atmosphere. So the crowded, multicolored sections, dense with unfamiliar letters, must be continents.

Sarah's world.

He flipped the book's pages, skipping the words and looking at pictures of streets and cities and people. Sarah's people came in a variety of colors, like his own people, but in a different set of hues. His people were blue or purple or brown; hers were various shades of brown and bronze and pink. He saw no one in the pictures with mods of any sort. No animal ears, no wings or centaur bodies, no gills or flippers.

He turned back to the map section. He might not be able to read the words, but he understood that the lines dividing the continents into blocks of different colors must represent political divisions. This world was vast, with many regions and provinces. The shapes of its continents corresponded to no world he'd ever studied.

Where *was* he?

Laughter and voices from below caught his attention. He leaned forward to look out of the loft, down into the pasture, where Sarah and the older native were dragging a hose across the field and chatting happily with each other in their incomprehensible language. The man pushed the end of the hose into a big metal tub and started filling it, while Sarah vanished briefly from sight—Rei heard rustling down-stairs—and came back pushing a little cart with a bale of hay on it. Various animals wandered out of the trees and from under the overhanging edge of the barn roof to snuffle around her. Some were large with short fur, others short and round with thick curly wool.

Rei was intrigued by the older man, who was petting some of the little curly-furred animals. He walked with a pair of sticks. Old age? A war injury? Those crude crutches were something Rei remembered from his childhood, but hadn't seen among the Galateans at all, with their prosthetic implants and external mech parts. Another sign of the prim-itive state of technology on this planet.

The older man was pink like Sarah. Rei felt a sharp twinge, which he tried to suppress, at the thought that this man might be her mate or spouse. But given the visible age difference, it was more likely the older male was her parent.

Sarah vanished beneath the overhanging roof again and reappeared leading the gray animal that looked like the bottom half of a Hnee plus the top half of something entirely different. She gave the animal a friendly slap on its haunches, and it trotted a few steps before lowering its head to nibble at the close-cropped grass.

Now that Rei saw this animal next to the other ones in the pasture, the kinship was obvious. He wasn't familiar with all the animals he saw out there, but they were all built along similar lines, with four legs and hooves and fur.

They were all Birthworld animals.

Actually, he hadn't seen a single animal on this planet so far that wasn't an obvious Birthworld species. Even the birds at the lake had gray and brown barred wings, like Rook and Kite.

Was it possible ...?

He shook his head to brush away the thought. No one knew the location of Birthworld; at least that was what Rei had been taught. All anyone knew was that the now-vanished alien species called the Founders had taken samples of many different kinds of Birthworld life and had seeded them across the galaxy, many tens of thousands of years ago, using entire worlds as their laboratories. The Founders were gone, and for all anyone knew, Birthworld itself was gone too, but the many laboratory worlds lived on, including Rei's homeworld and Galatea and many others.

That's all this is, just another world where the Founders put some modified Birthworld stock. Maybe they trans-planted a whole Birthworld ecosystem here. They did that in some places.

Which he knew from listening to Rook talk about it. Rei wasn't that interested in long-ago times and places, but Rook could never stop babbling about all the theories involving the Founders and their projects. He'd have loved this world so much—

Rei's chest clenched. For an instant, the soft rain falling outside the loft dissolved into the sparkling trail of Rook's destroyed ship, glimmering against the stars. Glittering embers, the stink of burnt flesh—no, that was wrong, he hadn't been close enough to smell anything, and anyway, you *couldn't* in space. That was from another place and time, when Haiva had died, shot in front of him—

He was sitting up, leaning forward, his heart racing out of control and his hands fisted in the hay. He blinked and blinked, erasing the sparks from his vision; or trying to— they still shimmered around the edges. *Slow breaths. Calm down.* He'd clutched two fistfuls of hay, and when he opened his aching fingers, he found that his fingers had shifted partway into claws, drawing blue drops of blood from his palms.

Lyr used to calm him at these times. But now the place in his head where Lyr used to dwell was empty. All he could do was try to calm himself.

When he could breathe properly again and his heart was no longer trying to tear its way out of his chest, he reached for the tools and scraps he'd salvaged. He couldn't stay on this planet, with its rain and its forests and its ... Sarah. He had to find out if Lyr had survived the battle.

Lyr was all he had left.

SARAH CAME BACK NEAR DUSK, bringing a plate of food: meat, bread, boiled vegetables, a gooey pastry with a red fruit filling, and some more of those hard little cookie things. Rei reached for one of those first, munching on it; they reminded him of Galatean ration bars. This time Sarah had put a small flat implement on the side of the plate, with three pointy bits at one end, but he had no idea what it was for or how to use it, so he went on eating with his hands as politely as possible.

Etiquette lessons had been part of his training after the

Galateans took him from Polara. He could still sometimes feel the sting of corrective shocks from the collar, or smacks from the long training rod that some of his teachers had used. The collar was more likely to be used on the battle-training ground or during formal affairs, and the rod at the regular dining table, where they'd whack the back of his hand or the top of his head when he tried to sop up gravy with his bread or reach across the table to serve himself rather than waiting for the serving dish to come around—perfectly acceptable behavior on Polara, not so much on Galatea.

The idea of Sarah correcting his table manners by hitting him made him smile slightly.

"Thank you," he told her in his own language, not yet knowing how to say it in hers.

Sarah smiled and said something that contained no words he knew. She reached into a bag she'd brought with her and pulled out some more books. She opened one of them to show him some pictures of forests and deserts, and then put them on a shelf and patted them.

"Thank you," he said again, and was privately delighted when it made her smile. She had a lovely smile; it lit up her whole face.

Rei finished the last bite from the plate and wiped his hands on a twist of straw. They had to get past the language barrier, and there was only one way to do that, at least if they didn't want to spend the next year learning each other's languages.

"Wait," he told her, holding up his hand as she started to pick up the plate and utensil. "Don't go yet."

He wasn't sure if she understood, but she was still in the barn, petting the cat, when he came back down from the loft with the toolkit.

Rei set the toolkit on top of the barrel they'd been using as a table and opened it. Sarah looked on with wide-eyed fascination, her gaze skipping from one item in the kit to another. She reached out, fingers almost touching a laser cutter as she asked a short question in her own language. Probably something like "May I?"

Letting the alien native play with a laser cutting tool didn't seem like the best idea, so Rei tapped the multi-wrench next to it. She picked it up with exquisite care and examined it for a moment, before she was distracted by Rei snapping open the translator chip's holder and fitting it to the tip of the injector.

How to explain?

Maybe analogy would do it. Rei laid the injector on top of the kit. As gently as he knew how, he took Sarah's hand.

She drew in a soft breath. Her fingers curled in his before relaxing, letting him guide her as he would.

Rei took the multiwrench from her unresisting fingers and set it aside. Her fingers were callused from farm work, not soft. Rei liked that, even though he knew at the same time that his killer's hands had no right to touch her.

But this was necessary. He guided her hand to his own face and touched her fingers to the skin behind his ear. All the while, Sarah watched his face with her wide eyes. The dim light washed out the blue in her irises and left only gray.

Rei guided her fingers to the small, hard nub of the translator implant under the skin. He was unprepared for his own reaction as her fingertips ghosted over his skin in that sensitive place. He wasn't used to being touched, especially not there. The fine hairs prickled across his entire body, a sweeping wave of electricity washing over him.

Sarah's pink lips were parted, her face very intent. Her

eyes flicked back and forth, searching his face as if she could find answers there.

Rei put his own thumb on top of her index finger and pressed against the translator chip. It hurt a little, like pushing on a bone spur. Sarah's sandy brows drew together in a puzzled frown.

He released her hand, but her fingers lingered on his skin a moment longer before she put her hand hesitantly down.

Now he reached to touch her in the same place.

With a quick, reflexive movement, Sarah tilted her head away, then straightened it and held still—eyes rolled to the side, trying to see what he was doing—as he felt behind her ear.

Her skull was shaped like his; he found the same ridge of bone just behind the ear, where his implant had been inserted. Her skin was distractingly soft. Trying to stay focused, Rei ran his fingertip around the underside of her ear, feeling for anything that might interfere with the implant, such as horn buds or other protrusions.

She didn't seem to have anything like that. Unmodified Birthworld human, like he'd thought, at least to all outward appearances.

Sarah was very still, except for her chest under her soft-looking sweater, rising and falling with quick, shallow breaths.

Rei took his hand away. "Sarah," he said, and she jerked, her gaze seeming to snap back to reality from somewhere else. "I need to do this so we can talk to each other." He picked up the injector. It was a simple one, shaped to fit in the hand, with a one-touch trigger to deploy its load. Rei held it between them, noticing with interest how she flinched slightly back from it, in a way she hadn't reacted to the cuffs. Did she recognize what it was, or did her people use handheld weapons? Perhaps she thought it was something dangerous.

"Talk," Rei said. He touched his mouth, then touched behind his ear again. Reaching out, he laid his fingertips across her parted lips (soft, so soft) for the barest instant before he touched the place behind her ear.

"Talk?" she whispered, her strange accent making the word sound odd, nearly incomprehensible.

"Talk," he agreed, and mimed pointing the injector behind his own ear. Sarah sucked in a quick breath.

Afraid of a common medical tool. Not afraid of energy bracelets that could fry her brain. What an odd woman; what an odd world.

There was no better way he could explain. He touched behind her ear again, then touched his lips, and held up the injector.

Sarah breathed in slowly, and tilted her head to the side, exposing the soft patch of skin behind her ear. With one hand, she held back her hair.

His heart flipped over at the vulnerability of that pose.

She was still watching him out of the corner of her eyes. He could see in her expression that she was scared as he touched the injector to her skin. It beeped softly as it found the right location. Sarah jerked, but stilled herself.

He pulled the trigger.

The injector made a tiny hiss, and Sarah flinched hard, jerking away. Her sharp "Ow! Fuck!" needed no translation.

"Ow, ow, ow!" Sarah yelped, stumbling away from him. She felt behind her ear, then tilted her head to the side and shook it like she had water in her ears.

Rei watched helplessly, wanting to calm her, but knowing he couldn't. He knew what she would be feeling now, the unpleasant pinched-nerve tingling as the translator extruded its wires and began to read information from her neurons. In a few hours, it would have finished forming its connections and would begin to engage with the language center of her brain.

"Ow!" Straightening up, she glared at him and babbled a long string of words in her language.

"I'm sorry," Rei said. "It won't hurt for very long. At least, mine didn't."

Sarah said something huffy. She touched her ear again, smacked it lightly with a palm, and snapped her fingers in front of one ear, then the other.

"It doesn't make you deaf," Rei told her. "It doesn't affect your hearing at all. At least, if I did it right."

The injector was supposed to make it foolproof, but she belonged to an unknown variant of humanity. What if he'd damaged her? Struck a nerve where other types of humans didn't have one?

There's nothing you can do about it, he told himself, stinging with guilt. *What's done is done.*

Sarah let out another long string of angry-sounding words, picked up the plate, and marched out of the barn.

Well ... he'd either given her the ability to understand him (eventually, when the translator synced) or he'd given his only ally on this planet brain damage.

He'd know by morning.

SEVEN

MORNING MEANT MONDAY, and Monday, for Sarah, meant driving an hour to Eau Claire for classes and her half-day shift working as a custodian on campus. It also meant leaving Rei alone all day to do God only knows what.

After he'd *already* done God knows what to her ear.

She was pretty sure she'd understood what he had been trying to convey last night. He wanted to use that gun-shaped thing to do something to her that would help them communicate with each other. Maybe they did have universal translators after all. But he hadn't warned her that it would *hurt!* The tingly, zinging pain felt like a bumped elbow, except it was in her *head*, and she couldn't make it stop.

The first minute or two had been the worst, but she could still feel it back there, tingling and throbbing. When she touched behind her ear, the little lump under the skin made her shiver.

I could cut it out. Just take a knife ...

But what if it was actually doing something in there? What if she ripped it out and took half her brain with it?

And what if it hadn't even worked? Before she'd stomped out of the barn, she hadn't been able to make any more sense than usual out of Rei's musical, lilting words. Maybe she had been completely wrong about what he was trying to do after all. Maybe he was the advance guard for an alien invasion after all, and he'd just planted something awful in her head.

Last night she'd made it through dinner with an effort, trying not to act too odd, and most of all trying not to reach behind her ear and grope at the sore place. Her dad was distracted anyway. He'd been listening to the radio all afternoon, where every DJ and news anchor in central Wisconsin had been speculating about the bright light at the lake. Which meant the only thing he wanted to talk about was the one thing Sarah wished he'd stop bringing up.

"Damned government flying things around. I bet it's some kind of military test plane. They just don't want to admit it." Her dad's eyes were bright; Sarah guessed that he would love to get his hands on experimental government technology to take it apart and see how it worked.

If you only knew, Dad.

She wished desperately that she could tell him the truth, but it felt like opening Pandora's box; once she told him, she couldn't stuff that knowledge back inside. Would he call the police? Maybe if she started telling people, aliens would come and kill them all for letting the secret out ...

Is it my father I'm worried about, or Rei?

It was, she decided, a little of both.

At least she felt better this morning, the pain unpleasant but not too distracting. It was still cold and raining outside, but the kitchen was brightly lit and smelled pleasantly of frying bacon.

"You look peaky, punkin," her dad told her, turning around from the stove.

"Maybe I'm coming down with something." *Or alien technology is destroying my brain.* "You didn't have to make breakfast for me," she added, giving him a quick hug from behind, and trying not to wish he'd stayed in bed this morning; she had planned on grabbing a piece of toast and going out to the barn to yell at Rei some more for putting alien tech in her head.

She didn't *feel* like she was being puppeted by an alien mind-control device. *But maybe that's what they want you to think!*

"Always happy to help out my college girl," her dad said, navigating between stove and table by hanging onto furniture as he dished up her breakfast. He'd pay for the exertion later, but she didn't say anything; it meant so much to him to be independent.

"I'll do the chores before I go," she said through a full mouth. Once the food was in front of her, she realized that she was *starving*. Something to do with the alien implant in her head? *Don't think about it, don't think about it ...*

"I got it, kiddo. You'll be late to class."

"How about I feed the chickens and get the eggs before I go, then? You can do the livestock in the field."

"Oh, givin' me the tough jobs," he laughed. "In the rain too!"

"You're the one who keeps saying you need the exercise," Sarah told him. Stuffing the last bite of bacon into her mouth, she scrambled to her feet and grabbed the entire stack of buttered toast. "I can eat this while I work."

Clammy autumn chill smacked her in the face when she stepped outside. Gray mist hung in the trees, and the animals were a huddle of damp fur and smoking breath under the lean-to along the side of the barn. This was a day for working inside. Hopefully her dad would spend the day in the house or the old mill, and not decide to go work on the tractor or some other project out in the barn.

As she crossed the yard in the growing light of dawn, she became aware of a deep thumping, felt through her chest and the soles of her feet. Sarah stopped and listened. Gradually it resolved into the chop-chop-chop of helicopter blades.

A helicopter—here? Flying in this terrible weather?

Sarah turned and peered through the gloom toward the lake.

She couldn't see anything, just the diffuse blinking glow of the radio tower in town. After a minute or two, she could no longer hear the helicopter. Either it had landed or flown out of hearing range again.

How hard *were* they looking into this crash, exactly?

If the government knew an actual alien had landed out here, the answer was probably going to be *very hard indeed.*

Her hastily eaten breakfast sitting uneasily in her stomach, she ducked into the barn, looking around for any signs of Rei's presence. Nothing was visibly out of place.

"Rei?" she called softly.

The barn cat, Mouser, mewed from the loft, and a moment later, Rei came down the ladder. "Sarah," he said, and she jumped when a sudden sharp twinge flickered through her skull. *"Hr'nalit se mreiti* me understand *ko?"*

"Whoa!" She was too astonished to even mind the renewed headache. "I understood some of that! Say something else!"

Rei flashed her a fast, bright grin. *"Hr'n toka* time taking *esteir* completely-all then."

She didn't hear the English equivalent in her head so

much as she just understood what the words meant. As she heard the alien sounds coming out of his mouth, comprehension of their meaning landed directly in her brain. She was still getting a sort of grammatical word salad, direct translations of individual words mingled with words she couldn't understand. But it was a vast improvement over trying to communicate with a two-word vocabulary.

"I forgive you for the headache," she told him. "This is amazing. Here, I brought breakfast."

He followed her around the barn, munching on toast, while she quickly fed the chickens and gathered eggs. "I have to leave today," she told him. "I need to go to school—do you understand that? School? College, to be precise. You probably don't have that in space. Or maybe you do. Anyway, I need to go to school and my part-time job. I'll be gone all day. Are you understanding any of this?"

"Leaving for a day cycle," he said.

"Yes, that's right! Oh my gosh, we can talk to each other. This is amazing. This is going to work better as this thing in my head learns English, right? Or whatever it's doing."

"*Lroa'tak* function-increasing *se tobit* two or three day-cycles."

"I hope you said it'll be working better in two or three days." She touched the side of her head. "Will it still hurt? Headache. Ow."

"Headache? Sorry." He really did look sorry. "I forgot *srikala se anatiya* too-long time."

"It's okay. I know you didn't mean to hurt me." He *wasn't* lying, she thought. He wasn't an invader doing something terrible to her brain. She didn't think it was possible to fake the soft sorrow in his eyes at the idea of causing her pain.

And they could talk to each other now! He could tell

her about his homeworld. He could tell her why he was here on Earth ...

... and instead she had to go try to concentrate on differential equations. She considered skipping class, but she would have had to drive to Eau Claire for work anyway.

"You have to stay hidden while I'm gone, okay? Stay up in the loft. My dad might come out to the barn. And ..." She hesitated. Trying to explain through the translator's wonky grasp of their languages that government agents might also be snooping around would probably scare him without giving him enough information to be useful. "Just stay out of sight."

"*Vaspar* hidden *kun to.*"

She was just going to have to assume that meant yes.

THE TRANSLATOR WAS STILL COLLECTING vocabulary and grammar from her brain, but the bits and pieces of her language Rei could now comprehend were enough for mutual intelligibility, of a sort. It was a start.

He fingered the implant behind his ear as he stood in the loft and watched her vehicle pull onto the road, its lights piercing the rainy-day gloom. He'd forgotten how much they hurt as they grew into the brain. In his case, the discomfort of having the translator implanted was just one small component of his general misery and homesickness in those early cycles.

Still, it bothered him that he'd caused Sarah pain, even with the best of intentions.

And you tried to attack her when you first met her, don't forget about that. Even though he hadn't meant to. It had been a deeply ingrained reflex, an automatic reaction to believing himself under attack.

But that was exactly why he had no business touching her. No business thinking about the softness of her skin, the vulnerability in the way she'd exposed the side of her head for the injector. The warmth of her lips under his fingertip ...

He pushed down the memories and went in search of something to cut the collar off with.

He'd thought about trying the laser cutter from the tool kit, but without a mirror he couldn't see what he was doing, and he wasn't quite desperate enough to risk slicing open his jugular ... yet. The barn held many scraping and cutting tools. Surely one of them had to work on the collar's tough yet lightweight alloy.

He found something he guessed was a primitive gas-powered cutting torch, but it suffered from the same problem as the laser cutter, only worse; it wasn't precise enough for cutting something right under his chin. There were some files and saws, and ... hmmm ...

Rei picked up a long-handled tool with curved cutting blades. He tested it on one end of a roll of heavy wire, and with a little effort, the blades snipped cleanly through. This might do it.

And if *all* the collar's functions hadn't been disabled by the power surge ... well, its anti-tampering measures would leave Sarah and her family with a blue mess to clean up.

He reversed the tool and guided the cutting end with one hand, settling the collar between its jaws. Gripping the handles at this angle was awkward; he couldn't get enough leverage to bear down properly. An idea occurred to him, and he braced one handle on top of the barrel, gripped the other, and—

The barn door opened.

There was no time to hide, not with the collar tangled up in the cutting tool. Rei wrenched backward, yanked on his own neck, caught the tool as its handles slipped off the barrel, and ended up tangled with it, staring helplessly as the elderly alien with the walking sticks limped into the barn, froze, and stared back at him.

For a long moment, they just looked at each other.

Rei straightened up slowly and worked the tool's blades free of the collar. He didn't have functional cuffs for defense anymore, but he could still run or fight. The barn was full of potential weapons.

But he sensed no threat from Sarah's parent. The alien didn't look hostile, just puzzled and curious.

Rei tried a tentative smile.

The alien said something. All Rei could catch was a female pronoun. Referring to Sarah? Since the male didn't have an implant, and with Sarah's implant out of range for syncing, all Rei could understand of their language right now were the scraps his translator had managed to glean from Sarah's translator so far. And it only worked one way. Rei should be able to understand a few words of the alien's language, but he could not make himself understood in return.

The alien was still babbling on. "I don't understand," Rei said, and that stopped the alien, who then said something else in a curious tone.

"No, sorry," Rei said. He touched his chest, echoing how Sarah had introduced herself. "Rei."

Hesitation, then the alien followed suit, and said something that sounded like "Garymetzger."

He raised a hand to point at Rei, in what Rei had come to understand was not a threatening gesture from people who didn't have wrist-mounted energy weapons, but it was still impossible to suppress his instinctive flinch. At least he managed not to raise a hand into shield posture this time.

Garymetzger saw this and lowered his hand. Instead he touched his own neck and nodded to the cutting tool. He said something, slow and questioning. All Rei understood was "off."

"Yes," Rei said. "*Yes.*" He nodded vigorously.

Garymetzger carefully closed the door behind him and limped closer. Rei took a few steps back, putting more space between them. Garymetzger didn't push it. He pointed to the cutting tool, shook his head, and then pointed to the tools on shelves along the barn wall.

"I hope that means you have something better."

Garymetzger smiled uncomprehendingly and went to the shelves. Rei trailed along, watching curiously as Garymetzger picked up a couple of small saws, examined them, and put them down again. The alien turned around and tapped his own neck, then held out his hand, palm open, and crooked his fingers in what Rei could only assume was sign language for "come here."

"You want to look at it?"

Baring his throat to an alien was the hardest thing he'd had to do on this planet so far. But Rei thought of Sarah's trust in exposing her neck and ear to him for the injector, and he fought down both his wolf instincts and his deeply ingrained caution. Tipping his head back, he let Garymetzger finger the collar and tap it.

"Hmmm," Garymetzger mused. He turned back to the tools and picked up something not unlike the bladed cutter, except this one had shorter handles and thick, heavy cutting tips. He put a chip of wood between the cutting tips and snipped it cleanly in half to demonstrate.

Rei nodded and tilted his head back again, baring his throat.

He had no way to warn this friendly alien that the collar might explode when cut. But he didn't think it was going to. He was pretty sure all its functions were completely inert.

He hoped.

Garymetzger gripped the collar carefully in the cutter's jaws and said something. Rei decided from the bits he could glean that he was being told to hold still.

Not a problem.

Garymetzger bore down on the handles, grunting with strain. The collar tugged painfully on the back of Rei's neck, and then with a sharp *Crack!*, it parted and fell away, thumping in two halves into the hay on the floor.

It was off.

Gone.

He touched his neck hesitantly, fingers brushing across skin that hadn't felt the touch of anything but the slave collar in fifteen years. He could feel the ridges of callus and scar tissue around the edges where the collar had rested, the little bumps where its electrodes used to connect with his nervous system for punishments.

"Thank you," he said. The words were inadequate. There were no words in his language, in any language, for how much this meant. "Thank you. *Thank* you."

Garymetzger smiled. He bent stiffly, leaning on one of his sticks, and picked up one half of the collar. He turned it over with thick-knuckled fingers, callused and scarred from years of work, examining the exposed wiring and twisted edges of the metal.

As Rei blinked away sudden tears and got a grip on himself, a thought occurred to him.

This was an alien who was curious about mechanical

things. If Garymetzger was the one who used the tools in the barn, then he must be some sort of mechanic or engineer.

True, he wouldn't know the specifics of Galatean technology; it was light-years beyond anything this planet had, at least from what Rei had seen so far.

But, with Rei to help and Sarah to translate, maybe Garymetzger could figure out how to fix a Galatean ship.

EIGHT

SARAH PULLED into the farm driveway in a dreary evening rain. The truck's windshield wipers slop-slopped back and forth, leaving a smeary trail in their wake. *Better add new wiper blades to the list of things to buy,* she thought. There was always some small thing to buy or fix on a farm.

At least the truck was still running smoothly under her dad's skilled hands. They used to have a second car back when her mom was alive, a newish Subaru that Mom used for commuting to her job in town. They'd had to sell it as crushing medical bills piled up on them, and now they were completely dependent on the aging truck. So far, none of her dad's project cars—acquired for free from neighbors, scattered around the farm in various states of disassembly— had yielded a second working vehicle.

Sarah shuddered at the thought of how close she'd come to losing the truck at the lake two nights ago. If Rei's ship had landed closer to shore—

But it didn't. It's fine. You couldn't have known.

It was so easy to forget about all this weirdness when she wasn't at the farm. Today had felt so *normal.* Like stepping through a portal, from the part of her world where Rei existed, to a world of normal classes and work, where the bright light at the lake on Saturday night was no more than a cause for idle speculation along with the latest international and political news.

As she stepped down from the truck and headed toward the farmhouse lights shining warm and bright through the rain, she could almost imagine the last two days had never happened at all. Aliens and spaceships! Maybe she really *had* lost her mind. Maybe it was all just a vivid dream.

But no. All she had to do was finger the little nodule behind her ear as a reminder. The headache had faded over the course of the day, helped along with some Motrin she'd borrowed from a classmate, but every once in a while it still sent a sharp twinge through her skull. This was real, all right, Rei and the implant and all of it.

"Dad?" she called, dropping the truck keys in the bowl on the kitchen counter, where they clattered among stray bolts and a detached carburetor. "Dad, I'm home."

The house was utterly quiet, the stove cold and dinner unstarted. He was obviously out on the farm somewhere.

Not in the barn, I hope! She'd left them both unattended all day. What Rei had been up to? She grabbed the sheepskin jacket off its hook and hurried out the door.

The lights were on in the barn. Whether that was a good or bad sign, she couldn't begin to guess. Surely Rei had the sense to stay out of sight? Sarah cautiously pushed the door open. Her dad liked to have the radio on while he worked, and she could hear country music coming tinnily from somewhere nearby.

Heart hammering, Sarah stepped into the barn, looking around. "Dad?" she called softly, then louder.

"Up here, punkin!"

The voice had come down from the loft. Sarah's heart hit triphammer levels. One of her dad's canes leaned against the wall beside the ladder. She scrambled up the rungs, her mind awhirl with all the terrible possibilities: Rei tied up while her dad called the police, Rei already packed away into police custody, her dad tied up while Rei held a laser gun on him ...

Instead, when her head popped over the top of the ladder, she beheld a scene of friendly tranquility. Rei and her dad had cleared away the hay and stored junk from the finished end of the loft—where the boards were solid and close together, without gaps between—and lit it up with several of her dad's bright shop lights. The two of them were sitting on the floor with the junk from Rei's ship spread out between them and an open toolbox by her dad's knee. The barn cat was curled up by Rei's leg, sleeping with one paw stretched out.

What the heck happened while I was gone?!

"Hi, sweetheart." Her dad waved at her cheerfully. "I made a new friend. Your friend too, right?"

"Right," Sarah said in a daze, turning to look at Rei. He smiled at her. "I, uh, see you two are getting along well."

"Looks like our mutual friend here got lost," her dad said. "We're seeing what we can do about that."

"So you, um ..." Sarah didn't know quite how to ask the question. She crouched down by Rei, draping her arms over her knees, and cleared her throat awkwardly. "Do you know Rei's an alien, Dad?"

"He's blue," her father said dryly. "And if that wasn't enough ..." He waved a hand over the pieces of spaceship junk spread out in front of him. "There's nothing like this on Earth. Not even in those newfangled computerized cars and miniature circuit boards. It's not that it's more advanced. It's just *different*. No way this was made here on Earth."

Of *course* it wasn't the presence of an actual alien that convinced him, but rather, the alien's technology. That was her dad, all right.

"You're taking this awfully well. I'm sorry I didn't tell you."

"I could tell something was bothering you, punkin. I just never woulda guessed what." He picked up one of the plastic scraps. It had an odd iridescent sheen. "How long's he been out here? Since Saturday night, that UFO at the lake?"

"Um. Yeah. Rei crash-landed his spaceship almost on top of me. The rest of the ship is at the bottom of the lake. We went out there again last night and picked up all this."

"Anybody else know about him?"

Sarah shook her head. "I've been keeping him as secret as I can."

Rei touched her coat sleeve.

"Yes?" she said. This close, she was acutely aware of all the subtle shades in his amber cats' eyes, the agatelike hints of blue and green, purple and gold.

"Lake," he said, followed by a couple of sentences in which she understood roughly every other word, out of order. He said it a couple of times.

"I'm sorry, Rei, I can't understand you."

"We were just waitin' on you, punkin," her dad said. "Blue here wants to run out to the lake tonight and get what I guess is the rest of whatever this all came from. We had to wait 'til you got back with the truck."

Rei nodded.

Sarah boggled at them both. "How can *you* understand him when I can't? I'm the one with the translator!"

"What's that, now?"

Sarah tilted her head and held her hair out of the way. "He put a translator in me, back here behind my ear. I'm starting to understand some of his language, but not most of it."

Gary scowled, his good humor evaporating. Rei looked startled when that scowl turned his way. "You put something in my daughter's head?"

"Whoa!" Sarah held her hands out with palms up for "stop!", noticing Rei's jerk—quickly covered—out of the corner of her eye. He definitely treated that as a threat gesture. She lowered her hands slightly. "Calm down. I agreed to it, Dad, it's okay. Really."

"Huh." Her father frowned at her. "Is that why you were off your feed last night? That thing hurting you?"

"Not much," Sarah said. She touched it, probing at the nodule with her fingertips. It hurt with a weird little *zing!* when she poked it the wrong way, but otherwise wasn't particularly sensitive. "It gave me a headache at first, but I feel okay now."

"Yeah, you *better* be okay." Gary pointed a thick, grease-stained finger at Rei. Sarah sensed Rei tensing up. "No more sticking alien doohickeys in my daughter's brain, got it?"

"Got it," Rei said.

It wasn't English—Sarah heard a lilting alien phrase while the translation unfolded in her mind—but Gary acted as if he'd understood anyway; he dropped his hand with a little headshake. "Good. Don't do it again."

"Did he give you a translator too?" Sarah asked him.

"Nope." Gary started gathering up his tools and putting them back into the box. "Hell, I used to work with ol' Lars all the time, the Mullers' hired fella, and he didn't speak a lick of English."

"Yeah ... but ..."

But he had a point. Sarah had grown up around Wisconsin farm folk, and half the people her dad called friends were men he hardly exchanged more than two grunts with. Working together in silence was their way.

Gary heaved himself to his feet with a huff of effort and the assistance of the one cane he'd brought to the loft with him. As he started to lean stiffly down to pick up the toolbox, Rei jumped to his feet and picked it up instead. Gary gave him a terse nod.

"What—are we going *now*?" Sarah protested. "Dad, I just got home. It's not even dark yet!"

"Soonest begun, soonest done," her dad said.

"Soonest *arrested*. Dad, there's cops all over at the lake. The last time Rei and I went out there, we had to go through a police barricade, and somebody spotted us poking around on the beach and sent a boat over to investigate. I had to take the back way home, through the fields." She paused, her mind drifting toward possibilities ... damn it. "We could get back the same way, if they haven't blocked it off. Which I bet they haven't. It's all private land out there, you just need to know which pastures to drive through ..."

"So let's hitch up the trailer," her dad said.

"No, wait!" Sarah blocked him at the top of the ladder. "Let's wait a little while, okay? Wait 'til everyone goes to bed tonight. We can do the chores and eat something and *then* go out to the lake. All right?"

Her dad glanced at Rei.

"It's better than being arrested," Sarah told Rei.

She wasn't sure how much of that he understood, but after a moment he said something her implant translated as, "All right."

HER DAD HEATED up some chili from a few nights ago, while Sarah hurried through the chores in the rainy dark, then backed the truck up to their big feed-hauling trailer. She would wait and let her dad hook it up; he'd always been much better at lining up the tow hitch with the trailer than she was, and she usually pinched her fingers when she tried.

She came inside to be confronted with the disconcerting sight of Rei, blue-skinned and barefoot and looking completely out of place, at the kitchen table with a cup of coffee and the tin of shortbread cookies in front of him.

"You're giving him *coffee?*"

Her father shrugged.

Well, it wasn't like she hadn't been feeding him everything in sight. Coffee probably wasn't any worse for him than pie or cookies.

She hadn't really noticed in the barn, but seeing him in the kitchen made her realize how dirty he was. Which was understandable—he'd been sleeping in a hayloft and walking around barefoot in the mud—but now the thought occurred to her that maybe he didn't like to be dirty. *She* certainly wouldn't.

"Rei, would you like to take a bath?" she asked him. "Get cleaned up? You can borrow some more clothes from us, like that shirt you're wearing."

"Probably be a good idea," Gary said over his shoulder. "Draw attention less if he's dressed normal."

"Dad, he's blue. He's going to draw attention everywhere."

"Yes," Rei said. "I would like to get cleaned up."

"Hey, I understood every word of that sentence!"

Rei flashed another of those glimmering smiles, lighting

his warm amber eyes. "Your language the implant will better understand *hran ki* your mind the more."

"Okay, there are still some grammar issues," she said, wincing. "Anyway, bath?"

Rei rose from the table and came with her obediently. He looked around with visible curiosity as she took him up the stairs. His eyes lingered on the framed photos hanging on the walls.

"Sarah?" he asked, fingertips brushing a photo of a small blonde girl sitting on the back of a horse.

"Yes, that's me. That's Dad," she added, indicating the bearded man holding the horse's head. "Dad. Gary. He doesn't have a beard anymore. And in that next picture, the woman pushing the little girl on the swing, that's me and ... my mom."

She finished in a whisper. After her mother's death, she had started to take down the pictures from the wall, and then, weeping, put them back up. Looking at them hurt, but putting them away made it like her mother had never existed. Like she didn't matter.

"She is beautiful," Rei said quietly. "Like you, she looks."

"Does she?" Sarah had never noticed. Maybe everyone with light pinkish skin looked alike to him.

But she'd been a teenager when her mother died, and perhaps she resembled her more as an adult. If her mother was alive today, maybe people would smile at them in stores in town and say, *"You look like sisters!"* Sarah had to blink the tears out of her eyes at the thought.

"She is dead?" Rei asked, his voice gentle.

"Yes," Sarah said, swallowing the lump in her throat. "She is dead. Are your parents still alive?"

Rei turned his face away. She wasn't sure if he didn't understand or just didn't want to talk about it.

"Anyway." She swallowed again, trying to push down the lump and the unshed tears that went along with it. "The bathroom is here. Do you have bathrooms in space? Well, you must. Actually ..." She hesitated and decided not to ask what he'd been using as a bathroom while he was staying in the barn. Probably a corner of the field, and it wasn't like cow pastures were known for being immaculately clean. "Anyway, I don't know what yours look like, but this is the, uh ... toilet, for—doing your business in—you know, pooping—"

She had no idea what the translator was doing with all of this, but one thing she knew for sure, from the heat in her cheeks, was that she'd started blushing. Rei looked a little extra blue himself. "I know what it is for," he said.

"Oh. Good. Well, that's for ... that, and then this is for washing your hands ..." She turned on the sink faucets to demonstrate. "And this is the bathtub. This is how you turn the water on and off, see? This knob is for the shower." She pulled; water sprayed. Rei gazed up curiously at the shower head. "What else do you need to know, let's see. Oh, these are soap and shampoo, for getting clean—*what are you doing?*"

"*Mehetesk'a* my clothes," Rei said, pausing in the act of unsealing the strips along the side of the gray garment. He looked baffled, while Sarah was pretty sure her blush was flaming all the way up to her hairline. "Do your people wash with the clothes on?"

"No, but we don't take our clothes off around other people." Even as she said it, a part of her brain wailed plaintively, *Why did you stop him?!* She was now vividly remembering the beach, and the flex of his smooth muscles under the blue skin as he'd gone in and out of the water. She could have had an up-close view of that, under good lighting ...

"No?" He hesitated, fingers on the strip-seal.

"No," Sarah said decisively, wrenching her eyes up to his face. "I'm—I'm gonna go get you some clothes, all right? Oh! This is a towel." She yanked a fluffy towel off the rack and thrust it at him. "For drying off with."

She left him holding the towel and fled the bathroom before her blush could cause her hair to spontaneously combust. She was into her dad's room before she realized she'd given him *her* towel, but, well, she'd only used it for this morning's shower, so ... that wasn't too weird, right?

Right.

As she rummaged through her dad's closet for anything that looked like it would fit a larger, more muscular alien, she listened to the sound of water running next door, and tried not to think of Rei with his clothes off, one thin wall away.

Peeling off the silvery-gray jumpsuit, exposing his wide shoulders and lean blue hips, the dark curls across his belly that were so like a human man's, tapering down to ...

"Gahhhh!" She tossed a wad of bundled-up clothing onto the bed. She really should be looking for underwear too, but while she didn't mind rummaging around in her dad's closet, poking through his underwear drawer was really a bit much. Plus, she'd have to think about everything those boxers would be wrapped around ...

Sarah whimpered quietly and left her dad's room with the bundle of clothing in her arms. She paused in front of the bathroom door.

The sound of running water had stopped. Now there was just a little bit of splishing and splashing, which was even worse. She could picture him all too easily, stretched out in the bathtub, lean and long and blue. And then he'd be pulling himself out of the water, strong arms flexing—

reaching for the towel, *her* towel, that she'd just rubbed all over her naked body this morning, and wrapping it around his long blue waist—

Sarah swallowed thickly and tapped on the door before cracking it open. Warm air came out, along with the citrusy smell of shampoo—oh no, he was using *her* shampoo, too. She took in a brief flash of blue as she pushed the clothes through the door. "Clothing!" she said, and shut the door quickly, stifling her urge to open it wider instead.

Rather than going back downstairs and facing her dad just yet, she fled into her bedroom and closed the door firmly.

Being back in her lifelong bedroom, home of all her teenage dreams and fantasies, didn't do as much to quell the lust surging in her as she'd hoped. She wanted to turn right around and walk back into that bathroom and ...

And what? she told herself. *He's an alien! He might not even know what sex is! For all you know, his people repro- duce using test tubes!*

But then she thought of the warm light in his amber eyes, the sideways looks, the way he smiled at her sometimes ...

Oh, Rei knew what sex was, all right.

You've known him for two days, she told herself, rational brain still struggling to assert itself over lust-brain. *You haven't even been able to have a conversation with him—*

And yet, she already felt as if she knew everything important about him. He was intelligent and resourceful and determined, even on an alien planet surrounded by people whose language he didn't speak. He was careful not to hurt her and respectful of her personal space. He was a little shy, but more than willing to take charge when he needed to.

He was drop-dead gorgeous, with a beautiful smile and shoulders to die for ...

Sarah flopped down on her bed and stared up at the ceiling, where little glow-in-the-dark stars were scattered in random constellations. Stars like the ones Rei came from.

She unbuckled her jeans and slid her hand inside them.

Unsurprisingly, she was wet to the touch. An electric shiver went through her as she stroked herself.

In the quiet of her room, she could hear the little splashes from the bathroom across the hall as Rei shifted around in the bathwater.

With vividness that shocked her, she pictured herself opening the bathroom door, Rei stretched out naked in the water, turning to look at her with those clear amber eyes. She saw herself close the door behind her and peel out of her jeans.

She could see the way Rei's eyes would widen with delighted surprise, his catlike pupils expanding and darkening ...

She slid one finger inside, then another.

She saw herself straddle him in the bathwater, slipping one leg inside the tub. Rei arched to meet her, his erect cock rising from a nest of dark curls. Like a human, but big. Huge.

A third finger joined the other two, pressing against her hot, wet walls.

Behind the darkness of her closed lids, she saw Rei pushing up into her, his hands clasping her shoulders to hold her steady as he thrust upward to fill her. Water splashed around them ...

Her breath quickened, her thumb stroking over her engorged clit, sliding between her folds as her fingers pressed inside. She spread her legs involuntarily, swallowing back a moan.

Rei's golden eyes were watching her as he thrust into her, his breath coming in a gasp with each thrust ...

In her mind's eye, Sarah bent her head down to kiss him, her curly hair falling on either side of her face. He rose up to kiss her, and as his lips met hers, they were just as warm and inviting as they looked.

She shivered into an orgasm with her mouth parted to receive an imaginary kiss, her eyes clenched shut and Rei's imagined taste on her tongue. The waves swept through her and when she finally shook her way out the other side, fingers buried deep in herself, it was not so much relief she felt as a desperate yearning to have Rei's arms wrapped around her in reality as well as fantasy, Rei's strong blue body pressed against hers.

Sarah pulled her fingers out of herself and sat up. She was still shivering with aftershocks. Her jeans were down around her knees.

I have a crush on a shipwrecked alien.

It was like a bad headline from those silly teen magazines she used to read.

Sarah quickly pulled up her underwear and fastened her jeans. It wasn't shame she was feeling so much as something else, something that was huge and warm and terrifying at the same time.

The moment she'd met Rei, her life had been swept out of her control, and now she was careening downhill on a runaway roller coaster, with no idea what was waiting for her at the bottom. And yet she was having the ride of her life.

She couldn't wash her hand in the bathroom because Rei was in there. Guiltily she wiped her fingers on several tissues and poked them into the bathroom trash can before going downstairs.

Her dad was in the living room, sitting at the computer. "Just need to fill in a few entries in the farm books, punkin," he said over his shoulder. "Dinner's hot when you and Blue are ready."

"His name's Rei, Dad!"

Her father grunted and turned back to the computer.

With relief, she hurried into the kitchen and washed her hands at the sink. It was easy to wash away the evidence, but not nearly so easy to ignore the slick feeling between her thighs and the hot lassitude in her limbs that was one part post-orgasmic relaxation and one part heightened lust, tingling through her whenever she thought of Rei toweling himself off upstairs.

To distract herself, she retrieved her phone from the bowl of rice where it had been drying out on the counter, with its charging cord trailing incongruously from the rice to the nearest outlet. She braced for disappointment and pressed the power button.

Victory! The screen came on right away. It had a few scuffs that hadn't been there before, but she'd happily take it. No need to go to the Verizon store the next time she was in town.

She dropped the phone in her pocket, and got busy dishing up the chili into three bowls and setting out garlic bread that her dad had been keeping warm in the oven.

When she turned around, Rei was standing in the kitchen doorway.

He was wearing an old sweatshirt of her dad's, the biggest thing she'd been able to find for him; though Rei wasn't enormous, his broader shoulders had strained at the seams of her dad's work shirt. His hands were shoved in the pockets, and his thick dark hair was wet and tousled.

He looked young, and cute, and vulnerable, like a freshly showered college kid instead of an intergalactic cyborg assassin or whatever he was.

After a moment of mutual staring, Sarah managed to boot up the less shallow part of her brain. "Hey!" she said brightly. "Dinner's ready. I don't know if they have chili in space—oh, what am I saying, of course they don't, but I bet there's something similar. It's beans, er, legumes, and meat and spices. And there's bread."

"It smells good," he said quietly, sitting down.

The translator, she was beginning to understand, did best with short, simple sentences. And Rei had been trying to speak that way, probably because he knew how the technology worked and was trying to make it easy for it.

There was something else different about him. It didn't click until she went to put the chili pan in the sink and turned around. Rei was turned away from her, reaching for the garlic bread and exposing the long line of his neck, wet black hair curling at the indigo nape above a slightly paler streak across the skin—

"Your collar's gone!"

Rei looked over at her. "Garymetzger helped me cut it off."

"Dad? His name's just Gary." She sat down across from him and picked up a piece of garlic bread to give her fingers something to do and stop them from twitching to touch the exposed soft skin above the sweatshirt's collar. "Metzger is our last name. Surname. Uh, family name. Do your people have those? A name that everyone in your family has?" *Do you?*

"Me? Just one name, Reian."

"Rei ... An?"

His smile glimmered; the dimple appeared briefly. "Reian. One name. Rei is a short name. Long name and short name. My people *hrsaka keth*. But not a ... family name."

"Oh, like a nickname? We have those. I mean, I don't, personally. Sarah is short enough as it is. But my mother's name was Margaret, and everyone called her Maggie."

"Maggie May," her father said quietly from the doorway.

He limped inside, using one cane and his hand on the wall for extra balance. "Maggie May. Like the Rod Stewart song. Her middle name wasn't May, of course."

"No," Sarah said softly. "I know that part. I'm named after her."

Gary nodded. "Margaret Sarah was her name ... but Maggie May was what I called her." He glanced at Rei, who was watching both of them, amber eyes flicking back and forth between, and forced a smile. "But we're being rude, talking about people our guest doesn't know."

Which meant *stop talking about your mother*. Sarah dropped her eyes and reached for her spoon. Out of the corner of her eye, she saw Rei studying what she did, and then carefully picking up his spoon in a clumsy approximation of her grip.

As they began eating in silence, she thought about how long there had been an invisible third person at their table: the ghost of her mother.

Now there really was a third person, a man from beyond the stars. And still the ghost was there, eating with them, following them around, a silent presence in their lives.

What does it take to move on? Sarah wondered, forcing down a mouthful of the chili that tasted like sawdust to her now. How did you learn to move beyond that, when you'd lost the person you'd loved most? It had been ten years since her mother died, and yet sometimes, for both her father and herself, it seemed as if it was only yesterday.

She raised her eyes to watch Rei eating quietly, looking at neither of them. The paler stripe across his neck was visible when he moved, appearing and disappearing above the neck of the sweatshirt. Sometimes his empty hand drifted up toward his neck, apparently without his conscious will, only to be jerked back down when his fingers touched his bare skin.

She still wanted to touch him, but less for her own sake than for his. She couldn't help wondering how many people he'd lost, and what kind of tragedies were hidden behind his golden gaze.

NINE

IN THE DARK of the night, as rain fell from the pitch-black sky, Rei hunched in a borrowed coat and stood out of the way while Sarah and Garymetzger—no, Gary, just Gary —hitched the trailer to their ground vehicle.

The entire evening was a whirl of impressions and thoughts he hadn't had time to process yet. He was clean and warm, with borrowed clothing brushing his skin—strangely soft, this fabric, yet not adhering in the way of Galatean smartcloth. He stood with his feet shoved into ill-fitting, borrowed boots and buried in a planet's dirt, with water falling from the sky; he'd almost forgotten about rain before this planetary excursion. And these two aliens were helping him retrieve his sunken battlepod.

He didn't know how he could ever repay them.

Lyr used to say his people believed in something called *amora*, which meant that you *couldn't* pay back someone for their kindness, so instead you helped others in turn. You couldn't repay your parents for raising you; all you could do was be a good parent to your own children. You couldn't repay someone for saving your life, but maybe you could save someone else.

Rei flexed his hands. Rainwater glistened on his dark skin like blood in the truck's headlights.

And does it work the other way, my friend? he asked the silence in his skull where Lyr used to dwell. *If you kill others, what then? Do you deserve to have violence visited upon you? Does it trail in your wake?*

Did it matter if you'd never wanted to do it in the first place? The dead were still just as dead.

He kept catching himself in the act of touching his bare neck, where the collar used to be.

"Rei, come on!" Sarah called softly. "We're ready to go."

He climbed into the truck and sat between Sarah and her dad on the padded bench seat. Gary pulled in his crutches and slammed the door.

"Maybe Rei on the outside should sit," Sarah said. He was now catching most of her words, though he could tell he sometimes lost the nuances of her grammar.

Gary shook his head. "Easier to hide him if we run into cops." He shoved a floppy-brimmed hat at Rei. "Here, put this on."

"Yeah, that's totally inconspicuous," Sarah said dryly as Rei pulled the hat down over his ears. She flashed him a sideways smile, her face lit up in the glow of the truck's instrument lights.

His shoulder was pressed to hers. Every time she spoke, he felt the gentle vibration of her voice.

Gary was right, it would've been easier to sit on the outside. Mostly because it would've saved him from driving to the lake while trying to hide a hard-on.

He hadn't been able to stop thinking of Sarah the entire time he was washing in the bathing room. Alien she might be, but she was also as human as his people—more so, even, since it didn't look like Sarah's particular fork in the tree of galactic humanity had been meddled with quite as much, lacking wolf DNA or his people's artificially designed, extra-efficient hemoglobin that gave their skin the blue tint.

She also lacked the perfectly symmetrical beauty of many galactics, the telltale signs that either her DNA had been modified at some point in her ancestral line, or her body had been modded after her birth. But those little imperfections made her more beautiful to Rei's eyes: the slight crookedness of her teeth, the way her nose was a little off center and her jawline slanted one way just a bit more than the other. Those were the details that made her Sarah.

It wasn't beauty that drew him to her, anyway. It didn't matter in the slightest what her face looked like. She was beautiful to him (would have been beautiful, no matter what) because of what was inside her, not the other way around.

She'd helped him when no one in their right mind would have. She'd sheltered him and fed him and—to the best of her people's limited ability—tended his wounds. And now she and her father were taking him out to retrieve his ship, risking imprisonment or worse. Considering how hard she'd been working to hide him, the punishment for harboring fugitives must be severe on this world.

Her shoulder flexed against his as she yanked the lever attached to the truck's steering apparatus. The vehicle lurched forward, the trailer rattling behind them as they got underway.

"I don't know how to thank either of you," Rei said, hunching forward. With the glow of the instruments affecting his night vision, it was utterly dark outside the truck, difficult even for his sharp eyes to penetrate. Through the rain, an occasional watery flash of lights indicated other houses along the road. "You don't have to do this."

"Sure we do," Gary said. He gave Rei a smile that was reminiscent of his daughter's, warm and friendly as his face creased around it.

Rei had assumed, at first, that Gary was quite old, but now he thought the old man was probably not very far past middle age. Living on a planet, in the sun and the wind, aged a person's skin faster than shipboard life.

My aunt might look that old, too. I wonder if she's still alive?

Until Sarah had asked, he hadn't thought about his people in years. It was easier not to. In the normal course of events, his servitude to the Galatean Empire would have lasted for another ten years. Afterwards, he could have gone home if he survived, but with most of his septmates dead, he didn't see any point in looking forward to it.

But now, possibilities began to open up in front of him. If he could fix the battlepod ... if he could get off this planet ... maybe he could go back to his homeworld. The smart thing would be to get as far away from the Galatean Empire as possible, but there was nowhere else he wanted to go.

To see Polara again, his chilly homeworld with its snow-capped mountains and tall trees and the three moons in the sky ...

Except that his people would never truly accept him if they knew that he'd run away. Polara gave the Galatean army a certain number of its young people every year so they would be left alone. A fugitive coming back to their world, bringing Galatean hunters behind him ... no, they would never hide him, not like Sarah and Gary had done.

Anyway, first he had to find out if Lyr was still alive.

And all of this meant leaving Sarah too. He didn't want to think about that.

He realized that he'd been softly flexing his claws where his hand rested on his thigh, popping them in and out of his fingertips with a light prickle through the fabric of his borrowed trousers, and made himself stop.

"Turn off here," Gary said suddenly.

"Really?" Sarah slowed the truck to a crawl. The headlights illuminated the edge of a field of tall grass, smeared through the streaks of rain on the truck's windshield. "I was going to turn at the county road and then go through the Gruenings' woodlot and pastures to the Muller place."

"Nah, there's an old logging road here. Takes you through the Kenner woods and comes out behind Will Hardesty's barn, almost all the way to the county line. Then turn left and you'll hit the Muller spread. It's shorter and a lot less likely to run into anybody."

"No kidding," Sarah murmured, maneuvering the truck onto two muddy ruts with trees on either side. The sides of the truck scraped against brush. "I didn't even know this was here. I thought it was just part of the Kenners' private farm road."

"Well, technically we are on Kenner land," her dad said. "I dated Kelly Kenner before I married your mom, you know."

"I know, Dad," Sarah sighed. "That was the girl whose braids you tied to a fence post when you were a kid, right?"

"No, that was Tammy Wazlowski. Ah, Tammy. Girl had a good right hook on her."

Rei let the banter wash over him, his translation implant soaking it up. He knew what they were doing; he could hear the tightness in Sarah's voice. Idle talk eased nervousness.

How many times had he and his septmates done this before a battle? Or during one?

Lyr, Rook, Skara ... He pushed those thoughts away and tried to focus on mapping their route in his head—and not falling asleep. He'd barely slept at all for the last two nights, and now the truck's vents were blasting warm air at him, its growling engine and rocking progress easing him halfway to drowsiness—

The seat abruptly dropped under him, jolting him wide awake. He flung out a hand and clawed at the dashboard. For an instant, he'd been back in his battlepod, his stomach dropping as the pod changed trajectory with the dazzling light of plasma fire flaring on the screens—

"Whoa, sorry," Sarah said, glancing at him sideways. "Pothole."

Rei nodded, not trusting his voice. At least she was too busy driving to look at his face, but Gary gave him a lingering, curious glance.

A few minutes later, Sarah stopped and got out to open a gate in the rain. There were a few more instances of this as they drove through a succession of fields. At last she slowed the truck to a crawl and turned onto a smoother road. There were no other headlights in the darkness.

"This is the lake road," Sarah told Rei. "We're almost to the beach where I met you. I'm not completely sure we won't find any cops down there, just to let you know."

The translation chip gave him slang for Galatean military police. He merely nodded, wishing he understood more about her world's political structure and their relationship with Galatea. It was hard to believe her people had no connection to the Empire at all. If he was caught, would he be handed over to the Galateans immediately? Used as a political bargaining chip? Not that he was much of one.

There was nothing special about him; he was merely a fugitive slave-soldier. He had pilot skills, but those were nothing special either.

If they caught him, they'd probably just kill him, or leave him to rot in a cell on this planet. Speaking of which ...

"What's your world's name?"

"Earth," Sarah said, with a brief smile.

Earth. He tasted the word carefully on his tongue. His implant gave him connotations of soil and a meaning that was simply "the world." Well, that was understandable; many planets' names meant something like that. Polara meant a great forest in one of his world's old tongues, but it was the same thing. His people were hunters; hers were farmers, with their fields and settled towns. So of course her people thought of the world as a lot of dirt, while his kind thought of theirs as a huge hunting ground.

He'd never heard of a planet called Earth, but that didn't mean much. There were many inhabited planets in the galaxy. And the Galateans might call it something different than the natives anyway.

One thing he did know for certain, though. He had no intention of bringing danger to this two Earthers who'd helped him, not if he could help it.

Sarah turned off the road and jolted down the narrow track that he knew led to the beach.

"Stop," he said.

Sarah slammed on the brakes so suddenly that Rei had to throw out his hand to avoid being flung into the dashboard. "What? Did you see something?"

"No. Let me out. I'll walk from here."

"The heck you will. It's pouring rain." She put the truck back in gear and crept forward.

"If there are 'cops' on the beach, they mustn't find me in your vehicle."

Gary gave a rough snort. "I think that ship has sailed, kid."

"I don't understand."

"What Dad means is that nobody's going to believe we're innocent at this point, Rei." Sarah took one hand off the steering wheel and started to rest it on his thigh, changing it at the last minute to a quick pat on his arm before she jerked it away. "We've got a truck and a trailer and a winch, and we're driving down to the beach at midnight in the rain. It's pretty obvious that we're not hanging out here for our health."

He wasn't sure he understood every word, but he got the gist. "You'll be in danger."

Another snort came from Gary. "Fine time to worry about that, kid."

"Dad!"

"What?"

"I didn't mean to cause danger to either of you," Rei said, feeling wretched. She was right. They were both right. Every moment he spent with them, he was risking their imprisonment and, perhaps, death. He should have just left that first night.

But it was easy to second-guess himself when he had clean, dry clothes and a full belly. Self-preservation was a powerful instinct.

Still, he vowed one thing to himself. He'd die before letting Sarah and Gary get hurt.

"Here we are," Sarah said softly. She killed the head-lights and then the engine. The only sounds were the drumming of rain on the roof of the truck and the soft pings of the cooling engine. A few distant lights glimmered smearily in the rain, across the water, but there was no sign of anyone closer.

"No one's here," Rei said.

"You sure about that?" Gary asked, reminding him of something he'd noticed about Sarah earlier. Their unenhanced vision couldn't pierce the dark as well as his could. To them, the night was pitch black.

"I'm sure."

Sarah opened her door and leaned out. "I'm thinking we back the trailer down to the edge of the water. We have a winch on the back of the truck to haul your ship out, Rei."

"Trick's gonna be whether this engine is up to the job." Gary patted the dashboard. "If she can't do it, we might have to bring a tow truck down, or even rent a bulldozer, and that's gonna be a damn sight harder to arrange. How big is your ship, son?"

Rei's implant translated their word "ship" as "water vessel," but he understood by now that they meant the battlepod. "Not too large. And not very heavy. Your truck is heavier." He still couldn't get over how solidly constructed everything was here, made out of metal and wood and dense, primitive plastics.

"We'll have to take your word for it," Sarah said. "You're going to have to do the hard part, though. Someone has to dive underwater and find the ship and hook the winch cable to it. I could probably help—"

"The hell you will," Gary said promptly. "That water's probably forty-five degrees at this time of year. You sure the kid can swim in it without killing himself?"

"He can," Sarah said. "He did before. And I wish you'd stop calling him a kid, Dad. He's no more a kid than I am—"

She broke off as Rei started to remove his borrowed

shirt. He stopped in the act of pulling it off, remembering that these people had a strong nudity taboo.

"... Anyway," Sarah said, and though the night was dim even to Rei's enhanced eyes, he could tell that she was blushing. "Let's just get the truck backed down to the water, and then you can—er—take things off in here, while Dad and I get the winch cable ready."

Their nudity taboo must make their sex lives difficult, Rei thought. He would very much have liked to see Sarah naked. In fact, he was thinking about it now, which was going to make disrobing somewhat awkward.

Especially in the close confines of the truck's cab, with her body so near to his. He'd almost ceased noticing it on the drive over. Now, with his interest freshly awakened, he couldn't stop noticing.

Sarah didn't look at him and, once the truck was turned around with the trailer pointed at the water, she departed the cab at a great rate of speed. As soon as she was gone, Rei stripped quickly, despite the awkwardness of doing it in the truck when undressing on the beach would have been so much easier. No wonder she had acted so strange about it earlier, given how strong their nudity taboo seemed to be. There was no way to retrieve the pod without getting naked to go into the water, but he hoped it didn't offend Sarah and her father too badly. He tucked the floppy-brimmed hat behind the seat where it wouldn't get crushed, and then found the door handle after some fumbling, and stepped down to the sand.

Wet, cold wind blew past his naked body, eliminating the last traces of his hard-on; in fact, it felt like his genitals were trying to crawl up inside his body. He focused on using the nanites to raise his body temperature a degree or two. His shivering eased, and the wind grew more comfortable. With wet sand and pebbles squishing between his toes, he walked to the water's edge.

"Rei?" Sarah called. She sounded slightly choked, and he didn't want to look around at her, to see her expression of disgust at his nakedness. "Rei, uh, we've got a flashlight in the truck. I don't know how well it'll work underwater—"

"It's all right," Rei told her. He didn't recognize the word she'd used, but whatever it was, it would probably be unnecessary to the pod's retrieval. "I'll dive first to find the battlepod, then again to hook your hauling line onto it."

He waded in, step by step. The water climbed his calves and crept above his thighs, making him stagger against its pressure. He pushed his metabolism up another notch or two, and took several deep breaths, oxygen-loading his tissues. With the nanites at full capacity, he was capable of holding his breath for several minutes. They were barely working at half capacity right now, based on the slow speed of his healing—he was still limping on his injured leg, and his arm twinged a warning when he moved it, when it should have been strong enough for normal use by now. So he'd better not count on their usual level of assistance. Still, he should be able to easily stay under for a couple of minutes at a time.

And he had another asset that he didn't want his hosts to know about.

Two of them, actually.

He dove forward into the water, slicing cleanly through it. His inert cuffs glinted under the water's surface. Rei kicked himself beneath the surface, and as he sliced deeper into the black water, he shifted.

Suddenly it was no longer a human figure kicking through the water, but a huge, lean wolf with a shaggy, blue-gray pelt.

The cold of the water was suddenly much less acute, though it dragged at his fur more than his bare skin. With water clogging his ears and nose, he didn't notice the sharpening of his senses as he normally did. His night vision was about the same in either form.

But oh, it felt good to stretch his legs as a wolf again.

He'd been allowed to shift occasionally during his time as a Galatean slave. It was known, or at least believed, that Polarans had to shift regularly to maintain their sanity, and if it wasn't true, Polara certainly wasn't disabusing outsiders of the notion. But the tightness of the collar made it impossible for him to shift at will. His wolf neck was thicker than his human neck, so he needed to have the collar unlocked for every authorized shift.

Now he could shift whenever he wanted.

But he had to be careful. He didn't know if this world had shifters or not. They were rare among the human worlds. He knew of only a few shapeshifting races, including his people and his dead septmate Skara's, as well as rumors of shifters among the Galateans themselves. And of course there were Lyr's people, the dragons, but they weren't even remotely human. They had evolved independently rather than coming from Birthworld stock.

Like all Birthworld shifters, Rei was restricted by his human mass. His wolf was exactly the mass of his human body, no more, no less. Dragons had no such limitations.

It still made him a big wolf, two hundred pounds at least.

His implants ached as always; they made the shift with him, but never quite seemed to settle into his wolf body the way they did when he was human. But he didn't care. It was a small discomfort that he pushed aside, glorying in the strong grace of his lupine body.

Running would have been better. He could have stretched out along the shore and run; oh, he could have run. The wolf was less well suited to swimming. But its endurance and natural cold resistance made up for it.

Even so, his lungs began to ache. How far had he come? Not far enough; he kicked deeper. The lake bed dropped off steeply here, and his battlepod was down there somewhere in that blackness. As man or wolf, his night vision, however acute, couldn't penetrate the gloom when there was no light at all.

But he had another way.

Staying up late last night hadn't been in vain, because with the tools from the kit, he'd managed to get one of the damaged cuffs back online. It still didn't have most of its functions; he couldn't yet use it to produce weapons or shields. But the cuffs had a homing function. In the absence of other data, they defaulted to the battlepod they had last been linked to.

His internal nanites might be damaged, but they were still capable of utilizing the cuff linkage, giving him a rough sense of the battlepod's location. With the cuffs fully functional, he could have built a three-dimensional map of the surrounding area, delivered directly into his brain for unerring navigation. This was much more limited, but it could still do what he needed it to do.

He blew the air out of his lungs to force himself deeper. Silver bubbles streamed surfaceward, dimly glimpsed in the faint light coming down from above. Beneath him was only blackness.

And then his paws brushed something that was not lake bottom. Victory!

Rei kicked upward. There was a ringing in his ears now, and his chest burned with a rapidly growing urgency to inhale that would soon, and fatally, overwhelm his self-control.

His snout broke the surface. He opened his jaws wide, gasping as he dog-paddled.

He was far enough out that he didn't think Sarah and Gary would be able to see him. He gulped air in great, greedy heaves before he risked shifting and swam more slowly toward the shore.

Sarah came running to meet him as he stumbled out of the water. "You were down there for so long! Are you okay?"

Rei nodded wordlessly. He was still panting. His nanites were more damaged than he'd thought. He had guessed they were at fifty percent efficiency, but now he revised his estimate downward to thirty or even twenty percent.

"Here." Before he could stop her, Sarah shrugged out of her heavy fur-lined coat and put it around his shoulders. She seemed to have a habit of doing that, he thought dazedly as she led him, stumbling, through the sand to sit on the end of the trailer.

His shivering began to ease as he hunched into the coat. Rain was still falling on his head, but he was so wet that he hardly noticed it. Sarah's sweater was soaking through as she stood beside him, one hand on his shoulder. He wanted to tell her she should get out of the rain, but with the shivering and the way his teeth were chattering, he couldn't seem to get enough air to speak properly yet.

He really had come within a hairsbreadth of staying down too long. He wasn't used to having his nanites so badly damaged.

"You shouldn't go down again," Sarah was saying anxiously. "You should at least warm up first. We don't have to do this tonight. We can find another way."

"She's right, son," Gary said, coming up on his other side. "We could go out in a boat tomorrow. Got a neighbor with a nice Grumman and a fishfinder. We can borrow it."

Rei shook his head, wet hair slapping against his ears. "I found the battlepod," he finally managed to say. "I can dive again to take your line down with me. Show me how it works."

Sarah and her father exchanged a look, a whole word-less conversation passing between them, before Sarah brought him the end of the cable. It looked strong, he was pleased to see, made of braided metal strands with a sturdy hook on the end.

"You need to find something on your ship that won't break off and wrap this around it," Gary explained. "Set the hook and come back up."

Rei nodded impatiently. As if he couldn't understand how a simple rope worked!

"Are you sure?" Sarah asked. "We could wait for a while. You can warm up in the truck."

Rei started to answer, but fell silent as he became aware of something else, a low thrumming vibrating in his chest.

"Helicopter," Gary said softly.

The word was unfamiliar, but they were both looking up, so Rei did too. Through the thick mist and clouds, he couldn't see what it looked like, but fog-dimmed lights passed over them and across the lake. The chop-chop-chop of the vehicle changed pitch. It was circling somewhere over there.

"We've got to get this show on the road," Gary said softly. "There's no telling what they have up there. Infrared cameras, sonar, who knows. They might've already spotted us."

Rei nodded. He took off Sarah's coat and handed it back to her with an apologetic grimace.

"Please be careful," she said. There was the briefest hesitation, as if she wanted to say something else, do something else, but all she did was reach out to give his hand a quick squeeze.

He could still feel the warm pressure of her fingers on his cold ones as he walked back into the water, the cable unspooling behind him.

SARAH WATCHED ANXIOUSLY until Rei disappeared under the water.

"How can he stay down there so long?" she asked her father as she put the coat back on. She was shivering, and tucked her fingers into her damp sleeves for what little warmth they had to offer.

"Get in the truck, hon. Warm yourself up while we wait."

Sarah shook her head. She looked anxiously across the lake, where the helicopter could still be heard but not seen, and then out at the ruffled gray waves. "I need to be here in case something goes wrong."

"Nothing you can do for him if it does," Gary said gently. "You dive in there, you'll be a popsicle in minutes."

"I pulled him out of the water on Saturday night."

"Really?" He gave her a long, searching look. "You know, there's still a whole lot you haven't told me about how this alien kid ended up in our barn."

"It's not that much of a story," Sarah said as the memory of Rei, limp in her arms, flitted through her mind. "He crashed in the lake, I fished him out and took him home."

"How long was it gonna take you to tell me if I hadn't found him on my own?"

"I ... don't know," Sarah confessed quietly. "I just didn't know *how* to tell you, or what you'd say if I did. 'Dad, there's an alien in our barn' isn't an easy conversation to have."

Gary patted her shoulder. "Punkin, you know I always tried to make sure you could bring your problems to me, but this sure is a new one."

"For you and me both, Dad."

They both looked out at the lake. There was no sign of Rei breaking through the surface. The winch cable had stopped playing out into the water, nearly at its full extent, and hung limply off the end of the trailer.

"Can you understand what he says?" Gary asked. "That up-and-down talking of his."

"Sort of. I can catch most of it now, but sometimes it's too scrambled to figure out what he's trying to say. He says it'll get better as I adjust to the translation thingie."

"Mind if I have a look at where he put that gadget in your head?"

"Sure, be my guest." Keeping one eye on the water, she tilted her head to the side as her father's work-roughened fingers probed around the injection site while he held a flashlight in his other hand. "Ow. Be careful. It's still sore."

"I don't like him putting alien crap in your head."

"Me neither, but things are a lot easier when I can talk to him."

"He tell you anything about himself yet, since he can talk to you so great?"

"I haven't really asked." Deep down, she wondered if she was avoiding the question intentionally. What *was* Rei, really? An escaped criminal? The advance scout for an invasion? Like revealing his existence to her father, asking him about his true mission on Earth meant opening a can of worms she could never close.

Her father started to say something else, then broke off as the winch cable jerked and went taut. "Ah, there's our cue, kiddo. I'll put 'er in gear. You stay back here, handle the winch an' make sure the cable don't tangle up."

"All right," Sarah said, but she was still scanning the wavetops, hoping to see Rei's dark head in the water. So far there was no sign of him.

Her father was an old hand at towing things with the truck. The winch whined, the cable vibrating over the end of the trailer. As the weight of the unseen ship threatened to drag both truck and trailer toward the lake, the truck's wheels spun and it ground slowly forward instead.

Come on, Rei. Where are you?

Something dark began to breach the ruffled gray waves, sending white foam rolling in all directions. Sarah craned forward, her worry about Rei temporarily subsiding beneath her curiosity about his ship.

This was her first chance to see it when it wasn't either an incandescent fireball crashing on top of her, or glowing wreckage sinking rapidly beneath the lake.

It didn't look big enough to be an actual spaceship. This must be some kind of escape pod, she thought as the truck ground onward and the dark bulk rose, inch by inch, from the lake's depths. It was bubble-shaped, perhaps eight or ten feet in diameter, bristling with projecting fins, antennae, and stubby bumps all over its surface. Most of the longer projections were warped and twisted, though Sarah had no idea if they were meant to look that way or if they'd been damaged in the crash.

Then her attention was drawn from the slowly rising pod to something in front of it, a wet dark shape that looked like it was tangled in the winch cable, rising and falling limply on the waves rolling up the shore.

"Rei," she gasped and ran into the water. It was shockingly cold, soaking through her sneakers and jeans as it climbed up her legs until she was waist deep. Heavier waves rolled over her, wetting her to mid-chest, pushed ahead of the vessel that the truck was now dragging into the shallow water by the beach.

The closer she got, the less it looked like Rei and the more it looked like some kind of trash or flotsam, wrapped around the cable. An old carpet? A shaggy coat like her sheepskin jacket? A ...

A big *dog*?

She couldn't believe it until she actually dug her hands into the dog's thick fur. It was draped over the cable just in front of the ship, its front legs hanging over the cable and back legs trailing loosely in the water. She couldn't tell if it was alive or dead, but it looked drowned, a mass of sodden fur rolling limply on the waves.

"Rei!" she screamed across the glimmering wake trailing behind the pod. "Rei, where are you?"

Her first thought was that he might be inside the pod, but now that she was closer, she could see how badly damaged it was. Its side had been torn open, and muddy water gushed out as the winch and the truck dragged its bulk inch by inch toward the beach. She kept pace with it, walking backward through the roiling water so it didn't roll over her, still holding absently to the drowned dog.

There was no sign of Rei anywhere.

He couldn't have drowned, not after all of this. That's— that's not right.

The depth of her shock and grief startled her. She'd only known him for two days. But she could finally *talk* to him. She could hear about the alien planet he came from, and find out what it was like to fly between the stars.

She'd never gotten to comb her hands through his dark hair, or run her nails across his long blue back ...

She'd finally had wonder and magic at her fingertips, all the exotic adventure she had craved for her entire life, and it had vanished forever into the dark, cold waters of the lake.

"Rei!" she screamed again.

As if in response to her cry, the dog jerked suddenly under her hand and gave a wet cough. It was by far the biggest dog she'd ever seen, bigger than even the most enormous Husky or Rottweiler. The glow of the trailer's taillights made it look black, but she thought it might be more like a dark gray or ...

Or blue, maybe?

It was an *alien* dog.

Well, of course it was. What other kind of dog was going to get dredged off the lake bottom along with an alien space pod?

The dog was coughing and panting now, its body writhing weakly as it fought for breath.

It breathed air. It couldn't have been in the water all this time. Had it been in some kind of stasis capsule in the pod? (She hadn't read all that science fiction for nothing.)

A glint in its fur caught her attention, and she leaned forward, closing one hand over its lanky foreleg. A silver bracelet dangled loosely around its ankle.

It was an exact copy of the bracelets Rei wore.

A copy, or ...

"Rei?" she whispered.

The dog groaned. Its ears pricked forward, lifting from its skull.

They were so close to shore now that she was stumbling

in a rising heap of sand scraped up in front of the pod. Sarah wrapped her arms around the dog's wet bulk and tried to heave it off the cable. It was so heavy that all she managed to do was break its fall as it splashed into the shallow water. Sarah gripped the dog behind the forelegs and began dragging them both out of the way of the pod as it ground inexorably onward.

"Sarah?" her dad called. "You okay back there?"

"I'm fine!" she shouted back, stumbling out of the water with her arms full of the dog's sodden forequarters.

Rei couldn't have gone into the water and come out as a dog. He *couldn't* have. That was impossible.

As impossible as a spaceship falling out of the sky on top of her?

As impossible as blue people and injectable translation technology?

She collapsed to the sand with the dog half on top of her. They were both so wet by now that she could barely tell where its soaked fur ended and her coat began.

The noise of the winch stopped, and she remembered she was supposed to be keeping an eye on it to turn it off when the pod was out of the water. It must have run out of cable, or else her dad had shut it off. Lying on her back, she could feel the low thrumming of the truck's idling engine through the sand. She raised her head after a moment and saw her dad standing with a cane in one hand and his other hand hooked through his belt, gazing at the dark dripping shape of the pod. It was taller than the truck, with sand churned up around it and water streaming off its sides.

"Gettin' that thing on the trailer is gonna be a whole barrel of fun," he remarked. "Sarah, hon? Where are you?"

"Over here." She sat up, with the dog's forequarters

sprawling across her lap. Dog, or ... something weirder and far more wonderful.

Its fur was definitely blue.

"Awww, punkin," her dad said, slogging toward her, his cane sliding on the wet sand. "I'm sorry about your alien friend. He didn't come up, did he?"

"I ... I don't know." She stared down at the mass of wet fur in her lap, as if she could make sense of the whole situation that way.

"What's that you've got there?"

The dog raised its head weakly, ears pricking forward.

Gary let out a surprised yelp. Starting to crouch down with the cane's support, he instead lost his balance and landed hard in the sand.

"Dad!" Sarah lurched up, and then back down, with the dog's unyielding weight pinning her legs. The animal was impossibly heavy ... about, say, the weight of Rei's dense, muscular body.

"'m fine," her father grunted. He didn't look fine—falling like that must have hurt—but he sat up stiffly and reached out to scruff the dog's wet fur. "Where'd you come from, boy? Man alive, you must'a got fed the right kind of dog food when you were a pup."

"Dad, I ..." Sarah hesitated, and then took the plunge into the crazy unknown. "I think this dog *is* Rei. Somehow."

"Sarah—"

"No, look." Sarah held up the dog's massive paw, with the bracelet dangling around its ankle. Its anklebones were smaller than the wrist of a man, but the large paw stopped the bracelet from sliding off.

"What the heck," her father said slowly.

It had to be Rei. She couldn't be wrong. If it wasn't, then Rei was dead beneath the waves on the cold, dark lake bottom ... or dying, even now, abandoned while his would-be rescuers exclaimed over a dog on the beach.

But she didn't think she was wrong.

"Let me check something." She felt behind the dog's ear. If this was Rei, there should be something she could feel where his translator ought to be, the same way she could feel hers under the skin.

And there it was: a little bump, rolling under the skin like a subcutaneous cyst.

Sarah burst into relieved laughter. Her eyes stung. "It *is* you. Oh, thank God. Rei, can you change back?"

The dog blinked dazedly, closing and opening eyes that were, come to think of it, exactly Rei's amber color. Sarah didn't think he was quite all there yet.

From across the lake, the low chop of the helicopter's rotors changed pitch. Gary looked up. "We gotta get that thing on the trailer and get out of here."

"Yeah—yeah." She pulled her legs out from under the dog and draped her coat over him before giving her dad a hand up.

They'd brought heavy boards in the truck bed to serve as a makeshift ramp. Sarah steadied the pod while her dad winched it slowly onto the trailer. Rei was right, it was lighter than it looked. No way she could have moved it on her own, but the boards didn't crack under its weight, and the trailer didn't settle too badly.

She had trouble concentrating on the work, and kept glancing over her shoulder at the huddled shape under her coat, as slow waves lapped up the beach against his paws.

How?

Maybe something on the ship itself had caused him to transform? A ... an Infinite Improbability Drive or something like that?

That's from a book, Sarah, you nitwit.

But aliens and interstellar spaceships were supposed to be fiction, too.

"Crap," Gary muttered. "Chopper's comin' this way."

They heard it pass over the lake, a little way down. Sarah glimpsed it for a moment, a sleek black shape like a hunting shark gliding through the thinning fog beneath the low bellies of the clouds.

It's an actual, literal black helicopter, she thought in disbelief. She pinched her finger painfully as she fumbled with the straps, trying to get the pod ratcheted down as quickly as possible.

"I got this," her father snapped, shaking out one of the tarps that had been wadded up in the pickup's bed. "You see if you can get Blue into the truck."

"I'm here," Rei's voice rasped.

He was standing right behind her, with the sheepskin coat draped over his shoulders. He looked like he could barely manage to stay on his feet, and that probably wasn't his healthiest shade of blue, but he was there. Alive. Not a dog.

A quick glance along the beach assured her that the dog had vanished. The dog was Rei. Somehow.

Sarah flung her arms around him, catching him in a quick, wet hug.

Rei jerked in surprise, which provided an instant for her logical brain to catch up with the rest of her and make her realize that she was hugging a wet, naked man, in front of her dad. She dropped him just as quickly and stepped back. "You need to get in the truck," she said. The rumble of the helicopter was getting louder. It sounded like it was right above the trees and coming their way. "We gotta get out of here."

She was pushing him into the truck as the helicopter suddenly roared overhead at treetop level. Light speared down at them and then was gone, but she could hear it circling around for another pass.

"Dad!" Sarah yelled, sliding into the driver's seat. "Get in!"

"Comin'!"

Rei pulled him up into the passenger's side of the truck. She still wasn't sure if Rei was completely tracking on what was happening, but he'd definitely picked up on the urgency. Sarah killed the truck's headlights and stomped on the gas, lurching forward into the wet, dark woods.

The very, very dark woods.

"Damn," she whispered, braking. She'd been driving this old road a few times a year ever since she got her license, but she didn't think she could do it blind. The minute she turned on the headlights, the helicopter would find them and could follow wherever they went. It was her desperate hope that if they kept the headlights off, visibility was so poor in the fog and the rain that it wouldn't be able to find them by the glow of the taillights alone.

Except it won't matter if I kill us by driving into a tree.

Paralyzed by indecision, she clutched the steering wheel. The chop of the helicopter's rotors shivered the air. It sounded like it was either landing on the beach or hovering right above it.

"Sarah, we gotta move," her dad said.

"I can't. If I turn on the lights, they'll find us."

Rei spoke up suddenly. "Can't you see?"

"No," she said, surprised. "Can you?"

"Yes. I'll guide you."

"You sure this is a good idea?" her dad asked as she put the truck in gear and began to creep forward.

"Rei says he can see." She kept forgetting her dad couldn't understand him. "He can help me drive."

Rei reached out a hand to curl his fingers over the steering wheel beside her own. With small tugs, he guided the truck as Sarah crawled at less than ten miles an hour—horrifically slow, and yet much too fast. She couldn't see a thing beyond the glow of the instrument panel and the rain slopping on the windshield in the wipers' wake.

From the sound of things, the helicopter was on the move again, cruising above them. *Very low* above them. The noise rattled her teeth.

"The road is ahead," Rei said quietly.

"Hold on. I'm stopping."

She braked just before turning out onto the lake road. The side of Rei's hand rested against hers on the steering wheel; his shoulder, through the jacket, was pressed to hers.

The helicopter skimmed across the treetops in a flash of lights, ghostly in the mist.

"It's behind us," her father said. "Go."

Sarah gunned the engine, turning out onto the road. She glimpsed distant taillights far down the road, but there should be few people out in this weather and at this time of night.

Yeah, more opportunity for the Men in Black to grab us. Lucky us.

The truck responded sluggishly with the weight of the trailer behind it. Not that she *wanted* to go fast. In pitch darkness and rain with no headlights, thirty-five felt more like eighty.

"Rei," she said, her voice breathless with tension, "I can't see if we're coming to a curve. You've got to tell me when I need to slow down."

"I will," he answered softly.

"Turnoff to the Muller place is coming up," her dad said.

"How do *you* know? You can't see either!"

Gary flashed her a quick grin. "You might think you know this corner of the county pretty good, kiddo, but you ain't got nothin' on the old man."

"I'm slowing down, then," Sarah declared.

She braked, her heart rate slowing markedly with every five miles that the speedometer dropped. At least until headlights appeared in her rearview mirror, making her realize that with her headlights off and the trailer blocking her brake lights, other vehicles couldn't see her. It was coming up fast behind her.

"There," Rei said quietly, just as her father said sharply, "Turn here!"

Sarah wrenched the wheel and pulled off, wincing as the bottom of the truck scraped something in the dark. The trailer rattled along behind them, and the other vehicle, whatever it was, roared past on the road with no awareness of their presence.

They also seemed to have lost the helicopter. Sarah could hear it flying a search grid as they jolted along the shortcut through the Mullers' back pasture, but it was staying behind them, at the lake.

"We got away." Sarah discovered she was grinding her teeth when the words came out indistinct. She forced her jaws to unclench. Her teeth were chattering, her whole body shaking.

"I'll take over," her dad said, reaching over Rei to pat her arm. "Hear me, hon? You did good, but I got this. You take a break now."

"Your hips," she protested shakily. "Driving is—"

"Something I've been doin' for forty years. Take a break, punkin."

She was too shaken to argue. It was all hitting her now, the chase and the fear and—and being *hunted*, that helicopter had been *hunting* them, and Rei vanishing into the cold dark water and not coming out—

"Hey, sweetheart. It's okay. You did good, kid."

They stopped to change drivers, and she ended up on the outside, with Rei's arm around her. That was awfully nice, wet though they both were. She leaned, shivering, into his solid side. He was shaking too, but from cold, she thought, not fear. She squeezed her eyes shut, feeling like a terrible coward.

"You were very brave," Rei said quietly.

Sarah opened her eyes, looking up into his warm amber ones.

"Hey, kiddo," her dad said, "think you can ask Blue to do for me what he was doing for you back there, show me which way to go and all that?"

Rei put a hand on the steering wheel. "He can understand you," Sarah said. "It's just that you can't understand him."

"Yeah, well, keep that in mind, so if he says I need to do something in a hurry, you gotta translate."

The truck jolted into motion.

It was a less seamless process with her dad driving. Rei guided them around obstacles, but Sarah had to translate any detailed instructions, such as the need to stop for gates blocking the road. Still, they managed, with Rei as their eyes and her father's strong, capable hands on the steering wheel, and Sarah as the translator mediating between them.

When she thought back on this night afterward, the fear was not entire gone—but it had been eclipsed by the memory of those last miles, and Rei's quiet voice, guiding them home through the dark.

TEN

SARAH WOKE to honey-colored sunlight bathing her bedroom walls, turning the old yellow wallpaper to molten gold.

It was rare for her to sleep past sunrise this late in the year, when the sun rose after seven. As a farmer's daughter, normally she was up at dawn. But this morning, she lay in bed for a few drowsy, indulgent moments.

It had been long after midnight when they'd pulled into the farmhouse driveway. All of them were too exhausted to think about unloading the trailer. Gary had backed up to the big door at the end of the barn, and Sarah and Rei dragged enough clutter out of the way that he could back the trailer into the barn, unhitch it, and then park the truck in its usual place beside the barn.

They didn't have a guest bedroom, as such, so she'd made up a bed on the couch for Rei. "Sorry we don't have anything better. At least it's not the barn, huh?"

His smile was rueful. "You have been too kind. I don't know how I can ever repay—"

"There's nothing to repay. We haven't done anything

except be decent human beings. If I were stranded on an alien planet, I'd hope someone would help me too."

She'd run upstairs before she could give in to the temptation to sit beside him on the couch and try to comb the mud out of his stiffening hair with her fingers. She had so *many* questions, a million questions. And now that they had retrieved his ship, would there be time to get answers to any of them?

Was he even here now? Maybe he was already gone.

This made her sit bolt upright. "Ow," she groaned aloud as her stuff body protested.

There was mud embedded in the creases of her palms, and her hair had dried into a mess of tangles that resisted the brush she tried to rake through it. Outside the window, leafless branches of the old maple tree outside her window glimmered in the morning sun, still wet from last night's rain. The sky was a vivid blue between patchy clouds that sent a brief chill across the world when they temporarily hid the sun.

Sarah opened her window and leaned out so she could see the barn. Everything looked fine. Perfectly normal. You'd never guess there was a trailer with an alien spaceship hidden inside those old wooden barn walls with their peeling paint.

He couldn't possibly have left already, she reassured herself. Not with the ship in the condition it was in last night. But maybe it would be better for him if he had, because she could hear helicopters, not close, but definitely out there. Flying around. Searching. Their buddy from last night had come back with friends.

They know we took something out of the water. They just don't know where we went.

She pulled on a sweater, determined not to lose her

good mood. They'd escaped with the ship, the sun was out, and it was a beautiful day. She supposed Rei would probably want to work on his ship, but maybe later she could talk him into letting her show him around the farm a little. If he was leaving soon, she wanted him to have some nice memories of Earth to go with the terrible ones.

There was no one in the kitchen, but she found bacon and scrambled eggs in a covered skillet on the stove. Sarah made herself a bacon sandwich and stepped out into a fresh, glorious morning. The air had a hint of chill, fading rapidly as the day warmed, and a crisp smell of autumn leaves ... and also manure, but long familiarity meant she hardly noticed it except when the wind blew directly from the pasture.

Ringing hammer blows echoed from the barn. Sarah nudged open the side door. The noise escalated to deafening levels before cutting out abruptly, to the sound of a ringing clatter of something falling. The radio was playing country music quietly in a corner.

The spaceship was off the trailer on the floor of the barn. It looked much bigger indoors than it had on the beach, and even more wildly out of place. Nothing about this thing belonged in a barn on a Wisconsin farm. In better light she could see how filthy it was, festooned with lake weeds and mud. A clutter of junk surrounded it, regular metal farm junk mixed with pieces of the matte gray metal and plastic the ship was made of.

"Dad? Rei?"

She couldn't see Rei anywhere, but her dad popped up over one of the ship's side fins, with a welding mask pushed up on his forehead. "Hey, punkin. Playing hooky?"

"Tuesday. No class."

Her dad nodded toward the shelf beside the utility sink,

where the coffeepot lived along with its attendant collection of cracked mugs. "Grab a cup of joe, then, and have a look."

Coffee was a lot less interesting to her right now than the spaceship. When she circled around to her dad's side of the ship, she found it gaping open, exposing the interior. It was impossible to tell how much of that was crash damage and how much had been done afterwards by the one-man/one-alien wrecking crew disassembling the ship.

"Are you taking the whole thing apart?" she asked.

"Just takin' off the damaged parts. Can't go to space with shielding that doesn't work."

"Since when are you an expert on spaceships, Dad?"

"Since an alien started tellin' me how to build 'em."

"I thought you still couldn't talk to him." Sarah leaned inside the ship to get a better look; her voice echoed in the small space. "Or did he find a translator for you?"

"Nah. We get by."

"Where is he, anyway?" Sarah asked, looking over her shoulder.

"Up in the loft, gettin' some stuff for me."

Sarah nodded and turned back to her exploration of the ship. Not that there was much to explore. If the outside of the ship had surprised her with its small size, the inside was downright tiny. There was just enough room for the ship's pilot to sit in a cradle made of gray material, resilient enough to spring slowly and soggily back when Sarah poked at it. Water beaded on the surface where her finger had left a dent.

She couldn't tell how the ship was controlled. There was no steering wheel or joystick-type control, no panels of buttons like in a spaceship on TV. There were some switches and levers, but the main feature of the controls was a pair of holes in the molded console panel in front of the seat. They were placed where someone sitting in the seat could insert their arms, so Sarah cautiously reached into one of them. Her fingers squelched in slime and mud from the ship's immersion in the lake, but she also felt mechanical bits and bobs, and finally a handle. Experimentally, she gripped it, and tried to imagine clutching those handles with the ship sealed up around her.

It would be like being trapped inside a tin can. She wasn't claustrophobic, but it still made her shudder. How did the pilot see where they were flying? She couldn't see any signs of windows, ports, or screens. Just a molded gray cradle and two handholds. Maybe that part there, about face height if you were sitting in the cradle, folded down over your face? She shuddered again; that was even worse.

How could Rei bear it, flying through outer space trapped in this cramped tomb? It had to be an escape pod, not an actual spaceship. Maybe there was, even now, an alien ship up there in Earth's orbit somewhere, looking for him.

"Sarah?" said a voice from outside the pod, in a musical, lilting accent.

Sarah banged her head against the pod's ceiling. "Ow," she muttered, backing out, rubbing her temple. Yeah, this was exactly the view of her that she wanted Rei to have, just her ass and feet as she rummaged around in his spaceship.

Rei was standing behind her with a toolbox. He wore a jacket of her dad's, too tight across the shoulders and a little too short in the arms, revealing the bracelets he was never without. Under the cuffs of a pair of rumpled sweatpants, his feet were bare as usual.

"We can get you some shoes that fit," Sarah said. "Unless you like going barefoot all the time. Or is that, um, traditional for your people?"

"Ah." Rei set down the toolbox in the straw. "Your shoes are uncomfortable for me. On the ship, we mostly wear light slippers, as there is no need for heavy footwear when one is indoors all the time. For the slaves, particularly."

"Slaves?" Sarah repeated. Her dad glanced up at her shocked tone as much as the word.

Rei froze. That was a deer-in-the-headlights look if she'd ever seen one. One of his hands started to come up and then dropped down again.

A few different thoughts spun through her mind:

He was right, the translator seemed to be picking up more of their languages, because she could understand him with near fluency.

Which meant she could ask him questions about who he was and where he came from.

Except now, she thought she knew. At least she knew a lot more than she had a minute ago. Rei was an escaped slave, and he was scared.

"Don't be afraid," she said quickly. "We aren't going to send you back. I promise. We're not going to do anything to you. You know that by now."

Rei's hand still hovered at about waist height, fingers clenching and unclenching. He started to raise his other hand toward his neck, but quickly lowered it. "I thought you might know," he said quietly.

"No. We didn't." Sarah glanced at her dad, who was watching them, able to understand only her half of the conversation. "Rei, do you want to take a walk? I think it's time for us to have a proper discussion about things."

"The pod—" Rei began, gesturing to his ship. Then his face twisted into a rueful grimace. "As if it's ever going to fly again. Yeah, come on. Let's walk."

As the implant picked up more English, it seemed to be

translating his speech in more colloquial ways. That couldn't possibly be what he was really saying, could it? Well, the implant had learned English from her; presumably it picked up Sarah's speech patterns as well.

"Yeah," she said, "let's walk. Hey, Dad? We'll be back soon."

"Don't forget the hat," her dad said absently, working on a piece of steel with a cutting torch.

"Hat?" Sarah asked, but Rei was already picking up the floppy-brimmed hat from last night. He settled it over his ears and smiled at her.

"Dad," she said, trying not to start laughing, "he's blue. I *really* don't think it's going to help."

"Better safe than sorry," her dad said serenely. "Be careful out there, kids."

"I'VE BEEN a war slave since I was nine standard years old."

They were in the back pasture, walking through the wet grass. Sarah's jeans were sodden from the knees down. Through the trees, their barn and other outbuildings could be glimpsed now and then, but otherwise it felt as if they were the only people in the world.

But they weren't, of course. Sarah reminded herself to turn back at the old mill, because just beyond it they'd be able to see into the Haverfords' hayfield, which meant someone might see Rei.

"You were stolen from your people?" she asked, looking over at Rei's profile, his gaze downcast as the high meadow weeds whispered past their legs. The hat looked ridiculous, perched on top of his dark hair, but she could see her dad's point; it would help disguise him from a distance. People would see the hat before they'd see the telltale blue.

"No," he said. "I was taken as taxes."

"I think the translator didn't get that right. I'm not sure what you mean." Tribute, perhaps?

"The people who rule my world, the Galateans, leave us mostly alone, but we don't have much that they want. Mine is a primitive world. So they take their taxes in the form of young people to be cannon fodder for their wars."

She wasn't sure what he'd said in his own language that her implant translated as "cannon fodder," but she didn't need to know more. Didn't want to know more. "Those assholes," she snarled, clenching her fists. "They took you as a *child?* How dare they! You were nine!"

"My years are not the same as your years," Rei reminded her. "Unless you have the standard calendar here."

"I doubt we do, but—okay, so, is nine years old still a child? Pre-pubescent? You were a *kid?*"

"Yes, I was." Rei turned his measured amber gaze on her. "You seem very shocked by this. Your people don't keep slaves?"

"No!" she exclaimed, horrified. But then honesty compelled her to add, "We used to. We don't anymore. I guess we still do, in some parts of the world. People are trying to end it."

"Different planets have different ways. I don't know how it was for your people, but unlike some parts of the galaxy, Galatea doesn't have hereditary slavery—that is, a slave's children are free. It's also not lifelong. They consider it very humane. For war slaves like us, we owe twenty years of service from the time we become old enough to fight, at fifteen standard years."

"You've been fighting since you were *fifteen?*"

He shrugged.

"And how old are you now?"

"Twenty-four," he said quietly.

She wondered how that compared to her twenty-six Earth years. He looked about the same age she was.

She tried to imagine knowing she would have to spend the next ten or eleven years of her life as a slave, fighting in a war she'd never signed up for, trapped in that tiny, awful tomb of a spaceship. No wonder it looked so uncomfortable. Nobody worried about a slave's comfort.

"Humane is *not* the word that comes to mind. How could your people let this happen? What kind of people would *do* that?"

Rei shrugged again. The pain that ghosted across his face was old and deep. "They didn't have a choice. If it wasn't me, it would have been someone else's child. Some see it as an opportunity, a chance for their children to get a galactic education and come back with useful skills after their twenty years of service is up."

"You. Were. *Nine.*"

Rei smiled very slightly. "I like that you're angry for me."

"Of course I'm angry," Sarah said. "Any sane person would be."

"I'm used to being around people who consider this situation normal."

"It's *not*," she said heatedly. "I don't care if some people think it's normal in Galatean or in yours. That doesn't make it right. There is *no* planet where it's morally okay to take a nine-year-old child, put a collar on them, and send them off to fight in someone else's war."

"Yes. Well." He looked down at his hands. "The universe is an unfair place."

It had never really hit Sarah, until now, what a safe and

comfortable life she had lived. She knew bad things, terrible things, happened elsewhere, but they had never touched her life. Ordinary deaths, yes. Tragedies, yes. But nothing like this. Sidonie was so small it hadn't even had a murder in her lifetime.

"Do you have friends out there?" she ventured. "Others like you?"

"They're all dead," he said, and it was the calmness of his voice, more than anything else, that brought bile to the back of her throat. "All but one. I don't know if he's still .... But I have go back and try to find him."

"Yes," she said, when she could speak. "Yes, you have to try."

They had been walking alongside the old millstream, and now reached the footbridge that her dad had built years ago to replace the old, rotting bridge that had once been able to accommodate wagon traffic. He'd dragged the old bridge out of the stream with the tractor, leaving it to rot beside the path. It was little more than a snarl of wild roses and black-berry brambles now, with mossy timbers poking out like the spars of a sunken ship. Someone who didn't know it used to be a bridge couldn't have guessed; it looked like a tangle of brush at the edge of the cleared pasture.

Her mother's ashes were scattered here, along this very stream. She took a breath and tried to turn her mind away from that.

"Is there any chance that they might be able to find you here?" she asked Rei.

Rei hesitated. His fingertips glided over one of his bracelets, back and forth, in what looked like an uncon-scious habit. "I don't know. My collar and cuffs burned out at the moment I fled. That was why I escaped when I did. Normally they would have been able to find and punish me from afar. And the collar would kill me if I got too far from the mothership."

"Kill you?" Sarah repeated weakly, while a cold voice in the back of her mind said, *What did you* think *being a slave meant?*

"Yeah, but it didn't happen, so I know the collar is nonfunctional. I don't think they have a way of tracking the pod, not from a distance, anyway. They'd have to jump to the same system I fled to. And I set the coordinates randomly. I don't think they could do it by accident."

"So ... they can't find you?" Sarah ventured.

"I don't think so. But we are within Galatean space, so it's possible they have a detachment in your system—"

"Wait, wait, *what?*" She stopped in the middle of the footbridge, turning to face him. "What do you mean, we're in Galatean space?"

"The pod's jump drive didn't have enough power to jump far enough to get me out of the Empire," Rei said. "Wherever your planet is, it's within Imperial space."

"No. No *way*. We're not part of some galactic slave-trading empire!"

"They might not know you're here. Space is vast, and habitable worlds are many. They may not have found you, or they might still be planning the conquest of your world when resources are available. They might just be watching and learning about your people right now. They do that."

"Wow, when you start talking, you really don't mess around, do you?"

"I don't understand?" he asked hesitantly.

"Nothing, just—this is all a lot to dump on a girl, you know?"

There was a large rock on the far side of the footbridge, a glacial erratic that she'd used as a makeshift bench to sit and watch the water ever since she was a little girl. Just downstream, the water swirled into the old millrace, past the dark bulk of the tumbledown mill. Sarah sank down on the rock and patted it in wordless invitation. After a moment, Rei sat beside her. He cocked one leg over his other thigh to rub his foot. In the sunlight, the silver traceries in his skin glinted and the gold spots on his face, trailing down from his eyes to his chin, held a hint of metallic green.

"I see why your people wear shoes," Rei remarked, chafing at the sole of his foot with his thumb. "Walking on a planet is not like walking on a ship."

"Dip your feet in the water," Sarah suggested. "It feels nice when your feet are sore. More so on a hot day, it's actually pretty chilly for it at this time of year, but you said your people come from a cold planet."

"Your planet is very comfortable for me." Rei stepped down to the water's edge and waded in, holding up the cuffs of the sweatpants. "You're right, this does feel pleasant."

"If you think that feels pleasant, then your world *must* be cold."

He made an amazing picture like that, his indigo skin contrasted against the green pasture and blazing fall colors behind him. Even the hat no longer looked so odd to her.

It was a picture she could never take, of course. She wasn't about to record any photographic evidence of their otherworldly visitor.

Their amazing, beautiful alien visitor.

"Rei," she said, leaning back on her hands on the sun-warmed rock. "Did you really turn into a big dog last night?"

Rei had been starting to lean down to dip his hand into the stream; he froze before he continued rinsing his fingers in the water.

"I assume from your reaction," he said slowly, "that you don't have *jaegan* on your world."

"Apparently not. I don't even know that word. We do have, um, legends of people who can turn into wolves, but they're just stories, you know? Fiction." At least she'd always thought so. "Just to be clear, that *was* you? You really did change?"

"I did." He smiled briefly. "Would you like to see again?"

"I'd love—" Sarah stopped, alarmed. She'd been hearing helicopters off and on all morning, but this was much louder. It sounded like it was coming their way.

"Is something wrong?" Rei asked.

"I don't know. I hope not."

She scrambled off the boulder. Now she could see it, a dark shape against the blue sky. It was low, barely above the treetops and rapidly getting larger, the thunder of its rotors thumping in her chest.

"Quick, Rei, the mill!"

She hurried to open the door. They didn't usually keep it locked. Even with her dad's hydro project, there was little inside that thieves might be interested in.

Rei crowded in on her heels, and Sarah shut the door almost all the way, leaving it open a crack so she could peek out.

The helicopter sped toward them, its shadow flitting across the fields underneath. It passed just to the south, arrowing onward toward the neighboring farm. Sarah waited a moment and then cautiously opened the door. "No, stay inside," she told Rei, and went around the edge of the mill, watching the helicopter cruise across the fields without slowing or stopping.

"Your people are seeking me," Rei murmured behind her.

"They sure are. I wonder if they know about *you*, or just about your crash landing the other night." She stared after the helicopter. "Does your ship put off any signals that people of my world might be able to detect? Like some kind of radiation or a distress signal or anything?"

"Not that I am aware of. But I'm no expert."

The helicopter dwindled against the sky until it could no longer be seen. After straining her eyes to recapture the tiny shape in the blue bowl of the sky, Sarah reluctantly turned away.

"I guess it's probably not a good idea for you to be outside too much, even on the farm. You need to stay close to somewhere to hide." She gave him a critical look. "Maybe Dad wasn't wrong about the hat."

Rei spread his hands, glancing down at himself. "But as you said, I'm still blue. There is no one this color on your world?"

"Nope. Not in the slightest." She gave him a light shove, herding him back into the mill. "We should stay in here for a few minutes in case it comes back."

He let himself be maneuvered into the mill, but kept looking over his shoulder. "Is there any chance your people might have contacted the Empire about me?"

"*My* people? No, of course not. People on Earth don't even know that life on other worlds exists."

"Are you sure?"

"Very sure," she said firmly, even as a tiny worm of doubt squirmed in her stomach. "If we'd found life on other planets, it would have been all over the news. They couldn't possibly hush it up. Now let's just wait 'til they're gone and go back to try to get your ship working."

Rei took off the borrowed hat and looked curiously around the mill's shadowed interior. Sunlight slanted across the high ceiling through windows near the roof, and the sound of rushing water was almost as loud as outside.

"What is this building used for?" he asked.

"It was built to grind grain, a long time ago. Now my dad's trying to make a power plant out of it. For generating electricity, you know?"

The smell of fresh-cut lumber was strong; her dad had been out here off and on all summer, shoring up old timbers, fixing rotten floorboards, and otherwise doing work that his doctors undoubtedly would not have approved of. His original plan with the old mill had been to restore the former grinding equipment and use it as a gristmill again, to demonstrate to tourists how flour used to be made in the old days. Part of the mill's interior was taken up with the scaffolding from repairs for that project, but at some point he'd switched over to his new idea of turning the mill into a power plant, supplying power for the farm and maybe even enough to sell back to the local power company. So now there were coils of wire and Rubbermaid totes full of electrical components scattered around, along with shop lights and a sleeping bag on the floor. Sarah worried for a minute that he'd started sleeping out here—surely she would have noticed!—but she decided it was just for insulation from the floor, so he could sit and work on his project.

And it was cold in here. In midsummer she loved coming into the mill to cool off, but at this time of year the icebox chill was much less welcome. She shoved her hands into the sleeves of her jacket, warming them against her opposite wrists, and sat on the sleeping bag. "Aren't you cold?" she asked Rei. "Your feet must be cold, at least."

Rei shook his head. "I'm fine. This doesn't feel unpleasant to me. As I told you, my world—"

"—is a cold world. I know." Sarah crossed her arms over

her knees. "How cold are we talking, exactly? Like Hoth?" He looked blank. "I mean, ice and snow all the time."

"No, our winters were long and cold, but the summers were not so different from your world."

"This is actually fall. Our summers are a lot hotter."

"Oh." He smiled shyly and bent to pick up a voltmeter, examining its leads absently. "I don't know what else I can tell you. I left when I was nine."

"I know, but you must remember some things, right? I can't even imagine walking on an alien world. This is the only planet I've ever known—the only planet any human has ever known. What was your world like?"

"A lot like yours, really. There were trees and mountains. The colors of the trees were a little different. More green and blue, less red and yellow."

"Our trees aren't that color all the time. Just in the fall."

Rei tipped his head to the side. A distant look of wonder crossed his face. "That's right. Trees change the color of their leaves before winter. I had completely forgotten about that."

Sarah's heart clenched. He was, if anything, even more beautiful in the dim light inside the mill, lit up by a shaft of sunlight speckled with dust motes, a blue-skinned angel from an alien world.

Rei took a sudden deep breath and shook himself out of whatever world of memories he'd gone to. "Anyway," he said briskly, "I don't remember much after all these years."

"Can all your people turn into ..."

"Yes, most of us are *jaegan*—shapeshifters." His smile was quick and shy, infinitely human, endlessly beautiful. "Do you still want to see my *jaegan* shape? I'll have to take my clothes off."

Her mouth dry, Sarah said quietly, "I don't mind."

Without a word, he began to strip out of the borrowed shirt, the borrowed sweatpants. His body emerged, muscular and blue, glistening with the silver threads embedded in his skin.

"What are those?" Sarah asked.

Rei paused in the act of folding the shirt. "What are what?"

"Those metal things, on your arms and shoulders." And everywhere else. Glistening silver threads ran between his ribs, formed intricate patterns on his chest, curved around his knees.

"Oh. Those are surgical implants. They're where the nanites in my body live. And they do other things too." He tapped the silver bracelet around his left wrist. "They help me talk to the cuffs. They also power the cuffs, gathering up energy from my entire body. They make me stronger and faster than I would be without them."

"For fighting?"

"Yes," he said softly. "For fighting." He dropped his arm to his side, the silver cuff gleaming against the indigo skin of his hip. "Do you want to see my wolf now?"

Sarah nodded.

Rei leaned forward—and flowed.

There was no other word for it. He was like a blue and silver waterfall, his natural grace turned supernatural as his entire body ran forward like water and pooled into a new shape. Sarah had imagined there would be an element of the grotesque to it, but there wasn't, just a grace and elegance that took her breath away.

Rei ended his shift on all fours and turned his head to look at her.

He was a huge wolf, long-bodied and lean, like something out of the prehistoric past, run through a photographic filter to add colors never designed by nature on Earth. Had he been uniformly blue, he might have looked painted, but he wasn't; his fur was brindled and variegated, deep blue mixed with gray and black, with a darker saddle over his shoulders and back.

In the dark-masked wolf's face, his amber eyes gleamed as if lit from within. But they were still Rei's eyes, looking at her with intelligence and warmth.

"You're beautiful," she whispered.

The blue wolf paced toward her with a slow, rippling predator's grace, dark body moving in and out of the shafts of sunlight and patches of shadow. When he reached her, Rei sat on his haunches like an enormous dog, and then carefully, slowly, lay down at her feet.

Sarah reached out cautiously and brushed his fur with her fingertips. It was coarse at the tips, but when she sank her fingers into his thick ruff, the underfur was luxuriously soft. *Adapted for cold weather,* she thought.

Rei blinked his luminous eyes slowly, and then closed them as she dug her fingers into his pelt, scratching him like a huge dog. He laid his head on his paws, nestled between the silver bracelets gleaming through the fur on each wrist. Up close she could see that the iridescent gold-green patches on his face were replicated in his fur, a sweeping pattern of small patches like the eyes in a peacock's tail that curved away from under each eye to vanish into the thick ruff around his neck.

"How did a creature like you evolve?" she asked softly, unable to contain her curiosity.

Rei's body rippled and flowed—and he was Rei again, sitting up, naked and blue, while she jerked her hands back guiltily.

The spots on his face darkened to the color of his skin in

a rippling blush. "My clothes are over there; I know your people—"

"It's okay," Sarah said. "I don't mind if you don't mind." She flipped back a corner of the unzipped sleeping bag. "Sit with me and use this to keep warm."

Rei hesitated, then settled crosslegged next to her, his knee touching her thigh, and flipped the corner of the sleeping bag over his lap. "The answer to your question is that we didn't evolve. We were made."

"By the Galateans?"

He shook his head. "No, by the Founders, a long time ago." When she looked at him blankly, he asked, "Don't your people have stories of the Founders? Or have you forgotten it, the way you forgot about other worlds? Some of my genetic material is a wolf's, but most of it is human, put together by the Founders long ago. They made you too, you know."

"Made," she repeated. "No, that's not possible. Maybe your people didn't evolve on your world, but *we* did. We have lots of evidence for it. Fossils. Do your people know what fossils are?"

"Of course we do," he said, smiling. "But that's the point. My people *didn't* evolve on Polara. Neither did the human inhabitants of any other world in the galaxy where humans live. Sometimes we were modified to fit the ecosystem of the world where the Founders put us, and sometimes they built a whole ecosystem around us, like on my world. But either way, we were put there a few tens of thousands of years ago."

"Ten thousand years?" She shook her head slowly. "No, Rei, we weren't put here by aliens, not that recently. I mean, maybe a few *million* years ago—but no, that doesn't fit either. This is our world. We've always been here."

"My people thought so too, until the Galateans attacked us. Now we know better, and we've met human cousins of ours from worlds across the galaxy. Before that, we thought we were alone. Like your people do."

"No, Rei, that doesn't work. Archaeology isn't my field, but I know we have an unbroken fossil record going back hundreds of millions of years into the past. And humans are too closely related to other species on the planet not to have come from here. We all have the same basic DNA and everything. We definitely evolved here. There's solid evidence for it."

"Then perhaps my suspicions are true." His eyes gleamed. "When I first woke up on your world and saw your people and your animals, I thought this might be Birthworld itself—the planet where humans originally came from. I've never seen so many Birthworld species all in one place. And your people look as close to base human stock as anyone I've seen anywhere."

"But—no—are you saying Earth was visited by aliens? And they took humans to other planets? That's impossible!"

"Is it?" he murmured. "Impossible as a Galatean battlepod landing in your lake?"

"We—I—but that means you're not an alien at all. Not really. If that's true, you're as human as I am." She reached out to touch the back of his hand lightly, shyly. "Okay, maybe with a few extras. Even after seeing you change shape, I can't believe you can do that. How does it work? Do you change genetically or just on the outside?"

"I have no idea," he said with a quick smile and a self-deprecating shrug. "I don't know much about the science of it. All I know for sure is that we don't change size, only shape."

"Oh, of course," she said, excited. "You can change your

shape, but not your mass. That's just basic physics. The mass would have to go somewhere, or be released as energy, and then you couldn't get it back. So as a wolf, you must weigh the same as you do now, right?"

He nodded. "As far as I know."

"Are all your people wolves?"

"Most of my village was. Some people elsewhere on Polara can shift into other kinds of animals, such as—" and here he said several words the implant couldn't translate. Sarah wondered if those were animals that didn't exist on Earth, or if the translator simply hadn't learned the English words for *tiger* or *meerkat* or *star-nosed mole* yet.

"What does it feel like," she asked, "to change shape like that?"

"I don't know how to explain it. How would you explain breathing to someone who doesn't need air?" He spread his arms, and smiled suddenly, wide and dazzling with dimples in *both* cheeks. "It feels like freedom."

Sarah had to catch her breath. He was gorgeous like that, so bright and alive. She felt as if she'd just caught a glimpse of the person he might have been, if he hadn't spent most of his life as a prisoner in an alien war.

The look vanished as quickly as it had come, locked down beneath his usual surface calm, but his eyes still sparkled with exhilaration. He was happy, she thought, dazed. She wasn't sure if she'd seen him happy before.

"I still feel the same under the surface," he went on. "I can hear and smell better. Some *jaegan* can shift to forms that have gills or wings, so they can breathe underwater or fly. But I still get tired about as quickly, and I still have to breathe. Not like dragons. They aren't like us at all."

"Dragons?" she echoed in amazement.

"Yes, they're an intelligent species who can also change

their shape, but they aren't from Birthworld stock, and they don't follow the same rules we do. They can change their mass as well as their shape, and they can survive in hard vacuum without having to breathe."

How many mythological creatures were actually real? she wondered. Maybe some human in the distant past had met actual dragons. Or maybe the translator had simply picked up on the closest word and he wasn't actually talking about dragons at all. "What are they like? Are they big lizards that breathe fire? Have you ever met one?"

"I'd rather not talk about dragons right now," he said quietly.

There was no emotion in his voice, but the pain that flashed in his eyes cut her to the quick. She wanted more of that bright joy from earlier, not this. Never this.

"No," she said, and moved a little closer to him on the sleeping bag. "No, we don't have to."

They sat in silence for a little while. The helicopter hadn't come back. It really was peaceful in here, with the rushing of the stream outside, the dust motes drifting in the sunlight shafting down from the mill's high windows.

Rei was close enough she could feel the warmth of his skin. If she moved over just a little, his bare leg would be pressing against hers.

So she did. Just that little bit, closing the gap between them, his skin electric against hers.

She was half afraid he'd pull away, but he didn't.

Sitting like this, their usual height difference—six or seven inches—all but disappeared. His eyes, she found, were even more fascinating up close, a hundred shades of gold and green and brown. The iridescent patches on his face fascinated her. At the moment they were a warm gold, close in tone to his eyes, glimmering with iridescent hues of blue and green when he tilted his head.

"Can I touch these?" she asked softly, lifting a hand to gesture to his spots.

"What, my *tsinde*? Go ahead. Just be careful; they're sensitive."

She touched the skin of his cheek very lightly, beside the spots rather than on top of them. His skin felt soft and human despite its indigo color. Up close, she could see the pores and the subtle darkening over his cheekbones, much too complex for the stage makeup it otherwise resembled. She realized suddenly that she had never seen him shave, and there was no stubble on his face. Instead his skin was very lightly fuzzy.

"Do your people grow beards?"

He gave his head a small shake, not enough to dislodge her hand. "Not in my part of Polara, anyway."

"That seems odd," she said, smiling. "Since you turn furry when you change, to have no hair on your face."

"I have some hair." He took her other hand and placed it lightly on his chest. "Here."

The coarser, curly hair on his chest felt very human. But of course, from what he said, he *was* human. A long-lost distant cousin of the humans on Earth.

With one hand on his chest, the other on his face, she leaned closer. The *tsinde* spots were almost reflective, but not quite. "How sensitive are they?" she asked softly.

"Very." His voice was a breathy whisper.

She brushed the juncture where the *tsinde* met regular skin and felt him give a little shiver. Darker color flushed the spots, occluding their gold with blue.

"But what *are* they?" she murmured, running her

fingertip around the edge. There was no seam, as if they'd just grown there.

"Regular skin cells, I guess. Just flatter and shinier." His fingertips brushed her lower lip. "Why are your lips pinker than your face?"

"I don't know," she whispered. With every word, her lips moved against his fingertips. "They just are."

The *tsinde* spots were almost the color of his skin now, with faint green and purple overtones. "What does it mean?" she asked, daring to brush one of her fingertips directly across the one just below his eye, and felt him shiver again. "When they change colors?"

"The same thing it means when your skin changes colors."

"But that could mean a lot of things."

"So does this," he whispered.

She leaned closer—he moved his hand away from her mouth, threaded the fingers lightly through her hair instead —and touched her lips to the *tsinde* just above his jaw, near the corner of his mouth. It was slightly warmer than his skin. Her fingers couldn't feel the difference, but her sensitive lips could.

His breathing quickened as she explored the *tsinde* with her mouth, feeling the difference between the slick, firm color-changing skin and the softer skin around it. One by one, she traced the line of spots to the corner of his mouth— and kept going. His lips were incredibly soft on hers, and incredibly, perfectly human.

I guess kissing isn't just an Earth thing.

It was gentle and slow and a little awkward; they bumped teeth, making her laugh softly into his mouth. His hand was still in her hair, fingers laced through it; hers was cupped along the side of his face. She trailed her fingers through his hair and made an unexpected discovery.

"What?" he asked, when she pulled back in surprise.

"Your hair is ..." She trailed off, stroking her fingers up from beneath, through soft fluffy hair close to his scalp and into the layer of coarse guard hairs on the outside. No wonder his hair looked so thick. It was like the fluffy, two-layered coat of a Husky dog ... or a wolf. "It's *layered*. Like a cold-weather breed of dog. The same as you do when you're a wolf. You've got underfur."

"I told you, Polara is a cold planet."

"Yes, but—" She stopped before telling him that humans didn't have that kind of hair. Earth humans didn't, anyway. But Polarans did, and what did it matter if they'd been given the gene for it, or if they had evolved it naturally?

"It's nice," she said instead, running her fingers through it. "Different from what I'm used to."

His fingers stroked lightly across her scalp, making her lean into the petting like a cat. "Your hair is very soft," he murmured.

"So is yours, on the underneath. Like you."

She kissed him again, combing her fingers through his hair. It wasn't like anyone's hair she'd ever touched before; it was wonderfully, uniquely Rei. She loved the contrast between the soft undercoat and the coarser hair on top.

A sense of unreality settled over her like a blanket. *I'm making out with an alien in the old gristmill! How is this my life?*

And then his lips closed over hers, and his tongue probed her mouth, and she didn't care. Not in the slightest.

They kissed and kissed. Rei kept stopping to look at her, stroking her face, touching her hair, gazing at her with soft amazement in his eyes as if she was the most beautiful thing he'd ever seen.

No one had ever looked at her like that before.

And he—he was beautiful, he was amazing, he was *everything*: the grace of his long blue body as he leaned into her, the strength in his hands as they cupped her face gently, so gently.

He broke their kiss again to fumble with the buttons on her shirt, breaking into a shy half-grin when his fingers kept slipping off. Sarah folded her hands over his and showed him how to undo them. He'd never actually buttoned the shirt he'd borrowed from her dad, she realized. He might not know how they worked.

She stripped the shirt off her shoulders and saw that wonder in his eyes again as he gazed at her torso, at her breasts spilling over the cups of her bra and the little rolls above the waistband of her jeans. Her nipples were erect, pushing against the cotton fabric of the bra.

"How does this garment work?" he asked, running his hands around the sides.

"It's cleverly designed to baffle even ordinary Earth humans." She started to reach around to undo it herself, then thought better of it and turned around, leaning forward to display her bare back. "There are little hooks under the band. Lift it up a little and push them in to unhook them, then pull them apart."

With her back turned and her head bowed, curls hanging in her face, she couldn't see exactly what he was doing. The sight-unseen feeling of his callused fingertips on the skin under her bra band was unexpectedly thrilling. There were some little tugs against her breasts and then the cups loosened. Heck, she'd had Earth boyfriends who had more trouble with it.

"You're a natural," she told him.

"Your planet," Rei murmured, pressing kisses to her back and shoulders as he carefully slipped each strap over her arm, "is in desperate need," more kisses, "of some proper clothing-fastening technology."

"How does yours work? That thing you were wearing when we—oh—" He'd reached around from behind her, cupping her breasts in his hands. Her aching nipples pressed against his fingers. "It was ... sticky? Down the side ...?"

"The fabric adheres to itself." He spoke into her hair, nibbling at the back of her neck between words. Heady tingling flowed through her with every touch of his lips, with the brush of his breath across the fine hairs on the nape of her neck.

"Where did it go? I'd like to—ah—" He'd figured out that she liked her nipples played with. Concentrating on the conversation required a concerted effort of will. "—see it."

"It's in the ... *hailoft*." That was English; he must have learned a few more words from her dad. His breath huffed in a soft laugh, tickling her nape. "Right now? Are you sure?"

"No, I—nngh—" She pushed back against him, her whole body tingling now. His hardness pressed against her buttock; she wasn't the only one. Rationality managed to reassert itself a moment later, despite the neck-nibbling and his attentions to her sensitive nipples sparking a growing heat between her legs. "Rei, I—oh—I don't have a condom. Do you know that word? Condom? Protection?"

The neck-nibbling paused. "Are you talking about protection from pregnancy?"

She twisted her head around so she could see his face. "Pregnancy, yes, and STDs—I don't think you could actually get me pregnant, could you? I mean, Earth humans and your kind of people—"

"I should be able to, in theory." He sat back, settling her more comfortably in his lap, and kept lightly stroking her nipples as he spoke. "Most types of humans are cross-fertile with each other. I couldn't right at this moment, of course. All slave soldiers wear contraceptive implants."

"Removable?" she asked, leaning her head back against him. Not that she wanted his—she just wanted to—It was scientific curiosity, damn it.

"With permission. Though ..." He mouthed lightly at her neck. "I don't need anyone's permission now that I'm free. Except yours, of course."

"What about diseases? Do you have space STDs?"

His gentle biting and kissing moved down to her shoulder; he spoke between kisses. "I don't know that last word, but you don't need to worry. I've never had sex before, except for the—" and he said a word that didn't translate.

Sarah's eyes opened. "Except for the *what?*" She squirmed around in the circle of his arms until she was straddling his lap and facing him; she couldn't have this conversation if he was talking to her neck. "Rei, are you telling me you're a *virgin?*"

Rei kissed her forehead. "I don't know that word, but if it means inexperienced, yes, I am. I've been taught but I haven't had an opportunity to put it into practice with a partner yet. Is something wrong?"

"Taught? Taught how? By whom?" The sexual energy between them hadn't ebbed—she still had her arms around his neck, her face mere inches from his—but if he was an actual virgin (good God, with a body like that, *how?*), she didn't want to make him feel like she was springing Sex-Crazed Earth Humanity on him all of a sudden.

He was frowning now, looking worried. "Is that a problem for your people?"

"No, no, of course not." She kissed him to make sure he knew she wasn't upset, nibbling at his lips. "How did you learn?"

"With robots." It translated this time; she wasn't sure if he had used a different word or if the translator had managed to pick up an equivalent meaning from her mind this time. "That's how it's done on Galatea. You learn with robots before you have sex with a person. Not just for slaves; for everyone. You have to practice before you do it for real. I guess it's not like that here?"

Sarah couldn't help the nervous laugh that escaped her. "No, it's definitely not like that. Although maybe the sex would be better if we did." She'd lost her virginity in a fumbling encounter in the back of a pickup truck the year she graduated from high school. Not her most shining moment, especially since they'd broken up two weeks later when she found out he was also having sex with two other girls in her graduating class.

"Do you mind?" His golden gaze searched her face anxiously.

"No! No, of course not." She kissed him again fiercely, letting her body say what her words couldn't. "Do *you* mind," she asked in sudden worry, her cheek pressed to his, "that I've had other partners before?"

"Different cultures do things differently." He kissed the side of her face, lips trailing across her skin, leaving a shiver in their wake. "My people, we don't ... we tend to cleave to one partner. Sex without attachment is not easy for us. Not like some of the other races of humankind—my friend Skara's people, for example, who have sex as casually as breathing." There was another twist of pain in his voice that she didn't ask about. "For us though, for Polarans, we don't have sex without love. Perhaps it's something in the way we were made. Wolves mate for life, they say. I only know that I never really had much interest in it until ..." He hesitated.

"Until now?" she whispered. *Love.* The word bounced around in her mind, unable to settle.

"There was one other," he whispered. "Before you. A girl in another sept. But we never—she wasn't—she was transferred elsewhere. I didn't have a chance to get to know her. Learning about sex with the training robots was pleasant, the physical sensations at least, but it wasn't ... I didn't *want* ..." He trailed off, frustration written in every line of his body, the spots on his face cooling to subtle shades of pale blue and gold.

"Shhhh." She pressed a kiss to his shoulder. "We're both here now, and that's what matters. You can show me what they taught you, and I'll show you what I've learned here on Earth, all right?"

"All right." His voice was a ghost of a breath against her hair.

She kissed him gently all over his neck, his collarbone, his chest. If he'd never had sex except with robots, she wondered, had anyone ever touched him like this—tenderly, with love?

He was certainly responsive, his breath quickening as she trailed kisses over his blue skin. His hands were all over her, one gliding down her back to cup her buttock over the fabric of her jeans, the other fondling her breasts and fingering the sensitive nipples.

If the dual-layered hair on his head was different from what Sarah was used to, his body hair was just the same, dark and close-curled on his chest and in a narrow stripe down his flat abdomen. He wasn't as hairy as some guys;

along with the lack of facial hair, his chest hair was sparse, his shoulders and back smooth. And his cock was just like anyone else's—erect and ready, large but not tremendously so.

Eagerness pulsed through her. She wasn't used to guys who wanted to take it slower than she did. The slow pace heightened the need, leaving her wet and aching, struggling not to do what she really wanted to do, which was to fling herself on him and rub on him all over like a cat in heat.

She showed him how to undo the button and zipper on her jeans, and rose to her knees, hands on his shoulders, so he could pull those down.

"Can I look at you?" Rei asked.

"Look at me? Like this?"

"Just like that." His hands resting lightly at her waist, he slid back a little on the sleeping bag, gazing at her with that same look of wonder.

Smiling, Sarah put her arms over her head to lift up her breasts and give him a bit of a show. He sucked in his breath, his cock lifting eagerly in its nest of wiry curls. When he leaned forward, she let him take the lead, laying her down on the sleeping bag so he could strip her the rest of the way out of her jeans and underwear.

There was a considerate gentleness in him that she hadn't encountered in her previous boyfriends, the boys and young men her own age who seemed more concerned with their own pleasure than with hers. Inexperienced though he might be, it was obvious that Rei was interested in pleasing her above all else. With hands and mouth, he explored her body, and when he made his way down her body to the soft place between her legs, she found that, whether through training or instinct, there was nothing at all lacking in his technique. She arced her head back and let go, releasing herself to pleasure as he took her apart.

HER SKIN WAS SOFT. So soft. Rei kept losing himself in the wonder of it. Warmth flooded him, not just arousal, but the sheer delight of touching and being touched.

His people were not meant to be alone.

Her hands combed through his hair as he tasted her salt, learning to match the strokes of his tongue to the soft sounds she made and the responsive jerks of her body. He was delighted to find that he could read what she was feeling by her reactions, and adjust his own movements to draw more of those soft, ecstatic little sounds out of her.

Making love to robots was nothing like this. It wasn't *love* at all. This ... this was what he was meant for; he was made to give himself wholly to a mate, body and soul. Her touch consumed him. Her scent and taste filled his world.

There was nowhere he wanted to be, nothing he wanted more than this. His own aching need became one with the pleasure he sensed rising in her, until she bucked under him and he had to jerk back, drawing slow breaths to stop himself from joining her as she fell over the edge.

Sarah's gasps of delight faded to softer breathing. She pushed herself up on her elbows, looking at him through tousled sandy bangs. "Rei? Are you okay? Why did you stop?"

"I just ... need a minute," he panted. "They said ... a woman might not be ready again right away, depending on species, and I don't want it to be uncomfortable for you. I need—"

"Rei." She lifted her hips, spreading her legs to expose

her inviting pink folds, all but shoving herself at him. *"Please."*

He needed no more invitation to slide into her. It was ...

It was everything.

She enfolded him in her warmth, and for that first instant he couldn't have moved if he'd wanted to. All he could do was lean forward, shuddering, to press his forehead against hers, as her arms wrapped around his neck. Her fluttering eyelashes tickled his sensitive *tsinde*, sending tiny electric thrills through his body, coalescing around the heat at his core.

"I didn't know ..." he whispered, and felt her stir beneath him, *around* him. "I didn't know it could be like this."

She moved her hips, and he jerked in a pleasure so great it bordered on pain. For years he'd tried not to feel anything, physical or emotional. He had taught himself to focus on things outside himself, to detach himself enough to stop caring that his body was nothing but a possession for others to use as they wished.

Now feeling swept over him in a tidal wave, the physical and the emotional.

He had almost forgotten that bodies could feel *good*.

Sarah pushed against him and he met her thrust for thrust, feeling out her rhythm as he'd matched himself to the rhythm of her pleasure-pulses when he was tasting her earlier. They moved together as one body. It was not so different from sparring for pleasure, in certain ways— moving in sync, matching parry for thrust. But sparring was never like this ...

Heat and urgency grew in him. He breathed out her name, and heard her gasp his. He couldn't tell if she was approaching another climax of her own, but he knew that he wouldn't be able to hold himself back much longer. He didn't *want* to. He wanted—needed—to feel this. All of this.

He went over the edge with a white-hot burst of sensation that made him cry out involuntarily, breaking the habits of a lifetime. *Be silent. Be in control. Never let them make you scream.* Now this rush of impossible feeling tore a cry from his throat, and Sarah added her own soft cry to his.

They came down slowly, together. He could feel her pulsing around him, sending shivery aftershocks through his body. Afraid that he might hurt her with his greater weight, he rolled to the side and lay beside her on the sleeping mat as he softened gradually inside her.

"I didn't know ..." he whispered. "That it could be like that."

"Me neither," she murmured back.

Rei propped himself up on his elbow to look at her face. The shadows were almost as clear as daylight to his dark-adapted eyes, showing him every freckle on her pink skin. She gazed back at him with sleepy eyes, their deep blue-gray making him think of the often stormy skies of his homeworld.

"But you've been with others, correct?" he asked. "You said I wasn't your first."

"You're right; you aren't. But Rei, I'm not with those men now. None of them were like you."

He couldn't help smiling. He felt light, almost effervescent. He couldn't ever remember feeling like this. "Blue?"

Sarah smacked his shoulder with her hand and rolled against him, pressing her cheek against his skin.

They lay like that for awhile, as the shadows of the moving sun crept across the wall. The flying vehicle did not come back. Finally Sarah gave a little shiver. "I don't know about you, but I think we might want to put some clothes on. I'm chilly."

He wasn't, but he sat up and watched her clean herself with a handful of disposable towels from a roll she found behind a crate, before putting her clothes back on. It was unexpectedly erotic, a strip tease in reverse, covering up each part of her gorgeous body in turn.

She kept stopping to smile at him, as if she sensed his thoughts—or maybe, he thought as her gaze lingered on his bare chest, because she liked looking at him, too. She *wanted* him. She *liked* him. He could still smell that wanting on her, along with the powerful scent of sex.

When all her clothes were back on, he reached reluctantly for his borrowed leggings. "Will your father be upset?"

"About what?"

"About ... this."

"We don't have to tell him," Sarah said.

"He'll be able to smell it."

Sarah wrinkled her nose. "Ewww, Rei. Mood-killer."

"He is very protective of you," Rei said, refusing to be distracted. "Will he ask me to leave?"

"I'm a grown woman, so it's none of my dad's business who I have sex with." She fell silent for a moment as she tied the thongs on her shoes. "Maybe we'll just ... not tell him yet."

"He'll be able to—"

"Rei, no, humans can't just smell sex on people, okay? Not unless they get really close. Dad's not going to be sniffing my neck, and I'll take a shower back at the house." She took his hand. "Don't worry, I won't let Dad come after you with a shotgun. He'll be cool about it. I promise."

IN ALL HONESTY, assurances aside, Sarah *couldn't* quite figure out how to tell her dad that she'd been banging their alien guest in the mill. She brought the sleeping bag back to the house with her and stuffed it into the washing machine. It seemed *way* too weird to just leave it there for other people to sit on. But not as weird as her dad smelling her; *ewww*, Rei.

She could figure out how to tell Dad later. The afternoon slid past in a pleasant haze. She'd forgotten how *good* sex made you feel. Her whole body felt like it was bathed in midsummer sunshine, even when the sun went away and the gray late-October clouds rolled in again.

Rei and her dad spent the rest of the day working on the spaceship in the barn. Sarah helped them for a little while, but she really couldn't do much more than fetch, carry, and hold things—granted, that was all her dad could do either; Rei was the one who actually knew what he was doing. When that started to wear on her, she did some homework and put in a load of laundry while the sleeping bag dried, and then worked on a little bit of long-deferred farm maintenance. One of the hens had turned into an escape artist, so Sarah checked every inch of their pen until she found the escape route and blocked it with rocks. She called in an order to the feed store for more of Princess's special feed to help with the mare's chronic colic, and scribbled a note to herself to pick up a case of oil the next time she was in town, or preferably in Eau Claire, where it would be cheaper; the truck needed an oil change before winter. She peeled some potatoes and put a pot roast in the oven, before chopping some of the last of the summer's cucumbers and tomatoes for a salad.

Simple routine, as if it was an ordinary day.

As if her heart didn't sing every time she moved, the slickness between her legs reminding her of the secret delight she and Rei had shared.

What is Dad going to say?

If it had been anyone else—one of the local farm boys, say—she knew he'd be overjoyed for her. He didn't talk about it much, but she knew he worried about her. He wanted her to have friends and a social life, go on dates.

But ... an alien? And one who was planning on leaving as soon as he got his ship fixed?

Sarah screwed her eyes shut to stop an unwanted prickling at the corners.

Don't set your sights too high, remember? If you don't want unrealistic things, you won't be disappointed. Live for the moment. Don't worry about tomorrow.

Always easier said than done, when there was something she really wanted.

The timer went off on the stove. She took out the pot roast and went out to the barn to let Rei and her dad know that dinner was ready.

"And dinner that I ain't cooked," her father said, grinning at her as he limped into the kitchen, grease-stained and cheerful. "That's a change."

"I even vacuumed the floor."

"Where is my little girl and what have you done with her?" Her dad peeked under the lid of the roasting pan. Sarah batted his hand away.

"Dad! At least wash the grease off."

Rei came downstairs from the bathroom, toweling off his hands. There was a moment of awkwardness when Sarah started to reach for him and quickly dropped her hand, spinning away to pick up the salad bowl and put it on the table.

"Oh, knock it off, you two." Her dad was washing his hands at the sink; he didn't bother looking around. "I can see what's goin' on. I got eyes."

Sarah noticed that Rei was—blushing? Yes, definitely blushing. His *tsinde* spots had turned a heated dark blue.

"I promised Rei you wouldn't be weird about it," she said quickly as she scooped up a stack of plates. "I'm a grown-up, Dad, and you *said* you want me to have my own life—"

"Honey." Her father caught her shoulder with a wet, soapy hand as she plopped the plates onto the table as if they'd done something to offend her. "I didn't say I mind. He makes you happy, does he?"

"Yes," she said, ducking to hide her smile.

"Well then." Gary turned to point a finger at Rei, who looked at it, puzzled. "Punkin, am I right that he does understand what I'm saying, even if I can't understand him?"

"Yes, as long as I'm in the room. I think?" She looked at Rei, who nodded.

"Good. You treat my little girl right, you hear me?"

"I would never hurt your daughter," Rei said sincerely. "Never."

Sarah blushed as she translated.

"Long as we've got that worked out." Gary dried his hands on a dish towel and reached for the salad tongs. "Let's see if that pot roast tastes as good as it smells."

After dinner, Rei quietly helped clear away the table. He seemed surprised by the process of washing dishes. "Don't you have machines for this?"

"Well, in the sense that they exist on this planet. We don't own one, though."

"Hmm." He reached for a plate and scrubbed it under the running water.

"Is this very different from what you're used to?"

Rei hesitated before answering. "It is very like my childhood. Your technology is more advanced than what we used in my village, but otherwise ... it is very like it."

"Is that good or bad?"

"I don't know. A little of both, perhaps." He smiled. "Many things are."

She leaned closer to brush his lips with her own. "I hope this is good," she murmured.

"This is good." He smiled back at her. "This is only good."

Only good. She felt the same way ... if she let herself. If she didn't remind herself that this was temporary, that he was going to have to leave soon.

After dinner, Rei went back out to work on the spaceship some more. Sarah did the evening chores and then watched TV with her dad, but restlessly; she kept glancing out the window, where light spilled out of the barn into the night.

Gary reached for the remote and turned down the volume. "Go on then. Keep him company."

"Am I that obvious?"

"More than you know." He grinned at her. "Don't think I'll mind if I notice the couch wasn't slept on, come morning."

Sarah threatened playfully to hit him with a couch pillow, then kissed his cheek and got up.

She took the sheepskin jacket and went out into the night. It was crisply cold and drizzling again; she shoved her hands deep into her jacket pockets. The barn, at least, was dry if not that much warmer.

"Hey there," she murmured, bending down to scratch Mouser's head as the cat twined around her ankle. She checked Mouser's food and water bowls to make sure both were topped up before going around the back of the dismantled spaceship.

Rei was sitting in the straw beside it, scribbling with a carpenter pencil on the back of a feed receipt. He let it drop into his lap with a sigh, then looked up and saw her. His smile was warm but distracted.

"Not going well?" Sarah asked, sitting beside him. The back of the receipt was covered with rough diagrams and what she guessed were notes, written in an angular, runic-looking script.

"It is not going to be easy to fix with the tools and materials that you have on your world."

"Will it be easier in the morning?"

His face softened; he took her hand. "Perhaps not. But it will keep."

The TV was off when they let themselves quietly into the house, the living room dark but for a single lamp. Sarah led Rei past the couch, and leaned close to whisper, "Dad doesn't mind. Really. We'll just have to be quiet."

It was hard to fit two people into her narrow bed, harder still to keep the bedsprings from squeaking.

They managed.

Outside the window, rain was falling more heavily now. Sarah fell asleep to the sound of water dripping off the eaves, and somewhere above the clouds, the dull chop of helicopter rotors, bound for destinations unknown.

ELEVEN

"WHERE ARE YOU GOING?"

Sarah paused in the doorway, clean clothes bundled in her arms. She hadn't meant to wake Rei, but she also hadn't expected him to sleep through her quietly slipping out of bed, into the bathroom for a shower, and back to the bedroom to collect a sweater and jeans from her closet.

He was normally so cautious, so alert. But it was she who had wakened a dozen times during the night, startled by the presence of another body pressed warm against hers in the narrow bed. Every time, Rei had been deeply asleep, limp and heavy, not even stirring when she propped herself up on an elbow to watch his lax face as he breathed softly and steadily in the gentle green glow of her lightning-bug-shaped nightlight.

As if he hadn't truly slept in days—weeks—months; as if all it took was having her beside him in the bed to relax him.

"I'm going to class," she whispered, closing the door. Her father was still asleep; she didn't want to wake him. She began pulling on her jeans in the dark bedroom.

Rei sat up in bed. The light coming in around the door

from the hallway, and the gray light of dawn through the lace curtain over her bedroom window, gave just enough light that she could see him shake his head.

"To class? I don't understand."

"Class? School? College? That's where I went on Monday, er, the other day, you know, when I was gone all day."

He nodded. "I remember that. I couldn't understand most of what you were saying then. It's a kind of training that you're going to?"

"Sort of. I'm studying astrophysics. That's a type of science, about stars and planets and gravitation."

"Science training?" He smiled, a flash of white teeth in the dark. "That's impressive. I didn't know you were a scientist."

"Just a rookie scientist who's still learning. And based on what I've seen so far of you and your spaceship, I now know that almost everything I'm learning is wrong." She pulled her sweater over her head and ran a hand through her damp curls. "But still, I paid for those classes, so I need to not flunk out. I won't be gone for long. Just a few hours. You can sleep for a while longer."

"I'm not sleepy," he began, and interrupted himself with a yawn.

"I can see that. Oh!" She looked up from tying her shoes. "I just had a thought. I'm going to be in the city today. It's not a big city, but much bigger than our little town here, with better stores. While I'm there, I can buy you some clothes so you don't have to keep wearing Dad's. Do you know what—oh, what am I saying, of course you wouldn't know what your sizes are. I need to measure your waist and leg length so I can buy you some pants."

"You don't need to obtain clothing for me," he protested

as she rummaged in her sewing drawer for a tape measure. "What I already have is fine."

"Move over and let me get this around your waist."

This turned out to be hard to do: he was so close, and so naked, and the skin above his hipbones was so soft, and now he was nibbling on her neck as she bowed her head over the tape measure. She turned her head to catch his next kiss on her lips, and he slid a hand into her hair, pulling her in closer—

—until she surfaced with a little gasp. "I have to go, Rei, seriously. I've got to drive all the way to the city, I'm going to be late for my class ... Come on, let me get your measurements written down, I'm not even going to have time for breakfast at this rate—"

He followed her downstairs with her dad's sweatpants sliding off his hips and a too-tight-in-the-shoulders shirt dangling its tails across his thighs. She was going to have to buy him better-fitting clothes for her own ability to concentrate, if nothing else.

"When did you say you'll be back?" he asked as she got out a loaf of bread and a package of sliced ham to make a quick sandwich to eat in the car.

"Early afternoon. I'm going to unload all my work shifts this week if I can. I wouldn't even go to class today, but there's a quiz." She shook her head and snatched the grocery shopping list off the fridge, where it was stuck on with a banana magnet so she and her dad could add items as needed. "And then I'll do some shopping and get back here. Is there anything you need me to pick up for fixing your ship?"

"Nothing that can be obtained on your planet."

"Oh well. Clothes shopping it is, then." She stuffed the

sandwich into her bag and gave him a long, lingering kiss before she dashed out the door to the truck.

———

ON MONDAY, going to class had felt like stepping back into the real world, with the farm and all its attendant weirdness receding like a dream.

Somehow, between then and now, everything had flipped. Now it was the university campus that felt unreal. Sarah drifted through it in a haze, unable to concentrate, all too aware of how young most of the other students were—sometimes the difference between nineteen and twenty-six felt like a thousand years—and how distant and unrelatable their concerns had become. Discussion about boyfriends and girlfriends, about politics and sports washed over her. She forgot she hadn't studied for the quiz until the paper landed on her desk, and then she just guessed at the answers she didn't know. It hardly seemed to matter; what point was there to a freshman physics class when she had an *actual alien spaceship* in the barn?

She escaped from campus as quickly as possible and hit the big box stores to pick up the items on her list. This was no less surreal, as she pushed her cart around harried-looking shoppers whose biggest concerns were which brand of cereal to buy. The garish displays of Halloween candy and decorations reminded her that the holiday was only a few days away, so she tossed a couple bags of mini chocolate bars into her cart just in case they got trick-or-treaters. Some years the local farm kids were more dedicated than others. She'd have to make sure Rei stayed in the barn, just in case ...

Wait a minute.

Sarah turned to the racks of costumes and thoughtfully fingered a witch's hat. Halloween ... the one time of year when no one would bat an eye if they saw a blue-skinned man running around town. She began to grin.

She could take Rei out in public. She could show him her world.

They could go on a *date*.

Laughing aloud in delight, she picked out a long pink wig and a set of fairy wings for herself. Rei would draw less attention if he was with someone else in costume. She didn't know what they could tell people he was supposed to be. One of the characters from *X-Men*, maybe? It hardly mattered. They could make something up.

For one day out of the year, he wouldn't have to hide.

And this might be his only chance. Sarah sobered as she pushed the cart toward the grocery aisles. If all went well, Rei wasn't even going to be here next Halloween. He'd get his ship fixed and go back to space.

That thought shouldn't hurt as much as it did. Rei didn't belong here. What kind of a life could he have, hiding indoors, unable to talk to anyone or go anywhere? And the authorities were actively hunting him. The faster they got his ship fixed, the better.

Sarah locked down *fast* on the next idea that came along: going with him.

She couldn't. No way. For one thing, she could see there wasn't room for two people in that cramped little pod. And what would her father do? He depended on her. She couldn't just run off to outer space.

But ... oh ... now that the idea had taken root in her brain, she couldn't stop thinking about it.

Space. With actual spaceships, real aliens, other worlds ... She could walk beneath alien skies, breathe the air of alien worlds, meet other people like Rei and these Galateans he kept talking about—

You mean the slave-keeping alien empire that's trying to find him so they can turn him back into a slave?

Okay, maybe not the Galateans. But there was so much else to explore, a whole enormous galaxy full of aliens and habitable worlds, with spaceships to take her between them ...

... and none of it was hers, not a single bit of it.

She couldn't let that dream get rooted in her head, she *couldn't*. It was never going to happen. There was no way Rei could take more than one person to space in his pod, and even if it was possible, she couldn't leave Dad. She would only break her heart if she kept fantasizing about this.

She carefully visualized pushing all of it into a little box in her head, closing the box, and locking it, the same way she'd locked up all her dreams since Mom died and Dad had his accident.

And if she had to blink away tears as she went through the everyday routine of shopping, she was only grieving for a dream that she never should have allowed herself in the first place.

ON THE WAY back to the farm, she gave in to the urge to check on the progress of the hunt for Rei and drove past the lake. They had no reason to associate her truck with anything suspicious, she reminded herself. She was just another curious local, out for a bit of rubbernecking.

But she couldn't even get close. There were roadblocks everywhere, and they were no longer staffed by local sheriff's deputies, but instead by ominous-looking strangers in suits and ties. Sarah had planned to chat with the local cops and find out what they knew, but she wasn't about to let any of these new guys get a look at her face.

Instead she turned around and drove into downtown Sidonie. Someone must know *something*. The town's local paper had gone out of business years ago, but the gossip network was more well-informed anyway. Sarah stopped into Duckworth's Food Mart to see if Bev Duckworth was working today. Bev knew everything and everybody.

No Bev, but her niece Britt was on the register, and Sarah had gone to school with her, which made her a good potential source of information. Sarah waved and looked around for something at random to give herself a pretext for being in the store. A display of school supplies caught her eye; she grabbed a pad of paper and a box of colored pencils. Maybe Rei would appreciate having something to draw with other than a carpenter pencil.

"So what the heck is going on out at the lake?" she asked as Britt rang her up.

"Totally cray, huh? They said something on the radio about a plane crash out there the other night, but I don't know. First it's a weather balloon, then it's a plane, and now the whole town is crawling with feds."

"Feds, really? FBI? Military? Department of Agriculture?"

"If you figure it out, tell me," Britt said, shaking out a plastic bag. "They're not even staying in town. They've got some kind of command center set up. Like I said, totally cray."

They both paused and looked up as a helicopter thumped its way over the town. In the small parking lot outside the store's front window, a little girl clinging to her mother's hand pointed up at the sky in fascinated interest.

"It's like they're looking for something," Britt said. "Like terrorists or Russians."

"I don't think there are any terrorists in Sidonie," Sarah said as calmly as possible, collecting her change. She tried to think how the old Sarah would have handled this. Laughed it off, perhaps? "Hey, maybe they'll find the homeless guy that Royce Muller claims is sleeping in his barn."

Britt laughed, so Sarah decided she'd chosen the right tactic. "He's working on that himself, you know. Got a game camera set up out there now." Something must have changed on Sarah's face, because Britt asked, "You okay?"

"Yeah, fine. I just realized I forgot to take the chicken thighs out to thaw before I went to class this morning."

She walked out to the truck thinking, *Shit, shit, shit.* Was that game camera angled so it'd pick up the shortcut across the Mullers' pasture? And would the Mullers tell anyone?

Most game cameras took very low-quality images. And it was night, and raining, which would have hidden the truck's color and most of its details. Even if the feds got hold of that image, they still wouldn't have much more to go on than they already had from the look they'd gotten at the truck by the lake.

Still, it might give them an idea of which way the truck had gone. And the shortcut across the Mullers' pasture was definitely off limits now.

Damn it, damn it.

But she saw no signs of trouble on the drive back to the farm. Everything was just as she'd left it, serene and calm. The sound of power tools and clanging metal came from the barn, and she hurried through putting the groceries away, eager to find out how the work on Rei's spaceship was coming along. She left the rest of her purchases in her room to give to Rei later, stomped into her farm boots instead of her town shoes, and grabbed a bag of Halloween candy before heading over to the barn.

It was hard to say whether things had progressed since she'd last seen the work area. Scrap metal and dismantled sections of the ship were scattered around in different arrangements, and it looked like more of the ship's paneling had been taken off. Rei was inside it, working on the wiring, while her dad was sitting on the end of the trailer with the cutting torch, trimming sheet metal to fit the damaged sections of the ship.

"Hey there, wrecking crew," Sarah called. "Just to let you know, everybody needs to stay away from the Mullers' pasture. They've got a game camera out there now."

Her dad pushed the welding mask up on his forehead. "Any trouble?"

"Not so far. Britt Duckworth told me about it. I don't think anyone knows we're involved, at least not yet." Sarah tore the bag of chocolate open and tossed a mini Snickers bar to her dad. "Anything I can do to help?"

"I don't even know what *I'm* doing," her father said, catching it. "Just pretty much whatever he tells me to do."

"Does that mean you can talk to each other now?"

"We can talk fine." Rei swung his legs out of the ship and smiled at her, sitting on the edge of the seat. "Hello. How were your studies?"

He was stripped to the waist, sweaty and smudged with grease; Sarah's train of thought temporarily derailed. She leaned down for a kiss and gave a happy little yelp when Rei put an arm around her waist and pulled her against him. Her dad snorted and turned to adjust the tank dials for the cutting torch.

I have a boyfriend. A space boyfriend. Who cares if the town is crawling with feds? My life is amazing.

"Do you like candy?" she asked when she came up from the kiss. "Chocolate?"

"I don't know. That's an Earth food?" He took one of the colorfully wrapped mini chocolate bars and turned it over in his hand.

"Yeah, candy. Sweets. These are my favorites," Sarah told him, holding up a Mars bar. She tore the wrapper off and took a bite before feeding him the other half.

He chewed. Swallowed. "Hmm. Interesting."

"Just interesting? It's chocolate. Most humans love it. Earth humans, I mean. Are you telling me you don't have chocolate in space?"

"I've never had it before." He smiled at her. "It's a very intriguing mix of flavors. May I try another?"

"You can have as much as you want. Uh, well, don't eat *too* much. It's got a lot of sugar in it and eating a bunch of them isn't good for you."

She left him tearing the wrapper off a Snickers bar and went around to the other side of the ship, where more of the paneling had been pulled off to expose its complicated guts. Since she'd last seen the ship, they had cleaned most of the muck out of it, although she could still smell the rank, muddy lake-bottom stink.

"Do you know if this is going to fly again?" she asked, lightly prodding at a clear tube that looked like glass but flexed under her fingertip. She knew how to do basic maintenance around the farm, but she was a physics major, not an engineer. Still, if even her dad was out of his depth with this stuff, she didn't feel too bad about having no idea what she was looking at.

"All we can do is try." Rei came around the curve of the ship, nibbling idly on another piece of chocolate and giving Sarah an eyeful of distraction with his bare blue chest. "It is not easy. I wish I had paid more attention to this part of my studies."

"You're still way beyond where I am, or any of my professors either. You probably know more about physics and engineering than anyone on our entire planet."

He smiled briefly. "Right now I wish that wasn't true, because what my pod really needs is a skilled technician and a properly equipped work station. Gary and I are doing our best, but this might be beyond our ability to repair."

Sarah tried to squash the little flutter of hope in her chest. It wasn't fair to ask him to stay—and it wasn't safe. Not with the Men in Black looking for him. "What needs to be fixed? Can you tell me what I'm looking at?"

"Well ... there are four main components of the battle-pod's systems that need to be functional for me to go to space in it. Life support, shielding, propulsion, and the jump drive." He patted the gray paneling of the ship's side. "Shielding's pretty easy. We just have to replace the damaged sections with something that can stand up to the stress of lift-off without coming apart. Your dad's been helpful at that. And life support isn't too hard either. These pods aren't meant to live in long-term. As long as it won't leak oxygen and I can breathe for a few hours, that's enough to get me somewhere."

"What about the other things you said?"

"Yeah. That's where my knowledge starts to run out. Without engines, I won't be able to get off the ground, and without a functional jump drive, I can't go anywhere outside your solar system. I'll just orbit your planet 'til I run out of air."

"Yeah, we definitely don't want that." She slipped her fingers into his and gave them a squeeze. What she really wanted to do was lean into him and put her arms around him, bury her face in his shoulder and enjoy his spicy male scent ... but maybe not with her dad right on the other side of the ship.

"Yes, suffocating in space is to be avoided," he agreed solemnly, though dry humor sparkled in his eyes. "But those first two are relatively easy. Your dad showed me some pictures of your world's space technology, and it looks like your people have solved those problems already, with relatively simple materials. The drives, though ... I don't know how I can possibly fix them with the knowledge I have and the technology you have." He brushed his thumb over the back of her hand and leaned down to point out something where the paneling had been pulled off the back of the ship. "That's a Vrik coil. I'm guessing your people don't have those."

"Not that I've ever heard of."

Rei tapped one of his silver bracelets. "I need to get the cuffs back to full operation. They won't replace a proper diagnostics rig, let alone a technician who knows what they're doing, but at least they'll allow me to scan the more delicate components for damage. A damaged coil or microscopically cracked heat plate might shatter under use, and strand me in space with no way to repair it."

Sarah shuddered. There were so many worst-case scenarios; she didn't want to think about any of them. Instead she brushed her fingertips across the silver metal on his wrist, warm from his skin. "Is that what these are for? It's a computer?"

"A computer? Is that what this is?" He touched the band of her wristwatch. "You and your father both wear them."

"What, this? No, that's a watch. It just tells time. It doesn't do anything else." She took her phone out of her pocket, unlocked it, and showed it to him. "This is a phone. Most of us have one. It's a communication device and it also takes pictures and plays games and, uh, other stuff, like you can have a calculator on there, or a flashlight app."

His face lit up. "Yes! My cuffs are very much like that. I didn't know your people had anything this advanced." He took the phone from her and examined the screen.

"You touch the icons to run the programs," Sarah explained. She tapped the flashlight icon. "See, this makes a light."

"Your father showed me a different tool for that, a small rod held in the hand." He tilted the light to illuminate what he'd called a Vrik coil. Sarah glimpsed colored reflections chasing each other through the flexible tubes she'd been poking at earlier.

"Yeah, that'd be a real flashlight. Because my dad is a Luddite!" she called, and heard a hoarse bark of laughter from the other side of the ship. "But seriously, the batteries on the phone don't last long enough to use it as a flashlight all the time. It's a good multi-purpose tool, but it's not always the best tool for the job. It's just a nice portable one we can carry around with us."

"I see." He handed it back to her. "Yes, my cuffs are similar, but more advanced. Rather than selecting pictures to access its functions, I use my mind. The cuffs are connected to my nervous system."

"Oh, wow." She looked at them with new respect.

"The collar was the same." Loathing filled his voice at the mention of it. "But unlike the cuffs, it was not useful. It had only one function, to keep me prisoner by limiting my ability to move freely about the ship and punishing me for disobedience." He stopped, and Sarah wasn't sure what to say. She put her hand on his arm, and after a moment he went on more calmly.

"Only slaves wear collars. But everyone in the Galatean Empire wears cuffs, because that's how you interact with most Galatean technology. Silver for non-citizens such as slaves or foreigners, and gold for citizens. I used to use my cuffs to fly the pod."

"Oh, but doesn't that mean you can't leave unless you fix them?"

"I can also fly the pod manually. But it's much harder, and most of the advanced functions are inaccessible to me, such as weapons."

"It has weapons?" She looked up at the curving side of the pod in surprise. "You didn't mention those earlier."

"I don't need to get the weapons working in order to leave your planet."

"No, I guess not." She tucked her phone away and looked down at the glimmer of the Vrik coil rather than at his face. "So ... best-case scenario, if you can get everything working, how long do you think it'll take until you're ready to leave?"

"It's hard to say. Perhaps a few days."

Sarah swallowed her disappointment, pushing it down to her core. She was used to the bitterness of giving up her dreams, and she reminded herself that even if Rei was gone in a week, she would always have the memory of that week to hold to her heart for the rest of her life. And it was always possible there was some equivalent of space email. Maybe they could write to each other. Maybe he'd even come back to visit. Long-distance relationships were a pain in the ass no matter what; did it really matter if one of the parties had moved to Ann Arbor or Alpha Centauri?

"So, I'll just go make some lunch, I guess—" she began, and stopped, frowning at his face. "Are you all right?"

"I think so," he said slowly. His face had gone gray under his dark blue coloring. The *tsinde* spots had paled to nearly white.

"You don't look okay. Do you need to sit down?"

Rei shook his head. "I need to go outside. Stay here."

With that he pushed away from her and strode briskly toward the door of the barn. Like hell she was staying behind; Sarah broke into a trot and then a jog to keep up with his longer legs. Had he heard something? Smelled something? Was danger even now bearing down on them? She didn't hear helicopters, but maybe Rei's keener senses had alerted him to something she couldn't hear.

He vanished through the half-open side door. Sarah rushed after him, looked around, and discovered him just a few feet away, leaning on the side of the barn, doubled over so he could throw up.

"Oh my God, Rei, what's wrong?"

He shuddered through the last few spasms, tried to straighten up, and doubled over again, one arm wrapped around his stomach. "It's all right," he gasped. "Go back inside."

"It's not all right. You're sick. Rei ..." She put a hand hesitantly on his back. He flinched, and she could feel that his muscles were knotted hard as iron.

It was more than just being sick to his stomach. She could feel him shivering, feel the rapid rise and fall of his ribs as he gasped for air. He started to pull away when she took his wrist to feel his pulse, but then yielded and let her press her fingers to his inner arm just above the bracelet. His heartbeat was racing, light and fast and fluttering.

"Is it the candy?" she asked anxiously. "Have you eaten anything else today? It shouldn't have made you this sick. You've been eating our food just fine—"

... Oh. Oh, *shit*.

"Rei." Now her heart was hammering, too. "The, the whatever they're called, the Founders, the people who made you, used some wolf DNA, right? Do you think something that poisons wolves would poison you too?"

"I don't know," Rei ground out, his head hanging down. "Why?"

"Because chocolate doesn't hurt humans, but it's poisonous to dogs. Oh God, Rei, I didn't think. I'm so sorry!"

All she knew about medicine was what she'd learned from helping take care of her parents and from doctoring farm animals. He'd ingested poison, so they needed to get it out of his body (looked like he was taking care of that already) and ... and he needed to take activated charcoal, that was the other thing, to absorb what remained of it. She was pretty sure there was some in the medicine cabinet.

"Dad!" she shouted into the barn. "Come help Rei! He's sick, I think it's the chocolate, like dogs—I can't explain, I'm sorry, I'll be right back. Just stay with him, okay?"

She gave Rei's arm a comforting squeeze and with that, she was off, running toward the house.

Stupid! Stupid! What was she doing, going around feeding Earth junk food to an alien? Just because he'd been able to eat everything they'd eaten so far—but he'd *said* he was human, he should be able to eat anything a human could eat—

But even humans had food allergies, gluten sensitivity, that sort of thing, and even if he was mostly human on a genetic level, his people had been separated from hers for tens of thousands of years. They were probably lucky they hadn't sent him into anaphylactic shock already.

She ransacked the medicine cabinet, throwing bottles into the sink until she found the activated charcoal behind a collection of ten-year-old painkillers and expired prescription meds.

I had an alien boyfriend and I killed him by feeding him chocolate!

He was going to be fine, she reassured herself. Chocolate wasn't necessarily fatal to dogs, only in large amounts, and he was bigger than most dogs and hadn't eaten a whole lot of it. He'd probably just be sick for awhile and then be fine.

She stirred a dose of charcoal into a glass of water in the kitchen, snatched her sheepskin coat off its hook, and dashed outside again.

Back at the barn, her dad had gotten Rei to sit down just inside the door on an overturned crate. He was no longer throwing up, but he looked terrible, grayish and out of it, his hair sweat-plastered to his forehead.

"Here," Sarah said, kneeling beside him. "Drink this."

"I'd really rather not," Rei mumbled. He was leaning on her dad, and when she put her hand on his chest, she could feel his racing heart.

"It's just charcoal. It'll help absorb the toxins."

He hesitated and then took the glass with a shaking hand and tossed back the black liquid in a couple of gulps. "Ugh," he muttered, handing it back to her, and swallowed heavily.

Sarah set the glass aside and draped the coat over his shoulders. "Can you walk? We should get you to the house so you can lie down."

"Just give me a minute." He closed his eyes briefly, took a deep breath, then gently removed Sarah's hand from his arm and stood up. "We can go back to work. I'll be all right."

"No way!" Sarah burst out, as her father said firmly, "Sit back down, son."

"I've done more difficult things than this while feeling worse than this." He grimaced, started to hunch over as a spasm of pain went through him, then straightened again.

"That doesn't mean you *have* to!" Sarah protested, trying to push him back down onto the crate again. "It's okay to take some time off when you're sick. It's okay to *be* sick. Dad, can't you talk to him?"

Gary stopped Rei with a gnarled hand on his arm. Rei sighed and looked at him with exasperated patience.

"Still can't understand a word out of your mouth," Gary told him, "but the meaning comes through loud and clear. Look, boy, I get you. Hell, docs told me loud and clear I shouldn't be doing half the things I'm doing. But Sarah's right. Don't take this wrong, but you look like the Devil himself stomped on your grave. Just lay down for awhile. I can get the rest of the replacement hull plates cut out on my own."

"You are both so stubborn." Rei's words came out on a sigh as he sagged against Sarah, making her realize how much effort he was putting into keeping himself upright.

"Would you rather stay here than go in the house?" Sarah asked. "We can make a bed with hay and animal blankets. Then you can tell us what to do, and we can keep working on the ship."

Rei hesitated, then nodded.

He sat on the end of the trailer, head in his hands, while she threw down hay and piled it with old blankets and towels from the ragged collection they used for sick or calving livestock. When Sarah slid an arm around him, he looked up at her wearily. "Come on," she said, helping him to his feet. "It won't be the most comfortable bed you've ever had, but you can nap while we fix the ship. Rei, I am *so* sorry I accidentally poisoned you."

"It's all right," he said, and laughed softly. "If you don't mind, I am very thirsty."

"Yes, of course. Hang on."

Under the old hand pump behind the barn, she rinsed the glass she'd mixed the charcoal in, and filled a clean jug. The pump drew on the same well they used for water in the house, so it would be perfectly clean; no sense in walking back over when she didn't have to. She left the glass and jug beside Rei on the barn floor and kissed his damp forehead. "Just tell us if there's anything else you need, okay?"

He nodded and closed his eyes.

Sarah took his pulse again. It had slowed somewhat from earlier and no longer had that frantic, fluttery quality that had so worried her. He really *hadn't* ingested that much, she told herself in forced reassurance, and went to help her father wrestle sheet metal around.

TWELVE

BY THE TIME the early October darkness came down, Rei was awake again, looking a little less gray and wan. He'd left the barn a few times to use the bathroom, and then lay on the pile of hay and blankets under a bright shop light, working on his bracelets with some of the small screwdrivers and other tools that Sarah's dad used to work on electronics.

Sarah had been helping her father cut sheet metal and install it on the damaged sections of the ship all afternoon. Her shoulders ached, and her fingers and forearms stung from small cuts and burns, despite the heavy leather gloves she was wearing.

"Think it's about time to throw in the towel for the night," Gary remarked, wiping the back of his forearm across his face and setting the welding torch aside. "Animals need fed, and I can hear Bonnie callin' out in the pasture for her evening milking. I could sure eat, too."

"Why don't you go put supper on," Sarah suggested. Since her father's injury, domestic duties around the farm had all but reversed; he did most of the less taxing housework, while she handled the heavy lifting of the farm chores. "I'll get the chores done and bring Rei over to the house."

Gary patted her shoulder and clumped off, weariness making him lean more heavily on his canes than usual. Sarah watched anxiously until he was out of sight. One of these days he was going to overdo it, have a fall, and set himself right back to where he'd been after the accident, but she knew from long experience that there was no use in trying to make him be more careful and use the walker when he was tired.

"Think you could eat something yet?" she asked Rei as she sat down beside him on the hay.

He grimaced. "Perhaps later."

One of the bracelets lay partly disassembled on a sheet of butcher paper. The bracelets looked seamless from the outside, like pieces of hammered silver jewelry, and she hadn't realized they opened up. She was used to seeing electrical components from old engines, fuse boxes, and disassembled kids' electronic games as part of her dad's various projects, but this looked like nothing she'd ever seen before. Like a smaller version of the electronics in the ship, it was mostly hair-fine glassy fibers embedded with colorful dots that made her think of the pearls in fancy body scrubs.

"Do you think you can get them to work again?"

"I'm not sure." He sealed up the bracelet's outer surface with quick strokes of his fingertips—Sarah couldn't even see what he did, but it appeared seamless again. With another deft twist of his fingers, he parted it at one side and then sealed it around his wrist, where it looked as if it had been welded in place there. "As with the ship's engines, this is far beyond my technical knowledge or the tools I have, and I drained its residual charge earlier while searching for my battlepod. But I think I've restored its ability to charge from my body, if my internal nanites are not too badly damaged to do so. It will need a little while to recover its charge, and then we'll see."

"You charge it with your body? Rei, your technology never stops amazing me."

Rei flashed her one of his quick grins. He looked much better than earlier. "I haven't shown you anything wondrous yet. These are nothing but everyday technology, like that communication device in your pocket. I should show you true wonders, like the great clan ships of the dragons, containing entire cities, or the winged warriors of the Tybor who joust with lances made of pure light. The Hanging Nebula on the edge of Iustran space, or the great gladiatorial arenas of the Hnee ..."

"I would *love* to see all of that," Sarah said wistfully.

The longing and sorrow in her voice stopped him in his litany of alien wonders. "But," he said in quieter tones, "there is only room in my pod for one."

Sarah nodded. "But I still want to hear about it, even if I can't ever see it. Let me just quickly do the chores, and then you can tell me all about it over dinner."

"I will help you with your chores."

She wanted to refuse; he looked much better than earlier, but he was still shaky and shivering under the sheepskin coat draped over his bare shoulders. She didn't want to hurt his pride, though, so she said, "Sure. I'll just divide up the jobs and tell you what to do."

She gave him the easier jobs—gathering eggs from the hens and herding the old horse, Princess, into her stall for the night—while Sarah refilled the water troughs, fed the livestock in the field, and milked the cow. It was very pleasant, working in quiet partnership in the cool October night.

After a dreary, gray day, the clouds had finally parted, letting through a silvery film of moonlight and the sharp pinpricks of the stars.

Sarah was standing at the last trough, gazing up at the stars while silver ripples spread outward from the hose, when Rei emerged from the moonlit shadows and came quietly to join her. "You like looking at the sky," he said.

"I always have. That's why I was at the lake, did I ever tell you that? I was watching a meteor shower when one of the meteors almost landed on top of me." She felt a brief pang for her lost telescope. It was probably gone for good, buried deep in the lake's thick silt for future generations of archaeologists to dig up, millennia from now.

"I'm glad I didn't hurt you."

"Well, of all the lakes on all the continents on this planet, I'm glad you crashed into mine."

Rei's fingers laced through hers. Normally he was slightly warm to the touch, but even with her hands chilled from handling the cold, damp hoses, his fingers felt like ice. She gave him a critical look, but it was impossible to see much in the poor light, other than the faint luminescence of his eyes, reflecting gold in the yard light, and the glimmer of the silver traceries on his skin.

"Do your people name the stars?" he asked, turning his softly luminous eyes to the sky.

"We do." She pointed. "That's the North Star. Our planet's axis points to it, so it doesn't appear to move. Sailors and travelers used to navigate by it, long ago. It's a saying for us, to be someone's pole star, their true north. What the compass of their heart points to."

"I like that," he murmured, his fingers tangling more tightly in hers. "Of course, when you travel long distances through space, the stars always change; only their official designations stay the same. But my people named the stars, too. We used to see pictures in the sky and tell stories about them."

"Us, too." She turned, looking above the horizon through the pale wisps of moonlit clouds, and pointed when she found what she was looking for. "That bright band of stars is the belt of Orion, the hunter. He has a hunting dog at his heels—that's Sirius, the Dog Star there, the brightest star in our night sky. We sometimes talk about the dog days of summer, when that star rises in the sky."

"Dog star. Appropriate." His quick smile flickered. "Dogs are your domestic wolves, right?"

"Right." She craned her neck, looking for other constellations he might enjoy. "That curving string of stars is Draco, the dragon. See the head there, that triangle of stars? I don't know any stories about it, but our scientists have found some planets among Draco's stars. We don't have the technology yet to tell if they're inhabited, but maybe some of them are even planets you might—oh!"

Cold water spilled over the edge of the trough onto her legs. She sprang back, releasing Rei's hand, only to realize he'd tensed into a combat position, one of his hands raised with the fingers lightly curled into a loose fist.

"It's okay. No worries. I just got myself wet." She picked up the hose off the muddy ground and looped it over the hook on the edge of the trough. "Come on, let's get inside. I bet Dad's done making dinner by now—Rei?"

He was still holding his hand out, the fingers now spread. Was it only the moonlight that made them seem to glimmer faintly?

Rei looked up and met her baffled gaze with a wide, brilliant smile. "It works," he said.

"What does?" Then a subtle gleam licked down the

band around his wrist. "Oh, your cuff thing? You got it working!"

"It works, yes. It wasn't so badly damaged after all. It just needed to charge." He let out a long sigh and straightened up, looking more relaxed than she'd seen him in awhile. "I need to test it. Stay where you are."

"Test—?" she began, but fell silent as he pointed his hand at a clump of grazed-down brush beside the trough. Before Sarah could ask what he was going to do, an eye-searing bar of blue-white light stabbed from his fingers and neatly zapped off a branch. The wood was too wet to burn, but it glowed cherry-red for a moment, and a tentative tendril of flame curled up from the bark before fizzling out in the damp. The acrid smell of woodsmoke reached Sarah a moment later.

Rei laughed aloud, with a harsh edge to it. "Let them come. I'm not helpless any longer." Then realization seemed to dawn on him that she was still staring, rather than sharing his delight. "Sarah? What's wrong?"

"It's a *weapon*?"

"You didn't know?"

"No," she said weakly. "No, I didn't know." Suddenly all of his defensive hand gestures made so much more sense. If his bracelets had been working, would he have accidentally fried her back at the lake, or that first time he woke up in the truck?

"I told you I was a soldier. You didn't think me unarmed, did you?"

"I just ... I guess I thought you must have left your gun behind or didn't have it in the pod, or ... something ..."

Of course weapons in a society with faster-than-light travel and cyborg augmentation wouldn't look like guns.

And she knew he was trained to fight. She knew he'd been in war.

It was just ... he was *so fast*, and—when he'd leaped into combat position next to her a moment ago, that had been a deadly weapon on the end of his arm, not a fist.

She hadn't known.

That was all: she hadn't known.

He was looking at her with uncertainty, and her confusing mix of emotions began to ebb away. This was still her Rei, of the gentle hands and the shy, warm smile.

So she let out a breath, and tried to let it go. "If you're happy, I'm happy," she said, and held out a hand.

Rei looked at her hand for a long moment. He didn't take it.

"Sarah—"

"I'm not afraid of you," she said. "I was just surprised." And she took his hand in hers, closing her fingers around it.

"You should be afraid." His voice was solemn, his eyes gleaming in the moonlight.

"Yeah, well, too bad, because I'm not." She pulled on his arm, tugging him close to her side. "Come on. Let's go see about something to eat."

IT WAS EASIER to let go of her lingering sense of unease in the kitchen, warm and familiar and bright, full of appetizing smells.

"I opened some cans of stew," her dad said, turning around from the sink. "Thought it might go down easy for Rei, maybe with a little toast."

In the brighter light of the kitchen, Sarah could see that Rei was still grayish and exhausted-looking. "Do you think you can eat?" she asked him. "Dad made something he thinks —oh wait, I keep forgetting you can understand him just fine."

"Perhaps later," he said politely. "I'd like to lie down for a while first."

"You can take a nap in my room. It'll be quieter up there where our voices and the TV won't bother you."

Rei nodded and went off without speaking. He was still feeling pretty bad, she thought, and guilt twisted in her stomach.

"Not your fault, kid," her dad said. He handed her a plate of toast and ladled a scoop of stew into a large mug, then stuck in a spoon. "Go on up there and take care of your boy. I'll have the rest on the table when you come down."

Sarah kissed his cheek and took it upstairs. The toilet flushed in the bathroom, and Rei came out, leaning on the wall. He straightened when he saw her; she could see him pulling himself together, forcing down the weakness to put on a show of strength.

"Still feel pretty bad, huh?" she asked softly. "I brought you some dinner in case you're hungry later."

"I'm just tired." He gave her a rueful smile and flexed his fingers. "In retrospect, draining some of my body's energy to power the cuffs wasn't the best idea in my current condition."

"Is there any other way to charge them?" she asked, following him through the doorway into her bedroom. "Could we hook them to an outlet or something?"

"Sunlight can also do it, but we don't have any of that at the moment." He sat on the edge of the bed. "You don't need to stay."

"I'm going down to eat in a minute. —Oh, right!" She'd completely forgotten about her shopping trip until the bags on her floor reminded her. "I got you some clothes, like we talked about, and something else too. I saw how you liked to draw, so I thought you might like to do some more of that."

Despite his evident exhaustion, Rei's eyes lit up when he saw the box of pencils with all its colors. "These are pigment sticks for drawing, correct?"

"Yep, that's right." She opened the box and shook out a few of the pre-sharpened pencils. "Have fun," she told him, kissing him on the forehead, and left him with the bedside lamp turned on and the pad of paper in his lap.

She and her dad ate in the living room while watching the news on TV. There was nothing about the crash at the lake; it might be big news in Sidonie, but it looked like it had already dropped out of the statewide news cycle.

The picture on the TV flickered as a helicopter thumped by overhead, reminding her that the world outside Sidonie might have forgotten about it, but the government sure hadn't.

"Do you think they'll come here looking for Rei?" she asked. "What are we going to tell them if they do?"

"Tell 'em they need a warrant if they want to go searching my farm," Gary said, switching away from the news to a sports channel.

"It's the feds, Dad."

"They still need a warrant. Or do we live in North Korea now?"

"They might not even ask. They might just go look. We should start locking the barn. Hiding Rei will be a lot easier than hiding his ship."

"Things go according to plan, neither one of 'em is gonna be here in a week or two."

"I know." She looked down at the bowl in her lap and

concentrated on swiping up the last of the stew with her bread.

"Honey." Her dad reached out to pat her arm awkwardly. "You know this is temporary, right? Rei can't stay here on Earth. This is no place for him. He belongs out there with his friends and his people."

"We could find a way," she said obstinately, refusing to acknowledge the tears prickling the back of her throat. "Dad, you don't know some of the things he's told me. I don't know if he has anything to go back to. His people sold him into slavery, and out there in space, he'd be hunted by people who want to put him back in chains."

"And here?" Her father's voice was gentle. Sympathetic. "What kind of life can he have, always having to hide?"

"Not *always*." She shoved the last piece of bread into her mouth, swallowing it past the lump in her throat. "I was thinking we could maybe go out in town for Halloween. Pretend he's wearing a costume."

"You think that's a good idea if the feds are looking for him?"

"But they can't possibly know what he looks like, how could they? And everyone else is just going to see a guy in face paint. Anyway, it doesn't have to be here. We can drive over to Eau Claire. I just feel like he deserves to see a little of Earth. He's hardly ever had fun in his entire life. I'd like to take him on an actual, you know. A date."

"He's got to go back to space, honey."

"Not right away." She straightened abruptly and began gathering their dishes.

"Didn't mean to upset you, honey. I like Rei too. But you know it's true."

She couldn't look at him. "I'm going upstairs to see how Rei's doing."

She expected to find him sleeping, but instead he was lying propped up on her pillows with the other cuff disassembled in his lap. He'd changed into the clothes she had bought for him, black jeans and a dark red sweater. The dark red color was, as she'd suspected, incredibly flattering on him, setting off the indigo of his skin. His feet were bare, his hair tousled as he bent his head over his work in the pool of warm lamplight.

She didn't think she'd made any noise, but he looked up and saw her, and flashed her a quick smile. Taking it as an invitation, she came over and sat on the edge of the bed. Half the piece of toast was gone, she noticed, though the stew didn't appear to have been touched.

"Fixing the other one?" she asked.

Rei nodded. He snapped it back onto his wrist and shook his arm to seat it into place.

Sarah told herself firmly not to be nervous about them. He could control those things just fine; it was no different from a cop or a soldier wearing a sidearm.

"Thank you for the garments," Rei said. "They're nice." He touched the sweater. "It's very soft."

"Well, maybe I just want to cuddle up to it," she said, running a light hand across the fuzzy sleeve.

He smiled and pushed himself a little higher on the pillows. "I would like that. But first I want to draw something for you."

"Oh, really?" She pulled up her feet under her as he reached for the pad of paper on the nightstand. "I'd love that. Nobody's ever drawn anything for me before."

Rei opened the pad of paper and dumped out the pencils on the bed. "You asked me about dragons earlier. I didn't want to talk about it then, because ... it hurt. My friend Lyr was—*is* a dragon. But I think I'd like to tell you about him now, if you don't mind."

"I would love to hear about your friend."

"You have time?"

"Always," she said firmly.

"Then ... let me show you Lyr."

He selected a pencil. Hands in her lap, Sarah sat raptly and watched him draw. Under his deft strokes, a human figure took shape. Humanoid, she amended, as Rei added spines to the head, forearms, and back. It was wearing a coverall that left the arms and feet bare, like the one Rei had been wearing when Sarah first met him. There was a collar around its neck, and a bracelet on each wrist. The face was nearly blank, just a sketchy suggestion of a penciled nose and eyes.

"This is Lyr," Rei said. "The head of my sept."

"What's a sept?"

"The Galateans divide the smaller children into groups and give each of them someone older to mentor them and look out for them. When they took me from my homeworld, I was put in a group of other children who were all about my age except for Lyr. He was an older teenager, maybe a young adult; hard to say because I was so young myself then. But he was like a big brother to the whole sept."

"How many of you were there in this sept?"

"Seven." He shaded Lyr's skin with a gold pencil, then added shadows of other colors—violet, green, brown, bringing to Sarah's mind the interplay of colors in a peacock's tail. Lyr's medium-length hair was delineated in careful spikes, folded down against his neck and colored in shades of dark blue. Sarah wondered if it *was* hair, or something else: feathers or scales.

Lyr's face remained blank, whether because Rei

couldn't remember Lyr's features well enough to draw them, or if he just didn't want to picture them closely. Sarah wasn't going to ask.

Rei glanced up and saw her rapt interest, bringing a trace of a wistful smile to his face. "Would you like me to draw them all for you?"

"Sure. I'd love to see them."

"Since Lyr was the oldest of us, I guess age is as good an order as any." Rei began sketching a slightly shorter figure beside Lyr; its head came up to his chin. This one was recognizably female, in a similar form-fitting coverall, with erect catlike ears and a short, thick mane of hair. Rei colored her skin light yellow-brown, her hair dark red, and added small clusters of brown spots to her face and arms, carefully working around the pale slashes of the collar and wristlets. Sarah thought at first that the spots were freckles, then realized they looked more like leopard spots.

"This is Haiva," Rei said, adding darker brown shading to her hair with deft flicks of the pencil. "She was the second oldest after Lyr. She was Galatean."

"I thought Galateans were your, uh—your slave masters." She cringed at having to say it, but Rei didn't even flinch.

"They are, but they also enslave their own people. Haiva was one of those."

The drawing was starting to look uncannily like Cheetara on the old Thundercats cartoons Sarah had watched as a child, but she knew Rei wouldn't get the reference. Instead, she said, "She looks like she's part cat."

"She is." Rei began sketching another figure next to Haiva. "Galateans were made from human and feline DNA, the same way my people were made from humans and wolves. But they don't shift like my people—at least most of them don't; there are rumors that the Sun King and his guard can turn into lions."

Sarah wanted to ask him more about that, but from the curl to his lip, she decided it wasn't a good topic to pursue. Instead she watched two new figures take shape. They were shorter than Haiva, one male, one female. Same gray coveralls, same bracelets and collars. But each of these had—

"Wings," she breathed, as Rei detailed the curve of sweeping wings rising above their shoulders. "Who are they?"

"Rook and Kite. They were twins." Rei reached for a red-violet pencil and began coloring in their skin. "Their people are called the Tybor." He colored gently over the red-violet with a brown pencil, adding darker undertones to their skin. The woman's skin was slightly darker than the man's.

"Can they really fly?"

"Yes," Rei said absently, as he detailed their hair in mottled gray and brown—barred, like a hawk's wings. "Yes, they could fly. And Rook loved reading, especially books about history. He was fascinated by how things were in the past. Kite used to get so impatient with him. She always wanted to be out there doing things."

The woman, Kite, had one hand extended, and Sarah soon saw why, as Rei began sketching a new figure holding her hand. This one was also female, very slender and taller than Kite—though not quite as tall as Lyr, who towered over all the others.

Sarah had thought at first that Rei had drawn Lyr so big because he was the oldest and the rest were children, but it was apparent from the curves of the female bodies and the broadness of Rook's shoulders that these were meant to be adults. Lyr was really that tall.

"This is Selinn," Rei said, coloring the girl's skin brown. "She makes portals. I don't know if all her people can do that. She's the only one of them I ever met."

"Portals?"

"Yes, to jump from place to place, like a ship. Except she could do it without a ship."

He had drawn the girl's opposite hand extended, and now he used bright blue and purple pencils to shade an oval as tall as she was, just beyond the tips of her fingers.

"You mean she could *teleport*?"

Rei nodded. He switched to a vivid green for Selinn's hair, and carefully detailed green nail polish on the brown fingers wrapped around Kite's dark purple ones.

"They were lovers?" Sarah asked.

"Yes," Rei said quietly. He reached for a purple pencil and added delicate shading around Kite's eyes. "Rook and Kite's people believe in soulmates. I don't know if there is any such thing, but of all the people I've ever met, I could believe it of Kite and Selinn. There was something between them from the time we were all young, as if they'd known each other in a past life and only now found each other again."

Sarah was starting to feel as if she knew these people. It was unbearably sad to think they were all dead—Rei's friends, his family.

Rei was adding vivid silver edges to Selinn's portal. "How could someone like that—" Sarah began, and then stopped herself.

He glanced up from the drawing. "How could what?"

Sarah touched the edge of the portal with her fingertips. "I just don't see how someone like that *could* be kept prisoner. Could she do that anytime she wanted?"

"Collar," Rei reminded her.

"Oh." Sarah touched her own throat, where the silver collar in the drawing slashed across Selinn's darker skin. "Yes. I see."

"But when they sent her somewhere, it was her attachment to us that kept her coming back. I sometimes wondered—" He broke off abruptly, shook his head, and began sketching a new figure next to Selinn.

"Wondered what?"

"If she could have teleported away from ... No." He answered his own question. "She's dead. If she was alive, we'd know."

"Is there any chance she could be?"

Rei reached for a red pencil and began shading the new figure's hair. "No. Trust me on this. Clinging to that kind of hope will kill you. She's dead. They're dead. End of story."

Sensing how tightly he was clinging to his self-control, Sarah let it drop. This new member of their little clan was the most colorful yet, with purple skin of a lighter, more vivid shade than Kite and Rook's, and brilliant red hair framing a square-jawed face.

"Who is this?"

"Skara. The little asshole," Rei said fondly. "Skara might have been the one of us they just couldn't break. It didn't matter what our overseers did to him. Locked him in solitary, beat him, starved him. He'd still play practical jokes on them, sabotage their equipment, and mouth off at the slightest opportunity. Looking back on it, I don't know how he managed to survive to adulthood. I think he got away with it because he was just one of those people who gets away with stuff. You know what I mean?"

Sarah nodded with a smile. She could see that Rei had a soft spot a mile wide for this Skara person. "Yeah, I went to school with a few of those. They could be awful, but being their friend was never boring, for sure."

"That was Skara," Rei murmured, touching the drawing lightly with his fingertip. "He *was* awful. He could be a real sack of dicks, especially when he was getting us all in trouble for some stupid prank. I think there were times when all of us wanted to strangle him, Lyr especially. But you couldn't ask for a more loyal friend. And he's also the reason why I know that Selinn and Kite didn't just portal somewhere. If they weren't dead, Skara would have known."

"How?" Sarah asked.

"Skara's people, the Iustra, are shapeshifters. Like my people, they can't change their mass, but unlike us, they aren't limited to just one kind of shift. They can rearrange their features to masquerade as other species. *Any* other species. And that's not all they can do." He shaded Skara's hair as he spoke, adding deft strokes of darker red. Like all of the other figures, he'd left Skara's face mostly blank, with just a suggestion of features. "Since an Iustra can look like almost anything or anyone, their people have a unique ability to recognize and find each other, no matter where they are or what they look like on the outside. And it's not just limited to members of their own species. Once he'd imprinted on us, Skara could find any one of us anywhere, even if we were halfway across the galaxy. But ... he couldn't find Kite and Selinn after they died. He said it was like they were just gone, like they'd vanished out of the universe. Lyr felt it too, like they just stopped existing."

The look on his face broke her heart. "If you need to stop—"

"No." He smiled at her, a wistful smile, but a genuine one. "It's good to talk about it. I haven't talked to anyone about them. Once we'd lost so many of them—Kite and

Rook, Haiva and Skara—those of us who were left didn't want to talk about them either. Especially Lyr." His fingers slid across the page from Skara to the blue and gold figure at the far left. Lightly he traced the spikes poking up through Lyr's hair; it looked like a caress. "He always felt responsible for the rest of us. And he was *there* with the lost ones when they died, in a way the rest of us weren't. I think losing so many of us broke him in some way."

I think it broke you too, Sarah thought, but didn't say. Instead she said, "What about the last one? That's only six."

"Oh, right. That'd be Thorn."

He began sketching again. This time the figure was a strikingly unusual one, a human male in basic outline, but colored like a patchwork quilt. One side of his face was silver, the other violet, bisected by a line down the middle.

"Is he a robot?" Actually Frankenstein's monster was the first thing she thought of, but she wasn't about to say that to his grieving adopted sibling.

"Chimera," Rei said. "He's made of organic parts—well, mostly. But he's a lab experiment." He paused, tapping the pencil against the page. "Out of all of us, I think Thorn might still be alive. Lyr couldn't contact him, but he always had trouble making contact with Thorn anyway. And Skara's people-finding ability didn't work on him either."

"What do you mean, Lyr couldn't contact him? I don't understand."

"Lyr's a telepath. He could talk to us all, as long as we were near enough."

"Oh," she breathed. "Can you talk to him now?"

"No. He's too far away. Or ..."

He left the thought unfinished, face turned away from her, carefully adding details to the picture. Hints of gold scales on Lyr, drawn with a yellow pencil; an elaborate bracelet on Kite's upper arm, left bare by her gray coverall; more details of Thorn's patchwork skin. Finally he laid the pencils aside and held the drawing out at arm's length.

With the figures all lined up in a row, facing the viewer with no background, it looked like a kid's drawing. But that was basically what it was, Sarah thought, a drawing of Rei's family, like a schoolchild might make.

"Do you mind if I put this on the wall?" she asked.

"On the wall?" he repeated, looking puzzled.

"Yeah, like this." She took down a framed 4H certificate that had been up there since she was in middle school, gathering dust. Rei gave her the drawing when she held out her hand for it, and watched curiously as she slipped it behind the glass in the frame and hung it where the certificate had been, at the foot of her bed.

There was a picture of her mom hanging next to it. Somehow that seemed appropriate.

"Like that," she said. "Do you like that?"

"I like that." His voice was barely more than a whisper.

She started to lie down beside Rei on the bed, got stabbed with a pencil, and sat up with a startled curse. Both of them laughed as they collected the pencils back into their box. Rei's laugh was so soft she could barely hear it, but it was there. He seemed lighter somehow, as if just talking about his family had lifted a weight off him.

"That's my mom there." She pulled the quilt at the foot of the bed up over both of them, and snuggled into the crook of Rei's arm. "On the wall next to your family. The pretty lady holding the goat."

It was a ridiculous picture and she'd always loved it. Her mom was young, about the age Sarah was now, with her hair pulled back in a sloppy ponytail and a baby goat in her arms, its knobby legs dangling. She was not, objectively, a beautiful woman, with a snub-nosed, farm-girl's face, a spatter of freckles over her cheeks, and a perpetual sunburn. But in every photo Sarah had of her, there was warmth and delight shining from her eyes and her smile, making her gorgeous. And it was vividly on display in that picture, as if the sun had lit her up from within.

"You miss her very much," Rei said, stroking Sarah's hair.

"I do. I can't believe it's been almost ten years since she died. I was so young. *She* was so young." She blinked her eyes fiercely, pushing back tears. "And then Dad has his accident—"

"That's why he walks with the sticks?"

"Yeah, the tractor rolled on him. After Mom died he got kind of ... reckless, I guess. Started drinking a lot and doing stupid things." She huffed a sigh against Rei's neck. "It could have been so much worse. If things had gone a little differently that day, I'd have ended up burying two parents within a year and a half, instead of just one. I'm not going to say that getting his back broken was a good thing, for Dad or for the family. It was a stupid, terrible thing. But it did make him start paying attention to the world again. It made him realize he didn't want to leave me alone."

Just like she couldn't leave him alone. There was no point in fantasizing about going to space. Her life was here, would always be here.

"What about your parents?" she asked to distract herself. "I know you haven't seen them in a long time, but what were they like?"

"I don't know. I'm an orphan." His chest hitched with a small, silent laugh. "My people might pass it off as an honor, but still, they don't send *wanted* children to the slavers."

"Oh, Rei." She turned her face into his neck, pressed her lips to his skin.

"It was a long time ago, like you said," he said quietly. "I did have an aunt who raised me. She was very angry when the village council selected me for the tax, even though they paid her a small stipend to compensate her for taking me away." Another small hitch of a laugh. "*Especially* because they paid her, I think. They had to put her in our village jail on the day I was taken, because she bit two of the men who came to take me, so I didn't get to say goodbye."

"Did they let you write to her?"

She felt him shake his head, a swish of his hair against the top of her head. "They didn't try to stop me, but I couldn't. Very few people in my village were literate. I wasn't, at that time, and she wasn't either. She's probably forgotten me by now."

"I bet she hasn't," Sarah said, her gazed drifting back to her mother, meeting the vivid gaze looking out of the past. Time didn't kill love, not if it was really love in the first place. "I bet she still misses you a lot. Maybe you'll get to see her again one day."

Her father was right. She couldn't stop Rei from going back to space. She couldn't even bring herself to nurture a hope that he would be unable to fix his ship and would have to stay. He'd have to live out his life on Earth as an exile, always wondering about his family, never able to see them again.

We come from different worlds ... literally. We were never meant to be together. At least we have these few days; it's more than a lot of people get.

She draped an arm over Rei's chest and pressed her body against his, as if she could somehow memorize the imprint of his skin, the shape of his chest and the way his arm fit so perfectly around her.

As if she could make a bulwark of memory against the lonely days ahead.

Time didn't kill love. Not if love was real. And she knew as well as anyone that a picture on the wall was no substitute for the real thing.

But he had to leave. She had to stay. There was no way around it.

THIRTEEN

THE BATTLEPOD WAS NEVER GOING to fly.

Rei's suspicions solidified into certainty over the next few days. He didn't say anything, as if admitting it would make it real. He and Gary, with inexpert but enthusiastic assistance from Sarah, spent most of the daylight hours and some of the night ones working on it.

But now that he had the cuffs working again, even if they weren't at full efficiency, he was able to use their diagnostic tools to get a better idea of the pod's condition, and it wasn't good.

He and Gary could fix the basic mechanical issues. This world already had the technical knowledge to construct crude pods capable of taking humans into space; there were pictures of them in Sarah's books. But, as he'd told Sarah, the engines and jump drive were beyond this world's technology or his own capability to fix, and he didn't think either one of those things were ever going to work again, at least not as long as he was trying to repair them in a barn with primitive tools.

Even if they jury-rigged a crude engine capable of

boosting the ship out of this planet's atmosphere—he could think of a couple of ideas, and Gary probably had more—there was still the jump drive to fix, and without *that*, he was going nowhere.

But would that really be so bad?

If he had to get stuck on a low-tech world outside the galactic mainstream, there were worse options. The climate was nice, the ecosystem compatible with his own biology (give or take a few local plant foods; he was now scrupulous about avoiding that bitter-tasting "chocolate" substance), and the world's overall level of technology was high enough to provide comforts such as long-distance communications and indoor plumbing.

And there was Sarah, of course.

It made him wonder why he wanted to get off this world at all. What was out there for him? There was Lyr, but he didn't even know if Lyr was still alive. As for the rest of his sept ...

Are you sure they're all dead?

Yes, he answered silently. Yes, they were dead. For a slave, hope was poison. He'd learned that long ago.

He could return to his homeworld and see if any of his family was still alive. But there, he'd be a fugitive. Not that he wasn't also a fugitive here, but according to Sarah, her world didn't have the capability to contact the Galateans. Her people didn't know what he was. The Polarans would know. Many of them might be sympathetic, but could he really expect them to shelter him knowingly, risking the wrath of the Galatean Empire? Much easier to just return the escaped slave and collect the reward. He wouldn't blame them.

If he was going to be a fugitive anyway, he might as well be a fugitive in a place where no one knew he was an escaped slave. Sarah's people were still looking for him, but even if they managed to find him, he could slip away into the woods and live as a wolf for awhile.

Why *didn't* he just make a new life here? He asked himself that multiple times a day, as he listened to Sarah and her father playfully bantering over the dinner table, as he helped Sarah feed her family's domestic fowl, as he lay in bed with her at night and stroked her sandy curls, more relaxed than he had been since those long-ago days when he used to sleep with his entire sept around him.

And yet he kept working on the pod, trying to make it spaceworthy again.

He didn't know what he wanted. He wished he didn't have to choose.

He hoped fate would make the decision for him.

If the pod couldn't fly, then he'd have no choice but to stay. And if he'd done his best on it, then no one (*Lyr*) could blame him for not trying harder.

And he'd live out his life on this world Sarah called Earth, never knowing if Lyr still lived, never knowing what had happened to anyone else in his sept.

So what? I don't owe them—

But he couldn't lie to himself, even in the privacy of his own head. They had been his everything: his pack, his family, his world. Polarans couldn't survive alone. His sept were the reason why he was still alive and still sane.

He couldn't abandon them.

But the longer he spent with Sarah, the more the mere idea of abandoning her felt like having his guts ripped out.

His future was in space. His future was on Earth.

He could only choose one.

"I can hear you thinking over there," Gary said, and Rei

sighed and straightened up from examining, for the two hundredth time, the pod's nonfunctional Vrik coils.

The older man came over, leaning heavily on his canes, and sat down with a grunt on an overturned crate beside the ship. "You can understand me, right?" he asked, eyes sharp on Rei. "Even without Sarah around."

Rei nodded. By now his implant had added English to its library of languages, though he still occasionally missed words when Sarah wasn't in the room. Without her brain to translate, he had to rely on the vocabulary and grammar it had already picked up.

"Good. There was somethin' I wanted to talk to you about."

Rei touched his own lips and gestured with a smile.

"Yeah, I know you can't talk back. You can just listen."

Rei smiled again and dragged over a barrel to sit on. He gestured to indicate "go ahead."

Gary hesitated, tapping his work-roughened fingers on top of the crate. "I don't know much about where you come from," he said abruptly. "Just what Sarah tells me, and she's not one for telling tales out of school. But I can tell you've been through some things. That right?"

Rei nodded.

"We had a war here, awhile back." Gary gazed off into the distance, not looking at Rei. "In a place called Vietnam. At that time, every young man in the country, when he turned eighteen, had to sign up for the draft. If you didn't have a good reason why not, they'd put a gun in your hand and send you off to fight. Sound kinda familiar, huh?"

Rei nodded again. He hadn't known they had things like that here. Sarah's world seemed so peaceful. He'd thought perhaps they had somehow found a way to live in peace, without wars. But perhaps there was no such thing, anywhere there were people.

"It's not like what happened to you, I guess. But it took me awhile to come back from that. Some guys, they never did. Came back broken in more ways than one." He smiled briefly and ruefully, and touched the top of the canes. "Not me, not like this, in case you were wondering. This is from a dumb accident on the farm."

Rei nodded, unable to answer any other way.

"Anyway," Gary said, looking straight at him now, "I guess the point is, I know what it's like to be taken away from your home and family when you don't want to go, and sent off to fight in somebody else's war. I know what it's like when the dreams wake you up at night. I guess what I'm saying is, you're not the only one around here who's been in that particular hell. I guess it doesn't do much good to say 'if you ever want to talk about it,' at least not unless you two find another of those things to put in my head, which, pardon my French, but hell no. But you ever want to have a drink and swap war stories—" He stopped, gave a short laugh, and shook his head. "Okay, can't really do that either. But I got a good bottle of Scotch in the house, and you ever want to pour one out for the friends we both lost and have a drink for old time's sake, one old soldier to another, you just let me know."

All Rei could do was nod, his throat tight. For the first time in years, he thought of the adults who had trained and raised him. Not all of them had been cruel. In particular, he wondered what had happened to Tamir, the old tiger-type Galatean who had been in charge of their sept when they were little, the closest thing to a father that most of them had ever known. Gary reminded him of Tamir a lot, now that he thought about it. He wondered if that old man was still alive, or was even so old as he'd seemed when Rei was small.

The language barrier hadn't been so frustrating since his early days with Sarah. He wanted to reply, but anything he said would be gibberish to Gary.

But he didn't have to be entirely mute, he realized. There *were* a few words of English he knew.

"Thankyew," he said. "Thankyew, Gary."

Gary looked startled and then smiled. "That's right. Guess you can talk a little after all."

Rei shrugged, and then Gary grinned at him, and Rei grinned back, and the language barrier didn't seem to matter at all.

SARAH COULD TELL something was bothering Rei. This felt different from his prickly reserve after she'd first brought him back to the farm. Then, he'd held himself apart because he didn't trust them. But now he alternated between warm friendliness and pensive quiet. She figured it had to do with leaving, and she wished he'd just talk about it. It would make it easier, a little bit, if she knew that he shared her mixed feelings about his departure. Was he looking forward to getting back to space, shaking the dust of Earth off his feet, or did he want to stay as badly as she wanted him to?

But as long as she could make herself focus on the "now" instead of the future, she had never been happier. The world outside the farm hardly seemed to matter. Her classes were nothing but a distraction; merely leaving the farm for a few hours was torment.

She'd gone from feeling trapped and stifled on the farm to feeling as if her entire life was here.

What more could she want? What purpose in dreaming of moving away when the entire universe's wonder and magic was right here? Rei *was* the universe; through his stories, he brought all the galaxy right here to the kitchen of her family's farmhouse. Sarah hung on his every word as he told her about the other worlds he'd been to, carefully glossing over why he'd been there (though they both knew: *See new places, meet new people, and kill them,* Sarah thought, paraphrasing from a war movie she'd once seen). He'd begun to open up about his dead friends, and he had her in stitches with stories of Skara's pranks or his portal-making friend Selinn's mishaps as she learned to control her powers.

She wrapped up every one of these glorious fall days in her heart like a pile of parcels, to comfort her if Rei *did* leave, if she never saw him again.

And secretly, quietly, in her heart of hearts, she let her dreams begin to expand, just a little, from the tiny, ordinary, safe dreams that were all she'd allowed herself, to start to encompass all the possibilities that had opened up to her.

What if she *did* go into space with Rei? Was there a way she could make that happen?

What if Rei couldn't go to space and stayed on the farm with them? Could they hide him? Get fake paperwork for him, maybe? She'd read books in which characters obtained fake birth certificates. She didn't have a clue how to go about it in a rural farm town, but the internet would probably help. They could use greasepaint to make him look human enough to go to town occasionally, once the government people got tired of looking and went away.

It felt so daring, so *huge* just to allow herself permission to daydream about it.

Especially going to space. She knew it wouldn't work. She couldn't leave Dad, and she wouldn't fit in the pod anyway ...

But what if she could? Maybe they could tear out some of the internal cushioning to fit two people. It would be cramped, but she didn't mind being in close quarters with Rei. And it wouldn't be for very long. The pods were not meant to live in. They didn't even seem to have a bathroom. Just a few hours of discomfort, and then she'd be ...

... well. Then she'd be *where*, was the problem. Just as Rei didn't fit into her world, she wouldn't fit into his. She looked at the picture he'd drawn for her every day, as if she could memorize the sketches of his family so she'd recognize them if she ever saw them, but the picture made it clear that regular Earth humans were going to stand out in space just as much as Rei stood out on Earth.

Just like Rei needed identification to do anything on Earth, Sarah would probably need an ID she didn't have to function in outer space society. Rei hadn't told her much yet about how Galatean society worked, but there was no telling what kind of things she'd need that she didn't have. Maybe you had to get your DNA scanned just to buy food. And what did they use for money in outer space? She certainly didn't have any, or any way to get some if she couldn't get a job without the space equivalent of ID.

Heck with this. It was a beautiful fall day, and she decided to forget the whole business for awhile and take a ride.

Princess perked up considerably when Sarah led her to the hitching rail and threw the saddle over her back. Sarah almost never rode anymore; it just seemed like there was always something else to do, and Princess—who had been her mother's horse, once upon a time—was old enough that she didn't need much exercise. But she still had some friskiness left in her, picking up her legs smartly as Sarah took her in a brisk turn around the pasture to check that the saddle was correctly tightened and adjusted.

"Hey, guys!" Sarah called through the open door of the barn. The radio was playing inside, punctuated with the occasional clang of a hammer on metal or the whir of a lathe. "I'm taking Princess out for a ride. Rei, you want to come?"

Rei appeared around the corner of the ship. It looked completely fixed on the outside now, all the damaged shielding replaced with new, shiny panels from her father's stash of scrap metal. If it was really as close to flying as it looked, she assumed there would be more of a party atmosphere in the barn—but maybe not. Her dad was a typical Wisconsin farmer, close-mouthed and not inclined toward wild displays of emotion, and he seemed to have found a kindred spirit in Rei.

"Do you mean on the Hnee?" Rei asked, looking at her as curiously as if he'd never seen someone on horseback before ... and maybe he hadn't.

"It's called a horse, and no, I don't think she can carry both of us. I was thinking you could run alongside as a wolf. You don't get much chance to do that."

Rei's eyes lit up. "Perhaps I could take a little time, if Gary doesn't mind working alone."

"Dad! I'm stealing Rei! You can have him back later!"

"Behave yourselves," was her father's only remark from somewhere behind the ship, and the lathe started up again.

Outside the barn—and out of sight of her father—Rei stripped and handed the bundle of clothing up to Sarah. He looked much healthier than the first time she'd seen him, she was pleased to note. By now, the bruises and other injuries were gone as if they'd never been. He had filled out and put on muscle, and his skin gleamed a smooth, healthy (she assumed) shade of blue in the sunlight.

Farm life, it appeared, was good for him.

"Ready?" she asked, and he nodded and shifted, flowing into the great blue-furred shape of the wolf.

Sarah had hoped she could pass him off as a dog if they encountered anyone back in the woods, but she had forgotten that he was quite so ... *vivid*. And also so huge. There was just no mistaking him for anything other than what he was: a big blue alien wolf.

"If we see or hear anyone coming, you'll need to hide, okay?" she said, and he nodded, a very incongruous gesture with his shaggy wolf's head.

Sarah wheeled the mare around and set a course for the upper pasture and the woods beyond.

It was a gorgeous day, one of those rare north-country fall days that has no equal, the sun blinding in a nearly cloudless sky and the red and gold trees like frozen fireworks. Princess's strong muscles flexed underneath Sarah, settling into a smooth canter. Sarah knew she'd have to rein the mare in eventually, to keep her from overworking and hurting herself, but for now she let Princess have her head. The blue wolf ran beside them, tail flying like a banner. His tongue lolled out of his jaws, not pink like a dog's tongue, but a deep purple as if he'd been eating popsicles.

When they reached the fence at the back of the upper pasture, Princess's shoulders tensed to jump. "Oh no you don't," Sarah told her, and dismounted to unlatch the back gate and lead the mare through. Princess's coat rippled and she shook herself as Sarah climbed back on.

"I forgot what a little spitfire you used to be back in the day, lady. She's a nice horse," she said to Rei, who had stopped to watch the whole thing, sitting canine style with his tail curled over his feet. "But she does have a few bad habits. Jumping over things is one of them. She can't do it with these old knees, she'll hurt herself, but she doesn't know enough not to try."

Rei made a little whuffing sound and stood up, ears pricked as he sniffed the air. The woods seemed to fascinate him, and Sarah realized that he hadn't been in an actual forest in all the time he'd been on Earth, except for their drive through the woods to the lake.

Not that this was forest primeval, exactly. It was just a little wooded strip that wound between the farms, criss-crossed with bridle paths, deer trails, and the beaten tracks made by farm kids heading to the local fishing holes or biking back and forth between their friends' houses. Sarah remembered when she used to do that, taking her bike over every afternoon to play with the Haverfords' daughter.

Susie Haverford was married and lived in Milwaukee now. Nothing ever stayed the same. Except her. Stuck in place, spinning her wheels ...

Sarah shook off the echoes of the past and pointed Princess's head into the woods.

She kept the mare to a sedate pace on the rough forest trails. They passed in and out of sun-dappled shade, leaf shadows flickering across Princess's silvery neck and Rei's brindled fur. A sudden crashing in the underbrush drew the attention of all three travelers as a startled deer bounded away, leaving a trail of snapping twigs in her wake.

Sarah took a left turn on the network of bridle paths that led to an old beaver pond. She hadn't been there in years, but she was pleased to see the pond was still there, perhaps a little more sunken and shallow than it used to be, the collapsed old dam a little more overgrown. The trees up here had lost more of their leaves than the ones down in the pasture, which were still at their full flaming glory. Brown and gold leaves carpeted the surface of the pond and lay thick under the trees.

She dismounted and knelt to feel Princess's legs, checking for signs of warmth or other damage from the unaccustomed activity. While she did that, and then took the bit out of Princess's mouth so the mare could browse a bit, Rei trotted around the pond on a mission of lupine investigation.

Sarah sat on a sun-warmed log beside the pond and watched him. His body language was doglike— sniffing things, investigating rabbit trails—but with a wild grace like no dog she'd ever seen. She could have watched him all day.

At least until he leaned down to dip his snout into the leaf-littered surface of the pond. Sarah burst into laughter and called across the pond, "If you're planning on drinking that, don't expect a kiss afterwards!"

Rei shifted back, on hands and knees. He grinned at her. "It's just water."

"It's *pond water*, you fool. Beaver pond water. Do they have giardia on your home planet?"

"Do we have what?"

"Apparently not. Look, it's not a good idea to drink pond water on Earth. It can make you sick. Come over here and sit with me instead." She patted the log beside her. "I've got your clothes here."

He sat at her feet instead, long blue legs stretched out in the meadow weeds. "I'm comfortable like this, if you don't mind."

"I definitely don't mind. Tell me if you get cold."

Rei nodded and leaned against her thigh. She played idly with his hair, petted his shoulder and the soft skin above his collarbone.

It was impossibly peaceful here, the only sound the soft rustling as Princess moved about the meadow, lipping at grass. A light breeze rattled the branches of the trees and sent a cascade of leaves showering across the pond, fluttering down onto Sarah's lap and Rei's hair.

"Your world is beautiful," Rei said quietly.

"It has its not-so-beautiful parts."

"Yes, perhaps, but ..." He hesitated and turned his face up toward hers. The *tsinde* spots glimmered in the sun, gold with hints of green. "I don't think I'm going to be able to fix my battlepod."

She was afraid to answer, not sure whether he'd be pleased with relief or disappointment. "Oh?" she said at last, noncommittally.

"It's as I feared. I don't have the expertise and your world doesn't have the tools."

"You're welcome to stay," she said, running her fingers through his hair, around the back of his ear. "I hope you know that. As long as you like."

"I know. I ..." A sigh escaped him and he leaned his head on her thigh. "I want to. And I also want ..."

"To find your friends. I know." She petted his hair, fingers separating the coarse outer strands to reach the soft, thick underfur. "I want to go to space with you, Rei. I want to see all these places you've talked about. I want it so much I could cry. But I can't leave Dad. And I want you to be able to find your friends and get back to your life, and ... and I know it wouldn't be much of a life for you here on Earth, but I—I wish you could stay."

He laid a hand on her thigh. She put her hand over it, and Rei laced their fingers together.

"There's no rush," he pointed out. "None of this has to be decided tomorrow. Maybe there's someone on your world who could help me fix the pod. Someone at the school where you study, perhaps?"

"Oh, I hadn't thought of that." She had been so careful about keeping him out of sight, so worried about anyone finding out, that the thought had never occurred to her that widening their circle of spaceship mechanics beyond Rei and her dad might be a good idea. The idea of introducing Rei to her professors caused a tiny twinge of proprietary jealousy. She firmly squashed it. He wasn't *hers*. And he was right, there was a lot more scientific and technological know-how on Earth than what was represented by Sidonie, Wisconsin.

"That's a good idea, actually. I can start looking around on Monday. Or—no—if we're going to talk to other people about you, especially someone with connections, we should give it a little more time and wait until those government people give up and go away."

"I don't mind waiting."

"Yeah, well, *I* mind. I don't deal well with uncertainty," Sarah admitted. "I try to make myself take life one day at a time, but I've always had my life planned out in detail. The plans keep changing, but I always hated not having them."

"And I've always tried not to think beyond tomorrow. You can't, when everything about your life is decided for you by other people."

She pressed a kiss to the top of his head. "Maybe I could use a little uncertainty in my life."

"Perhaps I need some stability."

Sarah rested her cheek on top of his head and closed her

eyes, listening to the rush of the wind in the trees, the faint jingle of Princess's saddle buckles as the mare moved about the meadow. Rei's thumb swept back and forth across the back of her hand.

"I had a crazy thought earlier," she said into his hair. "Have I told you about Halloween?"

"I know it's a holiday of your people and it's coming up soon."

"It's only a couple of days away. One of the ways we celebrate it is by dressing up in costumes. There are going to be lots of people out on the street in costumes, pretending to be monsters and fictional characters and all kinds of things." She hesitated. "You see where I'm going with this, right?"

"You think I could go out in public without causing alarm."

"All we have to do is add a couple of fake-looking touches so people dismiss it as a costume and don't look too closely. And then we can do anything at all. We could go out on a ... on a date." She could feel her cheeks flaming. "Do you know what those are?"

"Not in the sense you're using it."

"It's a—a courting ritual of my people."

"Oh?" he murmured. "What do you do?"

"You just spend time together. Often there's food. We could eat at a restaurant. And you could go shopping, if you want. You can pick out your own clothes this time." It sounded so banal, so unworthy of the risk of going out in public with him. And yet she wanted it more than anything. To be able to walk down the street with him, hand in hand ... "You wouldn't have to hide," she finished in a rush.

"I would very much like to see more of your world," Rei said.

"It would be a risk, though."

"My entire life is a risk."

"That doesn't mean it's a good idea to take *more* risks for very little reward."

"But there would be a reward." He tipped his head back, looking up at her. "I'd get to see more of your culture. And it would make you happy."

Her heart brimmed over, spilling happiness like a tipped cup. "It *would* make me happy. It would make me very happy. But only if you want to, Rei, do you understand? If you don't think it's worth the danger, then we won't do it."

"It's only one day." He reached up to trace her lips with the tips of his fingers. "I would like very much to go on a date with you."

FOURTEEN

"YOU THINK I will attract no notice if I go out in public like this," Rei said, eyeing his reflection in the mirror in Sarah's room.

"Absolutely," Sarah said. Her eyes danced with suppressed laughter as she carefully worked on his face with her little paint-stick. "It's from a movie, like I said."

The white dots she was painting on his face were, at least, similar to the *tsinde*. It was the ears that were deeply bizarre, pointed animal-like ears that stuck up through his hair.

"These ears are not very convincing," Rei said, reaching up to poke at one of them. She'd made them out of painted cardboard, cut from a box that had contained crunchy bits of breakfast food.

"That's the whole point. They're not supposed to be convincing. People are supposed to be able to tell at a glance that it's a costume."

Her phone was propped on top of the chest that contained her clothing, with a picture of the creature she was trying to emulate. It did actually look surprisingly similar to someone from Rei's homeworld. She had explained that the movie was called *Avatar* and it was about blue aliens.

"Are you sure it's a good idea to dress me as someone from another planet, even a fictional one?"

"It's called hiding in plain sight. Anyway, I figured it was this or a Smurf, and dressing you like a sexy Smurf would have given me nightmares for weeks, either that or a really disturbing Smurf fetish, so an *Avatar* alien it is." She put the cap back on the paint stick and looked around. "Where'd I put the wig? Let me see how it looks on you."

She had purchased a very cheap black wig and had spent an evening carefully stringing beads onto clumps of the wig's plastic hair. Now she settled it onto his head and arranged the hanging beads around the cardboard ears.

"Oh, yeah. Perfect."

"I still look very much like myself."

"That's the point. Just don't tell people that. Actually, you probably shouldn't talk at all if anyone can hear you, since all they'll hear is an alien language." Sarah smiled and gave the beaded hair a twitch over his shoulders, settling it into place. "If you do say something by accident, though, we can just tell people that you're trying to stay in character."

"The image on your communication device isn't wearing very many clothes." Rei grinned playfully at her. "Do you want me to walk around your town wearing a loincloth?"

Sarah's expression glazed for a moment. "I—uh—I'm sure that's a terrible idea. A very bad idea. Very bad." She shook herself and reached for the piece of blue rope dangling off the top of the clothes chest. "Let's put your tail on."

"I do not want the tail."

"I worked hard on the tail." She tied the rope around his

waist and draped the tail over his arm, fluffing out the ends; she'd made a knot in the rope and then unraveled the rest of it to create a tuft. "You'll probably have to carry it like this to keep it from getting tangled with your legs. Sorry about that."

"What's one small embarrassment at this point, more or less."

"You could've been a Smurf, buddy. Here, help me with my wings."

Rei helped affix the wire-and-gauze wings over her soft flowered dress. She tucked her real hair under a pink wig, and adjusted a pair of little curling antennae, cutely fuzzy on the tips.

"How do I look?"

"Not like any species I've ever seen."

"No fairies in outer space, huh? Too bad."

Her lips were as pink as the wig. They'd made love before putting on their costumes, and though they had both taken showers, he could still smell it on her, a delicious feminine perfume of sex and sweat.

When he touched her chin, tipping her face up to his, her pink lips parted. He leaned down to taste her, and himself on her.

"Ngghhh." She stretched and shook herself, and opened her eyes. Somehow the pink wig made her eyes stand out more brightly than her usual sand-colored curls. "If you keep that up, we're never going to get out of here."

"Would that be a bad thing?"

"Yes," she said firmly, picking up a little bag with a shoulder strap that matched her dress. "Got your spear?"

Rei sighed and retrieved the fake spear from the closet. Sarah had made it from a broom handle with a clumsily cut out cardboard blade. She grinned and reached to straighten a cardboard ear.

"Perfect. Let's roll."

Rei took a final look at himself in the mirror. He was wearing the red sweater and dark leg-coverings she'd bought for him. He didn't look like himself, but he definitely didn't look like an Earth-human, either.

Though, according to Sarah, that was the point.

They descended the stairs. Gary was on the couch, watching the entertainment screen. "So you two are really set on doing this, huh?" he remarked, looking up from a replacement part he'd milled for the jump drive to replace a mounting bracket that had bent in the crash. The original was sitting in his lap; he was comparing the two as he meticulously filed the replacement with sandpaper and a brush. "You really think nobody's gonna notice his blue doesn't rub off?"

"I think on Halloween, no one is going to look closely enough to notice." Sarah twirled, making the skirt and the pink wig stand out as she spun. The flashes of her legs, winking up to the thigh, left Rei dry-mouthed. "What do *you* think?"

"I think I'm glad nobody got a wild hare to drag me along on this foolishness," Gary grumbled, but he was grinning. "You kids have fun. I won't wait up. Just be careful."

Sarah grabbed a jacket off its hook in the kitchen, then hesitated. "I can't put this on over my wings. For that matter, I can't drive with my wings on. We'll have to take them off in the truck and put them back on when we get to town."

"Last chance to back out!" Gary called from the living room.

"No!" Sarah called back. She looked at Rei over her

shoulder as he helped her with the straps on the wings. "Unless you want to. We could call it off."

Rei shook his head. "I'm looking forward to seeing your world."

"Me too," she said shyly, and then laughed at herself. "With you, I mean. I've seen it before, of course."

"I know what you meant." He kissed the corner of her mouth lightly before turning to open the door.

The clear weather had held for the past couple of days, and they pulled out onto the farm road in crisp autumn sunshine, the truck's shadow as sharp as if it had been cut with a knife. Rei looked around curiously. He'd been on the road a couple of times now, but always at night. He had to suppress the urge to duck down in his seat when another vehicle passed them, shaped like Sarah's truck with a pile of squared-off hay blocks in the back.

Sarah leaned over and tapped the buckle next to his leg. "You should put your seatbelt on. Half the people around here don't wear them, but it is, technically, the law. Trust me, I'm not driving a half mile over the speed limit with you in the truck. No sense taking any chances."

Only some of that made sense, but he looked at how she was wearing the shoulder strap across her chest, and reached to find his own. Sensible, that the vehicle came with a restraint device in case of accident. It took him a few tries to figure out how to fit the buckle into its receptacle, but it was similar enough to the seat restraints on Galatean ships that he could figure it out.

Sarah turned on another road and they began passing more houses. There were people now, the first ones he'd seen outside of pictures in books and glimpses at night. Aside from their unusual color and foreign clothes, they weren't so different from people back home. A woman was walking two small bouncing moplike animals on leashes; an old man raked leaves in the yard of one of the houses. A girl passed them on the side of the road, riding on a high-stepping horse that looked even more Hnee-like than the smaller and more roly-poly horse back at Sarah's farm.

Sarah slowed the truck and made another turn. "And this is Sidonie," she said. "My hometown."

The buildings here were close together, some of bare red brick, others painted neutral colors. Most were one or two stories tall. The stores bore signs in the script of Sarah's world, which Rei's implant didn't give him the ability to read. Many of them were decorated with garlands of autumn leaves, bunches of straw, colorful fruits with faces carved into them, fake displays of small flying and crawling animals, and skeletons. It was eerie and primitive and fascinating, and for the first time he realized that this Halloween holiday of Sarah's was a harvest festival. His childhood village had done similar things in the fall, though the details were different.

Sarah drove slowly through Sidonie until the taller buildings gave way to scattered houses again.

"Don't you want to stop there?" Rei asked.

Sarah shook her head. "I think it's better not to. Everyone knows me, and that means they'll be wildly curious about you. What I was thinking is, I can drive up to Eau Claire, and if you see anything along the way that you want to look at, just tell me to stop. I'll take the scenic route so you can see as much as possible. And then we can get dinner in Eau Claire and maybe see a haunted house or a movie or something, and then come home. If we only get one night, we should make it count, right?"

Her enthusiasm was infectious. She loved this place, Rei could tell. And it had been a long time since he'd had someone to lift him up like this. The most optimistic and cheerful members of his sept had died years ago. It had just been himself and Lyr and Rook for awhile now, and despite their efforts to support each other, they'd made a dour triad.

"I'm looking forward to it," he said, a little surprised to find how much he meant it.

Sarah put out a hand on the bench seat between them. Rei laced his fingers through hers, blue on pink.

He hadn't prayed to the gods of his youth in a very long time, and had never found comfort in Galatean religious beliefs, but he offered up a small thought to whatever gods might be listening: *Let us have this day. Let* Sarah *have this day. Perhaps I don't deserve it, and you may take what you wish from me later, but she's helped me a lot and she deserves one day to be happy.*

IF THIS WAS to be their last good day, Sarah thought— before he managed to miraculously fix his spaceship and left, before they were discovered, before her father relapsed or some other terrible thing happened—then she couldn't have asked for a better one. She couldn't imagine being happier than she was now, Rei's warm fingers twined in hers, driving through the rust and gold of a Wisconsin autumn.

The harvest season was winding down, the roadside stands gathering in their baskets and shuttering their signs. Gourds were still out in force, row after row of pumpkins on tables or on their vines behind U-PICK signs, and fall mums added a dash of color to their drab wooden stalls. Homemade cheese and apples were also advertised in abundance.

"Just let me know if you want to stop," Sarah began, and then braked suddenly at a sign reading FALL FESTIVAL! CIDER & CORN MAZE! HAY RIDES! 0.5 MI! with an arrow pointing off to the left.

"What's this?" Rei asked as she turned onto the side road.

"An important tradition of my people. I thought you might like it."

She parked in a dirt lot with an array of other farm trucks mixed with the odd SUV or dirt-covered minivan. It was clearly all locals. Rei helped Sarah with her wings and started to reach for his spear, then looked at the kids running around and put it back in the truck bed.

The kids were mostly in costume, and some of the adults too, like the middle-aged lady with cat whiskers painted on her face and a pair of ears nestled in her piled chestnut curls who dipped hot cider for them. "Well, you sure went all out this year, honey," she told Rei. "What are you supposed to be?"

"He's an alien," Sarah said. "And I'm a fairy. We're up from Sidonie."

"Well, you two enjoy the fair, now."

Sarah curled her hands around the warm paper cup. The lightly spiced sweetness of the cider took her straight back to her childhood. "Do you like it?" she asked Rei quietly, and he nodded with a smile.

The advertised corn maze was kiddie sized, the corn no higher than Sarah's chest. She and Rei sat on a bale of hay and finished their cider. Sarah pointed to a hay wagon rocking in from the field behind the corn maze, pulled by two draft horses, with raucous kids scrambling all over the hay. "Want to try that?"

"How does one do it?" he murmured, leaning close to her so he could speak without being overheard.

"Do? Well, you just sit in the hay and ride around, mostly."

Rei gave her a look of bafflement.

"Maybe it's more fun when you're five. What can I say, I'm young at heart." She tossed their empty cups into the nearest trash barrel and pulled him up by the hand. "Hay ride! Come on!"

They scrambled onto the hay wagon, trying not to crush Sarah's wings. Most of the other passengers were teenagers, a couple of them holding onto little siblings.

"Cool costume," one of the girls told Rei. She was dressed like Dorothy Gale from *The Wizard of Oz*, complete with a stuffed Toto in a basket. "*Avatar*, right?"

Rei smiled and nodded.

"That's like my favorite movie ever."

"It's so lame," one of the boys complained, and the teens' conversation turned to movies, most of them involving science fiction or superheroes. Sarah noticed Rei looking intrigued but confused, and felt a little lost herself. She'd seen few movies in the last decade. Sidonie had never been big enough for a movie theater, and she'd lost touch with most of her high school friends as they had drifted in different directions; driving up to the city to go out to the movies by herself seemed like too much of an indulgence. Most of the movies she watched these days were old westerns, comedies, or sports movies—stuff her dad liked.

Is that all I do anymore? she thought, lying in the hay with her head in Rei's lap and looking up at clouds gathering in the blue bowl of the sky above her. *Take care of Dad, take care of the farm, make sure I get good grades in my classes …*

The classes, at least, were something she was doing for her own enjoyment. But at some point it had stopped really feeling that way. Even driving up to the university had turned into just another part of her daily responsibilities.

At least she still had her stargazing. If Rei stayed, she would have to teach him all the constellations. They could look for meteors together.

And there needs to be more of this sort of thing. More living for me, less wrapping my life around other people ...

She turned her head to watch the teenagers cheerfully quarreling over a candy apple that one of them had brought onto the hay ride, which was now, predictably, covered with hay. Someone had also spilled cider on someone else's costume. It seemed so long ago that she'd been that young, with one foot in childhood and the other tentatively feeling out the footing of young adulthood. And then her mother had gotten sick and suddenly she'd had to be the grown-up of the household.

Rei plucked a piece of straw out of her hair and bent over to murmur, "I think we're done?"

"Oh." She sat up as the laughing teens slid out of the hay. "I zoned out for a few minutes there."

Rei gave her a strong hand back to the ground and leaped down himself, a graceful catlike leap from the top of the hay pile. There were some appreciative cheers from the teens.

The clouds were starting to amass in earnest, blocking the sun, and the breeze had grown cool enough to cut through Sarah's light dress. She bought Rei a candy apple from a table selling them to raise money for the local 4H and they walked back to the truck arm in arm, while she tried not to watch the distracting way he was licking and nibbling at the apple, displaying little flashes of his purple tongue. The first drops of rain were striking the windshield as they pulled out of the parking lot.

"If it's doing this in Eau Claire," Sarah remarked, "we might have to forget about any more outside stuff. We'll get soaked."

"I don't mind being wet."

"Yes, but people might notice your greasepaint isn't washing off." She reached over to pluck a piece of straw off his sweater. He was covered with it; they both were. "So now you've been to a Midwest corn maze. Did you have anything like this back home?"

"We had an autumn festival in my village." Rei's voice was soft. "I remember there was a lot of food, and footraces, and lanterns with shapes cut in the sides, so they made patterns dance on the walls of the houses. We didn't dress in costumes. Usually the children would shift and play under the tables." He laughed quietly. "I haven't thought about that in years."

"Do you mind talking about it? Because I—"

"No." He finished the candy apple with a crunch, and Sarah realized too late that she'd forgotten to tell him not to eat the core. Oh well, it didn't seem like it had bothered him. "It's good to talk about it. I don't think about that time in my life very often. Perhaps I should more often." He took a breath and looked out the truck window at the passing woods and fields.

They drove in and out of patches of sun and rain. Sarah stopped at a U-Pick pumpkin farm and a bemused Rei trailed her as she examined the picked-over gourds.

"What are we going to do with this?" he asked quietly. There was no one else around. It wasn't actually raining, but the ground was wet.

"It's another tradition of my people. You can't do Halloween on Earth without picking your own pumpkin."

"Yes, but ..."

"We carve a face into it and put a candle inside." Crouched beside a large pumpkin, she looked up at him with a grin, enjoying the look on his face. "Yes, I know it sounds insane. Just wait. It's fun. I'll show you tonight when we get home."

He helped her load the pumpkin into the truck. The farmer had helpfully hosed it off for them when they brought it to be weighed, so at least it wasn't muddy.

"In Eau Claire," Sarah said, "we'll probably see more of the actual Halloween side of things. Part of Halloween is making things fake-scary for fun, like jack-o-lanterns and ghosts and skeletons and stuff, but you get that more in the city than in the country."

"Your world is strange."

"Oh come on, tell me your people didn't have strange holiday customs."

"The Galateans certainly do. They have a lot of Empire-wide civic and religious holidays. I never really minded those, since slaves get a half-day off on every holiday, and a full day on the religious ones."

Sarah bit the inside of her lip, *hard*, managing not to say anything about the implication that he didn't get days off otherwise. Instead she said, "Which holiday was your favorite?"

"Caruza," he said promptly. "The highlight of the Caruza festival is a fireworks display—do you have that here? Fireworks?"

"Colored lights and explosions, that kind of thing?"

"Yes." His smile was bright and a little wistful. "In the fleet, it's the pilots who do the fireworks. We release them from our ships. The cohorts compete to come up with the best display, the most striking and unusual, something the fleet would be talking about all the next day. We brainstorm and practice for months beforehand."

Sarah wondered what time unit he was actually using when she heard "months" through the translator. "That sounds really cool. I wish I could see them."

They compared notes on holiday customs all the way into Eau Claire, as the weather settled heavily around them, the clear bright morning turning into a severe gray evening. Unlike the holidays of Rei's homeworld, which mostly involved feasting and dancing, the Galateans tended to have holidays focused on fasting and contemplation.

"We're both warrior cultures," Rei said, "but while we Polarans like to enjoy our bodies and the gifts the gods gave us, their culture is more into things like staying up all night meditating or whole cycles where you eat nothing but a certain wheatgrass that grows only on their homeworld, that sort of thing. Lyr really got into that. He did all the fasting and cleansing rituals, every last one of them, while the rest of us mainly just did the ones that are required by law. I think for him it was similar to how he grew up. The dragons are a lot like the Galateans that way—well, actually, Lyr's people consider the Galateans very hedonistic and self-indulgent, so for him, the ritual fasting and all of that was the absolute bare minimum for responsible adulthood." He grinned. "Meanwhile Skara would sneak the rest of us sweets while everyone was supposed to be fasting. He'd almost always get caught, because Lyr's a telepath, so hiding things from him took a lot of concentration. Which is one of the things Skara was never good at, especially since his people are a little bit telepathic too."

"I can picture them so clearly when you talk about

them." And she could. It was easy to imagine Rei and his sept-siblings as kids, giggling in the dark, sneaking each other treats.

They *couldn't* all be dead. It was too unfair.

THEY DROVE into Eau Claire in the aftermath of rain, banks of dark clouds scudding south and eastward to leave the wet pavement glistening in late afternoon sunshine. The world was a watercolor dreamscape painted in shades of purple and gold.

Downtown swarmed with kids in costumes, running in and out of businesses designated as part of the town's municipal trick-or-treating event. For the first time since they'd left the farm, venturing openly out in public with Rei disguised only with the barest touches of cardboard and glue, Sarah felt herself starting to relax. They fit in here. She could feel it. The biggest Halloween parties would've been on the weekend, but there were still college kids and young adults dressed up for bar-hopping or partying. She and Rei slid right into the mix. No one gave them a second glance, beyond a handful of people offering appreciative comments on Rei's costume.

She didn't try the bars, since they couldn't risk Rei being carded, but they wandered the streets as the watercolor afternoon slid into a chill dusk. Despite having to leave her jacket in the truck because of her costume's wings, she wasn't cold; the air itself seemed charged with energy, lights driving back the darkness and Rei's warm fingers wrapped in hers. Since they couldn't partake of the free Halloween chocolate that was being handed out everywhere, she bought them both pumpkin spice lattes, after having a quick

Google on her phone to make sure pumpkins and cinnamon weren't poisonous for dogs. (Coffee apparently wasn't, since he'd been drinking it for a week with no ill effects.)

Rei looked nervous at the prospect of sitting in a restaurant to eat, surrounded by people, so Sarah bought them takeout burgers and fries. They ate standing up—the benches were too wet—in a waterfront park watching the lights glimmering on the river.

"The funny thing about seeing a place with someone new is that you see it as tourists do, and it's almost more fun that way," Sarah said as they wandered along a bike path after dropping the takeout boxes in the trash. "I've lived nearby all my life, but I've never seen downtown on Halloween before. Actually, I haven't really gone anywhere in Eau Claire except campus and the box-store shopping sprawl along the freeway in, I don't know, years? It used to be a big treat, going into the city to shop, especially around Christmas. Now it's just routine. I look forward to the days when I *don't* have to drive into town, but then when I'm out on the farm I think about the places I'd like to go in town. Which of course I never do, because once I'm here I just want to finish up what I need to do and get back home."

A couple went past them in the dark, neither in costume, close together with their arms around each other's waists. After they were gone, Sarah said, "I'm sorry. I'm hogging the conversation since you can't talk much in public."

"I don't mind," he answered quietly. "I really like hearing it. You don't talk about yourself much."

"I don't?" She leaned into him, enjoying the warmth as much as the contact. She was going to have to go back to the truck for her jacket soon.

"You do when I ask. You just don't volunteer information much."

He fell silent again as another pedestrian approached, a young man in a plaid jacket walking quickly, head down and hands shoved in his pockets. As he went by without slowing, Sarah marveled at how completely unafraid she was. Walking in a city park at night would normally have had her on high alert, fearing muggers and rapists behind every bush. But she'd seen what Rei could do with those bracelets he wore. With Rei beside her, she feared nothing.

"Pot, kettle," she remarked, and he gave her a curious look. "Sorry. Earth saying, I guess it didn't translate. What I meant was, you don't talk about yourself much either, unless I ask. But I understand why, and I guess ... I guess I feel like my life is so boring compared to yours. I'm just a farm kid from flyover country. You've been so many places and done so many things. How could stories about stargazing at the lake or Christmas shopping in a city that's tiny even by my planet's standards have any interest for you?"

"Sarah, I love hearing you tell me about yourself." He stopped and turned to face her, taking her other hand in his. "Everything about you is interesting to me. I'm the one who —" He stopped, his gleaming, reflective eyes focusing past her.

"What?" she asked, stepping closer to him and looking over her shoulder. They weren't entirely alone; a homeless person was digging in a trash container a little way down the bike path, and there were a couple of costumed party-goers in the park up ahead, visible mainly as silhouettes with fake cat ears sticking up against the light.

"I don't know," Rei murmured. "It's probably nothing, but ... step back into the shadows here."

She obeyed, allowing Rei to draw her into the inky darkness under the trees. Until now, she hadn't realized how well suited Rei's natural coloring was for night camouflage, the deep blue of his skin vanishing completely in the dark. The white dots she'd painted on for his Avatar costume had mostly rubbed off by now, and even his red sweater's vivid color was leeched to charcoal in the dim light. He was visible only by the glimmer of his reflective eyes and the fainter iridescence of the *tsinde* spots, picking out the line of his jaw and cheekbones when he turned his head.

By comparison she felt terribly exposed in her light-colored, flowered dress and long pink wig. She must look like a pale blur against the dark, where Rei was just another shadow in a night filled with them.

"What did you see?" she whispered.

"I don't know. That couple up there ..." He indicated the costumed pair. "Your people aren't normally that tall or broad."

"I think they're just bulked out because of the costumes." It looked like they were both wearing furry body suits. Smart, on a cold evening like this one, though they'd probably die of heatstroke if they went inside and try to dance. Still, they must be more comfortable right now than she was.

"I wish they'd step closer to one of the lights." Rei's voice was the barest murmur, stirring the strands of the wig above her ear. "My night vision is good, but all the lights around here make it hard for my eyes to dilate properly."

As if in answer to his comment, the pair did exactly that, moving over toward one of the lampposts illuminating the park. One of them was checking his phone, hands cupped around the glow of the screen.

Except no, his hands were ... empty? As they moved under the light, she caught the bright flash of bracelets around his wrist, around both their wrists. The costumed man was fiddling with one of his bracelets in a way that was very familiar to her from having seen Rei do it.

The streetlight illuminated tawny fur on both of them, one leopard-spotted, the other tiger-striped. They both wore armless coveralls of a type that was as familiar as the bracelets, although these were dark blue rather than gray, and each had a belt around the waist.

Next to her, she felt Rei's whole body go stiff.

"Are those Galateans?" she whispered, but she'd spent too much time looking at Rei's drawing of his dead Galatean friend—the cat-spotted fur, the ears—not to know the answer even as the words left her mouth.

FIFTEEN

IT WAS weird having the house all to himself again, after getting used to Sarah and her alien beau being around 24/7. Gary hardly knew what to do with himself.

He didn't want to work on the ship without Rei—and anyway, he had a feeling they were running up against the limits of what they could do with the tools they had. He'd machined new parts to replace as many as possible of the damaged ones, but some of those materials were things he'd never seen before, didn't even know what they were.

He thought Rei was coming around to the same decision Gary had reached awhile back, that they couldn't fix the ship using what they had to work with.

Gary wasn't sure how he felt about that. He liked the alien kid, and more importantly, the kid made Sarah happy. The poor girl hadn't given half a thought to her own happiness in longer than Gary wanted to think about. Rei made her happier than Gary had seen her in years.

But he had to think about her future, and what kind of future was there for her with a guy who could never go out in public except once a year, who they had to keep hidden all the time? Gary didn't mind—hell, he'd do anything if it meant keeping his little girl happy—but it didn't seem like much of a life for either of them.

Still, Sarah was an adult, and if being with Rei made her light up like it did, who was he to judge?

And it was awfully quiet with both of them gone.

He drifted around the house after they left, did some dishes, put out the bowl of candy in case any kids came by (they didn't get many trick-or-treaters, but a few of the neighbors had little ones and at least one of them usually stopped in). He'd finished machining the bracket for Rei's ship and checked to make sure it fit. He felt like he should take the opportunity to work on one of his own projects, but everything seemed dull compared to fixing an alien spaceship.

He was idly channel-surfing, looking for something better than game shows and old movies he'd already seen, when there was a brisk knock on the front door—*not* the kitchen door, which meant city folks, not neighbors. Gary levered himself off the couch, grabbed one walking stick (didn't really need both in the house) and limped over to answer it.

It had grown dark outside, a mist settling around the yard lights. A woman stood on the porch under the light bulb that he'd left on for trick-or-treaters. She was a few years older than Sarah, with thick dark hair pulled back in a ponytail and a badge held up where he could see it.

"Gary Metzger?"

"Yes, ma'am. And you are?" He kept the door cracked halfway where he could shut it fast if he needed to. There was a dark sedan parked behind her in the driveway, and a man leaning on it. Looked like just the two of them.

"Agent Anita Pradhan, Homeland Security. Do you have a few minutes, sir?"

"My show's about to come on," Gary hedged.

"This will only take a moment. I need to ask you some questions. May I come in?"

"What's this about? Am I in some kind of trouble?" He tried to sound baffled, playing "dumb farmer from the sticks" as hard as he could. The more this city lady underestimated him, the better.

"You're not in trouble, sir. We're just asking some routine questions. May I come in?"

He was strongly tempted to tell her "no." She couldn't force her way in without a warrant, not legally, at least. But he also didn't want to send up any flags that would make her take a closer look. Didn't want to give her a reason to go get that warrant and come back. At least Sarah and Rei were out.

"Yeah, guess that'd be all right," he said.

He held the door for her. She glanced back at her partner, but didn't invite him along. Gary took a quick glance around the living room, just to make sure there was nothing incriminating in sight, but the nice thing about Rei not really coming with much in the way of luggage was that he didn't leave a lot lying around.

"Coffee?"

"Sure," Agent Pradhan said. "Thanks."

She looked around with sharp eyes. Gary kept his own eyes roaming and alert as he limped through the living room to the kitchen, looking in particular for any telltale signs that the house was occupied by more than two people. Nothing stood out. The dishes were washed and in their rack, thanks to his earlier cleaning spree. He dumped the dregs of the old coffee and measured out a scoop for a new pot.

"Just have a seat. This won't take but a minute." He glanced over his shoulder and noticed that she was still standing. "So what's all this about?"

"A few routine questions, that's all. We think a fugitive may be in the area and we're asking around to see if anyone's seen anything suspicious. Have you seen any signs of an unfamiliar person in the area? Items missing, someone sleeping in an outbuilding, perhaps?"

"Nope. Nothing like that. This is a quiet town, ma'am." He wondered if it'd be suspicious to ask his own questions in return, decided it would look even odder not to. "Is this to do with all that business going on over at the lake?"

"I'm afraid I can't comment on that, Mr. Metzger."

"Course not. Sorry I asked." He fitted the coffeepot back onto its base. "You talk to the Mullers yet? Heard they had a homeless fella sleeping in their barn a few weeks back."

"I'll look into it," Agent Pradhan said in a polite way that suggested it had already been looked into. "Thank you for the tip. Have you seen anything yourself, heard anything perhaps? Odd lights in the pasture, tracks, animals acting strange?"

"Nope, nothin' like ... that."

As he turned away from the coffeepot, his eye fell on the mounting bracket he had been working on earlier. He'd left both it and the original sitting on the counter.

Which wasn't really a problem by itself. The replacement was just a piece of aluminum he'd milled into the right shape, and while the original was made of some glossy metal he didn't recognize, there was nothing about it to set off warning lights. It just looked like an engine part. He had 'em everywhere. He'd had to pick a rebuilt carburetor out of

the candy bowl earlier in the evening so he didn't accidentally hand it to some unsuspecting eight-year-old.

No, the problem was that he'd needed to make sure
the part fit, so he'd brought in the doodlyhickey it
attached to, a little glass tubey thing with a spill of what
looked like flexible fiber-optic cables coming off in all
directions. And the whole thing was all put together on
the countertop.

It still didn't look *that* weird, he told himself. Not to
someone who didn't know much about electronics. Girl was
a townie. She'd probably never taken apart her car's engine
or rewired a fuse box. What was she gonna guess?

Nothin', as long as he didn't keep staring at it. Agent
Pradhan clearly wasn't an idiot, and when his gaze had
dropped to the object on the counter, hers had gone to it as
if pulled along by magnets.

"Coffee's gonna be a minute," he said, moving quickly to
open a cabinet for mugs—and put his body between her and
the incriminating object on the counter. "Cream and sugar,
ma'am?"

"Cream, no sugar." Agent Pradhan moved in smoothly,
and Gary gave way, because he couldn't block her without
making a big deal about it. She reached for the object on the
countertop. "This is very interesting-looking. Do you mind
if I ask what it is?"

"Step-down capacitors from the starter motor on a '78
Lister diesel generator," Gary said promptly, without
pausing to plan or think. All he knew was, a hesitation
would've been worse. *Baffle them with bullshit,* as one of his
high school friends used to say, back in the days when they
used to sneak cigarettes and cans of beer, and lie to the
adults about it.

The problem with bullshit was that it did smell. If she

knew much about engines, he'd just made her even more suspicious.

But there was no reaction. Either she didn't know enough to recognize that what he'd just described wasn't an actual thing, or she had the world's best poker face. "Interesting," she remarked, and put it back down. "You're good with your hands, I take it."

"Something breaks on the farm, you fix it. And since it's useful to be able to, I like taking engines apart to figure out how they work." He grinned at her and reached for the coffeepot, which had finished percolating. "Hey, you want to hear about the hydro project I got goin' at an old ruin of a gristmill on the edge of the place? If it wasn't dark out there, I'd walk you over and show you. Gonna convert that thing to power this whole farm, maybe sell some power back to the utility company, even."

"It sounds fascinating," Pradhan said politely. "Perhaps later."

"You come back anytime you want to see it. Now, you said cream—?" He started to turn toward the fridge, and froze with a suddenness that he couldn't possibly disguise this time at the sight of light out the back window. Light shining from the cracks and windows in the barn, and a light about the size of a flashlight beam bouncing toward the house.

And Gary realized he was the biggest fuckin' idiot in the county.

Here he'd been worrying about Pradhan, and he'd just assumed the other agent would stay with the car.

There was a polite tap on the back door. Gary moved to open it, but Pradhan got there first. Her partner came in, flashlight in one hand, and in the other ...

Gary recognized it immediately. It was Sarah's old telescope, tucked under the other agent's arm, the one she'd lost out at the lake.

"You should go have a look in the barn," the male agent said quietly to Pradhan.

"You need a warrant for that," Gary said tightly. He never should've let them in. He should've turned them away, suspicion be damned. It would have taken them time to come back with a warrant. They could have moved the ship somewhere else, hidden it under a tarp at least ...

"Interesting that you assume we don't already have one," the male agent said. He set the telescope on the table with a clunk. "Recognize this?"

"Couldn't say," Gary said, heart beating fast, because he'd just noticed the neat row of letters scratched along the telescope's body in his daughter's handwriting.

SARAH M. METZGER.

Because of course Sarah had been the sort of child who meticulously labeled her things.

THEY'D FOUND HIM.

Ice rushed through Rei's veins, a sick cold spasm that choked him, closing off his airway and making him light-headed. Spots danced in his vision.

"Are they Galateans?" Sarah whispered, and it was her voice, along with the innocence of her question, that shocked him enough to fight back the cold fist of panic closing around his lungs.

He couldn't let them get Sarah. Couldn't let them find out about the farm.

They weren't looking in his direction yet. He reached mentally for his cuffs, making sure they were on their lowest power-saving setting. Maybe some process running in the background had pinged a Galatean server and alerted them to his location. Maybe they'd just tracked the pod's incoming trajectory, spread out over the surrounding countryside, and gotten lucky.

They were making no attempt to hide, even when another Earth human walked quickly through the park bound on some unknown errand, which meant they, too, had figured out that a night when everyone went abroad in costume was a perfect night for aliens to walk openly on a hitherto uncontacted planet.

Or *was* it uncontacted? Perhaps Sarah's government had been in touch with the Galateans for years, unknown to most of their people.

None of that mattered now. The important thing was getting away without attracting their attention.

Far, far away.

"Be quiet, as quiet as you can," he whispered.

Sarah nodded. She didn't ask again. It seemed that she'd figured out the answer on her own.

Slowly and quietly, Rei began to retreat, staying in the shadows and trying to maintain a slow enough pace that Sarah, too, could be stealthy in darkness that her eyes couldn't penetrate. He could have gone much faster on his own, but he wasn't about to leave her alone, not with Galateans nearby.

He was still holding Sarah's hand. Her fingers felt very warm and steady on his own, and he realized his hand was shaking and tried to make it still.

"Good God," Sarah whispered. Rei looked up quickly, but the Galateans still weren't looking in their direction. An Earth human had just passed the Galatean pair, jogging slowly in a way that Rei had already seen a few of them doing since he and Sarah had been in the park; it seemed to be a common form of exercise on her planet. This human was male, a full head and a half shorter than the Galateans, barely coming up to their shoulders.

"Rei, you didn't tell me Galateans are *huge*."

He decided not to tell her those two were actually on the short side. The Galateans must have picked agents who could blend more easily with this world's humans ... which also suggested some familiarity with the local humans already.

How many were here? There must be a ship in orbit. Not a full-sized battle cruiser, surely, just to capture an escaped slave. It was probably a smaller ship, a barque or a chaser-class ship. Most likely a chaser; they were small, fast ships used for courier work and small, stealthy missions—like, say, recapturing an escaped slave without attracting too much attention.

A chaser would have a detachment of around six or eight soldiers. None of them were likely to be authorized to take extraordinary measures or possess heavy battle armor. They would be moving fast and light, trying to conceal their presence on this world and get off with a minimum of fuss.

Unfortunately, they would still be well trained, competent, and hard to bribe. A fellow slave soldier might be convinced to look the other way, but chaser crews were usually Galatean citizen soldiers who trained as a unit. For them, he was a mission. And part of the Galatean warrior ethic was pride in a mission well done.

Maybe they aren't here for me.

Sure, they just happen to be on Earth for some other reason, and with a whole planet to choose from, they're here in Sarah's city? Yeah, right.

At last a twist of the path hid the Galateans from view.

Rei moved swiftly then, leading Sarah across a nearly empty parking field and onto the street. He'd hoped to mingle with the locals to obscure their visibility, but it was growing later in the evening and the crowds had begun to thin out. Most of the people who were still abroad seemed to be inside the restaurants and drinking establishments they passed.

"Can they track you?" Sarah whispered.

"If they could, I think they'd already be on top of us."

"Do you have a plan?"

"Get back to your vehicle. Get out of here." He paused and looked around. Despite his normally keen sense of direction, all these streets looked alike in the dark.

"This way," Sarah said, tugging on his hand.

Staying together, he told himself, was a mistake, putting Sarah at risk for no reason. He wasn't going to leave her alone in the city with Galateans around, but once they got back to the truck, he needed to convince her to leave without him. She'd be safer on her own.

... except no, she wouldn't, because his pod was in her barn. Even if the Galateans didn't have a way of tracking it directly, they had much better scanning technology than the locals, and they would find it sooner or later.

He and Sarah came around a corner, and he recognized the open-air parking courtyard where she'd left the truck. When she'd parked there earlier, it had been crowded with rows of vehicles in the big paved space. Now her truck was one of the few that remained.

Sarah made a startled sound when he gripped her wrist, pulling her to a stop against the side of the nearest building.

"What's wrong?" she whispered. "You don't think they found the truck, do you?"

"I don't know, but there's no sense taking chances." He nodded to her costume. "Take off your wings and wig so you can move swiftly. We don't want delays when we get to your vehicle."

"Yes, of course." She stripped off the costume, bundled it up, and barely hesitated before leaving it at the base of the wall. Rei abandoned his spear and fake ears along with it. The ears he'd thought about leaving on, in the hope of confusing the Galateans, but if they saw him the game was probably up anyway.

He scanned the street. There were a few Earth pedestrians around, each glimpse of movement giving him a sharp jolt of adrenaline before he identified them as not-a-threat and relegated them to the back of his mind. He wished he could use his cuffs to scan the area, but he didn't dare. It was Galatean technology meant for slaves to wear; the odds were good that they'd be able to detect a set of cuffs using an active scanning frequency. He'd never had to use Galatean tech against Galateans before.

"Let's go," he told Sarah softly, and they began to walk swiftly toward the truck. Sarah slipped her hand back into his, and Rei squeezed her fingers. It was good to know exactly where she was, by both touch and sight.

As they reached the edge of the vehicle parking area, angling toward the entrance, Sarah looked back and gasped, "Rei!"

Rei looked over his shoulder. He took in the scene in an instant: the damp street gleaming under the lights of the street lamps, the buildings glittering with their own lights, and in the middle of all of that, a hulking figure that had just come around the corner after them, ears pricked forward in its thick mane.

They are *tracking us!* was his first thought, tinged around the edges with panic, but then he took in the Galatean's companion, a hulking shape on all fours, head lowered to the pavement and tail curled around its hindquarters. It sniffed at the wall where they'd been hiding. It was a striped feline, bigger than Rei's wolf, and wore no collar or harness. Gold gleamed at its ankles.

One of them was a shifter.

They were tracking by smell.

He'd only ever heard rumors of shifters among the Galateans; he'd never seen one. His sept-sister, Haiva, had worn her cat traits openly on her human body, as most Galateans did. But he'd heard that some of them could shift fully into a big cat shape, and there was the living proof in front of him.

They hadn't been seen yet, but the parking area was brightly lit. It was only a matter of time.

"Keep walking," Rei told Sarah between his teeth, pulling her with him. "Stop looking back at them. We cannot behave differently from the others."

"But—" she began, and then her voice rose to a cry of alarm: "Rei!"

Rei spun around just in time to see the humanform Galatean assume a combat stance, and flung up his arms just in time to shield them both. Green light flared in front of him, and the Galatean's attack splintered on the air. Rei felt the fine hairs lift on his arms as static electricity crackled around him. Glimmers of light chased each other down his arms and over his cuffs.

He risked a glance to make sure Sarah was all right. She looked okay, but her eyes were enormous; she was frozen in place.

"Get to the truck! I'll be right behind you!"

Sarah snapped out of her paralysis and sprinted for the truck.

With a low, rumbling snarl, the cat-shifted Galatean

sprang forward, covering the distance between them in huge bounds. The other one fired off another energy attack. Rei dodged this one rather than depleting his shields. Blue-green light rippled over the vehicle next to him, which erupted in a piercing, wailing alarm.

Apparently Earth vehicles had defensive capabilities? He hadn't realized that. Whatever the vehicle was gearing up to do, its noise had distracted the Galateans. Rei took advantage of that instant of distraction to dash after Sarah and then duck behind another vehicle as another attack glistened over its surface. This didn't produce a new alarm, but the other was still wailing.

Some of the nearby Earth humans had sensibly taken cover. Others were holding up their communication devices, pointing them at the Galateans. Taking pictures? Preparing attacks of their own? It would do no good to shout at them; they couldn't understand him. Anyway, he doubted if the Galateans planned to injure the natives except in self-defense. They would be safe as long as they stayed out of the way.

An engine revved nearby. He hoped it was Sarah's truck. He just had to get to it—

With a tremendous thump and a snarl, the cat-shaped Galatean landed on top of the car, looming over Rei.

His fur was rusty orange, barred with black. Green eyes shot with gold, not so different from a Polaran's, gleamed at Rei over a snarling muzzle.

Rei brought up both hands and let him have it.

The Galatean almost managed to deflect it, flinging up his forepaws in an automatic defensive maneuver, except that the move itself threw him off balance since he was currently a quadruped. He fell forward and Rei's attack tore through his face and neck, sliding off the shield that the

Galatean had managed to bring up to protect part of his body—but not enough of it. He was dead before he hit the ground, stinking of burnt fur.

Rookie mistake, Rei thought numbly. They were probably just as unused to their enemies having Galatean weapons as Rei was. That was likely the last time he'd manage to get in a lucky shot at an unshielded enemy.

He closed his hands over the gold cuffs on the dead Galatean's paws. They resisted for a moment, but Rei poured mental energy into it, and the cuffs unlocked and came off in his hands. Gold ones were more powerful than silver. He could use the advantage.

The truck skidded to a stop beside him with a screech of tires. "Get in!" Sarah yelled through the open window.

Rei vaulted into the back. "Go!"

He crouched in the truck bed and deflected another attack. This one bubbled the paint on the truck's side as it slid off his shields. The first attacks had been meant to stun; now the remaining Galatean was using lethal force. Rei didn't blame him.

He didn't try to attack in return, just focused on shielding the truck as Sarah accelerated toward the swinging white-and-orange-striped bar blocking the exit to the street. She started to slow, then punched up their speed instead and slammed into it. The bar broke with a snap. Momentum flung Rei off his feet in a bruising tumble against the side of the truck as she cornered sharply and roared off down the street.

He sat up and looked back at the rapidly receding parking area. The alarm still wailed into the night. The Galatean was crouching over his dead crewmate; nearby humans had retreated into their vehicles. Then Sarah tore around a corner and Rei could no longer see them.

He looked down at the dead man's gold cuffs in his hands. They felt hot against his palms. He could still smell the searing scent of burning fur. He'd killed before in battle, but always while armored, always from a distance. He'd never fried anything up close except training robots.

But he hadn't even thought about it. Just fell back on his training, pushed the cuffs to full power and blew a hole in another living being.

Another living being who was going to take you back to slavery. Best-case scenario, you go back to being a slave, with an extra ten or twenty years tacked on for desertion. More likely, knowing what you know about this planet, they'll execute you.

He checked to make sure the gold cuffs were fully powered down, then slipped them into his pocket to deal with later. Already he felt tingling throughout his body as his nanites worked to replace the charge that he'd used in the fight.

The truck jolted to an abrupt stop, lurching under him as one tire went up onto the pedestrian walkway beside the street. "Get in!" Sarah called out her window. "You're too conspicuous back there. It's not legal to ride in a truck bed and we *really* don't want cops."

"Cops?" Rei asked as he climbed into the passenger side.

"Yeah, hear the sirens? They'll be all over that city lot in a minute. I hope they didn't have cameras back there." Sarah swallowed. Her hands were shaking on the truck's guidance wheel, and the realization struck Rei that this child of a safe and war-free world might never have been in a fight before, or even seen one.

"Are you all right?" he asked her.

"I'm fine." She swallowed again and pulled back onto the street. The truck wavered back and forth in its lane and then straightened out as she got control of herself. She glanced over at him, her face wan in the glow of the instrument panel. "How about you?"

"Unhurt." The stolen cuffs were still warm in his pocket, a reminder of what he'd done. In his initial escape, he hadn't hurt anyone. Now he'd killed a citizen. The likelihood they were going to even attempt to capture him alive had dropped to near zero.

But what else could he have done? They'd trained him as a killer. They had drilled him and drilled him in the training room to use lethal force in a fight. He'd almost instinctively fried Sarah when he first met her—might well have done so, if not for the cuffs being nonfunctional in the wake of Lyr's power surge. Nausea rolled in his stomach at the thought.

I will not be that, he thought, curling his hands into fists in his lap. *I will not be the killer they made me.*

But the Galateans might not give him a choice.

Sarah merged into the flow of vehicles on one of the fast roads she called highways, though they didn't seem much higher than the surrounding landscape. "Are they tracking us?" she asked anxiously. "Is it safe to go home? I don't know where to go, Rei."

"They are not tracking us." He checked again to make sure his cuffs were powered down, just to be on the safe side. "They were following us by scent before. They won't be able to do that now."

"Good. I don't want to lead them back to Dad."

Rei hoped to the gods he didn't believe in that they hadn't already done that. "I need to get my battlepod away from your farm. And myself with it."

"Rei, no. We're not going to abandon you to face this alone."

Fear and worry flared into anger. "Did you see what happened back there? Do you understand the threat you're up against? These people have weapons you cannot comprehend. Your people have no defenses against them. One Galatean with a pair of these—" He held up his hand, fist clenched, to display the silver gleam at his wrist. "— could kill hundreds of your people and lay waste to a city block. One of their ships, firing from above, could turn one of your cities to slag. And we have no idea how many of them are here."

"I think you underestimate humans," Sarah said, her voice flat. "We have guns. We have *armies*. We're not going to be that easy to invade."

"Sarah, your people are not going to risk war with an intergalactic empire to protect a fugitive who unlawfully stole himself and fled. I've seen what you call guns. Your father showed me how they work. Your little metal projectiles would bounce off our shields, and then we would effortlessly kill the person holding the weapon, because *they* have no shields. Do you understand?"

"We?" Sarah said. "*We* would kill—? You're not one of them."

"I was raised and trained to be! Anyway, does that matter now?"

"It matters! It matters a lot to me. We are *not* just handing you over—"

"I'm not asking you to—"

"—and we are not letting you run off into the night with a broken spaceship and—and two pieces of *wrist jewelry* to fight an intergalactic empire by yourself. You might have been alone all your life, Rei, but you're not alone now and I'm not going to let—I'm not going to—"

The truck veered and Rei realized with a shock that she was crying so hard she could no longer see the road.

"Sarah, please, be calm. Stop before you kill us."

He put a cautious hand on the wheel above hers. Sarah allowed the truck to be guided to the wide road-edge, pulling off as other vehicles roared past theirs in the night.

"I'm sorry," she mumbled, dashing at her eyes.

"You have nothing to apologize for." He slid nearer to her on the seat and pulled her against him—easily, readily; when had it become so easy to touch her? His people touched each other often, another thing he'd nearly forgotten about his childhood. It had been so hard to learn to live among the more reserved Galateans. As his sept left or died, one by one, and the remaining ones grew ever more tense and fragile, he'd learned to restrain himself until he almost didn't miss it anymore.

But Sarah unbuckled her restraint belt so she could throw her arms around him. She buried her head in his shoulder and pressed herself into him as if it was possible for two bodies to merge into one, and he held her back just as fiercely.

"I'll keep you safe," he promised into her hair. "I'll keep you and your father safe."

He had always been taught that soldiers, even slave soldiers, didn't learn to fight in order to kill. They learned to fight in order to protect. And that was what he meant to do. These people would not come to harm from helping him; he swore it.

"Oh! Dad! We need to warn him." Sarah pulled away, scrubbing at her eyes. She blew her nose on a paper towel from a roll she dug out from under the seat and then got out her phone. Still pressed up against Rei, with one of his arms around her, she tapped symbols on the screen and held the phone to her ear. He could hear a buzzing sound and then a voice, too low to make out the words.

Sarah frowned and tapped symbols again. She did this twice more before she put the phone back in her pocket and turned to Rei with worry on her tear-reddened face.

"No answer. I tried his cell and the land line. He's not picking up on either."

Rei didn't know what all of that meant, but it pointed to a likely possibility. "The farm might be compromised." He would not consider the possibility that Gary might be dead. He still felt it was more likely the Galateans would leave the natives unharmed, causing as little of a disturbance as possible.

Sarah nodded. "I'll understand if you don't want to go back. We could stop somewhere along the road, get a motel room, maybe. I can leave you there and go back myself—"

"Sarah." He gripped her hand tightly. "If you won't leave me, I won't leave you. We will go make sure your father is unharmed. I will not leave you to deal with this alone."

Sarah blew out her breath and slid over to the driver's seat. "Okay. Let's go get Dad."

"Together," he said.

"Yes. Together."

SIXTEEN

THE FEMALE AGENT, Pradhan, kept pacing and checking her phone.

"Got somewhere to be?" Gary asked dryly from the couch. Neither of the two agents answered. He hadn't expected them to.

They hadn't tried to tie him up or even arrest him. A guy could almost get annoyed at the way they'd instantly dismissed him as a threat, except he knew they were right. An old guy who walked with canes wasn't much to concern a couple of healthy young people. And they both had guns; he'd seen the bulge under the guy's jacket and had glimpsed Pradhan's when she'd frisked him and taken away his cell phone and stripped out the battery without a by-your-leave.

They had also unplugged the land line, even turned off the porch light to keep trick-or-treaters away. No way to get a message to Sarah and Rei. No way to tell them they'd be waltzing right into a trap.

He just hoped those two kids had a good time tonight, good enough to stay out all night. Get a hotel room in Eau Claire, don't even bother coming back 'til morning.

Not that it'd be any safer in the morning, but maybe he would have thought of some way to warn them by then.

Pradhan's phone buzzed with an incoming text. She glanced at it before tucking it into her pocket. "Incoming," she told her partner, who Gary had heard her address as Rhodes.

"Hooray," Rhodes said, leaning forward in Gary's favorite armchair to unwrap another piece of chocolate from the candy bowl on the coffee table.

Pradhan went to the window and looked out.

"You call for backup?" Gary said. "Can't handle one crippled old man by yourselves?"

He fell silent, looking up. There was a sound ... no, not a sound, more of a vibration. Similar to the deep vibrato of helicopter rotors as they flew over the house—the entire town of Sidonie had been getting used to that over the last week—but deeper, almost entirely beyond sound. It was more of a pressure, like the heaviness of air before a thunderstorm.

Pradhan let the front drape fall and walked swiftly toward the kitchen.

"Hey." Gary struggled to his feet.

Rhodes dropped the candy wrapper and tensed to get up. "You sit right back down, buddy."

Pradhan turned back from the kitchen doorway. "No, it's okay. Let him look. I'll keep an eye on him." She smiled at Gary. Pretty gal. Too bad she was a member of Club Fed, not to mention half his age with the gleam of a wedding band on her finger. "You're going to want to see this, Mr. Metzger."

"Better you than me," Rhodes said after them. "The less I see of those freaks, the better."

Gary reached for a walking stick. "Leave those," Pradhan said.

"I can't walk without 'em."

"They're also a weapon."

"C'mon, lady, what do you think I'm gonna do, use my karate moves to overpower you? I'm a sixty-four-year-old guy with a back injury."

The sense of heaviness and pressure was greater now, making his head ache. Pradhan looked like she was feeling it too. "Okay, yeah, whatever," she said, but watched him carefully as he limped to her with the stick in his hand.

When she turned around to go into the kitchen, Gary gave a passing thought to whacking her over the head with it. Trouble was, *she* probably knew all the karate moves he didn't. And there was still her partner back there with a gun.

So he didn't, and they went into the kitchen together. Pradhan opened the back door. "Stay here," she told Gary.

"Where you think I'm gonna run to?" he asked, with a pointed look at the cane in his hand.

Outside, night had fallen, dark as the inside of a black cat. It wasn't raining, but the air had the clammy thickness that meant it wanted to. Good night for Halloween, if not a good night for the county's trick-or-treaters, but all of that flew out of Gary's head at the sight of something in the pasture that wasn't supposed to be there.

Lights.

They weren't bright. A string of dim red and amber running lights traced out the lower edge of something big and dark that was just settling down in the pasture. Warm air rushed past Gary's face out of the cool night, blowing his hair back.

"What the heck is that thing?" He squinted as if he

could make his eyes pierce the darkness through sheer willpower alone. The yard lights penetrated only dimly back here, but as his eyes adjusted, he could make out the rough outline of the dark shape against the grass just as the red and gold running lights winked out. Its surface was faintly reflective, and it was too big to be a helicopter. Anyway, it hadn't made any noise, none at all except the heaviness which was gone now. And he didn't think it was his imagination that it had been in the air when he'd first seen it. It had flown here, not driven.

"What do you *think* it is, Mr. Metzger?" Agent Pradhan's voice was soft, and she was leaning forward intently. One of her hands, Gary noticed, had crept under her jacket to touch her gun.

Sudden bright light appeared in a door-sized block against the dark backdrop of the ...

Okay, fine, let's just call it what it is: it's a spaceship, a goddamn pardon-my-French spaceship sitting in my cow pasture, and those people walking out of it right now are probably more of Rei's blue guys.

They'd found Rei.

There were four of them, each one built like a brick outhouse. The door in the side of the ship closed behind them, and as they strode toward the ranch house, Gary kept revising his mental estimate of how big they were. Taller than NBA basketball players, wider than linebackers. The fact that two of them were female didn't seem to make an ounce of difference; the women were brick walls just as much as the guys. By the time they reached the back porch, Gary was trying to come to terms with the fact that all three of them were close to eight feet tall and probably three-fifty, four hundred pounds of pure muscle.

And they weren't Rei's type of alien. These guys were

big cats. He'd seen alien cat people like that on the cover of one of Sarah's science fiction novels once. The fellow in the lead was a lion-type guy; he even had a sort of mane. The others were a tawny-colored woman, a woman with tiger stripes, and a leopard-spotted guy.

Pradhan stepped forward, interposing her own body between Gary and the aliens as they reached the back porch.

"Sergeant Kyaroi," she said, pronouncing the word carefully. "This is Mr. Gary Metzger, and this residence belongs to him and his family. The Metzgers, their livestock, and their property are not to be harmed in the search for your deserter, are we clear?"

The lion-man, Kyaroi, answered with a flood of liquid syllables. Gary couldn't understand a word, and he also couldn't tell if it was Rei's language with a different accent, or a different alien language entirely.

Pradhan seemed to understand perfectly, which meant she either had one of those same things Rei had put in Sarah's head, or she'd known the cat-people long enough to learn their language. Whatever he'd said made her scowl.

Damn it, Gary thought. *And here I never used to listen to Sal Prouty down at the feed store when he'd go on about how the government was covering up alien moon landings. Looks like I owe ol' Sal an apology.*

"It was my understanding that your organization and mine would be working jointly on this," Pradhan said.

Kyaroi jerked his head at the lion-woman. She nodded and went past Pradhan, shouldering her unceremoniously out of the way. Gary moved hastily aside; the woman didn't even look at him and gave him the impression she would have gone through him if he hadn't moved. She was tall enough that she had to duck to avoid bumping her head in the kitchen doorway.

"As a representative of Earth—" Pradhan began. Her hand had drifted near the butt of her gun. Kyaroi reached out, almost casually, and gripped her wrist.

Inside the house, there was a sudden yell—Gary jumped— followed by a thump, and silence.

"Get your hands off me," Pradhan said softly. She didn't look nearly as freaked out as Gary expected any reasonable person to be with eight feet of alien cat monster looming over them.

Kyaroi said a few words, his voice low and calm, but Pradhan's face twisted in fury. She lashed a foot out at Kyaroi's ankle; he blocked it. Gary moved hastily as far from them as he could get in the confines of the porch, mentally calculating his distance from the one gun on the property, a shotgun he used for duck hunting, which was stored in the basement. No chance, he thought.

Pradhan lost her brief scuffle with the alien leader, leaving her with a bruise on her cheek and her gun and phone in Kyaroi's hands. At a word from him, the tiger-woman moved forward and shoved both of them unceremoniously back into the house. Once again Gary found himself being escorted through his own kitchen, this time in the opposite direction.

In the living room, Pradhan's partner was slumped in the armchair while the lion-woman prowled the room, looking at everything. Pradhan cried out in dismay and hurried to him, kneeling to feel his pulse. Gary simply sat down on the couch. Still wasn't much he could do. He didn't think Rhodes was dead; he could see the agent's chest rising and falling from here.

Pradhan had a brief, angry exchange with the two alien

women that ended with her being frog-marched to the couch and made to sit beside Gary.

Despite his fear for Rei and Sarah, who would be walking straight into an even more dire trap than he'd feared, Gary couldn't resist twisting the knife. "Still think it's a good idea making deals with aliens?"

Pradhan gave him a flat look. "Shut up."

DRIVING on the familiar highway helped calm Sarah's nerves somewhat, but it also freed her mind to keep replaying the fight in vivid detail. She gripped the wheel tightly, turned the radio to a talk station to see if anyone was going to mention the appearance of aliens in downtown Eau Claire, and most importantly, tried to keep Rei from seeing how shaky she still was.

It's so stupid. What's wrong with me? I shouldn't be reacting like this. I've helped butcher chickens since I was a kid, I sat with my mom when she was dying ...

But there was something different about having someone come after her with intent to kill. She kept seeing the green light shattering on the air in front of them, the flash of the alien tiger's fangs as it sprang after Rei.

"Are there tools in this vehicle?"

Rei's quiet voice jerked her out of her thoughts. "There's a toolbox behind the seat," she said.

Rei knelt on the seat and rummaged behind it. After that, he was quiet again. Sarah glanced over a few miles down the road. With a small flashlight clamped between his knees, he was working with a small screwdriver on one of his bracelets.

... no, he was still wearing both his bracelets. This one was gold.

"Where did you get that?"

"From the Galatean soldier I killed."

Apparently she'd missed some of the fight while she was starting the truck. "I didn't see that. How many of them were there?"

"Two," Rei said absently. His tongue poked briefly out of the corner of his mouth as he concentrated on prying something out of the bracelet; despite the circumstances, she couldn't help finding it cute. "The one I shot was the transformed one."

"The—wait, do you mean the *tiger* was a Galatean?"

"You know that I can shift. The Galateans have *jaegan* among them as well."

Stupid genetics-meddling super-powerful ancient aliens. "I thought it was some kind of bloodhound. Uh, a tracking beast, I mean."

"It was also that." Rei clicked the gold bracelet around his wrist above the usual silver cuff, then started tinkering with the a second gold one.

"What are you doing?"

"Among other things, I'm trying to ensure that I don't give away my position as soon as I activate these. They should be subsidiary to my usual cuffs, but this will give me much more power than I would normally have."

One Galatean with a pair of these could kill hundreds of your people and lay waste to a city block ...

"How many Galateans do you think are here?" Sarah asked, her mouth dry.

"Small military ships usually have a crew of six or eight. It depends on how many ships are here. I don't think they would send a heavy cruiser just to recover an escaped slave."

"How many on a heavy cruiser?"

"Around three to five thousand if it has a full complement of troops."

"Okay, yeah, wow, let's hope they don't have one of those."

She slowed at the outskirts of Sidonie. Nothing looked different than usual, but what did she expect: the town under martial law, swarming with cat aliens?

A white blur appeared suddenly in her headlights, and Sarah slammed on the brakes, then sat shivering in reaction as a party of costumed children, accompanied by a cheerful retriever and an older child as chaperone, ran across the road. A sheet ghost was what had flashed in her headlights.

"Will there be a great many children out of their homes tonight?" Rei asked as they started moving again. There was a small click as the second gold cuff closed around his wrist.

"Not for much longer. It's starting to get late enough that little kids are going to be in bed, even on Halloween night."

They were nearing the farm. She'd tried to call her dad a couple more times on the way and each time it went to voice mail. And yet, there were no roadblocks, no signs of anything amiss as she left the town behind for the deeper darkness of farm country. Only a paranoid worry buzzing in the back of her head that this wasn't like him, he wouldn't be out of touch this long.

Maybe it's nothing to do with the Galateans at all. Maybe he left his phone in the house while he was out working in the barn. Maybe he fell and couldn't get up, and he's been lying in the pasture all this time, while I was out on a date ...

The driveway was coming up on her left. She began to

brake, and then just as smoothly accelerated again, sweeping on past with her heart beating like a triphammer.

"The porch light's not on," she told Rei. "And there's a car out front I don't recognize."

Rei twisted around to look out the back window. "Your people, not mine?"

"Unless your people use cars now. It could just be trick-or-treaters, but the light's not on, and Dad *always* leaves the light on. He never forgets, he didn't even forget the year Mom died. Damn it!"

There was another turn coming up on the left. She slowed and took it. The truck swayed on deep ruts.

"Where are we going?" Rei asked.

"We're on an old road that goes up the back side of the Haverford farm, the neighbors next to our place. I used to be friends with their daughter when we were kids." She paused to concentrate on not getting the truck mired in a boggy place. The road was in much worse shape than it had been the last time she came this way, and it had been a wet fall. "We can drive through their back hayfield and park behind the old mill. Actually we might be able to drive all the way through our pasture to the house, if we can find a place to get the truck through the fence and it's not too over-grown back there, but I don't want to try. We don't know what we'd be driving into."

"Approach on foot and leave an escape vehicle at our back." Rei sounded approving. "You're a good tactical thinker for one who has never been in battle, Sarah."

Sarah hoped she wasn't blushing, but she knew she probably was. "Is it possible you could ... uh ..." She reached out to point at his bracelets. "Since you have an extra set now, could you give one of those to me and teach me how to use it?"

Rei shook his head. "I'm sorry. It won't work for you. You would need nanites and implants."

"Damn," she muttered. Briefly, she wished they kept a gun in the truck, as some of their neighbors did, but her dad had never been that type.

Anyway, from what Rei said and what she'd seen in Eau Claire, a gun might not be much help anyway.

She stopped to let them through the Haverfords' pasture gate. They jolted through tall grass, the truck rocking as it hit unseen ruts in the darkness. The Haverfords hadn't cut this field in years, from the look of it, and Sarah parked when it finally got too rough to drive, in the edge of a stand of brush and small trees along the property line with the Metzger farm.

"The mill is right on the other side of that fence," she told Rei quietly as she stepped down from the truck. She reached behind the seat and felt around until she found a tire iron.

"That's not going to be much use against energy weapons."

"Maybe not, but it makes me feel better."

Once she closed the door and the truck's dome light went off, it was utterly dark. Light from the town reflected off the low clouds and cast a dim, orangey light that her eyes slowly adapted to. Down at the bottom of the gently sloping pasture, the Haverfords' cluster of house and yard lights had a warm, homey look. Sarah wished she was heading that way instead of into the dark woods to face aliens or the Army or God only knew what.

With a small sigh, she squared her shoulders and followed Rei into the dark woods.

She regretted instantly that she was wearing a dress instead of jeans. Her legs were freezing, and the skirt kept snagging on brambles. It wasn't actually raining, but every-thing was damp, and even the dim town-glow was lost among the trees. She had to grope her way by feel, while roots tangled her impractical shoes and branches snatched at her hair.

She stumbled into the wooden fence rail and climbed over it, thinking of the long-ago days when she used to do that to go play with Susie Haverford. At the time, however, she hadn't been doing it in a skirt while cold and wet and carrying a tire iron.

"You're still here, right?" she whispered.

"I am still here, Sarah," Rei's quiet voice came out of the dark. He was perfectly silent. If he hadn't spoken, she would never have been able to find him.

The darkness was weirdly disorienting. She knew the farm as well as she knew her own face in the mirror, but without landmarks to guide her, she had to struggle to orient herself. She could hear the millstream, and she knew the mill was around here somewhere, but it seemed to appear out of nowhere, a dark shape framed against the faint amber glow in the sky. They'd come upon it from downstream rather than approaching directly from the back as she'd thought.

Rei touched her arm to stop her. He leaned close enough that she could feel the warmth of his body and see the faint shine of his eyes in the dark. "You must stay very close to me now," he murmured. "If my people are here, they will be able to detect us approaching by our body heat and other traces. I can shield us from that sort of detection, but only if you are very near."

Sarah felt in the dark until she found his hand and wrapped hers around it. His fingers felt very warm to her cold ones. "I will be."

REI ADAPTED his pace to Sarah's, exerting a small effort of will to keep her shielded along with himself. The sensor shielding was low-power enough that he could keep it up for hours, and it was passive, making it unlikely the Galateans would be able to detect his nearby use of the cuffs. He still didn't dare use the cuffs' scanning or communication functions, but he was fairly sure everything else was safe enough, including the weapons. The Galateans weren't used to having their own tech used against them.

However, there might also be sentries out here that *he* couldn't detect. Good to keep that in mind.

They crossed the stream with Sarah's small, cold fingers quiescent in his. Rei's eyes had fully adapted to the dark by now, and he could see clearly, if a bit fuzzily. Sarah seemed to be almost completely night-blind, so he guided her with small tugs of his hand as they retraced the path they'd taken a few days ago when she had first shown him the old mill.

Pleasant memories ... to be recalled at a later, less desperate time.

If there was a later.

They came out of the trees behind the Metzger farm. Sarah let out a tiny gasp just as Rei jerked on her hand to pull her down beside him. Maybe she could see in the dark more than he'd thought.

There was a Galatean ship parked in the long expanse of Metzger pasture between them and the house.

It was dark, all lights off, but he could see it well enough to tell that it was a mid-size chaser, an elongated teardrop shape with a pointed prow and smoothly rounded sides flaring out into stubby winglike extensions just ahead of the engines. Eight crew, probably, on a ship that size. He couldn't tell from this angle if either of the two skimmers were docked to the back of the wings in their usual location. Most likely, the team in Eau Claire had taken one of those, unless there was a second chaser in the area.

"Is that a spaceship?" Sarah whispered.

"Yes," Rei whispered back.

"Galateans?"

"Yes. Let me think, please."

The lights in the house were on. Some of the crew must be down there, probably with Sarah's father. Unless Gary was—but no; Rei refused to consider it. They weren't here to conquer, so they wouldn't want trouble. They were just here to recapture an escaped slave.

Unless they were *also* here to conquer. It was possible he'd led the Galateans straight to an undeveloped world they would happily add to their empire. But that wasn't a problem he could afford to deal with right now. Anyway, they clearly weren't out for conquest at the moment, not with one small ship.

With two soldiers in Eau Claire, that left six here, possibly seven if the survivor of the Eau Claire team had managed to return—

"Rei!" Sarah whispered, squeezing his hand.

She was looking back the way they'd come. Rei took in what was coming at a single glance and threw an arm over her, pressing them both to the damp ground and trying to stay as still as possible.

A skimmer swept over them, no more than fifteen feet off the ground. If the crew had looked down at just the right moment, they could easily have made a visual identification of the two intruders. Rei waited, heart in mouth, as the skimmer descended and vanished behind the chaser's wings, settling into place.

Sarah stirred after a moment, pressing closer to whisper to Rei, "Coming back from Eau Claire?"

"Probably." The chances were now quite good that they only had the one chaser to deal with. But he was still outnumbered seven to one.

... or seven to two, counting Sarah. Though he didn't know how much help she could be. Sarah was brave and intelligent, but she had no weapons or skills that would be useful. Her people were like his people had been when the Galateans came, clever but vastly outclassed by superior technology. Like the people of his village, Sarah didn't seem to understand the magnitude of the threat she was up against. Hopefully, unlike them, she would figure it out before it was too late.

The ship, he decided, would need to be their first target. It had powerful weapons, powerful sensors, and most likely the majority of the Galateans were on board. If they could take the ship, they might actually win this.

"Sarah," he whispered. "I need you to stay here—"

"Like hell," she whispered back fiercely.

He wanted her safe, but it wasn't worth fighting about. "All right, then stay behind me. In a fight, my shields will also protect you, and you won't be in the way of my weapons."

Sarah nodded and tightened her grip on the useless, primitive piece of iron she'd decided to bring with her.

They both rose to a crouch, and then Rei immediately pushed them down to the ground again when something moved off to his left. At first it seemed no more than a darker shadow detaching itself from the woods. Then he made out the shape of a Galatean striding across the pasture toward the ship with a predator's easy grace.

There had indeed been a sentry, and Rei hadn't even

seen him. His blood ran cold; they could so easily have stumbled onto him in the woods. By sheer chance he'd been stationed on the other side of the ship, across the pasture from the mill. The Galateans, unfamiliar with the area, didn't know there was anything else back here.

"Rei?" Sarah whispered. Night-blind, she probably hadn't seen the sentry at all yet.

"Shhh." Rei squeezed her hand and waited. The sentry vanished under the wing of the ship. There was a brief flare of light on the pasture grass—he felt Sarah flinch in surprise—that faded immediately as the door closed.

Rei waited a few moments longer to make sure it wasn't a shift change, but no one else came out, unless they were hidden on the house side. Since the Eau Claire party had come back, the sentry had probably returned for some kind of briefing.

Which meant there were now at least two more enemies in the ship than there had been a few minutes ago. Damn it.

It wasn't like waiting was going to make things better, though.

"Stay behind me, remember," he whispered to Sarah, and she nodded.

They moved swiftly through the grass toward the ship, Sarah a step behind with one of her hands resting lightly against his elbow. Rei felt hideously exposed under the too-large sky—anyone looking out at the right moment could see them—but they reached the ship without incident.

It sat flush against the ground in a wide circle of torn-up grass, marking the concussion radius of the anti-gravity repulsor shockwave from its landing. From a distance, the surface of the ship had looked opalescent and smooth, but up close the individual seams of the hull plates could be seen, as well as the inevitable damage that every ship accumulated from interstellar debris and from atmospheric landings like this one: small scratches and pits, burn marks, and charring along the lower edge of the ship's bottom skirt.

Sarah started to reach out to touch it. Rei caught her hand and lowered it back to her side.

She looked at him, wide-eyed. He touched his finger to his lips.

Whether or not the ship had a warning system that could detect intruders touching it from the outside, they'd find out in a minute, but he didn't want to risk tipping his hand before he was ready.

Instead he moved slowly along the curving line of the ship's hull, trying to reconstruct its internal structure from memory. He hadn't been inside chaser-type ships all that often; most of his life had been spent on the big cruisers or in battlepods. But he'd studied the layouts of all the common types of Galatean ships. They were generally built along very similar plans, for ease of manufacture at the big shipyards and to make it easier for personnel to switch between assignments. The Galateans were very focused on efficiency and modular interchangeability in their technology. The cargo areas should be just in front of the skimmer docking pods, on the lower deck of the ship—

The skimmers. Hmmm.

Both of them were docked in place, one under each wing. He'd originally planned on cutting through the chaser's hull, but that would take awhile and run down the charge on his cuffs. The skimmers, intended for traveling short distances in atmosphere, weren't even armored, and they were much less likely to have some kind of alarm system to detect tampering.

He drew Sarah's attention by touching her arm and

tapped his finger to his lips again to make sure she stayed quiet. She nodded and went back to staring up, wide-eyed, at the chaser's wings and engines. That's right, she'd never seen an actual ship before. She had been fascinated enough by the battlepod. He wished he could watch the play of fascination and wonder on her expressive features, rather than having to look out for hostile Galatean soldiers.

He powered up one of his newly augmented cuffs and poured the energy down his fingertips, concentrating it through the implants under his fingernails into a fine laser beam. It cut into the skimmer's hull with a sharp sizzle and a piercing smell of hot metal. Sarah transferred her amazed fascination from the engines to Rei using his hand as a cutting torch, as Rei cut a porthole in the skimmer's side just back of where he guessed the pilot's seat to be.

"Hold this for me," Rei whispered. Sarah planted her hands against the section he was cutting out, and helped him catch and lower it to the ground as it came free. She leaned forward to look into the small ship's dark interior.

Rei pointed to the red-hot, bubbling metal along the edge, and mimed caution. Sarah nodded, but that didn't stop her from staring into the skimmer's small cockpit with interest normally reserved for things that were, well, interesting.

But then, he'd been equally curious about her vehicle. Unfamiliarity bred fascination.

Rei stripped out of his thick sweater and used it to cover the sharp, hot metal edges so Sarah, with her bare legs, could crawl inside without hurting herself. He followed her and pulled the sweater in after them.

The lights came up automatically as they crawled inside. The skimmer was the same as the ones he'd learned to fly during his pilot training, a two-seater with a small cargo area and an airlock connected to the ship at the back.

He could just fire it up, he thought. No need for a fight. They could flee instead ...

—abandoning Gary, abandoning the farm, and leaving an enemy with a much bigger, faster, better-armed ship free to hunt them. No. Flying away would only delay the inevitable confrontation and give the Galateans time to summon reinforcements. Best to take them now, with the element of surprise.

Rei tapped the skimmer's airlock control experimentally, expecting it to be locked, but it cycled neatly onto the ship's cargo hold. He flung up his shields to cover himself and Sarah. No attack came. The hold was empty except for the expected crates and barrels of supplies, lashed neatly into place. There was also a tidy row of Galatean-height capsules arrayed vertically along the outer wall. Good thing he hadn't tried to cut through the hull there; it would have taken forever.

"What are those?" Sarah whispered as they crept silently from the skimmer into the cargo bay.

"Stasis pods." Used to contain prisoners or injured crew members, they could also be used as emergency escape pods and ejected to be picked up later. Small ships like this one typically carried enough to accommodate all of the citizen crew members. There were eight pods here, which confirmed his guess about the number of crew, now minus the one he'd killed in Eau Claire.

Sarah moved closer to the pods. At first he thought she was just curious—he was busy checking the charge on his cuffs—until she gave a soft gasp. "Rei, there's someone in one of those pods."

Rei moved instinctively, blocking her progress with an

arm, even though there was no way someone in a func-
tioning stasis pod could get out and attack them. She was
right; the first in the row of pods had a panel of lights and a
dim figure behind the transparent lid. Galatean, judging
from the height—well, Galatean or dragon, but he doubted
the pods would work on one of Lyr's people.

"Why is he in there?" Sarah asked, staring curiously at
the man in the pod.

"Could be a prisoner or a wounded member of the
crew." Rei moved close enough to determine that the sleeper
wasn't wearing a Galatean army uniform; instead he wore a
long leather coat, beat up and scarred with what looked like
old knife slashes. "Not crew. Must be a criminal they picked
up. They could've been pulled off another job to come hunt
me." He turned away; the prisoner was no threat to them,
and therefore need not be given further consideration. "I
don't suppose I can convince you to stay here."

"I want to help," Sarah said, tightening her grip on the
iron bar.

Perhaps she could be useful, as a distraction if nothing
else. "Very well, but stay behind me." He slipped off his
shoes, breathing a sigh of relief at the feeling of the deck
under his bare toes, and set out quietly down the cargo hold.

The hold ran the entire length of the ship's lower deck,
with the hulking mass of the shielded engine core in the
middle. As in the skimmer, the hold's lights came up automatically as they crept through it. Above them would be
crew quarters and the small amount of recreational space
that a ship like this could accommodate, with the bridge up
front.

There was a big lift in the back for raising heavy cargo,
and two man-sized access ports, one on each side of the
hold. Both trap doors were closed, with ladders leading up

to them. It was just a matter of picking the one less likely to lead to a bunch of Galateans—

"Rei!" Sarah whispered, but he'd already heard it: the clatter of metal as one of the ports opened.

With the lights on in the cargo hold, they didn't have much chance of concealing their presence. Rei powered up his cuffs as he dashed forward and stunned the tiger-striped Galatean soldier who was just setting her boots on the ladder. The woman folded up like a rag doll and plunged down the ladder. Rei caught her, knocking them both to the deck with a bruising impact.

Sarah scrambled up the ladder and struggled with the mechanism for a moment before figuring out how to pull the trap door shut. The whole thing took seconds.

Rei touched his finger to his lips. Sarah nodded. They both remained quiet for a moment, listening, but apparently it hadn't made enough noise to draw attention. The whole ship had pretty good soundproofing—useful when you were trapped in a confined space with a bunch of other people, but not so great when intruders were sneaking around on your ship. Rei made a mental note of that.

"Did you kill her?" Sarah asked softly.

Rei shook his head. "Just stunned. Quick, help me get her into one of the pods."

"Even the women are huge," Sarah murmured as Rei heaved the female Galatean over his shoulder. His strength enhancements were up to the task, but only just. "Are they all like this?"

"Most of them. Haiva was very short for a Galatean, but still taller than me." He grunted, dropping the woman on the deck next to an empty pod. "There are rumors the Galateans tinkered with their own genetics to make themselves into bigger, stronger warriors. I don't know if it's true."

Sarah took the woman's feet and helped Rei maneuver her into the pod next to the one with the prisoner. "You know, it's not that I *want* you to run around killing people, but ... is this really a good idea? All their friends have to do is let them out."

"I'll kill if I must, but I'd rather not. They're just soldiers doing their job. As far as they know, they're apprehending an escaped criminal."

"Escaped slave," Sarah said, her voice flat.

"They're still only following orders. Like I would be in their position. It's not their fault."

Before closing the pod, Rei stripped off the woman's cuffs and the power pack belted to her waist. He looked for a way to time-lock the pod so it couldn't be opened at all, but was unable to find anything, so he turned it to its maximum setting. Between stun and stasis, she would be severely groggy if anyone let her out, so that would have to do.

"What's that?" Sarah asked as he buckled the belt around his waist.

"Backup power for the cuffs. No need to wait until they recharge off my metabolism and—" He flashed her a quick grin. "—it makes a bigger bang."

"Big bangs are definitely what we need right now. Eight pods, so that means six more Galateans, right?"

She'd even thought to account for the dead one in Eau Claire; Rei smiled. "Yes. Most of them will be in the ship above us. Perhaps some are in the house with your father." And there it was: the perfect way to get her out of the line of fire. "We need to know where he is and how many are in the house. You can go down and scout while I take out the ones in the ship."

Sarah gave him a suspicious look as if she knew full well

what he was up to. "You said they can scan for life signs. Won't they see me coming?"

"You're a native and a noncombatant, and if it's just you by yourself, they may well mistake you for one of your domestic animals. Anyway, if they find you, they'll only capture you. Galateans have a strict code of conduct for prisoners—at least prisoners who aren't trying to attack them." He pointed at the iron bar. "Leave that here."

Sarah clutched it tighter. "I don't think so."

The Galateans might not even consider it a weapon. He probably wouldn't have, a week ago. "Fine, if it makes you feel better—oof!"

She kissed him first, fierce and passionate, and then hugged him until his ribs ached, the iron bar pressing into his spine. "The only reason I'm letting you talk me into this," she said into his chest, "is because I know you'll be able to fight better without having to protect me. So this way I can help Dad, *and* help you—just, you'd better not do anything stupid if I'm not here to stop you, okay? No pushing self-destruct buttons or throwing yourself in front of energy blasts. You're going to beat those bastards."

He held her tightly against him, felt the living warmth of her, the beating of her heart against his chest. "I'm not in the habit of doing stupid things," he murmured into her hair, and very deliberately did not think about the way he'd jumped his ship to unknown coordinates a week ago, the way some small part of him had almost *hoped* he'd jump into a supernova or collide with a planet ...

Now he could hardly relate to that desperate, hopeless person. He wanted to live. He wanted to *win*.

Sarah gave a choked little laugh. "You'd better not."

"Take your own advice too. Don't do anything stupid." There was nothing he wanted less than to pry himself out of her arms, but he separated regretfully and stepped back. "I must hurry before they discover their missing comrade. Go, Sarah, quickly."

Sarah started to open her mouth, then closed it and gave him a small, fierce nod, her lips clamped into a bloodless line. With both hands wrapped around the iron bar, she vanished into the skimmer.

Rei turned the other way to find the rest of the crew.

SEVENTEEN

AT THE SOFT thump of Sarah landing on the ground outside the ship, Rei felt a weight lift off his shoulders. It wasn't precisely safe for her to be outside, but right now, the least safe place on the farm was anywhere near him.

He started toward the nearest ladder, but then hesitated, and turned back toward the stasis pods. Even if some of the crew were in the house and not the ship, he was badly outnumbered. As the saying went, a stranded lifepod couldn't be choosy about where it landed. He needed all the help he could get.

And there was one other person on the ship who probably had as little liking for the Galatean army as Rei himself.

This is a terrible idea, Rei thought as he tapped keys, setting the prisoner's pod into a wakeup cycle.

The pod hissed open. Rei jumped back and powered up his cuffs, aiming both hands at the leather-clad Galatean. He needn't have worried. The prisoner tumbled out and fell face-first on the floor with a thud that made Rei wince in sympathy.

•

Keeping one of his hands ready for a quick stun if needed, Rei bent down and pushed up the sleeves of the leather coat to ensure that the prisoner's arms were bare of weapons. They were, though a shiny band was worn through the tawny fur of each wrist where a cuff had been until recently. The prisoner had no slave collar, nor signs of one.

The Galatean was a shaggy-haired lion type, huge even lying down. When he groaned and began to stir, Rei danced quickly back on light feet, cuffs at the ready.

"Attack me and I'll blow your head off," Rei said quietly. "Can you get up?"

After a hesitation, the Galatean pushed himself up to his hands and knees, then lurched unsteadily to his feet. Even wobbly from stasis hangover, he looked like somebody Rei didn't want to take on a fight, body-mods or not. His face was scarred with a set of parallel gouges like claw marks, scoring his cheek from just below his left eye to his jawline. They weren't fresh; the scars had faded to silvery, hairless lines in the tawny fuzz on his face.

"Who are you?" the Galatean asked, his voice raspy from the after-effects of stasis.

"Someone who'd like your help taking down the crew of this ship. Are you in?"

The Galatean smiled grimly, showing pointed canines. "I'm in. Name's Jeren."

"Rei."

Before he could say anything else, there was a clang of metal from the trap door where he'd stunned the Galatean woman. Rei grabbed Jeren's massive arm and pulled him behind a row of strapped-down barrels, where they both ducked out of sight.

"Suvi?" a male voice called.

Rei risked a glance around the barrels. A leopard-spotted male Galatean was just stepping off the ladder with his shields powered up; Rei could tell by the faint, opalescent glimmer on his skin when he moved, like the surface of a soap bubble. Even at full power, Rei wouldn't be able to penetrate those shields on his first couple of shots.

The shields were proof against energy attacks, but weren't nearly as effective versus blunt-force trauma, and trying to shield against it was a much greater power drain. Rei took a thoughtful, longer look at the barrels in front of him. According to the labels, they were filled with nutrient slurry for the ship's galley. Nothing explosive or incendiary. He was probably strong enough to pick up a full barrel, but he couldn't throw it, especially not that far.

However, right next to him, hanging on the wall, were a pair of power grippers for moving cargo.

Rei unhooked them from the wall. Each was a handle with its own small powerpack. He cut the barrels loose from the cargo restraints with a swipe of his cuffs' cutting torch and took a handle in each hand. Activated with a quick squeeze, they clamped onto the first barrel, a self-contained energy field holding them in place.

Rei hoisted it, stepped out from behind the row of barrels and reversed the grippers' charge at full power. The barrel shot from his hands as if from a catapult, slammed into the Galatean soldier, and smashed him into the wall.

Without the shields, he would have been a smear of paste on the wall. Even with the shields, he'd be reeling. Rei clamped onto another barrel and charged across the cargo bay, holding it in front of him like a shield. With the grippers buffering the barrel's weight, it felt moderately heavy and strangely unwieldy, like carrying something using a pair of forks.

The Galatean soldier rolled over and pushed the barrel off himself, just in time to be met full-force by a second barrel with Rei on the other side of it. Rei slammed the Galatean's head into the wall with the weight of another full load of nutrient slurry.

After a second blow from the now-dented barrel, the Galatean's shields flickered and vanished as he passed out. Rei stunned him on low power just to be on the safe side, then dragged him to the pods.

Jeren loomed at his shoulder. "You leaving him alive?"

"If I can, yes."

The big Galatean snorted. "Bad idea," he remarked, and reached for their prisoner's limp wrists, stripping off the soldier's cuffs to clasp them onto his own wrists.

"It's my call," Rei said, tensing. Now his maybe-ally was huge, dangerous, *and* armed. *Who have I allied myself with?* Jeren could be a rapist, a murderer, a slave-trader; there was no telling what list of crimes had gotten him locked up in that pod.

"Up to you." Jeren didn't interfere as Rei pushed the soldier into one of the empty pods and closed it. "But don't start crying if I kill a couple of 'em myself."

"Self-defense is fine. They'll be trying to kill us too."

Jeren didn't answer. He pointed at the open hatch, spilling light down from the ship's living area above them. "Your takedown wasn't quiet. They'll know we're here."

"I know." They had mere moments before the Galateans remaining on the ship worked out some kind of plan for dealing with the intruders they now knew were below them.

"Are we in space or on a planet?"

"Planet," Rei said. "Breathable atmosphere."

"Then we rig the engine core to blow and take a skim-mer. Get 'em all that way."

Rei shook his head. "I want the ship intact." Right now there was exactly one ship on this entire planet capable of interstellar flight, and he wasn't giving it up. "You can take a skimmer if you want. You don't have to stay."

Now it was Jeren's turn to shake his shaggy head. "I owe you an honor-debt for getting me out of that pod. Anyway ..." The sharp-toothed, feline grin flashed again. "I owe *them* for putting me in it in the first place. Let's go collect on it."

SARAH DROPPED out of the hole in the side of the space-ship—*a real SPACESHIP!* a part of her brain shrieked at her, not for the first time—and hit wet pasture grass in her imprac-tical, pretty shoes. One of them immediately jinked side-ways. Sarah wobbled and caught herself, clutching at sharp metal edges that scored the edge of her palm, and managed not to twist an ankle. Barely. She touched her tongue to the cut flesh at the side of her hand, decided it wasn't too bad, and clenched her hand into a fist to stop it from bleeding.

"Screw you, pretty shoes," she muttered, kicking them off. Rei had the right idea.

On quiet bare feet, she ran through the night toward the house.

Either the Galateans didn't detect her, or they consid-ered her no threat, because there were no lights or shouts or laser beams spearing the night. She crouched next to the raspberry bushes beside the back porch to think about her next move.

It was quiet enough out here that she could hear faint

voices inside the house, though she couldn't make out what they were saying or whether one of them was her dad's. The spaceship sitting in the pasture made no noise at all— though, she thought, a parked car wouldn't either. It was little more than a greater area of darkness against the dark pasture. Sarah wished she could see it by daylight.

She crept around the side of the house, crabwalking to stay under the level of the windows, and paused again at the base of the maple tree outside her second-floor bedroom window. As a kid she used to come and go that way all the time, not so much to sneak out—Sarah hadn't been a sneaking-out kind of kid—but just because climbing the tree was more fun than using the door.

She was no longer the agile little monkey that she'd been at age eight. Also, the tree had lost the big branch that used to extend toward the porch, the one that she always used to hop onto so she could reach the branch just below the one outside her window. Without that first stair-step, the trunk loomed above her like a cliff.

But she was also taller and stronger than she had been at eight.

Sarah stood up slowly with the tree between her and the house. The bark was rough and corrugated, with all the old limb scars and knots that aging trees accumulate. It shouldn't be impossible to climb, though doing it quietly was the trick. She regretfully laid the tire iron among the old tree roots. Stretching, she dug her fingers into the bark as high as she could reach and wedged her bare toes into an old knothole.

As she cautiously trusted her weight to her fingers and toes, her dad's old tree-climbing lessons came back to her. *You got two hands and two legs, Sarah, so make sure you've always got your weight on three of 'em before you let go with the fourth one.*

Three points of contact at all times, she translated into the lingo of adult, college-educated Sarah. That wasn't so hard. Set both feet, make sure she had a good handhold, then move her other hand up. Repeat with one of her feet. Next hand. Next foot.

Like the little monkey she'd once been, she crept up the tree, one handhold and toehold at a time.

Getting onto the branch outside the window was harder and took a bit of scrambling. She froze as bits of bark showered under her, clinging desperately by her fingertips and all too aware of gravity dragging her, inch by inch, into the void.

But there were no shouts from below, and she gave it a last desperate scramble and draped herself over the branch. Her bedroom window was closed, but this part had never been hard. The lock had been broken ever since she could remember, and the window fit badly in its painted sash, warped from winters past. She reached out to pry it open—

"Awww, what are you doing up a tree, poor little thing?"

Sarah jerked so violently that she nearly lost her balance and plunged off the branch headfirst. Clinging to the bark with bruised fingers, she looked down. A male Galatean with leopard-spotted fur stood at the base of the tree, arms crossed, looking up at her. He could have easily looked up her skirt from his vantage point—her legs were spread-eagled to grip the branch with her toes—but he seemed to be very carefully *not* doing that.

Gold glinted on his wrists. He was, she reminded herself, armed and dangerous.

And she couldn't say a word to him without giving away that she could understand him. It was his tone that reminded her, that sweetly crooning tone, exactly like she would have used for a cat up a tree.

He didn't know she had an implant.

This was a complication she suspected Rei hadn't considered; they'd both gotten so used to being able to talk to each other that it was easy to forget most humans couldn't.

Well, he is down there, and I'm up here. It's not like he can make me—

The Galatean reached up and casually closed one of his hands around her ankle. She had forgotten how goddamn huge they were. This dude was almost eight feet tall. She had to be at least ten feet off the ground, but all he had to do was stretch a little to reach her.

She stifled a yelp and tried to kick him with her bare feet. All he did was clamp his other hand on her other ankle and pull her out of the tree. There was a terrible minute of falling—she let out a wordless cry—and then he caught her as if she weighed nothing and lowered her to the ground.

Sarah swallowed a couple of times and brushed her hair out of her face. She crossed her arms and stared up at him, trying to pretend he didn't have a couple feet of height and about two hundred pounds of muscle on her. It was all she could do to keep her mouth shut.

"Well, you're a little charmer," he said mildly. His voice was lighter than she would've expected for someone so huge. One big hand settled on her shoulder; she tried to shrug it off, but it felt like his fingers were made of steel. "C'mon, my baby tree bird. Let's go put you in a pretty birdcage."

Sarah twisted away—and managed to do it, this time, startling him enough that he didn't clamp down in time. She lunged for the tire iron. He might be huge, but even a leopard-bear-bodybuilder couldn't shrug off an iron bar to the face. She swung it with all her might—

—only to have him catch it in midair, stopping it with a grunt of effort.

"So birds on your world have claws." His tone was amused. He gave the tire iron a sharp wrench, ripping it out of her hands, and flung it away into the pasture.

The cuts on her palm tore open again. Sarah wrapped her other hand around the injured one and clamped her jaw shut on the urge to speak, complain, ask him questions—or even protest as he gripped her arm, not hard enough to be painful, but with a cage-bar strength that she didn't think she could break this time.

He stopped suddenly, head going up like he was listening to something. "Yeah, really?" he said. "I just caught me one, too."

Sarah stiffened, and hoped it would be taken for alarm at his behavior rather than understanding his words. *Does that mean they've caught Rei?*

"No, mine's a native. Caught her trying to climb through a window of the house. No weapons. She's probably part of the old guy's clan. Want me to come back to the ship?" A pause, then: "Yes, sir," the Galatean said.

Sarah wished desperately that the translator let her hear the other half of the conversation. Instead she put up with having him steer her toward the door of her own house. At least he didn't seem to be trying to hurt her. He wasn't even restraining her. He seemed to consider her no threat at all.

Oh, Rei, I hope you're okay.

REI COULD TELL Jeren wasn't a team player when the

scar-faced Galatean took off for the other ladder to the deck above them without saying a word.

There were only three ways out of the cargo hold: two ladders and the freight elevator. The trap door the Galatean soldiers had come through was still open, and Rei guessed that one would be guarded. The ladder Jeren had selected was the one most likely to lead to an empty part of the ship.

Unless they'd had the sense to guard all the exits leading out of the hold, but they might not have the manpower to do that.

There was a sudden clatter as something came through the trap door and bounced on the deck plates beneath. It was already hissing and spewing smoke. "Gas grenade!" Rei called to Jeren, who was working on getting the other trap door open; it looked like they'd sealed it, which probably meant the elevator wouldn't be working either.

Rei activated his shields. In a pinch, the personal shields could be used as a makeshift spacesuit, which meant they should be proof against poison gas as well.

Green light flashed, and sparks showered down into the hold. Jeren had given up on finesse and just blasted through the trap door. He was up and through in an instant. After a pause to listen for sounds of fighting above, Rei followed.

He emerged in a small galley, little more than an alcove with machines for heating food and cleaning dishes. Beyond it was a pocket-sized lounge with a few tables and chairs crowded together. There was no sign of Jeren, but Rei heard a sudden yell and the sizzle of laser weapons from somewhere nearby. Sounded like Jeren was keeping the Galateans occupied. Rei hoped his mysterious ally managed not to make holes in the ship while he was at it.

It was disconcerting to notice how lightweight and flimsy the spaceship's interior seemed to him now, compared to the solidity of planetside houses and furniture. Flimsy didn't necessarily mean fragile; most of the ship's furnishings and interior dividing walls were made of various tough, light alloys. But there was a permanence to planetary construction, a sense of weight and heft.

Maybe Sarah's iron bar wasn't such a useless weapon after all.

He didn't have an iron bar, but he did have a spare set of cuffs. Rei crouched behind a table, detached one of his silver cuffs from its coupling to the gold one, and snapped it open. He'd been shown during his training how to turn them into makeshift bombs—or suicide devices. It was a moment's work to rewire it to overload and explode.

With the bomb armed but not set, he left the lounge and went into a short hallway lined with doors. The ship was like a maze, subdivided into many little compartments. Rei knew that all the dividing walls were meant to provide an illusion of privacy and make the ship's limited space feel less oppressive on long deep-space missions, but it just made him feel like he was trapped in a jungle, with limited visibility and the possibility of enemies approaching from any direction.

There was a sudden loud thump and the door at the end of the hallway burst open. A Galatean soldier tumbled through, with Jeren on top of him. Both were shielded; their blows had little effect except to knock the other one down.

"Jeren!" Rei shouted. "Get back!"

He knelt and hurled the cuff along the floor, bringing back a sudden intense memory of playing some kind of similar game on the ice of a frozen pond near his village as a child. It was just the same move, the way they would set the flat stones against the ice and give them a little spin as they went flying—

But this stone was about to explode. Rei palmed open the door to the nearest crew compartment—he didn't expect it to be locked; on a ship like this, doors rarely were—and hurled himself into someone's living space just as the cuff-bomb went off with a deep *whump*.

The thought occurred to him that maybe he should stop worrying about Jeren ripping holes in the ship, if he was setting off bombs inside it.

He peeked out. The hallway was filled with smoke and the reek of burning plastic. The hull and floor were both intact, but the explosion had buckled the flimsy interior walls, opening up a gap into the ship's tiny gym. Jeren was just straightening up from the body of the soldier who had been caught in the blast.

Rei didn't bother asking if he was already dead or if Jeren had finished him off; it didn't matter now. "How many are left?" he asked.

"I took out another one on the bridge. There's at least one more on the ship." Jeren nudged the twisted, blackened remains of the cuff with his toe. "How'd you do that?"

"Something they teach slave soldiers. Show you later. Where'd the other one go?"

"Don't know. It's their captain, Kyaroi."

Wonderful. The person who knew the ship best and had the access codes to everything.

The door behind Jeren, nearly torn out of the wall, led to the bridge. A quick visual check showed that the bridge was unoccupied. Scorch marks on the walls and a charred section of console suggested this was where the bulk of the fighting between Jeren and the Galateans had taken place.

"He locked us out," Rei said, checking the main console, "but I think I can get us back into the ship's main systems, at least."

"You seem to know Galatean tech pretty well, for not being one."

"I'm a slave soldier and a pilot," Rei said shortly. "I was trained in it."

Jeren raised a hand. "No offense, pal. You know these ships well enough to guess where the captain might've gone?"

"No, but I might know a way to find out." Rei thrust his hands into the support cradles for the piloting system. Unlike his pod, a larger ship like this was flown mainly by automated systems, but there would still be a pilot on board and the ability to manually override the computer. His silver cuffs couldn't have gained access, at least not without a lot of work on his part, but the gold ones, with their more extensive access permissions, clicked right in. As he'd suspected, the pilot systems were not locked down. No one without pilot mods could've accessed them, and Kyaroi apparently hadn't bothered to learn that Rei had been given specialized pilot training, not just the basic battlepod mods.

Rei closed his eyes as the pilot tech enhancements in his brain came online, lighting up with information on the ship and its systems. He only had access to the flight-related systems, which meant he couldn't do anything to locate Kyaroi directly. But there were a few things he could do. The artificial gravity, for example, was part of the same system as the ship's inertial damping. It was currently off, since they were on a planet.

"Hold onto something," Rei said absently, as he hooked his feet around the base of the pilot's chair and turned on the gravity, then reversed it.

There was a startled yelp and a loud thump as Jeren proved that he had not, in fact, grabbed hold of anything. In the rest of the ship, Rei heard the crashing as unsecured items tumbled to the ceiling which had become the floor. Hopefully one of those tumbling items was Kyaroi.

Rei opened his eyes to the vertigo-inducing sight of an upside-down pasture and treeline through the forward viewport. He tried to tell his brain that the *pasture* was rightside up, it was just gravity in the ship that had turned topsy-turvy, but with the blood rushing to his head and his body dangling from his feet and wrists, it was very hard to convince himself that he wasn't hanging upside down.

Jeren scrambled to his feet, standing on what had until a moment ago been the ceiling. "Bet *that* surprised the bastard. I'll go find—"

"No need." Rei spoke absently, most of his brain taken up with piloting functions. It wasn't quite a trance, but it was close to it. He'd forgotten how much data was involved in piloting a larger ship, nothing like the bare-bones system of his battlepod.

"What? Why?" Jeren demanded impatiently.

Rei had picked up a cycling airlock on the level below them. Was Kyaroi leaving the ship? No—worse. It was one of the airlocks leading to the skimmers.

"He's taking a skimmer," Rei reported. "You'll never make it. He's already separating from the ship."

It was very hard to think. As well as the pilot functions now running in his brain, he was still struggling to get past Kyaroi's lockdown. It was never meant to keep out someone with pilot's permissions, just anyone who might try pushing buttons on the currently locked consoles, and the systems were falling into his control one by one.

LIFE SUPPORT .... UNLOCKED.

COMMUNICATIONS .... UNLOCKED.

The ship was sending a distress beacon. He quickly deactivated it and replaced it with the "all's well, false alarm" signal, hopefully in time; it couldn't have been running for very long. And he was also picking up a transmission between the skimmer and a personal comm somewhere nearby, probably in the house—

Rei choked.

"What?" Jeren said, seeing the look on his face.

"Kyaroi just ordered the soldiers in the house to kill the hostages," Rei managed to say, insulated by the artificial calm brought on by the piloting state. His emotions were there, but distant, even as their vehemence threatened to bring his carefully maintained mental discipline crashing down.

Gary! ***SARAH***!

And there was nothing he could do to help, short of firing on the house as soon as he got weapons systems back up. Even if he left now and ran as hard as he could, he wasn't close enough.

WEAPONS .... UNLOCKED.

"You son of a bitch," Rei snarled.

This was something he'd drilled on until he could do it blindfolded—*had*, in fact, done it blindfolded. These weapons were different from the pod's, but he was used to targeting across the distances between ships, moons, planets. Aiming at something as close as the skimmer was child's play.

The skimmer was just breaking away from the ship, soaring across the pasture as it gained altitude. Rei shot it down with a thought, just like a training simulation. A fireball flashed in the night, lighting up the pasture like a flashbulb before fading into a smeary afterimage.

IN THE HOUSE, Sarah was marched through the kitchen into the living room, where a second Galatean soldier, this one female but still scarily tall, guarded her father and two other people she'd never seen before.

"Sarah!" Her father started to rise from the couch. The female Galatean put on a hand, the gold cuff glinting at her wrist, and Gary froze, his welcoming smile becoming fixed.

Sarah gave her dad a little wave and went to hug him before looking curiously at the other two. The fierce-looking woman was impatiently trying to rouse a man in a suit, who stirred with a groan. Leaning close, Sarah whispered, "Who are these people?"

"Federal agents Pradhan and Rhodes," her father murmured. "Who have now learned a valuable lesson about trusting suspicious aliens. Why are we whispering?"

"Because I don't want the Galateans to hear me talk and realize that if they can understand me, I can understand them."

"If it works with them like it does with Rei," her father whispered back, "they're going to understand all of us now that you're in the room, right?"

"I ... uh. Maybe." She hadn't thought of that. "Can we trust those two enough to tell them?"

"Beats the hell out of me. Your call."

There was a sharp exclamation from the leopard-spotted Galatean, making Sarah turn to look.

"It's an order," the woman said, her face cool.

"They're cooperating," Leopard Spots retorted. "There's no need to kill them; we can just stun them and leave."

The woman turned her cool green gaze on the hostages and raised her arm. Sarah's blood turned to ice.

"They're going to kill us!" she screamed.

Pradhan reacted instantly. She whirled around, seized a

lamp on the end table, and flung it at the lion woman, who gave a startled curse and batted it aside. The stunned agent, Rhodes, tried to lurch to his feet and sank back into his chair. His hand went to his empty shoulder holster and then dropped away.

"Run!" Pradhan snapped. "There are four of us and two of them. Scatter!"

Half Gary's weight suddenly sagged against Sarah. He'd tried to take a step too quickly and lost his balance. He gripped her with strong hands. "Go," he ordered, eyes wide and scared—for her, not for himself.

"No!" she told him flatly. "I'm not going anywhere without you."

And anyway, there just wasn't time. The lion-woman held her hands toward them and spread her fingers. Sarah threw her arms around her dad as green light bloomed around the woman's cuffs and flowed into her palms.

There was a green flash—blocked by the dark shape of a fast-moving body.

Pradhan had thrown herself between them.

The federal agent hit the floor with a boneless thump and a terrible smell of something burning.

An instant later, green light flared across the lion-woman's body and skittered off, draining away like water from her shielded skin. The woman spun, startled, as Leopard Spots fired again, light splintering in all directions.

"I'm not killing unarmed civilians," he snapped. "And I'm not letting you do it either."

"We'll be gone from this world soon, it's not like it matters—"

"*Life* matters!" he snarled, showing fanglike teeth. "Honor matters!"

Sarah knew she ought to run, but her dad couldn't

move fast, it looked like Rhodes couldn't move at all, and Pradhan was crumpled at her feet in a charred heap. Sarah knelt beside the woman and was startled to discover she was still alive, but horribly burned. Her eyes were open, her mouth moving as she tried to speak. When Sarah tried to get a grip on Pradhan to move her, the injured woman gasped and lapsed into probably merciful unconsciousness.

I can't throw away her sacrifice by staying here. But I can't leave her, and I don't think I can move her on my own. And I have to help Dad.

Rei—

It was as if her desperate thought had summoned him. The door slammed open and Rei stormed through it like a blue-skinned angel of vengeance. He pointed both hands at the two Galateans and fired in a dazzling burst of colored light.

"Rei!" Sarah cried, trying to cover her head with one arm and Pradhan's with the other. Stray fire scattered everywhere, scorching the wallpaper and setting fire to the couch. "Not the spotted guy! Stop! He's helping us—*Rei, behind you!*"

But the Galatean looming in the doorway fired not at Rei, but at the lion-woman. Under the onslaught she was beaten backward to the kitchen doorway and fell to her knees as her shields failed. She looked up; her eyes widened as she appeared to recognize the Galatean newcomer in the long coat.

"You—!" she began, and he shot her.

Leopard Spots brought up his hands to aim at the two of them, as the lion-woman slumped dead to the floor.

"He helped us!" Sarah shouted again. "Don't kill him!"

"Drop your shields and surrender," Rei told Leopard

Spots. "We have the ship and your captain is dead. You're the last one left. You can't win."

"I won't surrender if I'm going to be executed like that."

"You won't," Rei told him. "You have my word."

Leopard Spots took a deep breath and there was a quick glimmer across his body as his shields fell.

The Galatean in the long leather coat brought his arm swiftly into firing position. Rei snarled and knocked his hand aside. "What did I just say?" he snapped.

"I was just going to stun him," the big Galatean said between his teeth. "You do it or I will."

Rei raised his hand, then hesitated. "How many of you were on the ship? Standard crew of eight, right?"

Leopard Spots clenched his jaw. His gaze flicked from Rei to the others; he seemed to decide there was no harm in answering. "Eight, yes."

"And who's he?" Rei asked, tilting his head at the Galatean in the long coat.

"A prisoner," the leopard-man said. "He—"

There was a green flash. Sarah jumped, but there was no crackle of electricity, no stink of burnt flesh; the Galatean folded neatly to the floor. The stranger in the leather coat lowered his hand as Rei turned a hot amber stare on him.

"A person could almost get the impression you're trying to hide something about yourself," Rei said quietly.

The Galatean shook his head and leaned down to strip the gold cuffs off Leopard Spots' wrists; he pocketed them. "You can question him at your leisure later, when we aren't standing at ground zero for reinforcements." He stepped over to the lion-woman's body and repeated the process on her. "You may be weak, but you don't need to be stupid too."

"He's not weak!" Sarah snapped.

Rei turned toward her, turning his back on the Galatean. His eyes met Sarah's, and something, some powerful emotion flashed in them—it was as if he'd been holding himself in check, and now, something in him folded, and his next words came out in a gasp. "Sarah, are you all right?"

She drew a breath that turned to a dry sob. Rei took three quick strides across the room and he was there, taking her in his arms. She clung; she couldn't help it. He was so solid against her. Real. Alive. *There.*

"I thought ..." he breathed into her hair. "I heard the order to kill you. I thought—"

"I'm okay." Sarah swallowed, pressed her cheek against his chest, and wondered if she'd ever really be okay again.

"Hey, not to break up the reunion, but we've got to get this woman to a hospital, fast," Gary said, looking up at them.

Sarah took a shaky breath and pulled away from Rei. "I can call an ambulance, but—" She turned to Rei. "I *wouldn't* be okay, Dad and I would both be dead, if not for Agent Pradhan. Is there anything on that ship to help her, some kind of advanced medical technology? She's really badly hurt. I don't know if she'll survive." Even if she did, she was going to be badly scarred for life.

"Let me see." Rei bent over the injured woman. Her breathing was so faint Sarah could barely tell she was breathing at all. Gary had covered her with a blanket. "There should be a medbay on the ship, but I don't know how to use the equipment. Jeren?"

The Galatean shook his head. "Sorry, not my area." He staggered to his feet with Leopard Spots thrown over his shoulder. "I'm gonna throw this guy in stasis. If it's okay with *you.*"

"Do what you like," Rei said shortly. He picked up Agent Pradhan, very gently, holding her bridal-carry style.

"Hey, wait!" Agent Rhodes staggered to his feet, holding onto the back of the chair. "You're just going to—*take* her?"

"I have to. You are right," Rei told Sarah. "From what I've seen of your world's medicine, there is not much you can do for her here. But I can put her in stasis on the ship and find someone to help her. She protected you. I promise I will take care of her."

The bottom plunged out of Sarah's stomach. In all of this, she had forgotten that the eventual outcome of all of this was Rei leaving Earth.

And now he had a ship to do it in.

EIGHTEEN

THEY LEFT Sarah's dad to deal with Agent Rhodes, who was still shaky from the stun. Sarah walked close beside Rei as he carried Pradhan with the injured agent's head tucked against his chest. She kept wanting to put her hand on his arm, just to touch him, to reassure herself that he was all right—that both of them were all right. She felt strange, dazed and shaky, as if the entire world had an unreal edge to it. The night seemed like some bizarre dream.

And the air in the pasture smelled ominously of smoke. "Rei, did you set something on fire out here?"

"It's a crashed skimmer. I shot it down. I'm surprised you didn't hear it in the house."

"If it happened while they were trying to kill us, I think we had other things on our minds." She could see a dull glow up the hill now, like a banked campfire. "That's not going to start a brush fire, is it?"

"Don't worry," Rei said. "It's too wet out here to burn."

Sarah hoped he was right about that, but he'd already reached the ship. No sneaking around this time; he opened a door in the side—she didn't see how; it seemed to just flow open in front of him—and they entered the cargo bay just in front of the stasis pods. The big Galatean in the leather coat (Jeren, Rei had called him) was just getting done tucking their other prisoner into a pod.

"He's still nice and healthy, just like you like 'em," he remarked, standing back and crossing his arms as Rei and Sarah carefully loaded Pradhan into one of the empty pods. She looked tiny in a pod meant for someone much larger.

"Can you try not being an asshole for five seconds?" Rei asked as the lid of the pod hissed shut. He touched a few buttons; a panel of lights turned pale blue. *The Galatean equivalent of green lights?* Sarah wondered.

Jeren shrugged and strolled off down the cargo bay. "Guess I'll take care of the dead guys upstairs," he said over his shoulder. "Since you're too busy canoodling with your local piece of tail."

Rei visibly bristled. Sarah squeezed his hand. "It's okay. Is that the guy who was in the stasis pod?"

"Regrettably, yes." He sighed and leaned against her. "I figured, under the circumstances, any backup was better than no backup. I hope we don't regret that."

"Uh ... how dangerous *is* he?"

"I wish I knew, but I don't want to spring an ambush on him and try to shove him back in the pod unless I'm sure I can take him. Maybe I'll stun him while he's asleep."

This made her smile slightly, as he'd no doubt intended. "What about the ship?" she asked. "Was it damaged in the fight?"

"Only cosmetic damage." He smiled down at her. "Want a tour?"

Her heart leaped ... then sank. "Yes. More than anything. But I need to get back to the house. I can't leave

Dad alone with Agent Rhodes, there's no telling what he'll do—and, um, there's a ... dead lady in our living room."

"Right. I'll deal with that. You shouldn't have to."

And somehow that was what did it, the reminder of the body in their living room. Sarah discovered that her hands were starting to shake, her teeth to chatter.

"Sarah?" Rei's voice seemed to come from very far away.

"I don't know what's wrong with me," she managed to say.

"I do." Rei's voice was infinitely gentle. "Sarah. Sit down."

He guided her to the floor; it was more of a controlled fall. She leaned into the circle of his arms, shaking as if her body wanted to fly apart.

"They tried to kill us."

"I know," he murmured, stroking her hair.

"We *killed* them."

"We had to," he whispered. "We killed as few of them as we could."

"I—I know. I thought—I thought you—I was afraid—"

"Shhh. Sarah, it's over."

"Is it?" she asked fiercely into his shoulder, her cheek pressed against the black T-shirt that was all he'd been wearing under the sweater. He smelled like smoke and sweat. "How *can* it be? You—they—"

The enormity of it choked her. *This* was what he'd been dealing with. All of this. The danger, the fear—the way Agent Pradhan had just *fallen down*, the smell of her burnt skin and clothes—

"Sarah, listen to me." Rei was still talking, had been talking, she felt, for some time. "I know what you're feeling right now. But it does get better. We were acting in self-defense. We *had* to. Your father told me he was in a war—"

"Vietnam," she whispered.

"And he came back from it. And he was all right again, eventually. Right?"

Sarah nodded, dimly aware that Rei's words weren't just for her. He was speaking to himself, too. And that was what allowed her to claw her way back out of her own head, reminding herself that neither of them had to go through this alone. Comforting her helped comfort him. And if she could just make herself say it, not just to herself but to him—

"It wasn't our fault," she said quietly.

"No. It wasn't."

"And it'll get better."

"It will."

"We're going to be okay."

"Yeah," Rei said quietly, and pressed a kiss to her hair. "Yes. We will be."

A LITTLE WHILE LATER, Sarah looked around the kitchen table at the odd, mixed group who had gathered there, holding cups of coffee while her dad thawed leftovers even though no one had shown any interest in eating. It always made him feel better to have something useful to do.

But what a strange, mixed bunch they were. Jeren and Rei had come in from dealing with the bodies (Rei hadn't told her what they'd done with them; she hadn't been able to work up the nerve to ask) and now the group around the table consisted of Sarah and her dad, one human federal agent, one blue alien (currently with his arm around her) and one enormous feline alien who dwarfed the chair he was sitting in.

"So you said they're leaving and taking Anita with them?" asked Rhodes. He was hunched in his chair with both hands wrapped around a cup of coffee. Sarah had given him some Tylenol from the upstairs bathroom cabinet; Rei had told her that being stunned could give you a hell of a hangover, and he still seemed to be a little out of it.

"Yes," Sarah said. She was serving as an interpreter since she was the only one of the humans present who could understand the aliens. "As soon as we—as they finish cleaning up here, they're going to be out of your hair forever."

And out of my life.

She felt Rei's arm tighten around her, as if he'd picked up her thought out of the air. Maybe he was having similar thoughts of his own.

Rhodes looked skeptical, as well as hung over. "I've got a job to do here. You know that, right?"

"Listen, Agent Rhodes," Sarah said. "They didn't tell me to say this, but we both know they could just throw you in one of those pods like they did with Agent Pradhan. I mean, if this guy here decided to do that, do you really think we could stop him?"

Jeren looked up from trimming his nails with one of her dad's kitchen knives. He smiled wide enough to show a flash of teeth that were much pointier than human normal. Rei had basically human teeth, but Galateans had *fangs*.

Rhodes blanched. "Can they understand what we're saying?"

"More or less, as long as an English-speaker with a translator in their head is nearby. Anyway," Sarah said, "we *want* to let you go. But we can't do that if you're just going to come back to my dad's farm with a dozen more agents and arrest him for hiding illegal aliens or whatever."

Reluctantly, the corner of Rhodes' mouth quirked up in a tiny smile. "I don't think there's a law to cover this. But even if you're willing to take my word on faith, I don't have a whole lot of control over what my bosses will do when they find out Anita's missing."

"That depends on what you tell them about where she went," Rei said, and Sarah translated.

"And how much control do you have over *your* people sending more ships to find out what happened to the last one?" Rhodes asked pointedly. "I've got a whole country to worry about. Hell, a whole planet."

"We can't promise they won't send more ships," Rei said. "Any more than you can promise your people won't send more men. We're going to try to stop them, but ..." He leaned forward, his amber eyes sharp as broken glass. "You have to give us a reason to *want* to help your planet. Locking up Sarah and her father won't do that."

Sarah sighed and translated.

"Or we could just stick you in stasis," Jeren said, flipping the knife from hand to hand. "Or kill you. I don't know why you two are trying so hard to negotiate with this native when there's nothing he can do for you."

"We could also stick *you* in stasis," Sarah told him.

"You want to try it, little girl?"

Rei made a growling noise deep in his throat.

"Sounds like negotiations are going well," Gary remarked. He set the tin of shortbread cookies in the middle of the table. "Sarah hon, I know you're busy here, but I hear Bonnie raising a fuss out there. We're way overdue on the evening chores. You want to take a walk with me, kiddo?"

THERE WAS A WET, clinging cold in the air, and Sarah pulled her hands inside the sleeves of her jacket as she and her dad walked through the damp grass to the barn. The next clear night would probably frost.

She had to resist the temptation to go to the spaceship instead of the barn. She wanted to look at it so badly, try to figure out how it worked, ask Rei to tell her all about it ...

But she could ask a thousand questions and it would never be enough to satisfy her curiosity. The ship was going to be gone soon, and Rei along with it. And somehow she would have to go on with her ordinary life and pretend that her heart hadn't been ripped out of her chest.

"We can get this done quickly if we only do the most important chores," she told her dad, using long practice to stop her heart from breaking by focusing on the small details of the here and now. "You can get the eggs while I milk Bonnie and round up the sheep if they aren't halfway to the county line by now—"

"Sarah," her father said gently. "Go with him."

Sarah stopped in the act of ticking off chores on her fingers. "What?"

"Honey, I remember standing with you in Walmart when you were nine years old and telling you that you could pick out a poster from that whole rack of 'em to put on your bedroom wall. And I remember how you flipped past the unicorns and ponies and fancy-pants big-hair singers to the posters of outer space. You begged me to please get you two instead, because you couldn't decide between the one with all the planets in the solar system, and the one of that comet or whatever it was—"

"Nebula," she whispered. "The Orion Nebula." She still had it.

Gary turned to face her. It was almost dark in the

shadow of the barn; she couldn't make out his expression, but she could see the glimmer of the whites of his eyes.

"Sarah, sweetheart, I know what you put aside because of your mother and me. I know what it cost you. Punkin, you can't spend your whole life looking after me, giving up everything. Not when a chance like this comes along."

"But ..." She couldn't believe in it. Couldn't *let* herself believe in it. "What will you do? How will you ..."

"I'll manage. I'm getting around well enough to do every-thing that needs doing around the farm, and if there's some-thing I can't do, I can get Bill Haverford or one of the Muller boys to come over. I can drive fine now too."

"But we need the money from my part-time job—"

"We've still got my disability checks. If that's not enough, I can pick up some cash fixing engines for folks, same as I did back when your mother was still—back when Maggie—" He paused, and when he spoke again, his voice had softened until she could barely hear it. "Thing is, with you so good-natured about doing what needs done around the farm, it's been too damn easy to do less than I can. Awful easy to sit around the house working on my projects, feeling like there's nothing that really needs doing, not worth getting up on these wobbly pins of mine. Tell you the truth, honey, I think you going out there and living your life is gonna be the kick in the pants that I need to start living mine again."

Somewhere deep in her chest, something fluttered, an emotion as delicate as a butterfly's wings. "Daddy, you know this might mean leaving really *soon*, right? Maybe even tonight, or tomorrow morning? I've got—I've got my job, my classes—and I'd be leaving you to deal with whoever the government sends, maybe even an actual alien invasion when they realize their ship's gone missing. I can't just ..."

"Sarah," her father said, and Sarah fell silent. "Do you want to go?"

She had to swallow a few times before she could get the word out. "Yes." *Oh yes, yes. More than anything.*

"There's a lot I haven't been able to give you. But I can give you this. You've been doing a lot of things around here you should never have had to. Trust the old man to clean up any messes that are left behind—*oof!*"

Sarah threw her arms around him and buried her face in his shoulder, like she used to do when she was a little girl. She was shaking again, she realized dimly, but for a different reason this time. It still didn't feel real: not the spaceship sitting in the pasture less than a hundred yards away, let alone the idea that she might be on it soon, with an entire galaxy full of stars, quasars, and nebulae spread out in front of her.

"You could come," she said into his shoulder. "If they can fix Agent Pradhan, they can probably fix your back."

She could feel him shaking his head. "Honey, if you find a miracle cure, you come right back here and tell me about it. I'll get on that ship tomorrow and go to whatever outer-space hospital you found. And then I'm gonna get on that ship and come back here. My life is here. But I don't think yours is. It never has been."

She was crying now, full-on sobbing, a pent-up flood of unshed tears.

"Hey. There, there." Gary patted her back. "Hey, kid. It's okay. It's gonna be okay." He kissed her hair. "What d'ya say we go milk that poor cow before she ends up with mastitis, okay?"

Sarah wiped her eyes and sniffled, and smiled through her tears. "It's a plan."

NINETEEN

SARAH'S FASCINATION with the ship glowed from her eyes, filling Rei's heart with shared joy as he escorted her through the cargo bay and took the antigravity lift to the upper deck. It was a vast relief to see her regain some of the sparkle she'd lost after the fight. She seemed to be handling things better now, but Rei knew from his own experience that it was going to be an up-and-down process. Sometimes she'd be fine, sometimes she wouldn't. It had been awhile since he'd had to help someone who was new to fighting through the aftermath of what the Galateans called battle shock.

But exploring the ship helped a lot. Everything fascinated her, even the most commonplace things. She touched the wall with wondering fingertips, stared at the galley fixtures, peeked into the tiny medbay with eyes round with wonder.

"This place is amazing."

"You're looking at the bathroom," Rei said dryly.

She punched him playfully in the arm. "It's a space bathroom. Shut up."

"Looks better without bodies all over the floor," Jeren remarked, coming in from the bridge.

Sarah jumped.

Rei growled softly at him. "Thanks, you're helping a lot. What were you doing up here, anyway?"

"Just checking out our new little friend here." Jeren patted the ship's battle-scarred bulkhead, and flashed a fang in a smile. "Seeing how we're going to be sharing quarters for a bit, or isn't that the plan?"

"The plan is to drop you off at the first inhabited planet we come to. Unless we just put you back into stasis—"

Now it was Jeren's turn to growl. Sarah moved closer to Rei.

"Nobody," Jeren said in a voice that was soft but full of menace, "is shoving me into one of those pods again. *Ever.*"

Rei made sure his hands were unencumbered, just in case he needed them for fighting in a hurry. "Yeah? If you expect us to leave you free, I think it's about time you told us what you did to get locked up."

"I'm a bounty hunter," Jeren said.

"Yes, and? Last I checked, that's not illegal in the Empire. What'd you do to make them shove you in a pod like a violent criminal?"

After a long silence, Jeren said, "They think I killed someone I didn't. I'm not a murderer."

Rei gave a short, disbelieving laugh. "Your behavior on the ship says otherwise. I literally *watched* you kill people. Not to mention your suggestion about blowing up the engines and killing everyone on board."

"Self defense is different. You said it yourself. Yes, I've killed. I'll probably kill again. You telling me those cuffs on your wrists are just for show? Every last dead Galatean on this planet was killed by me, huh?"

Rei curled his lip and said nothing.

"Yeah, thought so." Jeren stalked past him, with a parting shot over his shoulder. "Guess I'll go work on patching that hole you cut in the side of the skimmer so we can take off, huh?"

Sarah was quiet. Rei held her tight against him and kissed the top of her head. If that asshole pushed her into another battle-shock breakdown, Rei just might kill him.

"I don't like that guy," Sarah said softly.

"Yeah. Me neither."

"Do you trust him?" she asked, pulling away. She seemed steadier; Rei let her go.

"Not in the slightest. Especially since, as an escaped slave, there is a bounty on my head, dead or alive."

Sarah's eyes rounded. "I didn't think of that. Does he know?"

"I'm sure he's put two and two together. But he's right, we'd have a real fight on our hands if we try to get him back into that pod."

"I liked your idea about stunning him while he's asleep. I'm worried about him slipping into our cabin and slitting our throats."

"I'm not especially worried about *that*. Stunning me and stuffing me into a pod to take me back to the Galateans ... *that's* what I'm worried about. Fortunately he's still locked out of most of the ship's systems. I can only get in because I'm a pilot."

"Do the cabin doors lock?"

Rei smiled briefly. "Not usually, but I can make them do it. Do you have a choice of quarters?"

"Somewhere far away from wherever he's going to be."

"The cabin just behind the bridge is the captain's quarters and therefore the largest. We could take that one. We'll need to ... clean it out first."

The sick look was back on her face. "Oh no, I hadn't thought of that. All their things are still going to be—"

"Sarah." Rei took her face in his hands. "You can't change it. *We* can't change it. And we have to sleep somewhere. This is a military vessel, so the crew swaps out on regular rotations; they haven't been here long, either. It's not their house."

After a moment, she nodded. "What did you do with their bodies?" she asked quietly, looking up at him, her face still framed between his palms.

"Burned them," he said without hesitation. If she could handle the rest of it, she could handle this. "It seemed the best way. The Galateans cremate their dead, so that's what would have been done at home."

To his relief, she just nodded again. It was time, he thought, for a distraction.

"Want to see the bridge?"

"I know what you're trying to do," she said with a tiny pout and a scowl.

"Is it working?"

The scowl broke up in a smile, a little shaky, but sincere. "The bridge of an actual spaceship? Are you kidding?"

Rei didn't think the bridge was that much to look at. Its main attraction were the viewscreens, covering the entire width of the ship and wrapping around. The screens looked like windows, but weren't; the prow of the ship was heavily shielded against radiation, enemy fire, and stray space debris. At the moment the screens showed the dark pasture in front of the ship, but they could be set to any other view within range of the ship's sensors.

But Sarah looked amazed, wandering from one side of

the bridge to the other. "Does this ship have a name?" she asked. "Do Galateans name their ships at all?"

"They do." Rei slipped his arms into the pilot's cradle to make contact with the ship, and closed his eyes as text scrolled behind his eyelids. "According to this, it's called *Glory to the Empire 46.*"

"Well, we're sure not calling it *that*."

Rei opened his eyes to grin at her. "As this ship's new co-owner and co-captain, would you like to name it?"

"*Millennium Falcon?*"

"Sure."

"No," she said quickly. "That was a joke. One you wouldn't get. Um ... how about *North Star?*"

"Your planet's fixed star?"

"Yes. A fixed point to steer by. A star to guide you home."

"I like that," he said, and made a few tweaks to the ship's designation. "*North Star* it is."

———

JEREN WAS NOWHERE around when they left the ship. Rei hoped he wasn't off placing a call to the Galateans for the reward money. Of course, that'd just get Jeren thrown in prison himself, if he had told them the truth. *The enemy of my enemy is my friend ... maybe. Or at least less likely to kill me.*

Back in the house, they found Agent Rhodes and Gary on the couch, having coffee and talking.

"Really, Dad?" Sarah said. "You're making friends with the Men in Black?"

"Turns out Aaron here—"

"You're on a *first-name basis* with the Men in Black?"

Rhodes flashed a quick smile.

"—served in Afghanistan," her dad went on. "And me in 'Nam. Just catching up on old times. Seems like the more things change, the more they stay the same."

"Except we had better gear than you guys did."

"And better chow, from what I hear," Gary said with a grin.

Rhodes grimaced. "Most of the time."

Sarah glanced at Rei and then shook her head wearily and turned toward the stairs. "Have fun bonding, you guys. I guess."

Rei followed her upstairs as the quiet voices in the living room resumed.

"What do you think your government is going to do next?" Rei asked softly.

Sarah went into the bathroom and started washing her face and hands in the sink. She left the door open, which Rei took to indicate that she didn't require privacy. "I don't know," she said. "Maybe Dad can talk Rhodes into helping us. Maybe he'll turn us in. I'm just too tired to deal with it."

Rei took his turn at the sink, scrubbing at his hands until the skin hurt before he made himself stop.

Take the advice you gave Sarah. We did what we had to do. That's all.

What comes next will come.

He went into the bedroom to find Sarah stripped down to her underwear, gazing blankly at the wall as if she'd run out of energy in the process of changing into her night clothes. Rei stripped off his own clothes and, wordless, they climbed into bed and lay in each other's arms.

He was expecting a replay of today to fill his head as soon as he closed his eyes, but his mind was surprisingly cooperative as long as he grounded himself on the feeling of Sarah against him, breathing softly against his neck.

The sound of a vehicle door slamming outside made him sit up. Sarah pulled back the curtain, and they watched the red rear lights of Rhodes' vehicle turn out onto the farm road.

"I guess he and Dad came to some kind of arrangement," she said quietly. "Where's creepy cat dude, do you know?"

"Jeren? No idea. On the ship, I hope."

"What are the odds he'll figure out how to fly it and take off without us?"

"None," Rei said, then amended it to, "Very little, anyway. I don't think he has pilot mods or he'd be gone already."

"Pilot mods?"

"Special implants in my head that let me fly spaceships."

She nodded and settled sleepily in his arms again.

"Anyway," he said softly into her hair, "if he tries anything, I've had a rough day and I don't mind having someone to take it out on."

Sarah laughed quietly against his neck, and then slowly her breathing evened out and she slept. He held her as, a few minutes later, she twitched through a nightmare before settling down again.

It was very like sleeping with his sept, clinging to each other through their dreams, holding each other as they cried.

He wondered if any of his sept were still alive out there.

With a ship of his own, and Sarah by his side, perhaps he could find out.

TWENTY

IT WAS SUCH AN ODD FEELING, Sarah thought: trying to compress her entire life on Earth into a suitcase.

She could take as much with her as she wanted. There was plenty of room on the ship. But as she went through her closet, her keepsakes, her photos, she realized how little of it was meaningful enough to be worth taking to space. She took her favorite picture of Mom—leaving Rei's drawing of his family on the wall; it would stay safe here on Earth—and a picture of her parents together. Some changes of clothes went into the suitcase, along with her favorite soft, well-worn T-shirt for sleeping in.

There was no need to take a telescope, or any of her science books. She was leaving for a place where all the accumulated scientific knowledge of Earth was probably stuff that people learned in kindergarten.

She took a couple of her favorite paperback novels, and her ebook reader loaded up with books. Even knowing it was silly, with so much more advanced technology in the place she was going, she tucked her phone into the suitcase too. True, there was no service in outer space, but she had a bunch of games and photos on there. It would be nice to have that.

Was this was people used to feel like when they went on long journeys? Not knowing if you would ever come back, if you'd ever see your family again? Her ancestors had sailed to a new land and crossed half a continent to get to Wisconsin. Perhaps it only made sense that she was following in their footsteps; the urge to see new places was in her blood.

The last thing she put in the suitcase was her favorite stuffed toy from her childhood, a threadbare stuffed horse called Spot. She had always hoped she'd be able to give it to a child of her own someday. She still wasn't sure if she believed Rei that the two of them could have children together, but she'd like to have the option.

She closed the suitcase and clicked it shut.

Carrying the suitcase, she went down the stairs quietly, stepping automatically around the creaky step. She was wearing ordinary clothes: jeans, a sweater, sneakers. Somehow it felt like she ought to dress up for going to space. But she might as well wear something she felt comfortable in. Who knew what she'd end up wearing eventually, once she was out there?

No sign of the Men in Black, so apparently Rhodes hadn't sold them out yet. The whole house smelled like baking. In the kitchen doorway, Sarah stopped to watch her dad. He was wearing an apron and just putting a baking sheet into the oven with a pair of mitts.

"Hey, honey. I made your favorite oatmeal cookies. No chocolate chips so your boy can eat 'em too." He pointed to the baking rack with a mitt-clad hand. "Just let 'em cool and we can pack them up in Tupperware for you to take along."

That was what did it; that was what made the tears

come. "Oh, Dad," Sarah whispered, and threw herself into his arms.

They hugged for a long time, until the oven timer went *ding*! As her dad turned away and started getting the cookies out of the oven, Sarah noticed the table was covered with electronics. She didn't recognize most of what she was looking at, but she was pretty sure a lot of it was from Rei's pod, or maybe from the Galatean ship.

"What's all this?"

"Had a chat with your boy earlier—"

"His name is Rei, Dad."

"—about rigging up some kind of space phone. We gotta do it on the down low, don't want to get those cat folks after us, but I've got time on my hands and he left all this so I can see if I can put something together to talk to you two out there."

"That would be fantastic," Sarah said. She swallowed; she was pretty sure she'd gotten all the tears out of her system for now, but there might be more if she stayed here too long.

"Just let me get these cookies packed up, and I'll bring 'em out."

Her father's eyes were suspiciously wet, too. Sarah didn't mention it; she just nodded, and grabbed her sheepskin coat on the way out the door.

It was going to be cold in space. She'd need this.

"Your boy's at the ship!" her dad called after her.

"I figured!"

They'd moved the ship up the hill. Rei had landed it neatly straddling the stream, between the trees, where it couldn't be seen from the road or the Haverford place. They were definitely running on borrowed time, though. The weather was cooperating so far; it was another gray, rainy day. But the clock was ticking down fast until they were discovered.

Even though she got her shoes wet, Sarah took the scenic route up the hill, walking around the barn and petting Princess's soft gray nose. (She might have cried a little then, too.) She took one last look into the barn, inhaling deeply the mix of hay, grain, and animal smells that had been a part of her life as long as she could remember.

The battlepod was gone from the barn as if it had never been there. Sarah gazed into the shadowed interior for a little while before she quietly closed the door and turned away.

She wound her way through the pasture, petting the sheep and the cow one last time. There was a charred place where the crashed skimmer had been; it looked like someone had been burning off the field in that place, or maybe had a bonfire that got a little out of control. The damaged skimmer itself was back in the ship's cargo bay, along with the pod.

As she neared the top of the hill, Sarah noticed that she was being followed.

"No, Mouser. Go back." She crouched and petted the cat, but Mouser continued to fawn on her hand, and finally Sarah picked her up so that she wouldn't get wetter. "C'mon, you don't want to go with me. There are no mice in space."

The deep purr, surprisingly loud for such a small cat, vibrated through Sarah's chest.

"I wonder if Dad would mind getting another barn cat?" she murmured, scratching Mouser's ears. "I wonder if you'd be happy in space. I don't want you to be sad."

The ancestors of the Galateans had been part cat, she thought. *Someone* had taken cats to space, once upon a time.

Maybe it would be nice, having a ship's cat.

Carrying Mouser in one arm, and the suitcase with the other, she walked through the trees to the ship sitting incongruously in the middle of the stream, with water purling around it. Sarah splashed to the door standing open in the side. She set Mouser down inside, and smiled as the cat immediately set off into the dark space of the hold, exploring.

"Rei?" she called.

"He's up top."

Sarah nearly jumped out of her skin. "Don't sneak up on people," she snapped at the tall figure in the long coat who was leaning against the wall just inside the door.

Jeren's teeth flashed in the dark. "You're gonna have to learn to look around you, little girl. Space is full of monsters that'll eat you right up."

"You remember we're dropping you off on the first inhabited planet we come to, right?" She looked around. The ship's hold was much more crowded than it had been, with the battlepod and the twisted remains of the skimmer. "How are the repairs coming?"

"Done," Jeren said tersely. "We're ready to go, soon as loverboy gets done plucking feathers for his nest up there."

"What are you talking about?"

He nodded to the ladder leading to the nearest open trapdoor. "Go up and see."

Sarah climbed the ladder and poked her head up into the galley. "Rei?"

"Here!" he called from somewhere out of sight.

She walked carefully around the tables in the lounge. The door to the forwardmost cabin in the row of crew quarters was standing open, and something that looked very much like a Rubbermaid tote, made of something not unlike rugged blue-tinted plastic, sat outside the door, heaped with clothing and sundry objects. The dead captain's personal effects, Sarah thought. She shuddered and moved it gently out of the way with her foot. She wondered if Rei would object to contacting the dead Galateans' families to send back their things.

After taking a moment to get herself together, she looked inside.

Rei was fixing the bed. And everywhere Sarah looked were plants. It looked like Rei had potted them in anything he could find, and he hadn't been choosy about what kind of plants he took, either. Messy wads of grass stuck into coffee cans, thornbushes in shallow gray trays that must have come from somewhere on the ship—

"Rei, what is all this?" she asked, setting her suitcase inside the door.

"I can't take your planet with you, Sarah, but I can bring some little pieces of it." He snapped the sheet into place and turned around with a smile. "I thought it might make you less homesick to have a few things from your farm with you. I even thought about taking that gray animal in the barn—"

"What, the *horse*? No, she would be miserable on the ship. Horses need space to run."

"No, the little one. The cat. I couldn't find it."

Sarah laughed. "I have good news for you, then. She followed me up to the ship. It looks like we have a ship's cat whether we want one or not. I was just going to ask how you felt about it, but I guess this answers my question."

"Ship's cat? Is that a normal thing on Earth?"

She put her arms around him. He was wearing the battered red sweater, scorched and torn in places, but still soft and warm to the touch. "They're supposed to be good luck."

"That sounds like something we could use."

———

AND SO, here they were, ready to leave Earth.

It was early afternoon, the morning having vanished in a hundred small tasks. Her dad had dropped off several large Tupperware containers of fresh-baked cookies and muffins. Sarah had picked up a bag of cat food and a tray of dirt for a litterbox; they would have to find outer-space substitutes for both, but this would do for now. Rei topped off the ship's water supply from the stream, reassuring Sarah that the tanks would purify it of any surface contaminants. ("Refilling on planets is a standard procedure." "Yes, but *this* planet has giardia!") And still, Sarah kept thinking of more things to run down the hill to get. Deodorant! Sanitary supplies! Who knew what kind of substitutes they had in space?

Sarah's dad had somehow talked Rei into getting the pumpkin from the back of the truck. "Really?" Sarah said, coming upon them as Rei was helping him load it into the ship. "We're taking a pumpkin to space?"

"Bet you can't get them in any outer-space market," Gary said, dusting off his hands and reaching for his cane.

"Actually, from what Rei's told me about Earth-based ecosystems, I wouldn't be surprised if you can."

"Still. That's a good solid Midwest-grown pumpkin. Show the boy how to carve a jack-o-lantern and bake him a pumpkin pie. Then you can plant the seeds wherever you end up."

"Dad, that's called introducing an invasive foreign weed."

"Ain't a weed if it's useful," her father grumbled. He snapped his fingers. "You oughta take some spices too. Pepper. Where are you gonna get basic pepper in outer space?"

"Dad!"

"Oh hell," Gary muttered to himself, "almost forgot," and he was off down the hill, swinging along on his canes.

Sarah sighed, traded grins with Rei, and went to stow the pumpkin so it wouldn't roll around.

Her dad was back shortly, limping up the hill on one cane and carrying a box that must have contained all the spice bottles in the kitchen, along with a bottle of Scotch poking out of one corner.

"Give this to Blue," he said, tapping the bottle after Sarah took the box. "I promised him a drink one time, one old soldier to another. We never got to have it, but at least he can try good Earth whisky."

Sarah hesitated and then handed the bottle back. "Tell you what, Dad. You keep it here. It'll be a ... a promise you can keep when we come back."

"Coming back, are you?" There was a slight catch in his voice.

Sarah had to blink away tears. Damn it, she'd turned into a faucet over the last couple of days. "Of course we're coming back. We've got to visit. And you're building a space phone, so we can talk, right?"

Her father gazed at her for a moment with a smile.

"What?" Sarah said.

"Just thinking about how much you make me think of Maggie sometimes," he said quietly. "She'd be real proud of you, kiddo."

What finally put an end to the endless errand-running and cycle of goodbyes was a lightening of the clouds overhead. Blue sky was showing to the east. They needed to take off soon, or else they'd have to wait for nightfall. Already there was a risk of the neighbors noticing their takeoff, now that the rain had stopped.

"What kind of spaceship doesn't have a cloak, anyway?" Sarah asked Rei as he went through some kind of preflight checklist on the bridge.

"What do you mean, a cloak?"

"I mean, something to stop the ship from being seen." *Like on TV,* she didn't say.

"It has shields. Like the shields produced by my cuffs, they can confound many kinds of sensors. It's still visible to the eye, however."

We could wait, Sarah thought, and then: *No.*

If she allowed herself to think that way, she might never leave.

And she was ready.

She shut Mouser in their quarters for the takeoff, just in case the cat panicked. She wasn't sure what spaceship liftoff was going to feel like. Her dad was watching from the edge of the trees, at what Rei reassured her was a safe distance.

Jeren had joined them on the bridge, to Sarah's dismay, but at least he was just leaning against the wall and staying out of the way. She couldn't *wait* 'til they found a planet and got rid of that guy.

Rei buried his hands in the ship's innards. She still couldn't get over what an interesting way to fly a ship it was, nothing at all like spaceships on TV, or any Earth vehicles that she knew of. The pilot's chair held him like a sling, tilted forward with his hands encased in machinery.

Under her feet, the deck began to vibrate. There was a

distant sense of ... not even sound, exactly, but a great pressure she could feel in her chest and eardrums. Low-frequency sound waves?

What she didn't feel was any sense of movement, even when the trees outside the viewscreens trembled, losing leaves in great gold and red showers, and then fell away beneath them.

Rei tilted the ship so Sarah could see Gary, his hair blowing back, waving to them. She still didn't feel any sense of motion; it was like they were standing still. That helped a bit with the sense of loss as her father dwindled, as the trees dwindled, as the farm shrank to a handful of scattered toys and then vanished beneath a gray bank of clouds. She could pretend it was all happening on a TV screen rather than in real life.

The sense of pressure had begun to fade as soon as they were in the air. Now the only pressure was a tightness in her throat. Sarah swallowed hard and refused to cry. Rei was focusing on flying, but she was aware of Jeren watching her with his sardonic gaze. She definitely wasn't breaking down in front of *that* guy.

They really couldn't find an inhabited planet soon enough ...

And then they broke out of the clouds, and she gasped aloud.

She'd rarely had a chance to fly on a jet. Just a couple of times, once to Washington, DC for a school trip, and once to visit her grandparents after they moved to Florida. She had loved it, especially the way the sky darkened and deepened to a rich midnight blue as the plane reached cruising altitude. At the time, she'd thought it was the closest she would ever get to space.

The clouds spread below them like a soft cottony floor,

the same way she remembered from those trips, with gaps through which a hazy, distance-blued patchwork of farm and field could be glimpsed. Even those gaps were shrinking as they rose and rose, faster than any jet. Sarah still had the eerie sense that she *should* be feeling them move, but wasn't.

"The ship is somehow damping down our acceleration, isn't it?" she asked.

"Yes," Rei said, his voice distracted as he worked on flying. "The artificial gravity does it. Otherwise you'd be flattened to the deck, and probably crushed. We are traveling more swiftly than any vehicle on your planet."

They certainly were. She could already see the distant curve of the Earth, pale at the horizon, deepening to a dark purplish blue overhead. As they rose and rose, the clouds below them blurred to white and blue swirls, and above them, the stars began to come out.

The stars.

She had never seen stars like these before.

There was no atmosphere in the way. These stars didn't twinkle; they were clear and brilliant, each a sharp pinprick in the velvet blackness that had now lost all traces of blue.

"There's a satellite," Sarah gasped, pointing. They swept past it so swiftly she hardly got a chance to glimpse it. She couldn't believe their speed, still with no sense of motion at all. She could see the entire Earth now, looking exactly like photographs she'd seen: a great, swirly, blue-and-white-and-green sphere hanging against the backdrop of space.

Dwindling, dwindling ...

"The jump drive is charged," Rei said in that oddly flat, absent tone. "You should sit down or hold onto something. Are you ready?"

"Ready," Sarah said. She didn't sit down, but she gripped the back of the seat in front of her.

There was an odd wrenching sensation. Everything around her blurred, and along with it, her own sense of self: an instant's profound dislocation that reminded her of the disorientation that goes along with a high fever. The Earth and stars smeared like a watercolor in the rain, stretching, tearing—

And then everything snapped back into focus, and she was looking at two bright lights, one blue, one reddish.

Those are stars, she thought, blinking to clear her blurry vision. *No, suns. We're in another solar system, looking at other suns.*

Her grip on the back of the seat was all that kept her upright.

"Sarah, are you okay?" Rei asked, his voice sharpening. "Some people get sick their first jump."

"I'm fine," she managed to say. Her eyes were fixed on the viewport. Alien suns. Another solar system. The constellations still looked disconcertingly like the ones she knew. "Where are we?"

"I was about to ask the same question," Jeren growled.

"We're in an uninhabited system, the nearest one to your planet. The jump drive needs to recharge between jumps, and I didn't want to completely deplete it in case we had to move again in a hurry." Rei pulled his hands out of the mechanical cradles and shook them as if the fingers hurt. "We can spend a little time here, check the ship for spaceworthiness, and figure out somewhere safe we can drop Jeren off. Is that acceptable?"

"I don't care about safe," Jeren growled.

"I think he meant safe for *us*, you lunatic," Sarah told him. *Alpha Centauri,* she thought, boggled. *We're at Alpha Centauri. I can't believe it.*

Jeren shook his shaggy mane. "I'm going to my quarters. Wake me up when something interesting happens."

Sarah peeked down the hall after he stalked out, to see where he'd decided "his quarters" were. He was just vanishing into the cabin as far from theirs as he could get, all the way down at the end of the hall. Looked like the desire for privacy was mutual.

"I can't *wait* 'til we drop that guy off."

"Very soon now." Rei put an arm around her, and she leaned into him. "How are you handling your first space flight?"

"Excited. Nervous. A little sad." She smiled up at him. "Mostly excited. Not sick at all."

"Excellent. I've locked down the ship. Jeren won't be able to do anything, at least not without pilot-capable cuffs and pilot mods in his head."

"So we're safe." She grimaced. "Ish. I think I'd better go check on Mouser and make sure she got through the jump okay. After that ... can we fly around a little and explore?"

"Explore? There's not much to see. This system has some planets, but none support life."

"Show me those, then." She squeezed him tight. "I want to see it all. I want to see *everything*. And then we can start looking for your friends."

"It'll be dangerous," Rei warned her. "If Lyr's still alive, he'll be with the Galatean fleet. We aren't going to be able to get close in a stolen ship without setting off a hundred alarms. It might not even be possible—"

"Rei, until a week ago, I thought we Earth humans were alone in the universe. Until a day ago, I thought I would spend my entire life on the planet I was born on. Until ten minutes ago, I'd never set foot in another solar system besides my own." She looked up at his beloved face, all its familiar planes and curves limned with the light of two alien suns. "I don't think there is any such thing as *impossible* anymore. Not when I'm with you."

Rei started to say something, then let out his breath on a long sigh, and just held her, hanging here in the void of space, while all around them the stars moved in a slow, solemn dance as old as time.

EPILOGUE

THEY'D BEEN GONE for a month. Sometimes it felt longer. Sometimes it felt like no time at all had passed.

Gary kept busy. Truth be told, he was enjoying having the place to himself. Oh, the house was a little lonely at night. He'd gotten himself a new barn cat, a mean little tomcat the Mullers were getting rid of, and he'd also gotten a dog by accident. There was this box of black Lab-mix puppies outside the feed store with a teenage kid selling them for twenty bucks each, and somehow he ended up walking off with the first dog he'd had since before Maggie got sick.

You just went on with life. That's what you did. And life was pretty darn okay.

He was watching TV on the couch, the new puppy sleeping on a pillow by his feet, when there was a sudden knock at the door.

Gary heaved himself up with the help of a cane. He thought about going to get the shotgun, which he kept handy these days, then decided not to. If it was the feds, having a gun wouldn't do anything but risk getting his own fool ass shot. He knew they were still hanging around; all the business out at the lake was gone, along with the helicopters, but in a small town like this, you noticed strange faces. Oh yeah, they were still around. But they were leaving him alone so far. For that, he supposed he had Rhodes to thank.

He didn't have a single regret about any of it. He hoped Sarah and her boy were having fun out there in the wide, wide universe. Hoped he'd get an outer-space phone call from them one of these days, hoped like anything, hoped she'd find a way to cure his bad back too. But if none of that happened, well, that was life.

You watched your kids grow up and fly away; every parent had to. Your job, if you did it right, was not to keep them around forever, but to make sure they had the skills to fly fast and high. And Sarah was flying faster and higher than anyone he'd ever known, so yeah, he and Maggie had done all right.

He might get a little sad sometimes, might be a little lonely, but he had no regrets.

He cracked open the door. Under the porch light stood a slim, dark young man with a scruffy shock of curly hair, exhausted-looking, his eyes blue-shadowed behind his wire-rimmed glasses, looking as if he hadn't slept in weeks. Gary had never seen him before in his life.

"Yeah?" Gary said. "Help you?"

"Hi, my name is Neil Pradhan, and I'm looking for my wife," the stranger said in a soft voice with a trace of a British accent. "She disappeared in this area a few weeks ago. Her name is Anita. I have a photo, if you'd like to see it."

Gary hesitated for only an instant. He understood all too well what this kid was going through. Watching Maggie die in the hospital had been torment, but having her vanish, never knowing her true fate, might have been worse.

"Come in, son," he said gently, holding the door. "I'll put on a pot of coffee. We've got a lot to talk about."

Warriors of Galatea continues in *Metal Dragon*, available now on Amazon and Kindle Unlimited!

When a crash landing strands them on an alien planet filled with fierce, dinosaur-like wildlife, lonely dragon prince Lyr and Earth widow Meri find themselves struggling with feelings neither of them believed they would ever feel again.

Now Available!

ABOUT LAUREN

Hi, and thank you for reading! I'm a writer, artist, and life-long Alaskan, and I write my books in a cabin on the highway, surrounded by fireweed and birch trees. I also write as Layla Lawlor (urban fantasy and science fiction) and as Zoe Chant (a shared romance pen name with several other authors; my books as Zoe are the Bears of Pinerock County and Bodyguard Shifters series).

Join my mailing list for new releases, free stories, and sneak preview chapters! Get a free story just for signing up. https://www.subscribepage.com/LaurensList

Email: laureneskerwriter@gmail.com

Facebook page (*news and updates*)
https://www.facebook.com/laureneskerwriter/

Website: laurenesker.com

ALSO BY LAUREN ESKER

Shifter Agents

Handcuffed to the Bear

Guard Wolf

Dragon's Luck

Tiger in the Hot Zone

Shifter Agents Boxed Set #1

(Collecting *Handcuffed to the Bear, Guard Wolf,* and *Dragon's Luck*)

Standalone Paranormal Romance

Wolf in Sheep's Clothing

Keeping Her Pride

Warriors of Galatea

Metal Wolf

Metal Dragon

Metal Pirate (forthcoming)

Metal Gladiator (forthcoming)

BONUS DELETED SCENE

This scene originally appeared between Chapter Ten and Chapter Eleven. My first readers told me that it slowed the story down, so I decided to delete it and include it at the end as bonus content. This gives you a look at what was happening on the Galatean side of things while Rei and Sarah were getting to know each other on the farm, and also introduces Agent Pradhan.

Black Helicopters at Midnight

Homeland Security Agent Anita Pradhan had long since given up on the idea that her job would be glamorous, but it *was* occasionally exciting. Not to mention surprising. Being airlifted in the middle of the night to a remote location via helicopter was definitely a surprise. She tried to stick close to her boss, tried not to yawn, and stretched out her hand, which was still cramping from signing an entire stack of NDAs. Whatever the hell was going on, it was something big. A terrorist attack? she wondered. In the middle of rural ... wherever they were?

Somewhere in northern Wisconsin was her best guess. They'd taken off from Chicago in a large helicopter with no markings on it, and flew across towns and roads and a lot of dark woods to get here. She wondered if they could have even crossed the border into Canada. The weather had grown rainier and foggier as they flew north, but she'd been able to glimpse, from the air, a large floodlit clearing as the helicopter descended. Very large—a landing field the size of several football fields, in the middle of the woods. She just had time to get an impression of something parked in the middle of it, in the fog, before they landed at the edge. Anita looked around as she scrambled out, ducking beneath the slowing blades with the downdraft whipping her thick, dark hair around.

There were some low bunker-like structures along the edge of the woods, bristling with antennas. The fog was heavy enough that she still couldn't tell what kind of vehicle was parked in the middle of the clearing. A big cargo plane, maybe? She hadn't seen a runway, but the visibility was poor enough that she could have missed it. Fog haloed the floodlights, and now rain was starting to fall. Anita stifled a yawn and pulled her blazer around her as the cold wind cut through it, and wished she was back in Chicago with Neil.

For this, they'd pulled her away from date night with her husband. Neil had been great about it, he always was, but now she was teetering around in a cow pasture on date-shoe heels, shivering since she hadn't even thought to pick up a decent jacket. This was not the night she'd planned. By now they were supposed to be back in their condo, with candles burning next to the bathtub, enjoying Neil's hands all over her soaped-up, naked body ...

"Pradhan!" her boss, Leary, snapped at her, and Anita wrenched her mind back to reality. Like Anita herself,

Leary was former Army, a big brusque guy with a gray brush cut. She'd done a tour in Afghanistan before she decided she could better serve her country elsewhere. As for Leary, she wasn't sure what his story was, but sometimes she got the impression he thought he was still barking orders at new recruits—and there was a part of her that instinctively responded to it.

"Sir?"

"Show me your ear."

"My—ear?"

"Turn your head, Pradhan."

Puzzled, she turned her head, and jerked in surprise as one of Leary's thick hands took her jaw in an impersonal grip, steadying her head and turning it even further. "What—" she began, and then a sharp pain stabbed behind her ear. She cursed, jerked away, and turned to see Leary withdrawing some sort of injector.

"What the fuck!" she snapped, reaching up to feel behind her ear. It still hurt, sharp as an earache.

Leary swatted her hand away.

"Don't touch it for the first few hours. You're gonna have a killer headache. Don't make it worse."

"What'd you do to me, Leary?" she demanded, but her boss turned away as the door to one of the bunkers opened, spilling light into the night. Anita cursed again under her breath and scrambled to keep up. She had to catch herself on the doorframe as she wobbled. There was a buzzing sensation in her ears, and he wasn't kidding about the headache. Also, she was starting to shiver from the damp, chilly night. She hoped it was warmer in the bunker.

It wasn't, much, but at least it was brightly lit. The walls were cinderblock, the room crowded with folding tables. Extension cords for computer equipment snaked across the floor. The place had all the hallmarks of a hastily-established command center.

There were about a dozen people in the room, and a few of ... something else.

Anita stared.

Her first, crazy thought was: *Halloween costumes?* Six men, two women, all of them among the tallest people she'd ever seen; the largest of them had to duck his head to avoid bashing it on the ceiling. He had to be eight feet tall if he was an inch. All of them wore sleeveless, dark blue uniforms, exposing powerfully muscled shoulders; even the women were built like bodybuilders.

Their bare arms were lightly furred; so were their faces. A few of them had tails, and some had erect catlike ears. The huge guy was covered with tawny fur, and the hair on his head was thick and rusty brown; she could only think of a lion. Of the others, there was one more tawny lion type— one of the women—and the others had fur that was either leopard spotted or tiger striped. Each wore a gold belt with various gadgetry on it, and a pair of gold bracelets, but no weapons that she could see.

Unlike the others, Lion Guy had a sash across his chest, striped red and gold. Anita was willing to bet he was their leader.

Lion looked up and said something in a brusque voice that, even though he was speaking a strange language, instantly made her think of Leary; it had the same drill-sergeant cadence. It also sent a renewed bolt of pain through her skull, along with a weird sensation that was almost like distant whispering. Anita winced and clapped her hand over her ear.

"We just gave her one of your translators," Leary told Lion Guy. "It's not working yet."

Lion Guy said something. Anita tried not to wince, her eyes watering from the baffling mix of sensations. A translator, like, what, like on *Star Trek* or something?

The conclusion was inescapable. If she'd seen these guys on TV, she could have convinced herself that it was all makeup and CGI. But they were standing right in front of her, their fur rippling and tails twitching as they moved.

These were aliens. Actual, bona-fide aliens.

And she used to think government cover-ups were made up by conspiracy theorists with too much time on their hands ...

Lion Guy said something. "Look, we couldn't have you land any closer to the crash site," Leary snapped. "You think we want to explain your spaceship to a town full of curious farmers? Too bad your runaway didn't have the decency to go down in the middle of Siberia or something."

"Spaceship," Anita repeated in a whisper.

Movement on one of the computer monitors caught her eye. It showed a camera angle of the landing field. Tuned to some part of the spectrum other than the visual, the camera penetrated the fog, giving her a clear view of a ship unlike any she'd ever seen: all rounded curves, like it was made of silver teardrops. It was lifting off, levitating smoothly from the ground and kicking up a shower of earth and gravel from underneath.

"That's a UFO," Anita said in a tiny voice. No one paid any attention to her.

Above the monitor, on the wall, was a large map of Wisconsin. Two parts of the map were circled in red. One was far in the north, near Lake Superior. The other was somewhere around the central part of the state.

"Hold out your arm, Pradhan," Leary ordered, wrenching her away from her contemplation of the map.

Anita jumped. A leopard-spotted man had closed in on her, holding a device in one hand. He smiled and extended his empty hand, palm up, then nodded to her left arm and mimed pushing up his sleeve. The gold bracelets on his wrists glinted against his fur.

"Why?" Anita asked.

"They want a blood sample. Let 'em. They requested you, so give 'em what they want."

Anita swallowed and pushed up her sleeve. "What do you mean, they requested me? Why?"

"They want a broad cross-section of human genetic material. We promised samples from as many people as we could get on short notice. And you're the only agent in the area with a Southeast Asian background."

"*What?*" Anita said, too shocked to jerk away before the device stung her arm. "What in the hell are they going to do with it?"

"Ask him," Leary said, gesturing to the leopard guy, and turned to speak to an aide.

Leopard Dude smiled again and said something, which intensified the buzzing inside her skull. His hand was gentle, cupped under her wrist, and his green eyes, though they lacked whites and resembled a cat's, somehow seemed to have a kind quality. Anita scowled at him, refusing to be lured into liking him. Cooperating with DNA-collecting aliens sounded like a terrible idea to her.

He spoke again and mimed touching his own ear, then turning his head.

"Are you offering to do something about my headache?" She hesitantly turned her head, but mindful of what had happened the last time, tried to keep watching him out of the corner of her eye.

He touched something cold to the skin behind her ear.

She flinched, then reeled as an overwhelming wave of dizziness washed through her. The dizziness and nausea lasted a few interminable seconds before receding, leaving her standing shakily with the leopard guy steadying her.

"Sorry about that," he said. "Can you understand me?"

"Oh! Yes!"

"You might have—" She missed the next few words; they seemed to fall into a black hole of incomprehension, like a car radio losing reception under a bridge. She couldn't even tell how she was understanding him in the first place. She could hear the words he was saying, and knew they were in a language she'd never heard before, but she understood them anyway.

"—installing itself in your mind," he finished. "The basic kit is easy to use but ..." He grimaced. "Not at all comfortable. I've given you an enzyme to enhance the setup process."

"There's a thing in my brain that's translating your words for me," she said, amazed. A book she'd read in college came back to her. "Like a Babel fish."

"I don't know what that is."

"Nothing. Fiction. It's fiction. *All* of this is supposed to be fiction." She stared around wildly, at the tall cat-people talking to Leary, who looked even tenser than she was used to seeing him. At least he wasn't acting completely blasé about it; this made her feel a little better. "Who *are* you people? Was that really a spaceship out there?"

"How else would we get to your planet?"

"What *are* you? Why are you here? Why did you want my blood?"

His warm, ready smile flashed again, showing a glimpse of uncomfortably sharp-looking canines. "You can call us Galateans. I'm Legionnaire Rikos of House Teirn, the field medic for my team. As for the blood I drew from you, that's part of the deal we have with your people for their assistance with our small problem."

"What deal?" she asked, trying not to sound as panicked as she felt. "*What* small problem?"

"We are always collecting genetic material for our data banks so that our researchers can make use of it. As for the nature of our problem, one of our soldiers went missing on your world."

"How?" she asked.

"He ran away." Rikos's face was grim. "He may be dead, but if not, we're trying to recover him for discipline."

"I think he'll be pretty easy to find," she said, looking him up and down. "We don't have very many people like you around here."

"So I've been told. He doesn't look like me, though. He's Polaran. They're smaller than Galateans and blue-skinned."

"Blue skin, gold fur, or pink scales," Anita told him, "I can assure you, if your guy's gone AWOL here, he won't be able to hide on Earth for long."